MW00614368

The

Wizard's Return

Vol. 1 of the
Rowan Branch Trilogy

Pam Collins

Cover Art by Gail Grow

Cover Designer Gail Grow
Book design by Pam Collins

Printed in the United States of America
The Troy Book Makers • Troy, New York • thetroybookmakers.com

To order additional copies of this title,
contact your favorite local bookstore
or visit www.shoptbmbooks.com

ISBN: 978-1-61468-644-6

*Dedicated to Mother Earth, because we owe
her...everything.*

To Linda,
May you find
some joy in the journey,
Pam Collins

Author's Note

Short of creating a full-fledged glossary and potentially denying the reader the adventure of exploring internet rabbit-holes, I offer here a few explanatory bits. For instance, *Bru na Boinne* is the Gaelic name of New Grange in Ireland, and a currach is the Irish and Scottish name for a little boat. Some pronunciations that might help are Ceara (*key-AR-a)*, Naoise ('NEE sha"), Liadan (lee-A-din) and Cerridwen (*Ce-rid-WEN)*. "Pasties" are a deep-fried meat pie, pronounced with a short "a".

"The Yule Poems" book is not a fiction. It is a series of poems I wrote in 1998, one for each day between Thanksgiving and Solstice. That it became such an inspiration for both me and my characters was a complete surprise and delight. Finally, Raina's experience at the Chalice Well is not a complete fiction either. It reflects a similar experience I had when I visited there in 2017. Though I did not actually have a vision, I felt a strong presence of the Goddess and a call to make her more imminent in my life...hence, the book you hold in your hands.

THE WIZARD'S RETURN
Table of Contents
BOOK ONE

BOOK TWO

Book One

Pam Collins

1

A Birth

Wales
circa 500 AD

On a harsh and unforgiving night, the misty white of a corpse candle floated low over the fields, a chilling sight, casting its ghostly glow over the windswept earth as it passed. Who could say who marked it, if anyone at all? Certainly not the village midwife, bent over the bed of sorrow, nor the anxious presence that stood in the shadows as the midwife struggled to bring the child from the womb of its dead mother.

The babe, whose preternaturally open eyes glowed a startling green in the wavering candlelight, was deathly silent, but very much alive. The midwife tied her off from her mother and lovingly bathed her, cooing softly as she did so, as though to ease a grief the newborn knew nothing of. For all this child was likely to know, the woman who waited near the door would be known as "mother". The poor husk of a woman who had traded her life for the child's would hold no sway, cast no shadow, create not the slightest nagging memory in the mind of the infant girl. Even had the mother lived, the arrangements had already been agreed upon, for before she had succumbed to total madness, she had had foresight enough to know that she was unfit for motherhood.

Best that childbirth had taken her, thought the midwife. A life of madness and loss of child was no life to live. As the midwife swaddled the babe in the soft homespun the dead woman had so lovingly woven before the madness had seized her, the babe stirred and fixed the midwife with an uncanny stare. For the briefest moment, the midwife imagined she saw understanding in those eyes. Perhaps this child would remember her true mother after all. Perhaps this strange child had had a hand in her mother's release...

I'm getting too old for this work, the midwife reasoned, alarmed by her own thoughts. In her utter exhaustion she felt a contagion of madness knock on the door of her mind. Hurriedly, she finished her ministrations and brought the child to the waiting woman. Reluctantly, the midwife placed the babe in the woman's arms, then from her leather pouch fetched a handful of coins which she transferred to the pouch tied at the woman's waist. The woman took the infant and the payment without comment and turned to leave, but before she could cross the threshold, the midwife grabbed her arm.

"Have a care. Methinks this will be no ordinary child. See that not only does she survive, but thrives, for though you see a shell of a woman lying in yonder bed, she was once a good woman with pure intentions. This child would have been lovingly nurtured. If you cannot love her, at least be kind, for none of this is any fault of hers."

If the midwife had hoped for some sign of reassurance, a slight smile or nod, none was forthcoming. With the babe wrapped securely beneath her cloak, the woman stepped into the lane, knowing more of the circumstances of the child's begetting and likely fate than she would speak of. The wind whipped the snow into swirls as the midwife watched the darkness consume the child and the woman who carried her.

"God bless and keep ye, wee one," the midwife whispered, then turned back to the room and the corpse on the bed. Even in death, the woman was beautiful. No surprise on that point that the mage had succumbed to her charms. Still, thought the midwife, for the mage to be so careless as to beget a child then abandon both mother and babe...there must be more to the story. But that, she well knew, was not a tale for her humble ears and so she contented herself with lovingly washing and dressing the corpse, recreating as best she could the dignity she thought the woman must have owned before her ill-fated encounter with the powerful and mysterious mage. *May your soul find peace in its journey,* she whispered across the lifeless form.

Abertha hurried through the snow to the cart at the head of the lane where her husband, Derwen, waited to take her and the babe inland to their home. The horses grew restless at her approach, eager to complete their mission. Loath to expose the babe to the cold for even a moment, Abertha nevertheless handed her up to Derwen to hold while she scrambled into the cart. Only after she returned the babe to the folds of her woolen cloak would she take her eyes from the child and address the darkness.

"It is done," she whispered.

"And the mother?" Derwen asked.

"Dead, may she find peace."

"It is as she wished then."

Too heartbreaking a wish to make, Abertha thought. Then again, dealing with the likes of *him* is sure to bring thoughts and wishes alien to the human soul.

The couple rode in silence as Derwen urged the horses out of the village and into the wooded darkness. The snow had lessened some, but not the wind. It groaned through the oak and elder that lined the road and rattled the dry leaves that had yet to fall. So comforting in the daylight, the woods at night always frightened Abertha. But wasn't that the way of the world? In all things there was darkness and light. To dance the dance of the living one must surrender to beauty and delight while nevertheless keeping constant vigil. It was a paradox that had always nagged at her, but she thought she had gotten better at it with age.

Now she had accepted the charge of caring for this child. Light or dark, which would it be? She knew both would be at work in this tiny babe, because she knew its lineage. Some things should not be passed on, she thought. She drew the babe closer to her, against the howling wood, against the fate that she feared for the child. There were times when she had felt that the babe should have died with her mother, putting an end to an error in judgement, if not a crime against nature. Curse him, she thought, hardly for the first time. But now that the child was here, so precious and innocent and, admittedly, so uncannily beautiful, she couldn't help but treasure it. As the cart rolled and bumped through the darkened wood, she made a vow that she would surround the child with the things of light and goodness and do everything she could to defeat whatever darkness might lurk in her.

Half in a dream she said, as much to the forest as to Derwen, "I give her the name Annwyl -- beloved, for so shall she be, by us anyway."

"He's apt not to like it, you naming her," Derwen replied.

Abertha felt the anger rising in her, its heat fueling the love that was already growing in her for this child.

"I care little what the mage likes or dislikes, powerful as he is. He has charged us with her care and so Annwyl she will be to me...to us. He can't expect us to take on this task with cold hearts, even though his be cold as..."

"Caution woman. You know what lies ahead and these woods have ears, and voices that speak to him. Let us keep our counsel and discharge our duties as we do all things of importance in this life."

And so, they fell silent again for the remainder of the journey, but Abertha's heart was loud in her chest as she held the infant tightly to her. *Whatever your fate will be,* Abertha thought, *beautiful girl, for as long as I am able, I will see to it that your days are full of whatever joy we can find. I will teach you to weave and plant and know which wild things will give sustenance. For as long as I can, I will teach you that you are one of the Earth's beloved creatures, no more, no less.*

The forest did indeed hear Abertha's vow. Rock and wood, fur and feathers, all felt the passing of the magical child and through that influence became privy to what roiled in Abertha's heart.

Little do we think of what the forest makes of us as we pass through, but to imagine we go unremarked is folly. How much of the human animal's behavior is remarked there, it would, no doubt, discomfort us to know.

·2

Coming of Age

On an uncannily warm day in December, Annwyl awoke full of anticipation. It was her sixteenth birthday but it was also the day Annwyl had determined to test what had been a growing suspicion. Abertha had made quite a fuss about Annwyl "coming of age," although what this meant to the two women might have been quite different. For Annwyl's part, she had begun experiencing things that she thought best to keep secret.

She knew Abertha had been busy cooking special foods and preparing for a small gathering of friends that evening -- friends that Annwyl cared little about. But Abertha and Derwen had been good parents and taught her well, so lest she hurt their feelings, she would hide her boredom. In like manner, through the years, she had become expert in feigning an interest in domestic pursuits, and with application could do a fair enough job with needle and hoe, but took little joy in any of it. More compelling to her were Derwen's chores, caring for the animals, building and repairing -- anything that would get her outside. Mercifully, Derwen, bless him, let her fulfill the place of the son he did not have, even to the point of teaching her to hunt. She was as skilled with a bow as any boy her age, and, despite Abertha's suggestion that she not boast of it, she refused to hide her abilities. She would challenge the village boys to contests and laugh heartily when she beat them mercilessly.

To most who saw her, Annwyl had a blessed childhood, was even a bit spoiled at that. But for Annwyl, the sense that she was of a different sort than her parents had grown through the years, though why or how that could be true was a mystery to her, or at least it had been until recently.

That her parents loved her dearly she was sure of, but there was also a nagging and growing suspicion that could they see into the dreams that had begun to visit her -- dreams where dark things lurked -- that their love might be compromised by fear, for there was nothing dark in the hearts of Abertha and Derwen, of that she was sure. They were as pure as rain, as nourishing as the sun. Their hearts were as open as Annwyl's felt caged, like an exotic bird living in a land not its own, desperate to be free. In her younger years, she hid from the edginess she felt, throwing herself into learning everything she could and striving to please her parents. But in this past year, with the advent of the dreams, against her will she felt herself being pulled away from her familiar life and into something else. Even, sometimes, her dreams led her to wonder at her true parentage, for though she could not fault Abertha and Derwen on any count, a suspicion was growing in her that she was of different seed.

And now this. Vivid, insistent dreams that spoke of a strange power, whispered into her mind by a shadowy but somehow familiar figure.

Well, she was sixteen today. "Of age" as Abertha said. She could no longer stay caged.

"Annwyl, dear, rouse yourself! I need you to go to the market for me," Abertha called from the kitchen.

"But it's my birthday!"

"Oh, is that what day it is? Had I almost forgotten then? Well, you'll be the princess in the high seat this evening, but just now I'm up to my elbows in dough and need some special things."

In truth, Annwyl was all too glad to go to the small market at the village center. It was the perfect place to test the inkling that had come to her in the night. She dressed hurriedly and presented herself in the kitchen.

"There's my sweetheart. Now I want some of that lavender infused honey from the herbalist."

"But we have honey stored..."

"Not like this. Didn't you tell me this was a special day then? Here are some coppers. No need to bargain. She keeps her prices fair. It's pleasant out but take a shawl. The weather could turn."

But Annwyl was already out the door, without a shawl, the coppers jingling in her pocket.

"A small jar of your lavender honey, please." Annwyl smiled her best smile and looked, for all the world, like patience personified. But when the old woman brought the honey to Annwyl, the charming girl's smile faded and in its place a look like a darkened window sat upon her face like a mask. From her beautiful green eyes, the will of something ancient and impatient stared at the unsuspecting herbalist, as though it was pulling the soul from the old woman.

"You were going to charge me three pieces for this," Annwyl intoned, "but now you think that's too much. Two should do, shouldn't it?"

The old woman looked confused, but she took the two pieces and handed Annwyl the jar, who, as soon as she had the honey in hand, smiled her winning smile once more, her face again that of the beautiful young girl.

"Thank you, ma'am, and good day to you." Annwyl made a small curtsey and left the shop. Once outside, she fingered the extra copper still in her pocket. It worked, just as her dream had suggested. But her theory needed to be tested further. Not far away, she saw a young boy fighting his shadow with a wooden sword. She walked up to him, all smiling and friendly.

"Good day, young lad. How be it with you this day?"

"Right enough," he said, eyeing her a bit suspiciously. But then her countenance changed again, just as it had at the herbalist's.

"You're tired of that foolish toy sword," she said. "Throw it on the ground and run home to your mother." And the boy did. As Annwyl bent to retrieve the toy weapon, a raven landed a short distance away and fixed her with its beady eyes.

"Well it worked, didn't it?" she said defensively. "It was just a test." She let the sword lay in the dust and warily moved away from the crow who waited until she was well away before taking flight.

Once home, she delivered the honey to Abertha and offered to help in the kitchen, as she knew she should do. But she also knew that, it being her birthday, Abertha would send her on her way to do as she pleased, and what she pleased was to retreat to her room and contemplate the events of the morning. She also needed to find a place to hide the copper she had secured. Abertha would not be easily fooled, so the copper needed to disappear, as though it had indeed been spent. Not that the antics of the morning had had anything to do with securing the coin, for which Annwyl had little use and which, at this point, was more of a liability should it be found. No. What had been gained that day was the surety that there was more to Annwyl than she or anyone else had thought.

She would have loved to revel in the success of her new-found abilities, but the matter of the coin couldn't be put off. Looking around her room, she quickly realized that there was nowhere safe from Abertha's tidying ways. Sooner or later she would find the coin and Annwyl had no ready explanation for having it. Fingering the copper where it lay hidden in her pocket, she went back to the kitchen where Abertha was singing as she worked.

"Mother, if you won't be needing me, I'd like to take a walk. It's a beautiful day. It should be taken advantage of."

"See how even the sun smiles on your special day my dear! Of course, you should be out in it. Find Derwen to accompany you. Whatever he's working on can wait a bit."

"Of course, Mother." Annwyl did indeed keep a sharp eye out for Derwen, not to beg his company but to avoid him, which was easily enough done as she made her way to the edge of the woods. There she faltered, however, having never been into the woods farther than a few feet, always keeping the house in view. But an insistence gripped her. The caged bird in her was seeking a wild place and the body of the beloved girl had no choice but to follow, so into the woods she plunged. Thorns and scrub threatened to snag her, but she pulled her skirts tight around her and then, full of the same dream-inspired daring that had fueled her morning adventure, she stood her ground, squared her shoulders and with a voice she barely recognized as her own she spoke the command.

"Back."

Like some hidden hand reeling in the warp and woof of the forest, a path cleared before her. A bit surprised, but emboldened, she walked onward into the heart of the wood as though she belonged. Indeed, as though she ruled. So sure of herself was she that she never once looked back to see if the path remained open behind her, which, in fact, it did. The power held and the way home was no less clear than the path forward, at least for the time being.

When she came to a huge, three-trunked oak its very enormity stopped her in her tracks. This must be her destination, she thought, though she had no clear idea of a destination when she began, only that she needed to be in the heart of the not-human. The tree pulled at her, its vast trunk mother-like, comforting. Not having intended to, but unable to resist, she rested her back against the sunniest side of the tree and fell asleep with dappled golden rays upon her face. In such an abundance of light, her dreams should have been easy and welcome, but they were not. Black wings filled the air and a hunger that could not be satiated filled her belly and her heart. Her mind was filled with a want so deep and unfocused it felt like she would fly to pieces in the vain effort of finding its object.

As the day advanced, the cooling temperature wormed its way into Annwyl's dreaming, waking her with a start. The sun had westered significantly as currents of cool air drew away the warmth, like fingers drawing back a protective curtain.

Annwyl got to her feet and brushed off her clothes. To her immense relief the path was still there, if a shade darker than it had been. A few feet down the path, however, she remembered the copper in her pocket. Vague as it was, she had forgotten her plan to somehow hide the coin in the woods. Hurriedly, she made her way back to the oak. What better place than here, and if she marked the spot, should she ever want to, she could find it again. There, at the base of the tree, two roots forked, making what looked like a tiny cave. Surely, she would remember this fairy-like opening. She dug a small hole just inside the opening and buried the coin, then decorated the opening with bits of bark and pebbles. She imagined the copper piece comfortable there, waiting for her return, when...what? Annwyl's imagination didn't make it any further than that.

When she turned around again, it seemed that the path had shrunk somewhat, as though the woods had finally cast off the spell she had set upon it which now seemed so long ago. Her heart racing, Annwyl grabbed her skirts and ran down the path, her earlier bravado sinking as surely as was the sun. Just as a thorn scratched her cheek, she caught sight of her house and made a last dash for the familiar as the forest closed up behind her.

The day was not as far gone as it had seemed in the woods. Derwen was still at work fixing the wagon as Abertha continued toiling away in the kitchen. Thankful for small favors, Annwyl slipped into her room and set about playing the role of the birthday girl. She covered her cheek with a curl and put on her best dress, then sat at the window calming herself as best she could. At least the coin was gone. Surely no one would find it in the woods. Perhaps she would wake tomorrow and find that this day had been just another one of her troublesome dreams. Still, the hours persisted in being quite real as they passed on to the moment when she could hear the guests arriving.

Playing the little girl, she waited until Abertha called her to dinner, then roused herself from her lassitude and did her best to banish the boredom from her face. She knew how the night would progress. It would begin in a flourish of fuss over her, but quickly devolve into the usual adult gossip and storytelling. At least the food would be good. And there was the lavender honey, she thought with delight, as she made her way to the table. But when she found her seat among the assembled guests and looked up, there, across the table from her, sat the herbalist.

The candles burned brightly in Abertha and Derwen's cottage on the night of Annwyl's sixteenth birthday. No corner was left in darkness, no dust dimmed even the smallest trifle. No effort had been spared to make this night a special one, but despite the golden light that flooded the room and the bountiful feast spread across the table, Abertha's heart burned in her chest. She had feared this day for years, plagued by the premonition that when Annwyl came of age, the battle between light and dark that Abertha was convinced raged within the child, would at last be manifest. Either side could win, she kept telling herself, but knowing the power of the creature who had sired the child led Abertha to expect the scales would be tipped in his favor, despite her exhausting efforts to raise the girl surrounded by all the good Abertha could muster.

Now, as Annwyl emerged to join the guests, Abertha raised her eyes to meet those of her daughter and was stricken by what she saw -- a dark look on Annwyl's face as she faced the guests, most particularly, she thought, the herbalist. So changed was Annwyl's visage that Abertha's heartbeat quickened. Were her worst fears confirmed? Was what she had seen roiling in Annwyl all these years at last boiling over in some way on this fateful day? What had happened -- or what was yet to occur -- Abertha had no way of knowing. For now, the trick was to keep the worry off her own face and meet her foster child with the guileless smile of unconditional love she had worn all these years. The love was true, but the untroubled heart was not. Abertha had, since first holding the child in her arms, dreaded what now may have come to pass.

A scraping of chairs against the floor as the guests rose in honor of Annwyl's presence gave both women the cover they needed to arrange their masks. Had the herbalist noticed Annwyl's initial shock? Abertha would have to be extra vigilant tonight. Now she wished she'd talked to Derwen earlier, shared with him her concerns so that he might be an ally, a second pair of eyes. Then again, Derwen was not dependable where Abertha's worries about Annwyl were concerned. He was entirely smitten by his young charge, helpless against her charms, less innocent than one would hope as Abertha was now sure. Poor Derwen. He would want to fight her on this, she knew, but eventually the evidence would be overwhelming. Hopefully she could intervene before there was serious trouble.

Derwen was raising his glass. "To dear Annwyl on this special day! *Lechyd da*!"

"*Lechyd da*!" The cheer went up around the table as Derwen cast his adoring glance on Annwyl who sat, face flushed, for all the world a sweet maiden flattered by the attention. Only Abertha saw the quick lidded glance at the herbalist, who, glass raised, seemed to be fully in the sway of the celebratory joy of the evening, revealing nothing amiss. Whatever was the cause of Annwyl's apparent discomfort at sight of the herbalist was not shared by the old woman, or so at least Abertha had to presume from what she could witness. There was a puzzle here, but Abertha had to set it aside for the night, as much as it vexed her to do so. Then again, the night was young.

The evening continued in blessed banality until a guest, holding his bread reverently, declared, "My word this honey is delightful! A hint of lavender I think?" He aimed his suspended bread at the herbalist. "Yours I suspect?"

"It is," replied the herbalist. "Dear Annwyl came by this morning and..." for a moment the herbalist hesitated, her face clouding ever so briefly, "...and... bought some."

"Well," continued the guest, oblivious to the herbalist's stammering, "it's a fine contribution to this feast, by God! Let's raise a glass to our blessed herbalist who keeps us healthy and sweet!"

A cheer arose again from the assembly, as glasses were refilled. Abertha, however, kept her eyes discreetly on the herbalist, whose mirth did not quite keep pace with the rest of the guests. So, there was something here after all. A shadow of confusion sat upon the herbalist's features, but not once did she look across the table at Annwyl. In fact, Abertha noticed, the herbalist's gaze went anywhere but upon the guest of honor. And was that a tiny smirk on Annwyl's face?

The night continued on as such nights will. Many toasts were offered and there was much praising of the food and ale. When at long last dessert was served, attention turned again to Annwyl and much was made of her "coming of age." Abertha began to rise to give a blessing, but as she cast her eyes on her darling Annwyl, what she saw there made the words catch in her throat. Her daughter's eyes had turned stony, like a window with the curtains drawn, dark, giving nothing away, but casting their dark intent directly on the herbalist.

"If I may, I'd offer a blessing to our sweet Annwyl," said the herbalist, rising slowly as if half asleep.

Abertha nodded her consent, but her heart was beating furiously.

Let us raise a glass
to this fine lass,
may her heart know abiding love
and her hands honest work
may the sun and rain sustain her in turn

and may the angels be her constant companions.

"Here, here!" the guests shouted in all sincerity then drank heartily as the herbalist lowered hers, the far-away look slowly fading from her features.

Tears blossomed in Abertha's eyes, try as she might to hold them back. She would wish no less than such a blessing for this child, but what she had just seen put such hopes in doubt. *Oh, my love*, Abertha thought, *tonight you have won a dark victory. I sense the dark magic of the mage upon you. Clearly it is time for you to leave before trouble comes upon us all.* Still, she was glad of the blessing and prayed with every inch of herself that, from wherever it came, it would take hold.

As full bellies began to take their toll on the guests, Annwyl slid away from the table and took refuge in her room. Abertha let her go. The child must be wrestling with what the day had wrought and the guests were too far gone to care if their centerpiece had left the party. Derwen was at his best, so proud of his daughter, laughing and telling tales with his friends. Abertha did her best to play her part, but her heart was twisted into a knot of agony.

That night, Abertha lay awake, despairing that despite her best efforts she had not been able to save the child from her fate. Tearfully, she had to admit to herself that there were some things too strong for love to change. Everything had its own nature and while things could perhaps be shaped, taught to grow in certain ways, their basic nature could not be altered. To do that shaping, however, one must work knowledgeably with the natural drives. She could tease a vine around a post, prune a garden into abundance, but this dark art of influence she had no knowledge of. Worse, she had to admit, she had no sympathy for it. She was well aware of Merlin's power to influence the course of events, though she neither understood it nor cared to. All she knew was that to her mind, influencing the will of others was wrong, against the laws of nature. Life was hard enough. Individual sovereignty, she believed, is the one thing we have that is ours. For someone else to tread on that against our will...no one should have that power over another.

She knew the mage would argue that no one could impose on another's will, that if influence could be had, there was something in the other's will that acquiesced. On that point, she often wondered if he had worked his dark power on her to get her to take the child in the first place. And if that were true, did she not willingly surrender her will to his wish? Surely, she loved the child from the first time she touched it and would have cared for it had she been influenced to do so or not.

Now, however, all that was neither here nor there. She had nourished the child, taught her to the best of her ability and up to this point had kept her safe, but now she felt she was no longer equal to the task. Annwyl had grown beyond her. The dark power had asserted itself and Abertha had no idea how to deal with it.

After a sleepless night, Abertha woke Derwen.

"Dress yourself husband and walk with me. There is something we must discuss, but mind you are quiet about it. I would not wake Annwyl."

Tiptoeing past Annwyl's door in the dim light of early morning, Abertha walked Derwen well out of earshot of the house, then shared with him all that she had seen and suspected that night.

"Are you not making something of nothing wife? There's a world of other explanations for what you thought you saw."

Abertha lay her hand on her husband's rugged face. Poor sweet man who loved so blindly, both his greatest gift and tragic flaw. He had taken such care with Annwyl, taught her everything she wanted to learn, even things he thought it odd that a young girl would want to know. In his heart he knew she was different, gifted. Such a quick study, often understanding something before he felt he had finished teaching it. But just bright, not powerful, not like Merlin. Her mother, after all, had been a simple, common woman. Pure of heart, but also, he thought, weak willed, having fallen for Merlin in the first place and then sinking into madness when he left as she had to have known he would.

"From the very first we knew that dark and light would be at war in this child," Abertha contended.

"*You* knew, or thought you knew," he argued, though not unkindly.

"You must trust me in this. His power is awakening in her as is only logical that it would. She is beyond our care now. She is his child; he is responsible for her and it's time for him to act the part."

"But to place her in his world. That is no place for her." Derwen was struggling, grasping at straws.

Abertha fought the image that came to her and hated to place it in Derwen's mind, but he wasn't making this easy.

"It is this place that is no longer safe for her. She has no intention, or perhaps no knowledge of how to hide her powers. When they become obvious, what do you think the good people of the village will do to her? All those people who toasted her health last night...each and every one of them will vie to be the first to pick up a stone."

Derwen flinched at her words, but he knew the truth of them.

"How do we send for him, then?" Derwen asked.

"Conveniently, he never told us that, did he?" Abertha's frustration with the wizard all but consumed her at times.

"Perhaps the crows," Derwen suggested. "Or the old oak in the forest? I cannot believe he has dropped us from his vigilance. There must be some way to send for him."

"Send for whom?" Annwyl asked from behind them.

3

The Forest of Broceliande

Armorica
(modern day Brittany)

"What troubles you, my love?" Nimue lounged on the richly upholstered divan, her golden hair loose and glowing, her gown arranged artfully around her. Her casual pose was staged to belie the anxiety she felt at her lover's recent and growing agitation.

"What makes you think I'm troubled?" Merlin snapped, not even pausing in his pacing.

Nimue merely lifted an eyebrow, but in that eye a spell was brewing to pull the truth from the wizard.

Merlin caught sight of it. *Think fast*, he thought, *she cannot know about the child.*

"It's Arthur as always," he barked, twisting his hand under his cloak to cast his counter spell and disguise the lie.

"Ah, the great King who cannot lace his own trousers without the help of his wizard." How Nimue loved to taunt, but Merlin was in no mood to engage in bedroom warfare. He had been called to Wales, which meant there was something amiss with the babe he thought he had left out of harm's way -- and out of his hair. And there was urgency in the wind. An uncomfortable storm was brewing. But he returned to his excuse for leaving which he would build on the ground of some truth.

"He has gotten it into his head to send his knights out on some quest or other."

"Better that than sitting idle or bashing at each other in the lists."

Ah, she's taken the bait, Merlin thought with relief.

"Is it? Better? Sending his knights all over creation and leaving his court undefended? We may be at relative peace for the moment, but you know how things can change."

The minute it was out of his mouth he regretted it. Damn this woman who can leave him so unguarded, so undefended himself. And what a lover of chaos she was. Had he planted a seed of mischief in her impish mind? Unwise at a time when he had to leave her to her own devices. Unwise. Not the way one likes to think of a wizard. Certainly not a word that was often pointed at him, and yet here he was, creating more trouble for himself by the minute.

"Well, you should go to him, of course," she said, smoothing her hand across her skirt.

This was too easy, Merlin thought. Either his spells were still getting the best of hers (to be ardently hoped for), or she had seen through him and was plotting something -- he dared not think what. Either way, he could not defer the impending mission. If she was planning trouble, he'd have to deal with it later. Not for the first time he cursed himself for the weakness he had for her, but curses did nothing to loosen the bonds that kept him firmly doomed to orbit the sun that was her, as though he was some minor planet with no other purpose than to decorate her sky.

He left at dawn. True to his deceit, he would make an appearance at Arthur's court, for he knew well that Nimue had her spies there. In the meantime, he had to be on the lookout as well for any being (human, animal, or, worst of all, bird) she might send to follow him. At the coast awaited a small craft, just big enough for his horse and himself and enough magic to get them across the channel to the coast of Cornwall, a short trip made even shorter by a landing at the island mount just off the coast. He knew of a hidden harbor there where he would moor his craft, safe for the return voyage, then spend a blessed night awash in the charms of sea and hazel wood, lost in a peaceful sleep that he feared would not be his again for a long time.

He awoke at low tide and rode the causeway to the mainland. As his mount splashed through the shallow water, he knew that while it had been difficult so far for anyone to follow him undetected, once on the mainland, there was little he could do to escape whatever eyes she might employ to keep him in sight.

Was love always so possessive? But then, it was not love that bound him and Nimue, but something even more grasping. She didn't want him, she wanted his power, his knowledge. He knew that. Nor was it enough for her that she could seduce a wizard of his power and hold him emotionally captive. She wanted more. He wanted to believe he could hold out against her, but hadn't he proven himself a fool already to have fallen this far? As he rode on, he imagined never returning, staying at court with Arthur where he belonged, but...what was the point? He had played his part in Arthur's story; the world was moving on, away from the old ways. He deserved...what, to be enchanted as he had enchanted so many others? He had to laugh at himself, giving in to his own undoing. But then there was this trouble in Wales. How he would have liked to have forgotten that.

"Merlin! You've come at last!" There was both a gentle chiding and a sincere welcome in Arthur's greeting. Arthur knew of Merlin's involvement with Nimue, as who did not? But he was too gentle and respectful of his mentor to mention it. In Merlin's presence, there was always something of the young lad in Arthur, despite all he had accomplished, both with Merlin's help and without it. As for Merlin, he loved Arthur too dearly to even begin to show it. The arrangement was always to maintain his gruff facade.

"What's this foolishness I hear of sending your knights out chasing after some damn cup?" Merlin quipped.

"Hah! Merlin! Not just any cup! 'Tis said to be the cup The Christ drank from at the Last Supper, brought to our uncivilized little isle by Joseph of Arimathea for safe keeping."

"Better to seek the Cauldron of Cerridwen if you want a magical quest," Merlin muttered under his breath, then, "By whose authority are you privy to this astounding piece of information?"

Arthur was bursting with the wonder of the story he was about to tell, but held himself in check for the moment.

"Merlin, come. You've had a long ride, let's eat and drink and get comfortable and then I'll tell you the whole tale."

Arthur drew Merlin into the great hall, where he expected Nimue's spies were well in attendance. He'd rather have ridden into the woods with Arthur to have a chat in private, but this was, alas, a necessary part of his ruse, to be seen at court, and, he thought with glee, make plenty of people wary. For while Arthur had clearly established his sovereignty and the new religion had gained credibility, increasingly Merlin was perceived with distaste, a relic of the early years of turmoil, and purveyor of the heresy of Druidism.

Once in the hall, Merlin could see that this quest of Arthur's had already drawn off many of the knights. Still, the board was richly set and even more victuals were sent for as though Merlin were not one man, but a ravenous army. Clearly, Arthur had missed his mentor and despite Merlin's expressed skepticism about the quest, was eager to tell the full tale, well garnished with robust drinking.

"I actually thought it would have been you who initiated this quest, Merlin," Arthur began as he poured them each an ample tankard of mead.

"Hardly," Merlin growled, careful to appear to take a healthy swig from his cup but letting most of it run into his beard and disappear.

"Well, as has happened more than once in this court, we were at this very table, feasting away, when a hag came in and accosted us. A hag she appeared, but in truth, Merlin, I suspect it might have been the Lady of the Lake."

"And what makes you think that?"

"You told me yourself, she is the source of all things."

"In a manner of speaking, yes."

'Well, it's logical. First the sword and then the cup."

"And what is the relationship do you think?"

Arthur hesitated. "On that point, I am not clear. It's on the tip of my thoughts, but I can't quite get it."

The same old Arthur, King or not. Unstoppable in battle, a leader of men, but when it came to metaphysics...

"But Merlin, don't you see? That's the beauty of it! Somewhere out there is this wonderful thing. Finding it will be just the beginning. And anyway, when we do find it, you, in all your wisdom, will unlock it's mystery for us."

"This Christ is out of my purview. I am of the old ways." But it was not Merlin's intent to deflate Arthur's enthusiasm, ill-advised as Merlin thought it was.

"But you're right, King. This is a noble quest and no doubt your knights will find many adventures along the way. As for me, I'm spent. I'd truly love some isolation for a spell. Perhaps I will consider your *cup* and what it might mean. Is there a place where I can rest undisturbed for a few days?"

"Here at court? Usually you're off to your cave in Tintagel."

"If it's not imposing. I need some..." he almost said 'cover' but caught himself. He was more distracted than he thought. "...Kingly hospitality!"

"Say no more! It's yours! Stay as long as you want, emerge when it suits you. I'll give the order that you're not to be disturbed. It's good to have you here in whatever form."

And so, it was let about that Merlin was sleeping off the exhausting experience of being in the clutches of the most beguiling woman in the Kingdom, while he conjured a dense mist and rode under its cover to the home of Abertha and Derwen.

A murder of crows dappled the sky above the cottage and the wind blew dust and strange scents under the door and through any crack it could find. It didn't take Abertha long to sense what was coming and decide what she must do in preparation. Derwen must be found and Annwyl gotten out of the house long enough for Abertha to gather her courage and confront the wizard. She had no intention of sparing his feelings, if he had any.

"He's near," she told Derwen when she found him.

"You figured out how to call him then?"

"No, not at all, other than whispering it to the trees and pleading with the birds. And maybe that was enough. At any rate, he has been summoned and is on his way. I know the signs. You must take Annwyl somewhere for the day. I'll not have her hearing everything I have to tell that wizard."

"But the weather is threatening, and where will we go?"

"That's your part in this. Think of something," Abertha said, trying to temper her impatience.

"I've been meaning to visit my cousin. I have a tool to return to him anyway. But what if she doesn't want to go?"

"I'll tell her I'm turning the house out to scrub the floors and want the two of you out of my hair."

"In this weather?" Derwin said, eyeing the darkening sky.

"Well, it started as a fine day. See what trouble that man is..." Abertha said, her exasperation on full display.

"I'll hitch the horse while you get our daughter." But the words caught in Derwen's throat as it dawned on both of them how hard it would be to face what was coming.

Merlin brought his horse to a walk as soon as the cottage came into view. He needed time to sense what he could of the situation, although the signs had been insistent. He could see the figure of a woman standing in the doorway, arms crossed, her skirts pulled askew in the wind. Could that be his child? How long had it been? But a few paces closer and he could see that it was Abertha, alone and unsmiling. He nudged his horse into a canter. No point in drawing this out any longer.

"Did you bring this annoying wind?" Abertha asked, accusingly.

"Hello to you too, Abertha. Is there illness?"

"Not exactly. Come in then. Let's at least pretend to be civilized."

Merlin followed Abertha into the cottage, a cozy and loving home, he could see. On that score, at least, he had chosen well. To his right, through an open door he could see a single bed covered in a blanket woven in blues and greens and walls adorned with painted leaves and flowers.

Even with no sun coming through the windows, it had a feeling of brightness.

"It was a girl then?" he asked.

"It *was* a girl child and is now a young woman. Quite beautiful I might add...surprisingly." She looked Merlin up and down as though he was a troll, horribly out of place in her house.

"So, we might as well cut to the chase, Abertha. May I sit?" But he was already dropping into a chair, not waiting for the invitation. He dreaded what was coming. He could see in Abertha's eyes that she had a dressing down in store for him. He could smooth that over, but in his heart, he was sorry that she was so distressed. She was a good woman and he owed her much.

Merlin wasn't the only one whose heart was changing, now that he and Abertha were face to face. As Abertha eyed the old man and considered what he would now have to deal with, her anger wavered and melted into the sorrow she had so far held at bay. This daughter whom they had loved and nourished with such hope could no longer be theirs. The parting would be bitter and now the tears flowed and washed away many of the angry words she had intended for Merlin.

"She is no longer safe here," she said, finally. "For some time, there were little inklings that she was going to be more than the simple woman her mother was. But then, on her sixteenth birthday, a power came alive in her and since then she has been testing it out...on people, on the weather. If I didn't know better, I'd think this wind was her doing and not yours."

Merlin opened his mouth to tell her that it wasn't his doing at all, but decided to keep his counsel for the moment and not give Abertha anything more to struggle with. Clearly, she was struggling enough.

"So far no one has made any connection to her -- she has been much beloved by all who have known her -- but that won't last forever. It may be different in Arthur's court, but out here there are those who look askance at magic and are quick to..."

"I know all too well, woman, what ignorant people will do. What do you propose?"

"Well, you must take her of course. What other options are there? She is yours, after all, and only you will know how to handle her and this power she has inherited."

Merlin let himself imagine bringing this girl to Nimue. She would play with her as a cat plays with a mouse before devouring it, leaving only her severed head. How she would fair at Arthur's court was less easy to guess, not knowing her...Merlin felt a tinge at the admission. Not knowing her. Had he not anticipated this day all along, try as he might to keep the thought at bay?

"Then, Abertha, tell me about her."

And she did.

The hours passed in surprisingly gentle conversation as Abertha recalled the wonderful years she and Derwen had shared raising their Annwyl. Here and there Merlin would ask a question, genuinely wanting to know his daughter at last, or so it seemed.

The peace they had created between them shattered, however, with the sound of voices at the door.

The object of their conversation had returned. Abertha's heart beat like a trapped bird in her chest. How would this play out? Merlin and Abertha both rose to their feet as Annwyl walked into the house, shadowed by a sad-eyed Derwen.

"Annwyl, darling, this is..." Abertha began.

"My father, I know."

Abertha and Derwen exchanged a startled glance. Had he told her? But Derwen, still behind Annwyl, shook his head "no."

"It is I who summoned him," Annwyl said, standing her ground just inside the doorway, her self-assured woman-self barely gaining ascendency over the role of loving daughter. But barely was enough.

Abertha and Derwen were shocked into silence while Merlin chastised himself for falling into the seductive comfort of the cottage and letting his guard down. He had let this whole thing throw him out of himself. Time to regain his balance, though to do so would not be easy. This young woman who stood before him was the mirror image of her mother and, though not fully into her womanly beauty, glowed with the promise of the same compelling beauty and grace that had so enchanted him years ago. *Come now,* he thought, *you're the most powerful mage in these lands. Surely this young girl will be no match for you.*

"Then it was you who brought this wind then," he accused her, though not harshly.

"Well...I....not intentionally. I think it came of my anticipation."

She was indeed powerful, he thought, and quite out of control. Abertha was right, but she could have saved her breath. This encounter told him all he needed to know about this child -- his child.

"Annwyl is what they call you?"

"Yes."

"And do you like the name? Are you comfortable in it?"

Annwyl stole a glance at Abertha. She had done her best raising her, and while Annwyl was anxious to leave the confines of their love and mundane expectations, she had feelings for them nonetheless. She would keep the name, at least for now.

"It will do," she said, striving to keep her aloof demeanor.

Merlin sighed. "Do you ride?"

"Of course."

"You'll need to ride with me. I did not bring a second mount. Are there things you wish to pack?"

"A few clothes and my warm cloak. Nothing burdensome I hope."

"Then be about it."

Abertha and Derwen stood clutching each other in their grief. As the wizard and the child rode out of the yard, Abertha spoke, "Our poor Annwyl...carrying the legacy of madness on the one hand and magic on the other."

"She was never ours, was she?" Derwen said, defeated.

"No, not really," Abertha said, her eyes never leaving their retreating forms. "I just hope he hasn't come too late."

As Merlin and Annwyl rode away from the cottage, Annwyl kept her eyes straight ahead, lest the weakness of sentiment find its way into her heart, but as they passed the edge of the forest, she glanced ever so briefly toward the path that led to the three-trunked oak and the single copper that lay buried among its roots.

4

The Cave

Cornwall, England

They should have taken the journey easy, two to a horse as they were, but Merlin was wary of discovery and so rode his mount harder than was wise. Every bird that flew overhead, every fox that dashed across their path he imagined would carry the story of him and his young charge straight to Nimue. He gritted his teeth against the disgust he felt at his own failing. There was a day when he would have ridden at any pace he damn well chose, with any kind of baggage he desired, unafraid -- only wary -- of prying eyes, spies, or traps, and confident that all but a few of nature's creatures would readily do his bidding. Foolish man. But Nimue wasn't his first mistake, as his current freight reminded him. Curse the weakness of the flesh, made all that much worse as one's power diminishes which surely his was doing. He could feel the power he used to take for granted radiating from the girl pressing herself against him as she clung to his waist, wordlessly enduring the hard ride.

As reluctant as he was to do so, he knew they would have to stop. Food, rest, and, if possible, a horse for the girl. She had said she could ride and he doubted she would take advantage of the freedom, having been the one who called *him*.

He knew of a place, not a bustling inn, but a quiet place with simple food and rough but serviceable rooms, though nothing like Abertha's and Derwen's cottage, blessed reprieve from the ills of the wider world that it was. To arrive there before nightfall, he would have to urge his horse to a gallop.

"Hold tight," he growled to his charge.

At the inn, Annwyl ate in intense silence and went to her room without a word. Still, over dinner she had fixed him with those uncanny eyes, as though she would dig into the depths of his soul and pull his thoughts from his mind. *Give her a few years,* he thought, *and perhaps she will be a match for Nimue after all. She has the beauty and the latent, raw power. Whether she has or will have the cunning remains to be seen.*

That night though Merlin's body found some rest, his mind could not. Helplessly, he stared into the darkness as though he might find some clue there as to what lay ahead, but even with his prescience, he could conjure nothing. So much of what he had dealt with in his life had come from his own orchestrations. He would choose his pieces and set them on the board then use his cunning to move them as best fulfilled the needs of the moment. But this...a child, *his child.* This had not been his intention at all. What might arise from this circumstance was entirely and maddeningly hidden from him.

The next day they rode the coast road at a smart pace. Mercifully, the day was crisp but clear and the horses were pleased to carry their burdens without complaint. After the sleepless night, Merlin chose to let his mind go to stillness, thinking of nothing, hearing only the beat of the hoofs and feeling only the blessed sun on his face, hopeful that insight would visit him soon enough.

When they reached a small town, Merlin told Annwyl they would be leaving her horse there, for reasons that would become obvious later.

"We haven't much farther to go."

Again, wordlessly, though frowning slightly, Annwyl obediently dismounted and pulled herself up behind the mage once again, and onward they rode. Higher and higher they rose above the sea until they saw a castle in the distance. At the sight of it, Annwyl's heart quickened. If this be their destination, then she was more than glad she'd set these events in motion. To be at court! Fine dresses, great feasts and plenty of opportunity for intrigue and scheming. How she would delight in her escape from the confines of the simple life.

"Is that where we're going, to that castle?"

Merlin was jolted out of his trance as Annwyl addressed him at last. Quickly recovering himself he answered,

"Near there, but not there exactly."

"What is it?"

"Tintagel."

"Is it splendid?"

"Splendid enough."

"Where are we going then?"

"You'll see." For the time being, it seemed to Annwyl that they continued straight toward the castle despite what Merlin had said, until they came to a place where the path to the castle went uphill and another forked down toward the sea. To Annwyl's surprise and chagrin, they stopped on the verge of the latter.

"Best dismount. It's too steep for the horse to manage with both of us riding."

"But there's nothing down there except the sea!" Annwyl protested.

"Ah, but there is. Have a little faith my dear."

Annwyl wasn't sure whether she was terrified or mesmerized by the pounding surf that seemed to be their destination. The salt-laden wind was exhilarating, but the rhythmic whisper of the waves made her sleepy. Merlin was already well ahead of her so, despite her trepidation, she grabbed her skirts and angled her way down the steep cliff. When her feet touched sand, she stood in amazement. The sea came within just a few feet of where they stood. To her left, Tintagel Castle loomed above them, and directly below it, rising from the sand, a great black mouth yawned in the side of the cliff, seemingly sipping the sea as the waves teasingly advanced and retreated from its lip.

"Follow me if you don't want to get soaked." Leaving the horse on the beach, Merlin led the way into the mouth of the cave. At first, Annwyl was blind in the darkness, but slowly her eyes adjusted as they followed the shafts of sunlight fingering their way into the cave. Just once, she turned back to the opening to see a rainbow flickering in the sea mist.

"Can you conjure some light for yourself?" Merlin asked as he opened his palm to reveal a butter-colored orb that emitted a surprising amount of light. But Annwyl just glared at the magician, anger, fear and excitement burning in her mind.

"No matter," he said, as he led the way deeper into the cave until they came to what appeared to be a dead end. Merlin muttered a word Annwyl didn't quite catch, and pushed gently as the wall gave away to an opening already filled with crystalline light. When Merlin set his orb on a pedestal just inside the opening, the warm light, punctuated by pinpoints of shimmering crystal, revealed a large, well-appointed room, more alluring than she had imagined even the castle would be. Annwyl's anger morphed into something even more terrifying and consuming. Here was a glimpse of what she most feared...and most desired.

"What is this place?" Annwyl whispered, afraid to chase away what could only be an illusion.

"Home, more or less."

"Is it real?"

"Define real..." but Merlin caught himself, reminded himself that he was dealing with a child, one that was part of him to boot.

"Real enough then. I think you'll be sufficiently comfortable here until I return."

"Return? I'm to stay here? Alone? In a cave?"

Merlin drew Annwyl over to the hearth. A wave of his hand ignited a welcoming fire. He pulled up two comfortable chairs, sat Annwyl down in one and took the other himself. This was it then. Neither of them could skitter around the situation any longer. Annwyl was his...and his responsibility...but so much else was as well and so much more than one girl-child's feelings was at stake. He would have to muddle through this unknown territory as well as he could for now, until he could get some clarity on what was best to be done.

"There's much I need to tell you and not much time, for now at least..."

So he began, and as the firelight played across his face Annwyl listened as Merlin explained, however haltingly, that he needed to return to Nimue before she could fret over his absence, but that he would soon return. In the meantime, she was to make herself at home. There was plenty to eat and she could begin her lessons. There were manuscripts explaining the druidic Ogham markings that she should study and, well, the place was full of magic. Soon enough, he continued, he would return and they would study in earnest. He cautioned against her attempting to leave, gently suggesting that he would place a spell on the "door" so as to keep her safe.

As Merlin talked, he watched Annwyl for her reactions. Despite all the other claims to his attention, he had to make at least some effort at understanding this child. He wanted to discount her as silly, as typical, as something he needed only to clothe and house until he could figure out what to do with her, but the piece of her that was him reached out like tendrils and caught at something deep inside him. He had felt her power, sensed it as one might sense a crouched animal in the woods. Thrown off by her as he was, on this score, at least, he believed he could still trust his intuition.

He understood, too, that Annwyl chafed at being held prisoner in a cave, but he also sensed that her youthful curiosity was piqued by the abundant artifacts in the room.

There was plenty here to explore and he wondered...to what extent did she feel the magic? How much could she already manipulate? Clearly, something had awakened, else why would he have been summoned? But to what degree, and did he dare leave her here? It would be a test of his own magic to trust that with hers so untried, so misunderstood, that despite the power inherent in the cave, confined here as she would be, she would be safe...and the outside world would be safe from her.

Perhaps the warmth of the fire, or the promise of so much to explore, softened Annwyl and encouraged her. Being left to her own devices in what appeared to be a playground of magical things -- how could that not appeal? It seemed to her that his promise to return was sincere. He was, after all, her true father, of this she was certain. Every molecule of her being told her it was true.

As he prepared to depart, he hesitated, then kissed her gently on the forehead. "I will return. I promise." Then, before she could speak, he disappeared into the darkness.

Moments after Merlin's departure, Annwyl slid into a restorative sleep before a fire that never seemed to need stoking. How long she slept, or if she dreamed, she couldn't say, but when she awoke, she saw that there, on the chair Merlin had recently vacated, sat an owl, his enormous eyes trained directly upon her. As Annwyl stirred, shaken by the sight of so large a bird in such close proximity, the owl unfurled his cloud-white wings, shook himself, then majestically refolded them, as if to say, "now you see that I am not to be abused, nor is the home of my Master which I am here to protect." Not that Annwyl needed the warning. The oversized bird was quite menacing enough. For a long time, she sat there, afraid to move, until hunger got the best of her. Slowly she rose, all the time keeping her eye on the owl, who, in turn, kept his huge amber eyes on her, but did not move. Rather, he swiveled his head this way and that, prepared to keep her ever in his sight. Cautiously, Annwyl backed away from the hearth, wanting for all the world to turn her back on the owl so that she could search in earnest for some food, but as she thought that, the owl nodded, or so she imagined, and somehow let the threat cool in his eyes. Well then, at least for now he didn't seem disposed to do her harm.

5

The Tower

As the days wore on, Annwyl found the cave fascinating, with seemingly endless possibilities for exploration, but always the Owl watched her. She pulled books from the shelf and leafed through them, grateful that Abertha had taught her to read...but not everything in these books was in an alphabet she recognized. Then there were all the strange amulets and trinkets. She touched each one but was careful to return them to their exact placement. She'd learned enough from her dark dreams to know that objects held power and must be treated with care...and then, too, there was this nagging desire to please her mysterious father, as much as she still harbored a tinge of anger at him. Perhaps the two emotions were born of the same seed.

There were maps and instruments she couldn't even begin to imagine their purpose. In a seemingly disorganized array, she saw liquids and powders, crystals, rocks, sticks, dried leaves and flowers, strange figurines, and things she couldn't name. At first the abundance thrilled her, but soon she found it overwhelming. If she'd hoped to understand all this, where would she begin?

As she tired from exploration, Annwyl turned to finding something soft, something she dared move that she could put in her arms or beneath her head when even the mysteries and magic of the cave could keep her awake no longer...something to comfort her, for she feared the return of the dark dreams that had come to her in Wales and left her feeling both not herself and more herself than she had ever dared imagine. But night after night, despite her fears, she slept in comfort, her head nestled on a sheepskin robe she found neatly tucked on a shelf, far from the busier part of the cave. It was almost like her dreams had found their concrete reality in the cave and so left her in peace.

And always the owl stood watch.

At last, she could stand it no longer. Too young to have developed comfort in solitude, she longed for companionship and the owl would just have to do. Trying to keep the exasperation from her tone, and failing miserably, she gathered her courage and from what she hoped was a safe distance, found her voice, craggy from disuse.

"So, Owl," she croaked, "are you my jailer then?"

Nothing.

"Certainly not a pet."

Nothing.

"Dinner, if I felt like pulling all your feathers out?" She offered brazenly.

To this Owl ruffled his pristine feathers ever so slightly.

"What then?"

To her shock, Owl spread his wings and flew over her head, lifting her already tousled hair, and landed on a shelf -- one within her reach -- then swiveled his head, first to her, then to the various manuscripts and back again.

Annwyl approached cautiously. Almost respectfully, Owl backed away slightly to give her some distance from his formidable beak, but nodded as though pointing to a bright red book easily within her reach. It was warm to the touch, its worn leather a comfort in her hand. On the cover was a strange glyph of two interlocking circles over the title, *As Above, So Below.*

She couldn't have returned the book to the shelf if she had wanted to. Even had Owl lunged toward her, she would have clung to the volume. But nothing of the sort happened. Owl stared at her from his perch on the shelf, a penetrating, demanding stare.

"I can read it then?" she asked, as though Owl would answer. But he did blink, once, and nodded his silky white head ever so slightly.

"You *want* me to read it?" Another nod, deeper this time.

Annwyl smiled for the first time since she had set foot in this strange place. She strode to the fire and curled into what she'd come to consider *her* chair and with trembling hand, opened the book feeling like she was opening a door to a magical realm, which indeed she was. Owl closed his eyes, as though to give Annwyl some space, or as a display of trust. Annwyl fell deep into her reading and lost all track of time and place as she read of the connections between earth and sky, water and air, how all the creatures and plants of the earth were interconnected, how energy flowed between everything and how humans, so large in their own minds, were but a small part of the whole.

The anger and darkness that had engulfed her these past years, loosened its grip. There was a comfort in these words, these ideas of connection between all things. She felt wrapped in a blanket of wholeness, woven of threads of animal fur and sea foam, sunsets and bone, stone and birdsong. In her own being, she felt both small and large, as though her troubling thoughts were of little concern, but her being as large as anything she could imagine. She had only to embrace it. As the words entered her mind, there crept into her heart, ever so slightly, something like a breath of rain-washed earth -- a glimpse of the joy of living into this description of a larger reality.

When she awoke, the book had slipped from her lap into the space between her leg and the side of the chair. Owl was exactly where he had been...how long ago? The cave was exactly the same as it had been, the fire burning its usual, unchanging perfection of wood and flame. But Annwyl felt slightly different. Lighter. As though her foot might not completely touch the floor when she rose to move to her makeshift bed. A sweet exhaustion filled her and as she slept, in the place once haunted by darkness there was only sunlit sky against which tree branches seemed to spell out magical incantations that were almost, but not quite, decipherable.

Over the next days, Annwyl and Owl developed a tentative relationship. Owl seemed to invite her into new discoveries and she became somewhat better at reading his avian gestures. To her delight, Owl lead her to an alcove she had not noticed before, on the floor of which was a tiled chessboard, and scattered across the floor were carved chess pieces, some of wood, others molded from a gray clay flecked with black. The pieces were roughly a foot tall, like dolls Annwyl thought. Owl could easily move them with his beak or leaning his weight against them and so, leaving the glittering pieces to Annwyl, Owl became her formidable opponent.

And so, the days passed.

"I need a name for you," she declared one night. Owl gave her a skeptical look.

"Oh, I expect you already have one, but I don't know it and who knows when father will return? So, I think I'll call you 'Perch' because that's what you do."

So much more than that, Owl thought, but until Merlin returned, he resigned himself to being called by the humiliating name.

"So, Perch, I'm tired of moving pieces around the floor. Teach me a spell. Perhaps one that would open the door?"

Perch looked at Annwyl with unflinching stoniness.

"Have mercy on me. I've not seen sunlight for days. Maybe it's weeks. Who would know locked in here?"

But Perch was resolute. He knew Merlin's wishes and they did not include letting Annwyl free, not that she would get very far.

Annwyl pouted, but it was not that which moved the owl, rather a recognition that of course, as a human, sooner or later she would need to see the sun, to breathe in the sea air. There was a way to bring her such -- not to set her free, but to give her the daylight if only for a little while.

Perch flew to be in front of Annwyl, but in her pout, she turned her back on him. Again, the same maneuver. Again, she turned. Owls can show immense patience waiting for their prey, but alas, this child was not prey, but his charge, like it or not. Perch swept his massive wing across the chessboard, scattering the stone pieces across the floor, the clatter echoing out of the alcove and into the entire cave.

An angry owl was nothing to taunt, that much Annwyl knew for certain. She unfolded her arms and faced him, waiting for this next move, hoping it would not be to sweep her into a corner as he had done with the chess pieces.

Perch flew to a far corner in the depth of the cave where the magic cave-light did not quite reach; an area of the cave that Annwyl had not even been aware of much less explored. From its murky depths, Perch turned his head toward Annwyl and fixed his piercing gaze upon her.

She hesitated to think what might befall her if she did not follow. Not willing to find out, she went to him and followed as he moved into the deeper darkness, barely able to see his brilliant white feathers. Gradually, she felt the walls tighten around her until she could sense that she was in a narrow passageway, now dimly lit by crystals embedded in the stone.

After a particularly sharp turn, Annwyl found herself at the base of a stairway. Her heart beating wildly, she began her ascent up the stone stairs, struggled to keep up with the owl. Up and up she climbed, until she was quite out of breath, but excitement sustained her. When she thought she could climb no more, she saw a shaft of light --

sunlight! Suddenly, Perch shot through the hole in the darkness, his wings glistening in the sun. Annwyl took the last few steps to emerge through the same hole to find herself looking out from a high cliff, the sky gloriously lit with the same sunshine that scattered diamonds across the sea below.

In the near distance, she could see the castle of Tintagel, but if she had any thought of adventuring, there was no hope for it, for she stood on a tower of land that made a sheer drop on every side save the one she had emerged from. There was nothing to do from here but to sit and enjoy the view, unless, like Perch, one could fly. So, sit and enjoy the view she did, glorying in the warmth of the sun and the colors of the earth.

Perhaps she fell asleep, or just dozed in the sun, breathing in the sea-fresh air with pure joy. Perch had disappeared, but Annwyl was too besotted by the light and the air to care. Having been so long in the cave, she had almost forgotten how precious all this was, how for granted she had taken the special warmth of the sun, the salt-tinged air, the sound of the wind through the sedge. She loosened her hair to the wind which tossed it about like wings while new thoughts played at the corners of her mind. Lying on the ground, she could almost imagine melding with the earth, the molecules of human and nature interchanging, drawing energy from one another. Perhaps she would never eat again, she thought, only draw her sustenance from the sun like all the green things of the earth. The thought made her feel light, limitless, free.

When at last Perch returned, the sun was nearly touching the horizon. She would have liked to watch it dip into the sea, but Perch made it clear that they were to return to the cave. Down the stone steps she made her way, the darkness more impenetrable to her eyes from having been so long in the daylight, her hands outstretched to the walls, her feet sliding ahead slowly to the edge of each step. The descent was much more frightening than the upward climb had been, but she was heartened by the joy she had felt above. She would conquer this for, owl willing, she was determined to make daily pilgrimages to the world of sunlight. Wrapped in this mood of joy and determination, she almost slipped when suddenly her right hand fell into a chill nothingness. For a moment she panicked. She didn't remember any turnings on the way up, but she had not been clinging to the walls then. Her heart pounding, she stood stark still, calling on all her senses to tell her which way to go.

"Perch?" she called into the darkness. "PERCH!" Surely, he must hear her, if not her call, then the drumbeat of her heart. She waited and waited. Nothing. Shaking with fear, she sat down on the step and when her feet found the next step below, her mind swam up out of her fear and into her head. If she followed the place where the steps went downward, surely, she would be on the right path. But what if the opening on her right also went downward? Which way to go and what if she chose the wrong way and fell into a hole? Finally deciding to avoid the opening on her right, she rose on shaky legs to continue her descent when Perch's whiteness came flying toward her from below. She was on the right path then after all.

"Stay where I can see you, you dumb bird!" she said, forgetting her manners completely.

After that, they made almost daily trips to the cliff. Sometimes Annwyl would take a book with her to study, although she usually ended up laying it aside after a short while and just lounging in the salt-laden air. On inclement days, Annwyl would sit just inside the tower stairs, delighting in whatever nature had to offer. But with each descent, she grew more and more curious about the opening she could sense on her right, about half-way down the tower. As her trips continued, she grew in confidence on the stairs and her eyes seemed to adjust more readily to the dim light, until one day, it occurred to her to count the steps from the strange opening to the bottom. Nineteen. In the days that followed, she would test her finding, counting nineteen steps up then reaching with her left hand until the wall fell away. Still, without some kind of light, she was reluctant to venture off the path she knew and Perch had shown no inclination to draw her in any new direction, despite the fact that she couldn't imagine for an instant that he didn't know about it. There had to be a reason he had not added that to the list of wonderous things he had shown her. Or maybe there was nothing there -- just an opening in the rock, an empty alcove not worthy of attention.

Then why did it haunt her so, dominate her thoughts, try as she might to let it be?

As Annwyl got more comfortable with her life in the cave, her typically self-absorbed thoughts eventually turned to concern for her companion. She never saw him eat but, surely, he must. Aren't owls creatures of the night? One has no visual way to measure the passing of day and night in a cave -- at least humans don't. Annwyl depended on Perch to mark the evening as he did each "day" by, just when Annwyl's energy was beginning to flag, he'd fly resolutely to his perch, fold his wings and close his eyes as though all matters were settled and there was nothing more for it but to sleep, which Annwyl generally welcomed. But now she wondered. Did he sleep all night, as she did, or did he follow the imperatives of his kind and take wing, up the tower stairs and out into the prey-rich darkness?

He must, she thought, and if he did, she would be free to explore the rest of the tower. That night, when Perch perched, she feigned sleep, but kept a covert watch on the owl, waiting to see if her theory was correct. The task proved more difficult than she had imagined, for the time passed without so much as a twitch from the owl. Sleep tugged at her, but her determination to explore the other passage was enough to keep her teetering on the edge of submission. After an excruciatingly long time, she heard the rustle of wings and when she finally dared look, the owl was gone.

As Perch disappeared up the tower stairs, Annwyl creeped up nineteen stairs, felt for the opening and edged in. There were no crystals embedded in the walls here as there were along the tower stairs, only darkness. Perhaps, she thought, her eyes would adjust if she stood there long enough, but this was a blackness like nothing she'd ever experienced. Reason dictated that, for now, she would have to turn back. Defeat wasn't an experience Annwyl took lightly, and as she grudgingly made her way back to the cave, she settled on a plan. A torch would smoke and might alert Perch. Also, it could go out, leaving her deep in a passageway, blind and lost. She had a better idea. She would tear the cave apart until she found a spell for the light orb Merlin had conjured that first day of arriving at the cave. He had done it so casually it couldn't be that hard.

Annwyl returned to the cave, relieved to find that Perch had not yet returned, and fell into a welcome sleep, realizing, nevertheless, that she would have to learn to be a night creature.

The next day, and for many days thereafter, she searched the cave for a spell of illumination. Surely there was something. The cave itself was lit by some unseen force, neither natural light nor fire, but a constant glow that seemed to rise and fall as needed. There had to be a spell. Keeping a calm attitude was getting harder by the day as her frustration rose, but she could not let Perch know what she was up to. More than once, however, she almost asked him to help her. Maybe she could make it sound like an innocent request, but she couldn't trust that her own duplicity wouldn't be guessed by the wise old bird, so she kept looking, feigning a scholarly interest that she hadn't previously shown. Perhaps the owl would believe the daily trips to the surface had awakened a liveliness in her, a narrative that Annwyl reinforced, never leaving for the cliff without a book in her hand. For his part, Perch was delighted to see his charge so eager and studious.

When at last she found the spell, the next thing was to practice it, again, without Perch's knowledge. During his night flights then was the time. Over and over she moved her hands and said the words as well as she knew how to pronounce them, and while she was, on occasion, able to call forth a feeble glow, a full-blown orb of light escaped her. Frustration threatened to derail her, to let loose the destructive tendencies that were always so on the verge within her, but something held her back, helped her keep focused on her goal. From that interior struggle arose a thought -- would, could, her dreams help? Since being in Merlin's cave, she had had none of her terrifying dreams. In truth, she had seemed to sleep dreamlessly and deep, arising refreshed and eager each day. But there was also a hint of loss -- not of the darkness and terror of the dreams, but of the power that lurked in them, a power that whispered to her and stirred in her mind.

What if her dreams could help her? Life in a wizard's workshop had inclined her to think that there was more possibility in the world than folks imagine. So, for the next week, she determined that before sleep, she would invite a dream that would help her to cast the spell correctly. If she feared opening herself up to terrors, she did not allow that to come to consciousness, so driven was she to explore the tower.

And before long, her dreams obliged. One wonderous night, she clearly heard the words and saw the hand movements. Victorious, she bolted from sleep, and seeing that Perch was still absent she cast the spell. Instantly she held an orb of light that lit even the darkest corner of the cave. For the next hour she played with the light, dimming it, bringing it to brilliance -- she even managed a slight tint of blue. Devilishly proud of herself, she crawled back into her bedding and lay awake until she saw the white streak enter the cave and alight in its usual place.

There you have it, bird, Annwyl thought to herself, *tomorrow night you will not be the only one to take flight.*

At the mouth of the opening, Annwyl cast her spell, so full of excitement her hand trembled, making the light flicker like a candle in the wind as it revealed a short passage ending in a flight of stairs winding upwards. If she thought she could keep a sense of where she was in relation to the cave, she was mistaken, for the upward staircase twisted and turned like a piece of string balled up and cast aside. Just at the point where Annwyl began to feel nauseous, however, the stairs stopped and settled into a straight passageway. As Annwyl peered down the length of it she could see pinpricks of light here and there. To see them better, she waved her hand over the orb to dim its light then made her way down the passage to the first of the lighted specks. The light was coming from behind the wall!

Annwyl put her eye to the hole and was amazed to see that she was looking into a large and richly appointed hall with a large table running down the center. The remains of a feast were scattered across its surface and chairs and benches had been left askew while candles and torches sputtered. When she had taken in every detail of the room that she could see, she moved to another hole, this one only a dim glimmer provided by the fire that burned within a bed chamber. Another and another until she came to a large room, alight with torches at regular intervals along the wall and at one end, opposite imposing and ornately carved doors was...a throne. This must be Tintagel, built on the hill above the cave, accessed by this subterranean warren of stairs and passageways. Accessed, she had to chuckle, by Merlin. The sly fox had spy holes through which he gleaned the comings and goings of the castle. It would take Annwyl a while to wrap her head around all that meant, but in the meantime, her understanding that that access was now hers as well, made her dizzy with delight.

But the night must be getting on. All this potential would be dashed, she feared, if Perch got back to the cave before she did. Though she had not seen anyone awake and about in the castle, nevertheless, she would keep the orb dim until she was well away from the peepholes, then raise it high and make haste on the return. All was going well until she was deep into the twisting passageway, when the light of the orb began to faulter. Annwyl passed her hand over it but to no avail. Instead of brightening, it went dimmer still. Why was it failing? The spell had said nothing that she could discern about a limited duration. Perhaps it was because she had lost focus. Certainly, she was in an elevated state, considering all the ramifications of what she had found. Whatever the cause, her concern now was getting back to her bed before the light failed completely. The faster she went, the dimmer the light became until halfway down the passage stairs, it failed altogether and Annwyl was cast into utter blackness.

Panic threatened to paralyze her, the darkness a hood blinding her and stifling her breath. Tears welled in her eyes and suddenly she was a little girl again, lost, alone, and unable to move forward. Her knees felt week, forcing her to sit. Her head in her hands, she knew full well she couldn't stay as she was, nor was there any one to rescue her. Precious moments passed until she could calm herself and find the courage to move ahead despite her blindness, one careful step at a time, keeping her palm pressed tightly against the wall.   She hadn't seen any other branching passages -- unless she had missed them, a thought which she banished from her mind lest it pull her to a stop once more. Heart thudding, palm scratched by the surface of the stone, she made her way through the dark as fast as she could until at last, she reached the fork and the crystal-lit tower. Nineteen steps to home and no light coming from the opening at the cliff. At the edge of the passage, she peered around the corner to find that Perch had not yet returned. Grateful but emotionally drained, she fell into her bed.

6

Discovery

As spying became a way of life for Annwyl, her studies diminished. Now, she was no longer interested in books -- she was learning in the school of life. As soon as Perch left, she'd fly into the tower and down the passage to the "hall of visions" as she'd come to call it. Since she could only go at night, she rarely saw people about, but used the time to explore a bit farther each time, naming each room and imagining as best she could the layout of the castle. Familiarity calming her excitement, she was able to keep the orb dutiful to her commands. On rare occasions, she'd see a servant tidying up or stoking a fire, and once or twice a small group of men huddled in conversation. Once, at a bedchamber, the door across from her eye-hole opened with the flash of candlelight which found its way to a night table while a ghostly figure slipped into the bedcurtains and disappeared into a muffled cacophony of giggles and groans.

The more she explored, the more she began to understand about castle life, limited as it was to night-knowledge. But as time wore on, and her investigation took her farther, it became clear that more goes on at night than one might expect. Clandestine meetings, errands, rounds, bedchamber intrigues, plots, petty thefts and strange rituals. Annwyl's glimmering green eyes took it all in and what she saw became the work of her "daylight" hours in the cave, puzzling out meanings and implications. Eventually, she began to wonder as well at Merlin's intention and use of the information *he* learned as such a silent witness. And of course, not constrained to night spying only, he was free to wander behind the lives of the castle-dwellers any time he chose. A mouse in the walls, privy to both public and private activities. Or was it a fox? Consumed by a growing and insatiable hunger, she chafed at her inability to travel the passage in the daylight hours, but Perch was steadfast in his habits, keeping Annwyl pinned to a similarly predictable routine.

Until the day that Perch did not return from his night flights.

Annwyl waited all day, expecting a blur of feathers and talons to arrive at any moment, but the day passed and the owl did not appear. Emotions roiled in the young woman. To lose Perch's company would be devastating. On the other hand, left to her own devices, she could explore the castle to her heart's content. But if something had happened to the owl, as of course it might well have, it would be the greatest loss Annwyl had experienced in her relatively short lifetime.

After three days of waiting and wondering, fretting and planning, she chose to fill the void of her loss with all the wonders that awaited her behind the tiny holes in the stone tunnel. What she discovered was far more than she had bargained for. There were more than just peepholes looking into the castle. At the end of the passageway, which she now had all the time in the world to explore, there was a door.

From the view in the last hole before it, she could see what looked like a storeroom, perhaps the safest place for a hidden entrance. As excited as Annwyl was to find a way into the castle, her heart beat a rhythm of caution. Best to make her entrance at night, she reasoned, and cloaked, so as to be as hidden as possible. *And yet...* how could she wait?

The moment she placed her hand on the door handle, she knew she could not wait. She would blend in -- pretend she was a servant. The handle was cool in her hand as she lifted the latch and pulled the door toward her. Surprisingly, the door made not so much as a whisper as it opened into...blackness. Incautiously, Annwyl lifted her orb so that light flooded the space, which, to her immense disappointment, was no bigger than a closet and, as far as she could tell, held no door into the castle. *This couldn't be*, she thought, once again furious with her missing father. This had to be a way into the castle. Was Merlin so powerful he could walk through walls? Somehow, she doubted it. Not to be defeated, she held the orb close to the walls, running her hand carefully over their cold surface, searching for a seam, a hidden knob, *something* that would indicate an opening, but found nothing. Youthful rage threatened to consume her, but she forced herself to calm down, aware, at last, that rage would do no good and moreover was likely to douse her light orb. Instead, she reminded herself that she was Merlin's daughter. His mind couldn't be entirely foreign to her.

Sliding to the floor, she dimmed the orb and willed herself into quiet, inviting the visions that had so often plagued her, keeping in mind her desire to find the opening to the castle that she was certain existed somewhere on these walls. It was as though she slumbered. Her head dropped, the orb dimmed to twilight, and the visions came. How long she suffered them was hard to tell but when she at last swam up out of a darkness blacker than the room itself, a phrase played in her head -- words that had no meaning to her, but she was sure they were what she needed.

Saying them aloud, she waited, then spoke them again with more conviction, twirling as she did so in order that she might scan the room and notice the slightest movement. On the third try, she heard a faint grinding of stone against stone as a sliver of pale light shone into her little closet. The opening was just wide enough for her to slip through, and once she was clear of it, it closed again of its own accord, showing only an uninterrupted wall in the far corner of a large storeroom full of cheeses and grain, and barrels of mead. Annwyl couldn't help but wonder if Merlin helped himself to bits of this wealth from time to time.

Now what? she asked herself. Was she ready to explore the castle without the safety of the hidden passage? Certainly, after all this, it would be foolish not to. Wishing she knew a spell of invisibility, Annwyl willed herself as inconspicuous as possible as she ventured out into the castle.

Tintagel was beautiful. Tapestries everywhere, high ceilings and ornate furnishings. She knew that to gawk would give her away and so she did her best to stride along the hallways as though she belonged, hoping she would be seen as just one of many servants or ladies' maids. She seemed to be getting away with it until she heard her father's name rise above the conversation floating into the hallway from a particularly beautiful chamber. She crept closer and hovered just outside the door, able only to hear fragments.

"Gotten his due at last...enchantress...finally rid...raise a glass...*To the end of Merlin.*"

Her indrawn breath gave her away. Before she could think to run, a guard just inside the door swung around and grabbed her by the hair, dragging her into the hallway and away from the door.

"What have we here, eh? Snooping about the Duke's council? I've seen people beheaded for less..."

Annwyl cried out as the guard tugged at her hair, arousing the interest of the men gathered in the chamber.

"What is this commotion?" asked a man, richly dressed, with an air of importance.

"A snoop, Sire," the guard answered, "she was listening at the door."

"Whom does she serve?" the man asked, clearly puzzled by Annwyl's plain attire. "She doesn't appear to belong to the court..."

At that a young man stepped up. "I know her," he claimed, a bit too loudly. "She is from the village, a seamstress's...apprentice."

"Really Gawen?" The man turned, clearly suspicious of the young man's claim. "What of the court seamstresses? Are they not good enough for you, or is there something more intimate she's here to measure?" With that the rest of the men now gathering around laughed heartily. But the young man remained self-possessed.

"I wanted a special garment...something out of the ordinary to please the Duke."

The guard had yet to let go of Annwyl's hair and now gave it a tug as though that would verify the truth of the young man's story. Again, Annwyl let out a cry.

"Enough of that, man!" the first man ordered. "If she is who you say she is, Gawen, then she is your charge. Take her from here and see to it that she better knows her place henceforth."

With that, the guard reluctantly let go of Annwyl, pushing her toward Gawen as the men filed back into the council room, leaving Annwyl and Gawen alone in the hall.

"Well, come then," Gawen said, under his breath, "let's find out who you really are and what your business is here. Mind you, I spared you the dungeon for now, but that fate may still await you. Come with me and if you try to run, I'll have you cut down like a stag."

"Where are you taking me?" Annwyl dared ask.

"Humph," Gawen replied, shrugging. "Anywhere I please."

Perhaps the dungeon would have been the better option, Annwyl wondered, when Gawen pushed her into a lavishly decorated and tapestried bedchamber. What little Annwyl knew of the world at least included the sense that privileged young men don't worry much about being kind to young women.

"Sit," he ordered, motioning her to a chair by the hearth. "Now, who are you and how did you get in here?"

Annwyl tried frantically to come up with a believable lie, but the extremity of her situation mixed with her lack of knowledge about the world left her with nothing. She couldn't even come up with a plausible entrance to the castle, only knowing Tintagel through tiny holes in its walls. There was nothing for it but to tell the truth...and a part of the truth was that Annwyl was painfully lonely, having lived so long in a cave with nothing but an owl for company. In her youthful innocence, she reasoned that either this young man would become an ally or he would throw her in the dungeon. Never had the two heads of a coin been so disparate.

"I will tell you the truth," she began, playing the only coin she had, "but you must swear to secrecy for what I will tell you includes knowledge of a secret long held."

"I think you are in no position to bargain, lass," but Annwyl could tell his interest was piqued.

"Then I shall remain mute and you can imprison me and my secret," Annwyl bluffed.

Gawen's face twisted into a half smile.

"Should we start with your name?"

"Annwyl is how I've been named." Then, after a pause, almost to herself, "I know this room."

"Whatever do you mean?" Gawen exclaimed, jolted out of his insolent posture by the audacity of this pathetic creature. "These are my chambers. I would know if you'd been here."

"I will tell you how I come to know this place and much of the rest of the castle," Annwyl said, a bit of her powers of influence creeping into her voice unbeknownst to her, "but first you must tell me of what was said in the Duke's chamber regarding Merlin."

Now Gawen was on high alert. No one in Tintagel took the mention of Merlin lightly. Even now, despite the news of his apparent incapacitation, one could not be confident that some mischief was not afoot. Annwyl, however, had no way of knowing of Merlin's reputation in Cornwall, although, by Gawen's reaction, she was beginning to guess.

"You're stalling," he growled. "What do you care of the magician's fate?"

"I promise you," Annwyl said, earnest now, "I will share with you a secret of great power, but I must know what has happened to m...Merlin."

"Well, what harm is there in it then?" Gawen mused. "The fool has been trapped by his own trickery. The Lady Nimue, with whom he has had an ill-advised dalliance, has, according to reports, used his own enchantments against him and bound him somewhere in the forest of Broceliande."

"Bound him?"

"Rendered him helpless, imprisoned him with magic."

It took some time for Annwyl to digest the news and what it meant to her. As conflicted as she was about Merlin, he was her only connection with the world, or with any possible future. All her hopes rested on his return to the cave, his teaching and, presumably, his protection as he brought her into his life. If he was imprisoned, what would happen to her? She could not...would not, continue to live like a mole in a cave, but to strike out on her own seemed impossible.

And now Perch's disappearance made sense. Had he flown to help his master, or had his own power been sapped by this Nimue?

She looked more closely at Gawen, trying to take his measure. He had rescued her, but to what end? If she told him the truth, would he conspire with her? For now, it seemed clear to her that she would have to try to rescue Merlin, if for no other reason than for her own future. It was then that she remembered the day of her sixteenth birthday, and the way she was able to control the herbalist and the young boy. Could she do that with Gawen, *make* him do her bidding? It had been a long while since she had tested those skills, and she had only done so with a foolish old woman and a young boy. Gawen might be another matter altogether. She would have to feel her way into this. For now, she was more convinced than ever that she needed to draw him in.

"May I rise?" Annwyl asked, feigning a humility she hoped would begin the process of winning Gawen over.

"If you must," Gawen said, but clearly on his guard and rising with her.

Annwyl walked to the far wall of the room and searched the space between the tapestries.

"Here," she said. "Look here."

Gawen came to where she stood and put his hand on the wall where she was pointing.

"There's a hole in the wall! I never noticed that." He looked at her questioningly.

"You certainly weren't meant to," she said, enjoying now the confirmation that she did indeed have something powerful to bargain with. "Behind this wall is a tunnel that winds around the castle. A person in that tunnel can see into the life of this place."

"Spying..."

"Exactly."

"How is it that you know this?" Gawen moved toward her menacingly, but as Annwyl backed off, she gathered herself and looked at him unflinchingly.

"You should not be troubled by this," she ventured, and watched for a softening of his features. Ah, just there, almost imperceptible. Gawen's shoulders relaxed some as his demeanor toward Annwyl eased from threat into curiosity.

"Still, I would know of this," he said.

"Not only will I tell you, but I will show you, in good time. For now, I beg of you, I must depart from here. If you would take me to the storeroom and leave me, I promise to return in... three days' time."

Annwyl's mind was racing. How to play this game? If she was to seek out Merlin and know his fate, she would need a great deal of help from Gawen. His reward for that help would be the knowledge of the tunnel, the cave, and, most likely, her connection to Merlin, but that bounty must be paid out gradually, strategically. In the meantime, and just as gradually, she would work her influence on him, until she was sure he was as obedient to her as a loyal hound. Whether it was a result of Merlin's distress, or her own brush with danger upon entering Tintagel, Annwyl could feel the power awakening in her, the truth of her parentage giving her the courage to use that power -- and to grow it. The time had come to claim her birthright.

Once in the storeroom, Annwyl turned to Gawen.

"Meet me here at sunset in three days' time. There is much to tell you, secrets to impart...secrets that will give you power over the denizens of this place, but you must keep your counsel and protect me above all else. Are we agreed?"

True to his station as the son of the Duke, Gawen held out his hand.

"Agreed, my lady. I will be here at the appointed time."

Annwyl took his hand, and, despite herself, was thrilled at the touch. How alone she had been, how bereft of human contact, now became painfully obvious. It was hard to let go of him, but she must, lest she betray any weakness to her prey.

"Now go," she commanded. Gawen gave a slight bow and departed.

Annwyl waited one hundred heartbeats then recited the words that she sincerely hoped would open the unseen door from this side as surely as they had from the other. After the third recitation, the opening appeared and Annwyl slipped through it, unseen, or so she thought.

7

Alliance

Surrounded by the trappings of Merlin's magic, Annwyl's frustration boiled over. What good was all this if she had no knowledge of how to use it? She had spent two of her three days before returning to Tintagel pacing and fretting, scanning the books and the detritus of magic for some direction in the way forward, but nothing brought her any closer to knowing how best to proceed. Without the master himself, all of this treasure was no more than the stuff of a dragon's lair, uselessly stored in the fetid hovel of myth.

"But this is my birthright!" Annwyl cried out to the unhearing walls.

Even her dreams were silent, despite her willingness to endure any kind of night terror if it revealed even the smallest secret. The conclusion was inescapable. She was on her own, left to her own devices, limited as they were.

"I am Merlin's daughter," she repeated to herself like a mantra. "His flesh and blood. What he knows, what he is capable of must surely reside in me in some measure at least."

Armed with this conviction, on the third day she awoke to prepare herself for returning to Tintagel, Gawen, and some personal agency at last. She brushed and plaited her hair, dressed in the best of what she had, and formulated a loose plan. Wrapped in the cloak Abertha had woven for her, before she plunged into the tower, she cast a last glance at the perch where she had grown accustomed to seeing the owl. What she wouldn't give for his companionship -- and wisdom -- now. But she was on her own, completely.

As well as she could judge, she arrived in the storeroom shortly before sunset and moved into the shadows to await Gawen. That he might not show up tugged at her thoughts, but she consoled herself with the belief that no one in their right mind would miss the opportunity to learn the secrets she had dangled before him, least of all a young man who no doubt was jockeying for position in court.

As the light dimmed, signaling the demise of the day, the door to the storeroom opened and Gawen slipped inside. Annwyl's heart jumped. He was indeed a handsome young man, with a regal bearing. Something unfamiliar stirred in her, an agitation that was not altogether unpleasant. As silently as he had entered the room, she slipped from the shadows and stood before him, struggling to regain her composure.

He was the first to speak.

"I assume you will not tell me how you manage this...this appearance."

"Not yet," she smiled, "but you will know in time. Can we get to your quarters unseen?"

If there had been any doubt about Gawen's commitment to their agreement, it was dispelled by what awaited her in his quarters. A table was set with bread and cheese and an aromatic beverage. In contrast to her first experience of him, Gawen now played the generous host, nor did he press her for her promise of secrets, but rather opened the conversation to a congenial sharing of their lives. However Annwyl had spent the last three days, clearly Gawen had used the time to plot his own strategy which, from what she could see, was designed to begin the process of a trusting relationship.

And so, they relaxed into friendly conversation. Gawen spoke of a noble childhood with all the luxury and comfort anyone could ask for, but lonely and in its own way demanding as he was groomed to one day carry the mantle of leadership. For her part, Annwyl shared the best of her life with Abertha and Derwen, avoiding any mention of troubling dreams and inklings of power, focusing instead on the goodness of her adoptive parents and, in so doing, feeling a pang of affection for them and the life they had given her. Warmed by the mead and the pleasure of the company of another human of her age she dared to wonder, could she learn to blend the goodness of her early life with the power of the magician? Lost in such thoughts she felt herself drifting into sleep.

The next morning, she found herself waking within the tapestried curtains of Gawen's bed, alone. Pulling back the bed hangings, she saw the young nobleman standing by the wall where she had shown him the spyhole.

"I trust you slept well?" he asked, turning to her with a gentle smile.

"I believe so," she said, barely awake. "And you?"

He pointed to a couch, not far from the hearth.

"All night," he said, guessing at her unspoken question.

Silence hung in the air between them like a robed presence, waiting for the next move. Annwyl knew clearly that what she had promised had come due.

"Will you be missed today if you come with me?" she asked.

"Give me a moment and I will make excuses," he said, bowing slightly and leaving the room. Annwyl took the time to arrange herself, though she was barely ruffled. Clearly, nothing more than conversation had happened between her and Gawen, she thought with relief. But now came the test. She would take him through the door, down the tunnel and into the cave. If so doing was in any way a betrayal of Merlin, it was in the interest of rescuing him, if that was possible -- or so she told herself.

Once safely in the storeroom, she recited the spell that would open the door, only a little thoughtful at Gawen's apparent lack of surprise at her behavior. Through the door and into the tunnel he followed her in silence, giving no clue as to his reaction at the revelation of the passage, or her ability to conjure light within her palm. In silence they continued, stopping now and then to put an eye to a spyhole. Whether Gawen was shocked or pleased Annwyl could not tell, nor dare she ask as silence seemed the best choice as they moved just behind of the lives of the waking inhabitants of Tintagel.

At the entrance to the tower Annwyl paused. Should she take him directly to the cave or up to the sea cliff? A moment's thought put her in favor of going straight to the cave. Time was moving on after all. If her goal was to find Merlin, then she'd best get on with the plan. Down the stairs she plunged, holding her light orb high above her head lest Gawen miss a step and send them both tumbling down the hard stone.

Once in the cave, Gawen could no longer hold his tongue, but exclaimed in a culmination of the wonders of the morning.

"Who are you, really?" he demanded as he swung around the room, as though he truly had landed among a dragon's horde. "You are no simple maiden, clearly!"

"Well, I guess the mead clouded my head before I could finish my story." Annwyl's attempt at coyness was a weak one, as Gawen's glare attested.

"Ok," Annwyl said, relenting. "Sit, and I will tell you all." And so she did, from the moment Merlin pulled her up on his horse and rode south to the day she found the hidden door into Tintagel. Omitted, however, was the story of her experiment in swaying people's will. That was her secret and must remain so if it was to be useful.

"And so you see, I must find Merlin and free him if I can. In exchange for the knowledge of this," she said, waving at the workplace, "I would ask your help. Indeed, I don't see how I can accomplish anything without it."

Gawen was silent for a long time, but Annwyl knew better than to say more until he had absorbed all that she had told him. When at last he did speak, it was not what she had expected to hear.

"You realize of course that what you ask of me goes against my family. Merlin has always been a scourge on Cornwall and now that I see he has had secret access to our private doings, it is clear how he has been so successful in his manipulations. And to think he has lived and plotted under our very noses all this time..."

"But surely, he has been helpful from time to time..." Annwyl argued.

"Only when it suited him, when it was his coinage in a bargain that benefitted him more than anyone else."

At that Annwyl felt her temperature rise. Wasn't this exactly what she was doing with Gawen now? Merlin's daughter indeed. She only hoped that Gawen did not see the correlation, that having access to Merlin's inner workings would be perceived as rich coinage indeed -- the better end of the bargain.

Now Annwyl caught Gawen's gaze and held it, gathering her power.

"You must see that I need to find him. What happens from there is open for discussion, but I must know his fate, confront him if that's possible." She held Gawen's gaze until she was sure her influence had taken, then released him.

"And now," she said, all sweet and charming, "I have one more thing to show you."

Taking his hand, she drew him back to the tower and up the stairs to the sea cliff. The day was sunny and warm, the sea whispered of peace, ignorant of the intrigues and sufferings of humankind. Together the two young people lay in the warmth of the sun and the privacy of the cliff as Gawen's home of Tintagel towered in the distance and Annwyl's birthright of magic and mystery lay hidden below. Lost to the murmuring freedom of the sea, the natural urges of the two could not be denied and they came together in their fullness.

In the days that followed the two worked as a team, scouring the workshop for helpful information, studying maps, seeking spells that Annwyl thought might be useful -- and doable with her limited experience. For Gawen's part, the searches included tactical and political observations he could use to further his influence at court. Without her awareness, Annwyl had given Gawen more than he could have hoped for.

While their days were full of research and study, their nights flew by in intimate comfort neither of them had known before. All their previous loneliness now became the fertile soil for the seed of passion to sprout in their respective hearts, opening them to dreams and desires hitherto unimagined.

Neither wished to leave the others' side, but circumstances dictated that from time to time Gawen needed to depart the cave and make an appearance at Tintagel, visits that were judiciously spiced with subtle hints and suggestions that would lead his father and his advisors to advantageous decisions, and moreover earn Gawen a greater respect for his privacy as well as freedom for his comings and goings. So, this is the power of knowledge, Gawen reckoned. Perhaps not magic at all, but rather well-placed and strategically timed information. That Gawen was learning powerful things from the absent magician did not escape him. It was the one thing, however, that he kept from Annwyl, in part because he knew how angry and disappointed she was at not having the opportunity to be mentored by her powerful father, but also, he had to admit, because he was learning that half the power of knowledge was keeping others in the dark about what you knew.

Among those things which the two discovered was a map of the tunnels that ran around the castle. Much to their delight, they found a second door, accessed by an offshoot of the main tunnel that was so situated as to be all but invisible unless you knew where to look, like a pocket in the rock. The door opened easily, without the use of magic, and let into an unused part of the castle behind a tapestry. Using that door, Gawen was free to go easily, undetected.

"It is said that Nimue resides in Armorica, in or near the forest of Broceliande," Gawen explained. "I have overheard conversation among my father's counselors that she has somehow imprisoned him in the forest, some say frozen in a crystal cave, others say woven into an oak." Gawen rubbed his chin as he spoke, thinking aloud as much as he was sharing what he knew with Annwyl.

"I have no idea how you would plan a rescue. Confronting Nimue would be insanity. If she can incapacitate one as powerful as Merlin, what defense would one such as yourself have against her?"

"I agree, of course. Could you not gently press someone for more specifics about where Merlin might be?"

"I don't think they know...or care really. As I've told you, there is little love for Merlin in the hearts of my father's court, nor does anyone have the stomach to cross Nimue. If we are free of the meddling of enchanters, we are happy to let that stand and do nothing to make Nimue turn her eyes to Cornwall."

Annwyl's silence was edging into a pout. It crossed her mind to accept things as they were, to leave Merlin to his fate and live in the castle with Gawen -- not exactly a simple or boring life, if not what she had imagined as the daughter of a great wizard.

"I need to return to the castle tonight," Gawen said, breaking into Annwyl's thoughts. "My frequent absence is beginning to be noticed."

"Must you?" Suddenly Annwyl felt bereft, blocked at each turning. If she had to give up hope of finding Merlin, at least she might find comfort in Gawen's arms.

"If anyone finds out about all this, about us..." he reached a hand out to Annwyl, "we must protect what we have with secrecy. And I promise, I will do my best to gather more information if I can."

Alone and despondent Annwyl fell into a troubled sleep in which she dreamed she was in Tintagel, reaching for Gawen but never able to touch him. Instead, she was forced to watch him go about his life from behind an invisible barrier. Anguish burned in her heart, always in sight of him, but unable to speak or touch. Then darkness spread across the scene and something awoke in her heart -- something dark and needy. *Use your power. Manifest your desires in the world. It is your birthright...*

When she awoke, her heart was set. She would find Merlin no matter what it took. It wasn't meant for her to live in the world in any way other than fully possessed of her birthright of magic. When Gawen arrived, she would ask his help in getting to Armorica. In the meantime, she packed what she thought might be useful -- a rough map of the forest, a knife, some dried food. As she was tying up the bundle, she heard a screech which was soon followed by Perch bolting into the cave, not from the tower as was his wont but from the seaward entrance.

"Perch!"

The owl flew directly to her and rested on her outstretched hand. His talons pinched her flesh, but she was so glad to see him she didn't care.

"Oh, Perch. You are a mess! What has happened to you?"

Indeed, the owl was much the worse for wear, his beautiful white feathers grimed with mud, and a nasty cut just above his eye. Annwyl tentatively moved her free hand to stroke his head. Not only did he suffer it, but leaned into it.

"Oh Perch, have you been looking for Merlin? Do you know where he is?"

He raised his golden eyes to hers. Indeed, he did know.

"And you will take me to him?"

Again, the look.

"But I can't fly, dear bird. How will I cross the sea?"

Where was Gawen? Now was the time for him to come to her aide. She paced the cave, debating whether she should wait for what she assumed would be his imminent return, or go to him? But he could be anywhere in the castle and they might miss each other unendingly...so she must abide.

Perch was as impatient as she was, if not more so. He'd ruffle his feathers, swoop around the cave, cry out in what Annwyl read as anguish. Obviously, he was signaling some urgency. Helpless, Annwyl continued to pace, only just avoiding crying out herself.

After an excruciatingly long time, Gawen finally appeared and was quickly brought up short by Annwyl's agitation and the presence of the owl.

"Perch has returned. I believe he knows where Merlin is. We must leave now. Can you get us some horses and arrange for passage across the sea? How quickly can we leave?"

Gawen was speechless in the face of Annwyl's urgency.

"Gawen," she pleaded, grabbing his arm and in the gesture remembering the dream, but he was real and she could touch him -- that much at least.

"Annwyl," he said, finally. "I...I believe I have a trusted man I can send with you..."

"No! You must go with me. I need you!"

"You must see that I cannot! I would be missed...and I have responsibilities. And honestly, I cannot risk it...nor do I think you should..."

"I have no choice," Annwyl said, suddenly unable to look Gawen in the eyes. "This is my...destiny. What else is there for me. A place at court? How would you explain me?"

"We could go away..." Gawen responded weakly.

"And yet you will not go with me now."

No, he would not, that was painfully clear. Perhaps it was his dislike, if not fear, of wizardry. What passed between them unspoken cut Annwyl to the quick. Their two worlds clashed, perhaps impossibly.

"Look," Gawen offered, "I can command a knight to go with you -- one more powerful and well-travelled than I. He will be armed and dedicated to your service. While you are gone, I will make arrangements and upon your return, we will make our life together. I think I can get my father to post me somewhere..."

He was grasping at straws and Annwyl knew it. So be it then. Even should she use her powers of influence, they would not work in matters of the heart, this much she knew by instinct. How foolish of her to have opened her heart the way she had, her heart which once had been not much more pliable than a stone. Let it be so again.

Suddenly, Perch took off through the cave, to the opening at sea level, then back again, signaling that that way was open to them.

"So be it," she said, turning dry-eyed to Gawen, her voice level and firm. "Perch and I will climb to the path above at first light tomorrow. Have your knight meet us there. Good day to you Gawen. We will see what shall transpire from here," and turning, she left Gawen to find his way back to the castle with no gesture of affection, only his orders for the following day.

8

Nimue's Curse

Despite her fear that there would be no one to meet her on the coast road, Annwyl rose early, and with Perch leading the way, exited the cave onto the beach where Merlin had brought her not so very long ago, but ages, if time were measured in the changes she'd endured. As she reached the top of the cliff, her fears seemed to be realized as there was no one in sight, but it was early yet. The sun was only just easing the sky from pink to blue.

Tintagel was barely seen in the near distance, and now Annwyl caught a flash of light in that direction, flickering with movement. Soon enough, the flicker became a rider coming her way. As he neared, Annwyl's heart quickened. For a brief moment she dared hope that Gawen was joining her after all, but of course, it was not him. The man who approached was much larger than Gawen, and sat his horse as though he was born to do so.

Dismounting gracefully, he faced her and made a slight bow.

"Lady Annwyl, I presume. They call me Tanan. I am at your service."

Lady Annwyl. She had no knowledge of courtly ways! She'd give herself away as a simple peasant the moment she opened her mouth. But she was not a peasant at all. She was a wizard's daughter. In that regard, perhaps she needn't worry about custom. She tried to imagine how one such as herself should act and did her best, relying on a straightforward manner, tinged with her power of influence, and spiced with just enough honesty to show respect, but prepared to turn cold at a moment's notice if the situation should require it.

"Well met, Sir Tanan. It appears the day favors our journey."

"For now, yes," Tanan smiled, a look that threatened to throw Annwyl off her guard. Dare she relax into a trust of this man? As angry as she was at Gawen, perhaps he had chosen wisely for her.

"But the weather here on the coast can turn in the wink of an eye. Shall we make good use of the sunlight while it lasts?" he said placing himself to assist her in mounting the handsome silver beast that was to be her mount.

With no more than a shared glance, the two urged their horses into a smart gallop, eager to start the journey. For Annwyl's part, the sea air on her face was a much-appreciated luxury. She rode into it as though she would become one with it. Sea and sky, all is one. Perch reluctantly curled into Annwyl's cape, all his aloof and avian ways reduced by his travails, whatever they had been. They rode that way until the sun began to warm them then, taking pity on their mounts, they slowed the pace.

Relaxed in the warmth of the day, Annwyl at last broke the silence.

"What has Gawen told you of my quest?"

Tanan waited a beat before he answered.

"Very little, only that you need to get to the forest of Broceliande. We had little time, and I think he felt it was up to you to tell me what you wished to share, no more and no less."

Exactly how much that would be, Annwyl herself did not know yet, and Tanan respected her silence.

"We'll need to stop for the night. The coast is not far, but more than we can make in a day and spare our horses. We'll need them well rested for what awaits us in Armorica. I know of a good inn that will give us rest and sustenance, and time to make our plans. In the meantime, let us enjoy the journey."

Annwyl smiled. This Tanan seemed an easy person to travel with, for which she was profoundly grateful. If she had been blessed with an older brother, Tanan would be the kind of person she would choose -- protective but not overly so, experienced but not arrogant. She could tell he was desirous of knowing more about her and her quest, but patience sat on him like a blessing. For Annwyl's part, she was content to ride in silence, keeping her fear at bay by the simple act of moving forward and swaying to the rhythm of her horse's gate.

When they arrived at the inn, Annwyl was nearly asleep where she sat, but once inside she gained her energy once again. The inn was a comfort, the stew flavorful, and the mead was warming. Perhaps too much so. At last, Annwyl opened up, and found herself telling Tanan more than she might have thought wise at the start of the journey. She could blame the mead, but Tanan himself drew her out, listening thoughtfully to all she told him, obviously strategizing where she was unable to with her limited experience. Even knowing that it was Merlin Annwyl was seeking failed to ruffle him. Someday, Annwyl hoped, she could sit at length with Tanan and hear his story. She could only guess at the wonders and adventures he had experienced.

Then there was Perch, never far from them. There was no doubt in Annwyl's mind that the owl would lead her to his master -- that he had returned to her for no other reason.

"There is of course," Tanan finally interjected, "the question of Nimue. She is not one to trifle with, nor do we have any information on where she is or what she is up to since enchanting Merlin. Perhaps she has gone about other business -- which we should fervently hope. But there is also the possibility that she has stayed nearby, perhaps still somehow drawing power from the great magician."

The two fell into silence as they contemplated the danger the enchantress represented.

"I will see you safely to your room, Lady Annwyl," Tanan said at last, "then I will go about and see what I can glean. I'll need to make arrangements for a ship as well. Rest well, for I expect tomorrow will try our wits to their utmost."

It occurred to Annwyl then, as it had not previously, how lucky she had been to have Gawen's help in getting to Armorica and the forest. Horses, a boat, someone who knew the way. She had been ready to find her own way, any way she could; now she knew she wouldn't have gotten far. How much more difficult would the rest of the journey be then she'd imagined?

It should have been impossible to sleep with those thoughts in her mind, but the sea air had done its work. With Perch keeping vigil at the foot of her bed, Annwyl fell into a deep sleep -- but not dreamless.

Moonlight danced through dense branches, only partly lighting the night, as Annwyl approached a cave -- not a sea cave like the one beneath Tintagel, but a woodland cave, no more than a cleft in a rock face, easily missed. To Annwyl's dreaming vision, however, the cleft was gilded in moonlight, vividly outlined, awaiting her arrival. Once inside, however, blackness totally enveloped her. "Are you here, child?" she heard her father's voice ask, weak but discernable. "I am, father, but I cannot see." She reached into the darkness but could feel nothing, nor could she recall her father's face. Vertigo brought her to her knees where she dared not move, having no sense of what lay before or behind her, above or, worse, below if she should move forward. For all she knew, she knelt on the head of a pin surrounded by unfathomable depths. Her father was near, of that she was certain, but she was frozen in place, blind and terrified.

On the edge of a panicked waking, she heard the gentle call of an owl that soothed her back into sleep.

When she opened her door the following morning, she almost tripped over Tanan who lay across the threshold. So -- she had been well guarded during the night, the only threat had come from the depths of her own mind, or at least so she believed.

"Dear Tanan," she said, offering the burly man a hand, as though she would help him rise. "And you cautioned me to rest! Are you fit for today's journey?"

"Fit as a fiddle, my Lady. I've slept less comfortably many a time. I'm distressed to report, however, that I was unable to learn anything of Merlin's fate from those I approached last night. Fear has locked every tongue it seems. Nimue casts a long shadow." His eyes held a question for Annwyl. Was she still willing to do this?

"I believe the owl will guide us," Annwyl said in reply to the unspoken question. "As for Nimue..." Annwyl searched for words. She had no sense at all of this infamous enchantress. Why had Merlin not told her more? When will parents learn that withholding information is not always the best way to protect their children?

And how to tell Tanan that she felt she had no future if she could not find Merlin? Whatever risk there was, she must simply face it, there was no choice. If she should perish in the process or meet the same mysterious fate as her father, so be it. That Tanan would be at risk as well, however, she sincerely regretted.

"Sir Tanan, I would have you know that I see no way to abandon this path, ill-fated though it may be. I'm in your debt for getting me this far, but I release you from further involvement. This is not your task, but mine alone."

"You forget, Lady Annwyl, that I am here at the command of Lord Gawen, who, apparently, is desirous of seeing you return! Should I return without you, my life would be forfeit I'm sure. So, you see, I'm at risk either way. Given the choice, I would rather take that risk in defense of one such as yourself." Then, smiling broadly, "Besides, to be one of the few men to face the enchantress Nimue and live to tell of it -- well, that will earn me a lifetime of toasts, of that I am sure!"

If the previous day's ride had been peaceful, today's was less so. Tanan urged them on, it being necessary to meet their ship before the day was out. He warned Annwyl that the voyage would take at least two days, depending on the weather. He had eyed her warily, suspecting that she had never been at sea, and worried that a difficult journey would leave her too spent to be ready for what awaited. But what else was there for it? She was determined, that much was clear.

Mercifully, however, the gods appeared to be with them. They arrived on the southern coast of Armorica the evening of the following day.

"I suspect you'd like to put feet on dry land as soon as possible," Tanan said, "but I suggest we take our rest here on the ship for the night and start out for Broceliande first thing in the morning. Once we set foot on land, we are within Nimue's reach. We'll need to ride with cautious but steady purpose. Will that suit you?"

As though I would argue with you, Annwyl thought, but Tanan's plan had merit. To her surprise and relief, she'd actually enjoyed the voyage. In truth, something stirred in her, as though she had been here before, made this voyage as part of a life of being a significant player in the affairs of the world. The rise and fall of the waves, the smell of the sea, the endless and variable dome of sky -- how much more thrilling than being so earth-bound as she had been until now. The sea was adventure itself.

Stone circles and grassy plains quickly gave way to misty woodland paths as they travelled inland from the coast. Perch flew just ahead of them, convincing both Tanan and Annwyl that he well knew where he was and where he was leading them. Soon the forest was so dense that even sunlight struggled to find its way through the foliage, leading Annwyl to wonder, had her dream been of the sun dimly lighting the way and not the moon? *Push the fear away,* she told herself, *it will defeat you before you begin.*

They rode in a silence born of awe, as the enchanted nature of Broceliande became undeniable. Trees reached out to them with gnarled arms, rivulets dripped from moss covered rocks, whispering in a language on the edge of understanding. Perch flew on, dodging branches here and there, but never faltering as he drew Annwyl and her knight closer to his master.

When the owl alighted on a rock outcropping, Annwyl almost choked on her indrawn breath. There, on the rock face, was a dark slit in the shape of a rowan leaf, identical to the one in her dream, though not limned with moonlight. Annwyl slid off her horse, unsure even if her legs would not buckle beneath her. Would the same black terror await her inside this cave as in her dream? Then she remembered. She could conjure light -- if she kept her emotions in check and her wits about her.

"Lady," Tanan said, quietly, afraid to speak too loudly in this bewitched place, lest he arouse all manner of demon and otherworldly being, "I fear I cannot fit through that opening if that's what you're about."

"I expect that's as intended, Sir Tanan," Annwyl agreed, never taking her eyes off the cave entrance. "Better anyway that you stay here and stand guard."

Tanan dismouted and drew his sword, following Annwyl to the cave mouth. Annwyl felt his unspoken protest, but they had already discussed this. Nothing could dissuade her.

"Here then, take this," Tanan said, pulling a short blade from his boot and handing it to her. Annwyl doubted that a metal weapon would do her much good against what she was likely to face, but to refuse it would be to cast doubt on Tanan's drawn sword as well, so she gave a slight bow of gratitude and tucked the blade into her belt.

Once inside, she steadied her breath and conjured a light orb which revealed an unremarkable cave -- thankfully, not the pinnacle of rock surrounded by a chasm which she had sensed in her dream. Nevertheless, she moved forward cautiously, slipping farther and farther into the cavern. In the distance, she saw a faint green glimmer. As she neared it, she saw that it was a tree, growing out of the rock and into the invisible heights. Strange tree to grow so, but stranger still as she grew nearer, for it was not a tree at all, but a man. Merlin. Half man, half tree, his arms scored with uncanny leaves that gave off an unnatural green glow, and his mouth, the mouth Annwyl had so longed to learn from, frozen into a silent howl. Only his eyes still seemed fully human and they looked upon her now, and in them Annwyl saw a look of recognition.

Annwyl's heart ached. Why had he abandoned her? Had he stayed and taught her she might now be sure in her ability to come to his defense. But what did she have? She could conjure light, open enchanted doors, urge someone to do her will, but what good was any of that against this wicked enchantment?

When she could manage to speak, she cried, "Father I'm here. What can I do?"

But the frozen mouth could not speak. In her mind, she heard her own phrase, *open enchanted doors.* Perhaps if she could see the tree as a casing, with a door that could be opened to free the man inside....

She let herself fall into a sleep trance, awaiting the words that she prayed would come to her. When they did, she clasped them to her heart, opened her eyes and prepared to speak them and release her father. As she spoke the words, that which was tree began to move, as though it might indeed open as a door. But what Annwyl hadn't clearly seen was that the tree did not encase her father, but was interwoven into his very being, so that as the tree moved, the man was stretched and pulled, ripped.

"NO!" she shouted, desperate to stop the spell as she saw it pulling Merlin to pieces. Frantic, she spoke the words backwards, once, twice, a third, panic-ridden time. At last the rending ceased and as though by some unseen hand, the entire process reversed itself so that all was returned as it was, except for Merlin's piercing gaze, which now held a sadness that defied all definition.

Annwyl fell to her knees before the tree man, reached out to feel that strange bark, part wood, part skin. Anguish ripped through her. To lose what she had never known left a hole in her even her dreams couldn't reveal the depth of.

It was then that she heard the voice in her head. *Go my child. I have failed you and myself, but this much I can tell you. Be not afraid of the dark, and seek the good. There is power in... but she comes. Leave this place! She will destroy you as she has destroyed me.*

Annwyl longed for more, but the voice was silent. Getting to her feet, she ran her hands over the bark one last time, raised her light to what illumination she could and dutifully made her way back to the cave entrance, though she felt as though she had left the better part of her heart at the base of the tree.

Tanan's relief at sight of her was shaken by the grief in her face.

"My Lady," he began, but she interrupted.

"We need to leave Tanan. Nimue approaches." But no sooner were the words out of her mouth then the enchantress stood before them, radiant, sizzling with power.

"What have we here?" Nimue spoke, her voice resonant and mocking.

Neither Tanan nor Annwyl could speak, but Tanan moved to put Annwyl behind him as he tightened his grip on his sword.

"Oh, no need to tell me, even if you would," she continued. "I see that the daughter has come to...what...free her father? Dear me. And how did that go?"

A laugh that was like no human laugh at all pierced their hearts.

"He tried to keep your existence a secret from me...and he almost succeeded, dear man. It was only as I was putting the finishing touches on his *transformation,* that I could feel his resistance, and it had a name...Annwyl I believe?"

Tanan took a step forward, but Nimue stopped him with the flick of her wrist.

"Stay little man. This is between the spawn and me. Perhaps," she said, returning her attention to Annwyl, "you would like to stay here...with...oh I guess you could call me your stepmother. That way you could always be near your father..." Nimue raised her hand as though to weave some kind of mischief, but Tanan lunged at her while he shouted to Annwyl to flee.

"GO NOW. Get to Gawen. Do not look back."

Annwyl hesitated, but Tanan screamed, "BE GONE."

Barely had she pulled herself onto her horse when she kicked it into a gallop, risking one last look back. What she saw tore apart what remained of her heart. Caught in a swirl of malevolent grey mist, Tanan and Perch were gradually decomposing, their flesh falling from them like dried leaves. What did she care to survive when what little she cared for was so torn asunder? But something stirred in her -- something that wanted to live, so she urged her horse onward, riding hard for the coast.

Nor did she stop when the forest began to recede, but raced onward toward the sea, until her horse reared and she found herself face to face with Nimue...or some ghost of her. Whatever it was, it had stopped her horse dead in its tracks.

"Let me go! I am no threat to you," Annwyl screamed.

But the vision of Nimue only smiled.

"No threat you say? Oh, but you are dear one. You don't know yet, do you? Shall I tell you? You are with child, daughter of Merlin. From you, his seed will be carried into posterity...if I let it."

Annwyl opened her mouth to speak, but Nimue silenced her with a look.

"If I had wanted you dead you would easily have suffered the same fate as that stupid owl and your precious knight. No. I have different plans for you, much better than simply eliminating you. You will have your child...you will continue Merlin's seed. But my curse is this...*from woman to woman born, no peace in motherhood will any have, each being plagued with the agony of power unrealized. Just as Merlin is not dead but trapped in limbo, so too your spawn will carry his torment through the ages. So be it.*"

And with that, Nimue's likeness vanished and Annwyl was left alone in the sunlight, for all anyone could see, just a young woman on a horse, making her way to the waiting ship.

9

A Different Light

America
The Present

A room with a view. As one of the highest places on campus, from this cherished alcove Professor Raina Quinn could look out across the university as the seasons passed, measuring her life in the rhythm of academic terms, on fire with new ideas for her courses, watching students move across campus like so many ants. But now she sat with her knees pulled to her chest, her head on her knees, her gray hair waving slightly in the chill December wind. Foolish to have opened the window, but she needed the air; her chest was tight with sorrow and anxiety.

She was exhausted from packing, but more than that a sadness tinged with terror had suddenly made it almost impossible to move. Her teaching had literally kept her sane...or so she fervently believed. Too fervently she now realized because the classroom was no longer to be her haven, her reason for being. Sure, there were rumblings throughout the years, but she never believed that the University would actually abolish the Humanities department, but abolish it they did, and rather abruptly. A week before the end of the semester she was given notice.

Tenured or not, there was no place for her in a curriculum devoted to science, computers and business.

She turned her head from the window to her disheveled office, once so well organized, so much an outer expression of the mental order she struggled to maintain, now a choking reminder of what interior disorder had been like. *Please, not again.* Boxes of books were scattered everywhere; the grime of years framed the spaces where posters and pictures had been. The edge of a lace curtain drooped from an open box. Lace curtains. What a joke. She thought she'd succeeded in projecting -- more than that, living into -- an atmosphere of calm and certainty, nurturance even. Illusion, all of it.

She felt her edges unraveling. Where the hell was this Art guy? She needed to get out of here before the reality of all she was losing completely overwhelmed her.

As she understood it, Art Fisher was the custodian of the cottage she was moving into -- her mother's cottage, which she had known nothing about until the letter from the law firm came, informing her of her mother's death and her resultant inheritance. A house on Aries Lake. Included in the letter was the name "Art Fisher" and a phone number.

Apparently, he lived nearby and had agreed to look after the place until she could take up residence -- which she hadn't done. That was three years ago. Now it was to be her home...and still she'd yet to see it. But in arranging things with Art and reluctantly explaining her circumstances as briefly as she could, he'd volunteered to help her move out of her office. Well, why not? He'd have to show her the way to this "Aries Lake" anyway since it wasn't showing up on the GPS. He'd already assured her he'd gotten the place cleaned up and suitable for her to inhabit until the rest of her belongings came from her apartment -- her over-priced apartment that she could no longer afford now that she was unemployed.

Unemployed. Her mother's cottage. A lake that wasn't on the map. She thought she might be sick.

"Good grief. Could they have given you a harder place to get to?" So lost in her musings was she that she'd failed to hear the footfall on the steps, but now, in the middle of her office, stood a rather comely man. So, this was Art Fisher, Mr. Helper. Better looking than she had imagined, not that she had given him much thought at all, she realized. But now here he was. Nearing sixty, to judge by the iron grey hair and creased smile, punctuated by sea-blue eyes.

He was acting like the climb to her aerie had done him in, but she doubted it had judging by his wiry build, covered in a flannel shirt and jeans. There was a look about him that was as comforting as his choice of clothes. Suddenly, she was unhappily aware of her hastily pulled up hair and frumpy clothes.

"You might be happy to be done with those stairs..." he offered.

"I like it -- liked it -- up here," she said. One last glance out the window, a deep breath to pull herself together, and then she slammed the window shut and walked over to the solid looking man who, she tentatively decided, she would allow to come to her rescue...for now.

"But yes...I'm done with it now. Raina Quinn," she said offering her hand, "nice to meet you face to face Mr.

Fisher." His grasp was firm but polite, conveying a comforting solidity.

"Art, for heaven's sake," he said, releasing her hand. "I believe the pleasure is mine." A slight smile played around Art's lips. He was parsimonious with his smiles, but that was a good thing. She suspected they could have a dangerous power.

"'I'm not sure how much of a pleasure this will be," Raina said, waving her hand at all the boxes. "There are a ton of books here. Sorry about that. Occupational hazard."

Art rolled up his plaid sleeves. "I'm prepared. Brought a hand cart. We can bounce about four boxes at a time down those stairs if no one minds the noise."

"The semester is over," Raina said. "Most everyone has left already. But anyway, make as much noise as you like." The sooner this was over the better.

As Art was making a final trip down the stairs, Raina took a last look around, not that she really cared at this point if she'd left much of anything behind. She did, however, spot a smudge of red and blue on the floor, obviously fallen from the bookshelf. Bending to pick it up she saw that it was her Wonder Woman action figure. Amazon woman -- hero of her youth, symbol of her hard-won adult strength, pop culture goddess, underdressed. Raina had always loved the modern myth, but suddenly saw it in a different light. Sure, a few women could claim super powers, but not unless they were young, sexy and -- underdressed.

"Ready Miss Quinn?" Art called from the bottom of the stairs. So, he finally had gotten tired.

Raina threw the rubber figure behind the shelf, out of sight but not gone, waiting to be rediscovered and perhaps reconsidered. Then, without another look at the room, her window, or her life there, she hurried down the stairs.

"Follow me close," Art urged as he pulled himself into his pickup. "You don't want to get lost in the mountains."

"Well, you'd best keep me in your rearview as well." Raina felt an overwhelming gratitude for Art's help, but wasn't ready yet to find a way to express it. Best to keep things crisp for the time being.

As they pulled out of the parking lot and headed off campus, Raina had an urge to check her mailbox one last time, but she hadn't alerted Art to the additional stop. And anyway, she'd cleared everything out yesterday. A silly urge. One last tug that it made no sense to give credibility to. She was finished here.

So, the letter, addressed in a shaky scrawl, lay alone and unread in the abandoned box.

The three-hour ride to the lake gave Raina plenty of time to wrestle with her feelings. The further she got from campus, the less she gave thought to her leaving. Anyway, what had the last few weeks been other than the torture of the loss of her life's work? What loomed before her was what her mind turned to now.

Her mother's cabin...her mother, who had left Raina to fend for herself when she was only in her teens; left without a word and had apparently lived up in the woods all these years. Raina kept her eyes on Art's taillights as the city dwindled away and the landscape grew more and more wooded. Small towns here and there, some as quaint as small towns are meant to be, others a jumble of barely livable structures. What would the cottage be like? Art had assured her it was quite the charmer, but what he considered "charming" might not have much in common with Raina's taste.

When they hit a particularly densely forested area Raina rolled her window down a few inches and was immediately treated to a strong sent of pine. It had a welcoming, calming effect. She drew in deep breaths as though she was trying to store up the scent for future need. The band of pain around her chest that had been so strong earlier began to loosen a bit. Just a bit.

Raina followed as Art made a turn into a barely visible road, then down an incline at the bottom of which sat the lake, December grey, gently rippling. Another thousand feet or so, past a few cottages marching up the hill, all dutifully facing the lake, then a turn into a gravel drive. Art's brake lights lit up like winter berries then blinked out. Raina realized she was holding her breath. This was it then.

The front door did not face the road, but rather faced east (as she would soon learn) down the lake. A well-maintained porch wrapped around from the front door to lakeside. Art was already at the door, standing to the side to let her enter. She stepped into a foyer that led directly into a great room with a river stone fireplace at the far end. To her left was the kitchen and overhead was a loft overlooking the great room. In the far-left corner was a door. Somehow, she knew it led to two bedrooms and a bath. Just a good guess perhaps, but somehow this cottage felt familiar to her, as though she had been here long ago, or had dreamed it. Or perhaps it was the daydream of the perfect home, the sheltering reflection of the soul we carry deep in our hearts.

Art's touch on her shoulder made her jump.

"Like it? Let me show you the 'lake room'."

Art led her through the kitchen and into an open room where all the windows faced the lake, bordered with the wrap-around porch. From here she could see that the lake was populated, but sparsely so. She judged it to be about a mile across, but its length wasn't entirely visible from where she stood.

"Well?" Art stood as though he might bolt any minute. So far Raina hadn't said a word. Perhaps this city girl, this fancy college professor, felt like she'd been cast adrift into no man's land.

"It's beautiful." It was almost a whisper.

Art's shoulders relaxed. "The heat's on, but I could set a fire if you like. There's a stew in the refrigerator. Just needs to be warmed up. It's venison. Hope that's ok."

"I don't want to put you to any trouble..."

"Not a bit." Art was close to a full-on smile. "Do you need a lesson in fire building or are you an old pro?"

"Never built one in my life."

The two of them knelt on the hearth while Art rumpled newspaper and arranged a triangle of kindling over it, all of which had been previously placed to be well at hand. It was clear to Raina that Art had done more than merely look after the cottage. Everything was clean and tidy, a bit of furniture here and there but plenty of space for her own things when they arrived tomorrow. She reminded herself that he had tended this place for three years. Did he feel an ownership that her tenancy would challenge? She made a mental note to go lightly as she claimed this as her space.

"So, you might have noticed there aren't any motor boats on the lake. Plenty of kayaks though and what we call "duck boats" -- nice narrow rowboats that slice through the water at quite a clip. I think there might be one in the shed. Not sure what shape it's in, though. I've got an extra kayak that's all yours if you want it." He struck the match to his carefully placed wood.

"I'm afraid I don't know any more about paddling a kayak than I do making a fire," Raina admitted. God, she sounded like a fool. A PhD in modern literature but she couldn't light a fire or paddle a boat, activities that seemed, as she sat there soaking up the warmth of the fire, much more basic, more real than postmodern literary criticism. It was like there was a whole new world on the other side of the life she had been leading. And here she was, well beyond middle age, just finding this out. And there sat Art, full of all the knowledge she didn't have. She felt like Alice or Dorothy, all those childhood characters falling into strange new worlds. A lot to take in. Were there road maps in the tales? Blueprints for how to proceed if one read them closely?

"Well then," Art said, standing up to brush the wood crumbs off his clothes into the wood box. "I'd better let you get settled in. My phone number is on the kitchen table, but my place is the next one over. You could probably give a yell and I'd hear you. Let me know if you need anything.

Oh, and throw a log or two on the fire from time to time. I expect the fire will be a comfort."

Raina hesitated. "You've got your truck full of my books yet."

"Oh, yeah," Art chuckled as he ran his hand through his hair. Raina could see that he had actually forgotten all about that, so intent was he on making Raina feel good about the cottage.

"I am rather tired," Raina admitted. "Do you mind keeping them overnight? We could unpack in the morning."

Obviously relieved, Art agreed. In truth, Raina wanted time to explore the house, decide if it was going to be a good fit.

The venison stew was delicious. She had eaten a bowl of it sitting in front of the fire. She'd even been successful in laying on a few more logs without smothering the flames. Her exploration of the cottage was more cursory than she had planned. Just sitting here quietly was its own kind of exploration. She may have dozed off, but suddenly she was awakened by a strange racket which seemed to be coming from the lake. In the dark, she couldn't tell what it was from the window; she'd have to go outside to investigate.

It was snowing, an early, heavy snow, filling the night with silver sparkles. The hillside cottages were all lit up and seemed to her like a tableau on a Christmas card, the light of the lives inside spilling out onto the gathering white. And who was she, out here all alone? Some other-worldly being making an earthly visitation, blessing the ordinary lives of ordinary people? A stranger in a snow-globe world...

But now the clamor was getting louder as the snow collected under foot and caught on her eyelashes and cheeks. The noise was coming from down the lake, towards Art's cottage. Still she could not make out what it was, the snow acting like a veil. She'd have to make her way down to the shore. To her surprise, Art was already there, staring out across the water.

"What is it?" she asked, the clamor now almost deafening.

"Snow geese" Art said. "Damn if it isn't snow geese."

Raina looked out over the water and there, glowing in the ambient light, she could barely make out a huge island of white in the center of the lake. From the intensity of the clatter and the size of the island, she thought there must be hundreds of birds.

"Is this usual?"

"Not at all, not at all." There was reverence in Art's voice. "I've never seen this in all my years here. I assume they've chosen to rest here, a different stop on their migration south."

"It's rather magical."

Art took a quick glance at Raina beside him and flashed a smile she didn't see. "You'll see that there's plenty of magic here on the lake, but yes, this is pretty special." Then, almost to himself, "Interesting that it should happen on the night you arrive..."

Raina doubted much of any significance would happen on her account. "A coincidence I'm sure, but a charming fairytale conceit."

"Is it?" Art said, under his breath.

They stood there then in silence, enchanted by the chattering of the birds and the swirling snow. Perhaps there was more to be said between them, but the geese were doing plenty of talking, and that was enough. Raina had a sense that they'd be gone by morning, as though they'd never been here at all, but Art, in all his solidity, was standing beside her, seeing this the same as she was, so this couldn't be a dream.

Hard to tell how long they stood there, but eventually the cold found its way into their bones. Art was the first to break the silence.

"Getting nippy. Best get inside. Damn magic night though. Want me to see you home?"

She did and she didn't. Best to err on the side of caution.

"Thanks, but I'll find my way. See?" she said pointing toward her cottage, "I found the switch for the porch light!"

Art laughed. "That you have. Be on your way then. But I'll say this...I think the lake welcomes you...you are part of it now."

Odd thing to say, Raina thought, but now the cold really was setting in. A few steps away though, she turned and said, "The stew was delicious. Thank you."

"Great, glad you liked it. See you in the morning. We've got boxes to unload."

10

A Hidden Door

The sun woke her. There was a brightness to the lake that was so different from what she was used to. Light was everywhere and the lake dominated her sight -- so open and exposed, at once freeing and a little terrifying. But she had slept her first night in this house dreamless and deep.

She'd just finished pouring a cup of coffee when a movement outside caught her eye. A mass of birds interrupted the morning sky, moving as one, collecting stragglers as they flew back and forth, not in a V formation, but in a cluster, like a giant white and gray scarf waving in the wind. The snow geese. They had stayed the night and were now presumably collecting to continue their migration. She watched in awe as the flock moved back and forth, back and forth, a murmuration, flowing, bending, playing in the wind until, according to some mysterious signal, after one last pass, they flew up the lake and disappeared beyond the southern horizon. Raina stood staring after them, a strange feeling in her chest, like something in her was flying away with them. She might have stood there for a good while, her coffee cooling in her hand, had a noise from the porch not roused her from her reverie.

Art was stacking her office onto the porch. Damn early riser that one.

"Did you see them?" he beamed at her as she opened the front door, wrapping her sweater more tightly around her pajamas.

"Yes -- fortunately! Pretty amazing the way they were moving." Then, against her better judgement, "Want some coffee?"

"A few more loads, then sure, I'd love one. What time are your movers coming?"

"Early afternoon, I believe."

They sat drinking coffee, looking out over Aries Lake, half wondering if the snow geese would circle back through but knowing in their hearts that they would not. Their visitation was of the nature of the ephemeral.

Screwing up her courage, Raina asked the question that had been haunting her since she had first crossed the threshold of the cottage.

"What was my mother like?"

This was also the question that Art dreaded hearing. Raina had averted her eyes when she asked it. *Tread carefully here* Art thought. He took a deep breath.

"Morgan Quinn? I didn't know her that well. To my knowledge, no one did. She kept to herself."

"Was she," Raina hesitated, "crazy?"

Art searched Raina's face for the subtext. That's not usually a question people readily ask, especially of relative strangers.

"What is crazy anyway?" he ventured. "She was eccentric, I guess. She kept a nice garden, went swimming in all kinds of weather, fed the animals, walked in the woods, but in all that time, she never asked me or anyone else I know of for help. When she...passed...and it fell to me to take care of the house, I was surprised that it was in excellent repair. How she managed that on her own is a mystery to me, but apparently she did."

Raina sat silently for a long while, staring out over the lake. Clearly, she wanted answers to questions she either didn't know how to ask or didn't want to and Art was not inclined to pry or offer more information than what was asked for, what little he knew. He did know that he would see Morgan from time to time walking out in the night, hair loose and blowing, a shawl wrapped tightly around her, or that a light in the loft would often burn all night long, seen through the skylights. Were those signs of madness? He wasn't eager to judge. He also knew that there was a feeling of strange energy when he entered the cottage in that first year of caring for it, but that dissipated as time wore on. He wondered if Raina's presence here would bring that back.

The moving van arrived right on schedule. It only took a few hours for the movers to get everything into the house and pretty much put where Raina wanted it. She'd decided that she would use the loft as her bedroom -- she liked overlooking the hearth. Like the geese, she could float above the landscape, seeing it all, but aloof, ready to fly if need be.

There was something about her present circumstances that was edging her into a less conventional way of looking at things. For so long she had played it straight, doing her best to be like everyone else. Ever since...well, she had learned the hard way that being different came at a cost, one that could nearly break you. But now, maybe it was the lake with its constant movement, or the breeze, so clean smelling it made her want to open all the windows, even in December. Or maybe it was the woods -- there was a kind of safety, surety, implied by it. Whatever it was, she felt something new stirring in her and just at the edge of it was a curiosity about her mother that could never be satisfied, she knew. But whatever insight was on the wind, she would do her best to catch it.

Raina worked tirelessly for three days settling herself in. The urge was strong to claim ownership here, to make the place hers. Art would stop in from time to time to see if she needed help, but this was the kind of work she had to do alone.

The loft was her favorite spot. She would sleep here, but there would also be a desk, a place to write and even draw if she liked. There were small windows on either side, but overlooking the railing, she could just see through the lake room and all the way to the other shore. Quite a perch. Not unlike her office, she realized, and the thought made her grin. The ways this house seemed familiar to her were piling up, coming together like an argument in a legal case.

There were a few pieces of her mother's furniture up here she thought might work nicely in her preferred arrangement: a wooden rocker, a small table with a pitcher and bowl and a rather large dresser against the back wall that looked too heavy to move. Perhaps that was as good a place for it as any, she thought as she set about her arranging. She wanted the bed and the desk to face the railing -- everything looking outward into the openness below.

116

Pulling and pushing she moved things into the arrangement she wanted but found that the dresser just wasn't right where it was. If she was going to use it -- and she thought she might -- it would work best on the side wall near her desk. She gathered her strength and tried to edge it away from the wall. It was surprisingly light, but as she moved it, she saw that behind it was a door.

A door? Here? Then there must be an attic. She moved the dresser out further into the room and then put her hand on the doorknob, but quickly pulled it back. She had never been a fan of attics and this one had been hidden by a dresser -- it had to have been so on purpose. If she was going to sleep up here though, she'd need to know what was behind that door. She stood staring at it, her arms folded across her chest. It was just a door to another space, she admonished herself.

And then it hit her that the cottage was curiously devoid of any of her mother's things. Had Art cleaned everything out? Was all her mother's stuff stashed behind this door? She was nowhere near ready to tackle this. She pushed the dresser back against the door telling herself that she'd be fine sleeping up here, attic or no. So far, she had felt surprisingly comfortable in the cottage. If there was anything amiss, she was sure she would have felt it. But why was the door hidden? Then again, maybe it wasn't. Maybe it was just an unused space and the dresser was put there for convenience. Nevertheless, despite the sun pouring through the windows like nothing dark had ever existed, still, she knew the darkness could lurk anywhere it wanted to. With everything back in place, she busied herself putting clean sheets on her bed, her questions pushed to the back of her mind.

By mid-day she was fairly decently settled in. She was tired, but not exhausted. Perhaps a little nap in the sunshine was all she needed. Then she would put together a decent meal and invite Art for dinner. He had been such a help and had checked on her religiously, but hadn't made a nuisance of himself. It seemed like the right thing to do and anyway, she had more questions for him.

Art showed up with a bottle of wine and plenty of praise for "what you've done with the place." More than once, Raina worried that perhaps Art would feel a sense of ownership, but she couldn't detect a note of that. He was genuinely pleased with the hominess he claimed she'd brought to it and, somewhat to her surprise, was especially complimentary about the bed and desk peering over the edge of the loft.

"I've always thought lofts were the coolest things and often under-utilized. From there you can keep an eye on pretty much everything," he observed.

Raina noted that "keeping an eye on things" was clearly a virtue in Art's eyes. Raina's questions pushed at her lips, but she was determined to get through dinner and whatever news Art might choose to deliver before she pinned him down with her concerns.

And what he brought was an invitation of his own.

"So," he began, shifting in his chair, "Christmas is coming."

"That it is," Raina replied, realizing she had let the holiday completely slip from her mind.

"Well, I don't so much celebrate Christmas. I like to mark the time of year with a recognition of Solstice."

"Solstice?"

"The ancient celebration that marks the longest night of the year -- the "sun's returning" as they say. Mostly Celtic in origin. Lots of things about the old Solstice celebrations made their way into all the little do-dads that are now a part of Christmas -- holly and ivy, lots of lights to chase away the dark. That stuff."

"I guess I have heard a little something about that," Raina admitted.

"So," Art continued, "I like to cook special foods, decorate the house, burn a log I've been saving all year...guess it looks pretty much like the usual Christmas stuff to anyone looking from the outside, but to me it reminds me that the earth is a pretty miraculous place and we ought to mark its events."

Raina could see that Art was struggling a bit -- maybe worried he was giving away more of himself than he felt entirely safe doing. She was perfectly willing to come to his rescue.

"It sounds interesting. I'd like to learn more about it."

"Well, lots of years I just do this stuff on my own, but now that you're here...well, I thought you'd like to come over for a "Celtic feast" of sorts. And, I might have a special guest coming as well that I'd like you to meet."

A special guest? But Art wasn't saying who and she guessed there was a reason he was being mysterious. Either way, her curiosity was piqued.

"I'd love it! Can I bring something? Bake a pie maybe?"

"You can leave the food to me. I consider it a pretty magical time of year. If you're meant to bring something, it will come to you."

How unusual this Art Fisher was, not like anyone she had known before and yet there was a familiarity to him that pulled at her. She had no notion how to respond to his suggestion that she would magically know what to bring to this event that she didn't really understand, other than it was going to have some interesting food...and a mystery guest. Besides, she could no longer hold back on her own questions. She suggested they move to the fire, so wine in hand, they settled in. Between the wine and the flames, Raina loosened up.

"So, I've been thinking -- there really aren't any of my mother's things around which seems odd. Do you know anything about that?"

"I'm not entirely sure, nor am I sure she lived here all the time. She may have come and gone. As watchful as I like to think I am, Morgan Quinn had her ways and they were undemonstrative at that. I do remember that shortly before I was contracted to take care of the place, I saw a woman come and carry some things from the house. None of this was in any way my business, mind you, but I did wonder what was going on. Then I got a visit from a guy who said he was a lawyer for the estate. That's when he mentioned you and asked if I'd take care of the place until you knew what you wanted to do with it. I always wondered if it was you who had been here, but now I know it wasn't.

"As for me taking care of the place, it was mostly tending to the outside. Didn't spend much time inside other than to just check around and be sure mice weren't getting in and that sort of thing. I kept thinking any day I'd hear from you but...well, when you finally did say you were coming, I took the liberty of cleaning things up, but nothing more than that."

"And I do thank you for that. Made getting moved in so much easier."

"So, I don't mean to pry, but you had no contact with your mother in all those years?"

"None at all..." Raina stared into the fire. That was one hurt that had eventually healed over or so she had thought. That her mother never came back into her life ultimately fit in pretty well with the rest of the narrative.

Should she ask about the room behind the dresser? She struggled with that. On the one hand, why not? It was just a room and Art was proving himself to be a helpful friend. But something pulled her into silence. What if there was something behind that door she wouldn't want him to know about? Why would there be...but still. And anyway, she suspected he hadn't been that involved with the house -- would not likely have moved the dresser, although clearly, he did clean the loft. It was spotless as was the rest of the place.

"I should be going," Art said, breaking into Raina's thoughts. "You must be tired. You've pulled this place together in no time. Dinner was excellent, thank you." But as Art pulled himself up to go, something caught his eye.

"This is interesting," he said, moving toward a small clay pot on the mantle. "May I pick it up?"

"Sure. What's so interesting about it?

"Where did you get it?"

Raina paused, her lips pulled together in embarrassment. "I made it."

"You made it?" Art was all smiles. "There's more to you than meets the eye, Raina Quinn."

"Don't tease. It's just a little clay pot. A child could make such."

"Not really -- wheel thrown?"

"Yes."

"Still doing it?"

"No... not...for a while."

"I like the etching on it. What inspired that particular design?"

"Nothing that I know of. It just came to me. Clay often seems to have a mind of its own, at least with me it does." Raina was shy about talking about her pottery -- it could open up too much of herself she wasn't ready to discuss.

"Well that design...I've seen the same on Neolithic pots..."

"Oh goodness...well it's a simple design isn't it? It must appear in all kinds of places."

"Maybe so," Art said, putting the piece back with great care, reverence even. "So, put Solstice on your calendar -- a week from tonight. Good to go?"

"Yes -- good." But, not entirely.

Raina lost herself in cleaning up the kitchen, avoiding the decision she had to make, whether to sleep in the loft or continue sleeping on the sofa as she had been. *Foolish woman, your comfy bed awaits.* But Raina opted for the sofa for one more night, promising herself that she would investigate the attic in the light of day.

That light of day came like the arrival of an ancient god. Mist rose from the lake to meet the rising sun, reflecting and multiplying its radiance so that the eastern end of the lake was a wall of an orangey pink light so brilliant one could only look at it askance. Inside the cottage, everything was tinged with a faint apricot glow. If Raina needed light to muster her courage, on this morning she had ample. Coffee, clothes, and up she went.

The dresser moved as though it wanted to, and the door opened equally as willingly. Raina stepped into the attic, curious, but no longer afraid. Skylights on either side of the peak let in the morning light, as did a tiny window at the far end, but there was also a pull cord just above Raina's head. She tugged it, but if she was expecting the light of a single bare bulb, that's not what she got.

Instead the attic burst into a glittering ambiance of hundreds of string lights. They ringed the edges of the room and moved across the walls and ceiling in strange pathways, revealing swirls of green and blue over every inch of the room, giving Raina a sudden wave of vertigo, as though she had stepped into the night sky.

The floor, thankfully, was not painted, however. By keeping her eyes on it, Raina regained her sense of groundedness until she could slowly lift her eyes again. Now she could see that all along the walls, from floor to waist high, were shelves, painted the same as the walls and only visible to her now because of the objects that were scattered on them. There wasn't much -- some books, crystals, clay pots, wooden boxes, but mostly the shelves were bare. Just inside the door was a bookcase. Unpainted and about the dimensions of a door, it stood at an angle, alone, as though waiting to be moved to its proper place, and on one of its shelves sat a thin book, bound in deep red leather and green cloth. If Raina had been in Wonderland, the book would have declared *read me*, but Raina was not Alice and this was not Wonderland. Or was it?

She would obey the suggestion and pick it up, surely, but not until she had wandered farther into the room, walking along the walls, touching the various objects on the shelves, marveling at the texture and mottling of the painted walls. To think she had been afraid! This was hardly an attic. No cobwebs or dark corners. No sea chests filled with the artifacts of past lives and dark secrets. No, this was like stepping into the immensity of the universe, like walking among the stars.

As she touched the stones and pots, a strange tightness gripped her chest. These were her mother's things, and these were the things left behind when everything else had been taken. Were they purposely left, or overlooked because whoever had come wasn't aware of the attic, blocked as it was by the dresser? Whatever the case, Raina was thankful for them, these strange clues to her mother. Strange and thrilling. If it had been her mother who had created this room, then there was more to her than she had imagined. The vertigo threatened to return, this time from the swirling winds of all the possible answers to the questions posed by this space, and the woman who had made...and used it.

Raina returned to the door, slipped the book from the shelf, pulled off the light and slowly closed the door. Back in the relative familiarity of the loft, Raina sat on her bed and stared at the door. She could imagine spending a lot of time on the other side of it, so it didn't make sense to have to move the dresser back and forth all the time, and yet she felt the door should be hidden somehow, at least until she got a better sense of what the space behind it was all about. A decorative cloth? That would hide it and be attractive, but it wouldn't entirely suit opening and closing. What about that bookcase? It seemed so like the door in size.

Raina bounced off the bed and muscled the dresser into the corner where she had wanted it in the first place, then returned to the attic. Lifting the bookcase, she found that it was surprisingly light. It was even missing a section of the back -- would it match the doorknob? Could it really be this easy? She edged the shelf out into the loft, closed the door and moved the shelf up against it. A perfect fit. How was it that everything was coming together so easily? Nothing in Raina's life up to this point had been easy. Everything had been a struggle...or worse. Raina had to fight back the thought that all this was an illusion, that something would intervene and turn it all to dust. But the wood beneath her hands was firm and the way forward clear and energizing.

Raina spent until well after lunchtime working on attaching the bookcase to the attic door. She gathered her tools from where she had stowed them in the kitchen and found the rest of what she needed in the shed -- again way too easy, but a shed is a shed and finding screws and brackets and odd pieces of wood is not to be unexpected. Screwing the bookcase to the door was fairly easy, given the surprising lightness of it. When she tested it, the door swung open easily, taking the bookshelf with it. The room within beckoned to her, but she resisted. Time enough for...exactly what, she wasn't clear about.

Now came the challenge of disguising the doorknob that protruded through the fortunate hole in the back panel. Then it came to her. She rushed to the bookshelf downstairs and decided that her Webster's dictionary was the perfect solution. It was the right thickness and she could easily sacrifice it to this greater good, making up for its loss by joining the modern world and using the dictionary on her phone. Making careful measurements and judiciously employing some rubber bands, she hollowed out enough of the pages so that what was left of the tome would fit over the doorknob and look like an ordinary book happily sitting on a shelf. Now all that remained was filling the bookcase enough so that it looked "used" but keeping it light and moveable without things falling off of it.

Suddenly noticing how tired she was, her intention was to get some lunch and peruse the book she had taken from the attic, but instead she curled up on her bed and fell asleep to dreams of doors upon doors, leading to rooms upon rooms, but none of them doorways to the milky way. Perhaps the next one, or the next...she slept until the early dusk of a December evening, and awoke ravenous.

11

Solstice Night

Art's cottage had been transformed into as close to a forest as one could get inside a house. Pine boughs hung from the ceiling, drooped from edges of every horizontal surface, and were tied into decorative swags that hung all over the walls. Candles were judiciously placed amid the boughs, arranged so as to decorate the greenery with their pulsing light but not threaten fire. The hearth was carefully set, the Yule Log balanced atop the concoction of branches ready for the match.

The odor of pine permeated the house, except in the kitchen where venison stew and soda bread took the stage. On the counter, a dozen brown bottles held Art's home brewed stout. Sirona had promised to bring plum pudding for dessert. In all the years that Art had celebrated the Winter Solstice, this one carried a special significance. He couldn't wait to introduce the tradition to Raina, at the same time that, whether she knew it or not, he sensed that she was a piece of the ancient tradition that Art had always felt was missing.

Sirona shared his feelings, his sense that Raina was a key to something. Though Raina claimed to know little about her mother, still, Sirona thought, she was Morgan's daughter. That had to count for something. And now she was here, on the lake and living in Morgan's cottage. Expectation flowed from those circumstances, though of exactly what neither Art nor Sirona was sure.

"Am I crazy?" Art had asked her.

"I've never known you to be," Sirona replied coolly.

"Then what is it?"

Sirona sighed. She didn't like not having answers, but even less did she like Art not having them -- Art who was always so calm and sure of himself. To see him this agitated was unsettling.

"I guess we'll just have to wait and see."

Raina was ready an hour early, but would never dream of showing up until the appointed time, if even a bit later. Completely unsure of what the dress code was for the evening, she had chosen a simple gray wool dress that had often been her default choice on such occasions and set it off with a white stone necklace and matching earrings. Now she stood in the lake room, staring into the dark, knowing the lake was there but barely visible. Since she hadn't seen Art in a number of days, she assumed he had left her alone to find her comfort in her new home. Little did she know the work that he was putting in on making this a special night. She had done a bit of research on the winter solstice and had to admit that it was a cosmically significant event, but one that modern American culture paid very little attention to. It withered in the shadow of the bright lights and bustle of Christmas. Who has time, four days before Christmas, to stop their preparations and mark the "turning of the year?"

Well, apparently this interesting neighbor of hers had the time, makes the time, marks the time. *And* there was to be a guest. That thought had Raina's stomach in a bit of a knot as well. Minutes before she was ready to leave, on a whim she ran to her closet and grabbed a simple green wrap that she hardly ever wore, but pulling it around her seemed to provide a kind of cloaking, a security blanket, and the fringe would be something to fiddle with. Oh, and the book from the attic. She decided it would be her "thing to bring." Now it seemed like a strange if not foolish choice, but there was no time to think of something else. She had over-dawdled; she'd be later than she had planned.

"Ah, there you are, neighbor! Welcome...come through!" Art was beaming and suddenly looked to Raina somewhat mythical, surrounded as he was by forest greenery and flickering candles. "Let me take your coat."

As Raina slipped out of her coat and adjusted her shawl, Sirona stepped out of the kitchen and into the hallway. So, this was Art's guest, a stunningly beautiful woman who was dressed as though she had just stepped off the cover of a Stevie Nicks album, only her hair was the color of a raven at midnight. Instantly, Raina felt like a mouse. If she could have scurried off into a hole somewhere, she would have. But of course. Why would a man as capable as Art not have a girlfriend, and a beautiful one at that? Raina felt a bubble burst that she hardly knew she had been carrying.

"Raina," Art said, gently putting his hand on her elbow, "I'd like you to meet...my sister, Sirona."

"Well met," Sirona said, moving closer and taking Raina's slightly trembling hand in hers. "Art talks non-stop about this charming new neighbor of his."

Raina hardly heard Sirona's greeting, lost as she was in the woman's face. Now that she was closer, Raina could see that Sirona was close to her in years, perhaps even older. The wrinkles on her face, however, only served to prove the timelessness of her beauty and the silver at her temples shone sterling against her hair. So, this interesting man has an even more extraordinary sister. She would have said they were both out of her league, but clearly, they were genuinely delighted to have her in their midst.

"Some libation before dinner?" Art offered. "You have a choice of my home brew or red wine from the Wine Barrel in town."

"Oh, my brother, you wouldn't foist on her that foul brew you mix up like some withered witch slaving over her cauldron, would you?"

"Then what is it you've been drinking since you got here?" he chided.

"Oh dear, you've found me out..." Sirona said with mock embarrassment. "Come," she said, taking Raina's hand and pulling her into the kitchen. "You can have wine any time. You haven't lived until you've tasted Art's stout. Straight out of the Celtic Isles. I'll give you your money back if you don't like it."

Raina loosened up and let herself be pulled into the fun. Clearly, Sirona was as light-hearted as her visage was dark and Art's talents seemed to know no bounds. The stout was delicious. They stood around the kitchen making small talk, bathed in the warmth of simmering stew and burgeoning friendship, until Art insisted that dinner was ready.

The table was set simply, but made magical by the pine boughs, red berries and pinecones carefully arranged down the center of the table with three candles evenly spaced among them. Perhaps she had been too appreciative of the stout, because to Raina, the whole evening was beginning to take on a quality of having changed from the world she knew into some other time and place, Art and Sirona her magical hosts.

In the muted light, she could see that of course they were sister and brother. In fact, so alike were they, that their features seemed to blend into one person. Twins? Raina had no intention of asking such a question tonight. This night she felt she should play the role of the spectator, present on this curious stage, but not an actor in the story that was unfolding. But what story was that? She couldn't quite get a grasp on it, surrounded by it though she was.

After dinner they moved into the living room. Art lit the fire that took immediately, then offered Raina more stout which she wisely declined.

Once they were all comfortably settled, Art gave Raina a look and asked, "Well then, what do you think of our Solstice tradition?"

Raina dared not even try to articulate how the night was affecting her. Instead, she reached into her bag and pulled out the red and green book titled "Yule Poems." She had almost forgotten she'd brought it, unsure as she was if it would be at all appropriate. Now, somehow, she was sure it was, and that this was the right time to produce it.

"I found this in... the house. It's a strange little book, obviously hand made. It has a poem for every day from November 26th to December 21st. Many of the poems refer to things I'm not familiar with, but the final one is written for the Solstice. I thought it would be appropriate to share that one. Would you care to hear it?"

"Absolutely," Art said as Sirona inched forward in her chair.

As Raina read, she lost herself in the rhythm of the words and the images they conjured in her mind. If she had worried about whether Art and Sirona would care to hear this, it didn't matter now. The words carried their own authority and their place in the evening's events could not be questioned. Indeed, they seemed to have always been here, just not yet spoken.

The sun stands still, the air is cold
Our present mind confounds the old...

In his grave the Warrior shifts
Wary of his fearsome gifts

Wizard rests in Winter lair
Stars for robes, tangled hair

Witch shakes seeds from herb and flower
Works away in magic tower

And what will you do, reader of these pages?
What have you learned from the journey of the ages?

What would you write to close the game?
What role in the Wheel comes with your name?

Now we begin with open heart
Merry Meet and Merry Part.

A heavy silence filled the room as each of the three sat with the images evoked and the questions asked, for on this special night, the words came alive and the questions went straight to their hearts, to be held there, for the time being, in secret. It was Sirona who finally broke the silence, her voice cracking as she did so.

"Merry Meet indeed Raina. We are indebted to you for sharing that."

"I'm not sure I really understand it," Raina admitted. "There are some clues in the other poems I think, but I haven't had time to work them through. They refer, I think, to a mythology I'm not familiar with. Still, the words grab at you -- at least they do me."

That the book was hand bound and the subject and verse style so unusual, raised a question in Art's mind, one that he felt cautious about asking, but he did so anyway.

"Do you think your mother may have written those poems?"

"It's possible," Raina said, "but I have no way of knowing for sure. It could have been a gift from someone else...but then why would she have left it behind? It's pretty obvious that it's special." Then after a pause, "Or maybe not. Maybe it's nothing...just some silly rhymes..."

"Oh, I quite doubt that," Sirona almost whispered. Then, more loudly, "We all felt moved by it, felt it's power. It may be written in old-fashioned rhyme and meter, but should not be discounted because of that."

"And that may be part of its allure," Art mused. "There is a power in words, especially when they're cast in certain forms."

A strange feeling began nagging at Raina. On the one hand, she was beginning to feel a warm kinship with these two, but on the other, she felt that things were moving too fast. Perhaps things were coming to light that she was not ready for. If her mother had written this book, she wasn't sure how much of it she wanted to share with others, especially before she had a better understanding of it herself. She slid it back into her bag and struggled to find a way to change the subject.

Ever vigilant, Sirona saw the move and read its meaning. Anyway, she had brought something for Raina. Now would be a good time to bring it out.

"Perhaps this is too bold of me, but I brought you a little present," Sirona said, digging into her own bag and handing Raina a small box.

Too surprised to protest, Raina opened it. Wrapped in green cloth was a silver brooch in the Celtic motif of the

Triskele. At the connecting center of the three swirls was a green stone. It was finely wrought and Raina fell in love with it instantly.

She heard herself say, "Oh, I couldn't," but knew it would take a considerable act of will to refuse it.

"Oh, but you can. You must," Sirona said laughingly. "Anyone with a name like Quinn needs a Celtic brooch. It is perfect for the shawl you're wearing."

And it was. Raina repositioned the cloth then pinned the brooch to her left shoulder.

"But I have nothing to give in return," Raina protested.

"My dear woman...you already have. You have completed us this night. Made us a jolly triad, as reflected in the Triskele symbol you now wear. Or...if you wish...consider it a house warming gift."

What Sirona didn't say was that the poem Raina had read was a gift of a value Raina could not imagine. Art had suspected that Raina held a key and the poem proved it. Sirona longed to read the rest of the pieces in the small book, but knew she would have to bide her time. She had waited ages; she could wait a bit longer...but not forever.

"Then again," Sirona continued, "Art tells me you are a potter. Perhaps I could barter for a piece of your work."

"I'm not a potter," Raina said, trying not to get flustered. "I worked on the wheel some years ago, but I can't claim an ounce of expertise in the craft. Sorry to disappoint."

Art came to Sirona's rescue. "Sorry I gave Sirona the wrong impression, Raina. I saw that work of yours and was enchanted by it. I mentioned it to my dear sister and as is so often the case, she ran away with it."

Thankful for Art's intervention, Sirona sat quietly, but it took an effort.

"So, the actual Solstice happens in an hour. We haven't dug into Sirona's plum pudding yet and I know a fun and easy to learn card game we could play. Shall we wile away the time in meaningless pursuits?"

Truthfully, Raina was ready to go home. It had been a lovely evening, but slightly overwhelming and the stout was beginning to make her sleepy. To leave now, however, would be ungracious. Sirona dished up the pudding while Art readied the table for the game which they played with much laughter and friendly competition while the Great Turning came and went.

12

Merry Met

Swirling tendrils of foamy seawater approached the mouth of the cave, nearly reaching the entrance before suddenly retreating. An Arctic Tern sliced through the air, its blood red beak opened in a warning screech. Was there danger here? Darkness whispered from the cave mouth, but the swelling sea held no threat, only the rhythmic hush of waves.

Raina's eyes flickered open. Sleep had not been her intention as she sat contemplating the patterns of lights across the walls, but odd states of awareness were becoming more common as she spent hours in what she had come to think of as the Mother Room. If she was ever going to get a sense of what her mother had been about, it would come from this room somehow, which was the conviction that had led to her dragging a chair and small side table into the mysterious space behind the loft. Since the Solstice dinner at Art's she had spent time nearly every day in the room, turning the chair this way and that, staring at the patterns on the walls, convinced they would speak to her in some way. But the dream frightened her, not because it was, in itself, particularly frightening, but because it evoked the terrors of the time before. Enough then for today. Time to move out of the rarified atmosphere of the Mother Room and back into daylight, the lake, and maybe some fresh air.

Any plans Raina may have had for the afternoon, however, were overruled by the doorbell. Sirona stood on the porch, attractively bundled against the cold.

"Sorry to come unannounced, but I was over at Art's and thought I'd stop by. If it's not a good time, I'll take no offense."

In truth, Raina was happy for the intrusion.

"No problem. I'm delighted. Come in."

"Oh, and Art made me bring this over." Sirona held out an aromatic paper bag. "Meat pie. Have you had lunch?"

Raina set them up out in the lake room. The pie was delicious.

"So," Sirona asked, "what have you been up to since the Solstice? Looks like you're well-arranged and comfortably moved in."

"Well enough. It wasn't hard, given the care your brother had taken with the place. And to be honest, I haven't been up to much. I thought I was dying to be retired, but I'm a bit at loose ends. Going from the intensity of teaching to having pretty much nothing to do is a bit unbalancing. If it was summer, I could garden or something, but," waving at the lake in the early, gray stages of freezing over and the colorless shore beyond, "one can only read for so long."

"Reading anything worth recommending?" Sirona asked.

Hesitating, Raina finally admitted,

"Actually, I've been reading the poems in the Yule book, trying to figure them out."

"Oh? Are they a puzzle?" Sirona tried to keep the eagerness out of her voice.

"It's just that much of it seems to refer to things I'm not conversant in." But Raina failed to mention that the biggest puzzle was who had authored the book. If it was her mother as Art had suggested, then this slim volume was everything to Raina. If it was someone else, then at least it was of interest to her mother because it had been in her possession.

Little did Raina know that Sirona was as interested in the book as she was, if not for the same reasons, but for urgent reasons of her own. Sirona struggled with how to move the conversation forward.

"Like what?" Sirona prodded, rather inelegantly.

This was it then. Either Raina would open up to Sirona and trust her, or deflect and stay safe, but the truth was that Raina couldn't abandon the mysteries that were pressing in on her. She simply had to pursue them and suspected she wouldn't get very far on her own.

She liked Art. He had been nothing but kind to her and seemed to have a sixth sense about when to engage and when to let her be. Sirona wasn't as immediately comforting to be around and yet there was an air about her of intelligence and...what was it...otherworldliness...that Raina was both attracted to and hesitant about. Then again, the stuff she needed help with was pretty otherworldly itself. Raina took a surreptitious glance at Sirona's face, the graceful wrinkles that spoke of a full life, the kindness in her smile, and the penetrating, almost bird-like quality of her eyes, full of the knowledge of things average folks would never know.

Gathering their empty plates, Raina said, "Why don't we adjourn to the living room? It's a bit chilly out here."

Sirona helped with the clearing and after making some tea, the two sat comfortably by the hearth. Sirona noticed that the book sat on a side table, with a pair of reading glasses folded on top. Her hands itched to hold it, open it, read the contents with her own eyes, but she sensed Raina's possessiveness and, with some effort, folded her hands around her teacup. Nor did Raina take up the book right away. As though she was reading her future in her own cup, she sat silent for a while, then finally spoke.

"My mother left while I was a freshman at college. Just left, gone. My father had left years before so I came home after term to an empty house. One would think I would have at least some sense of my mother from the early years, but I don't. She was a very closed person, emotionally and physically. I don't remember being hugged or held. There were even times when she locked herself in her room, so when I found myself permanently alone, it wasn't a huge shock, just a sadness that this was the inevitable culmination of everything I'd feared through the years. I do have a few vague memories of her and I together, laughing even, but they're like the dreams that dissolve as soon as you pull back the covers in the morning. I tried for years to recover them, but after a while I gave up. I had...troubles of my own.

"But now I'm back to grasping for her again. I thought maybe Art would know something of her, but I wasn't all that surprised when he said he barely knew her. It fit her pattern. When I learned years ago that she had died and left this cottage to me, I was angry. What did I want with her house, when it was only her I had wanted all those years and yet she kept herself away from me? Then, when my job at the University was eliminated, something in me broke. I lost heart and...well, I had lost my job as well...so why not come here and live out my days as my mother had apparently done? I thought I'd be a hermit like her, just curl up and wait for...it all to end."

"But my brother wasn't about to let that happen, was he?" Sirona said with a wry smile.

"No," Raina said, smiling back. "He is a good man. I appreciate everything he's done for me. But there was also something about this place. I felt it the minute I walked through the door. There is a feeling here that nudges me toward life, although I don't know exactly what it's all about yet. The lake is clearly part of it. Don't think me crazy, but the lake feels to me like a living thing." Raina paused, waiting to see Sirona's reaction, expecting a patronizing look at the least.

"Oh," Sirona said, sitting forward in her chair, "but it most certainly is! All lakes are living things, but this one is...special. But...do go on."

"So, yes, the lake, but also the house. I... well...I feel nourished by it as I never felt nourished by my mother. And yet, this is her place, and she left it to me. It has come late, but that it has come at all makes me wonder if I am wrong that she was *never* a loving mother...I just can't remember."

"And you feel this house and maybe the book may hold some clues?"

"I'm hoping so."

Now Raina's hand strayed toward the book.

"And you are sure there is no author named in it anywhere?" Sirona asked. If she wasn't careful, her eagerness might show and slam shut the slowly opening door between them.

"I've looked all through it. Even used a magnifying glass, and gently pulled back edges of the end papers...nothing. Not even initials. But it is clearly a hand bound book. It does have a date...December 1998."

Taking a deep breath, Sirona asked, "May I see it?" and extended an elegant hand.

Raina hesitated, then, "Of course," and transferred the book to Sirona as one might do with a newborn babe. With the same care, Sirona turned the pages. Each poem was accompanied by an illustration, some clearly drawings, others looked like photographs, but some appeared altered, whether digitally or by hand Sirona couldn't be sure.

In measure sweet this ancient creed,

began the opening piece,

Twenty-six couplets rule the Rede
From now 'til Yule, in days the same
Let us play a mental game

But Raina's hand was out and Sirona dared read no more, though she would have given anything to do so. A mental game based in some way on the Wiccan Rede. What gems were hidden on these pages Sirona wondered?

"Are there any clues in the poems themselves?" Sirona asked hoping that one way or another, she would hear more of them.

"I'm not sure. There is one that is clearly personal and makes a specific reference. Would you like to hear it?"

Sirona would like nothing better.

The tree is decked, the stockings hung
Countdown to Yule is now begun

What is it that we're looking for
In magic time, in ancient lore?

Some sense, I think, or some reprieve
From all the evil we conceive

I mind one Christmas, by blinking light
How I read Tolkien 'til late at night

Elves and Hobbits and Gandalf Gray
Filled my head, took me away

To lands where honor then did rule
the future spied in darkling jewel

Life had meaning in that place
Challenge and courage set the pace

And so I'd read with aching heart
To have the chance to play my part

To arm my spirit, the riddle to know
To fight for right and best the foe.

"Tolkien," Sirona sighed in admiration. "It's been so long."

"I've heard of him", Raina admitted, "but never read his book. But whoever wrote *this* book surely did and was much moved by it."

"As were so many..." Sirona shifted in her seat.

"You've read his book then? Raina asked.

"Oh yes, many times. And it was not just *a* book, but four actually -- The Hobbit and the Trilogy of the Rings. And not unlike your mystery author, I often read them at Christmas time. It just seemed fitting. All the magic...sacrifice and hope."

"There's a longing in the last lines of the poem."

"Oh yes, under all the magic and mythical beings, Tolkien's real genius was his call for us to heed our better angels even if it means incredible sacrifice and almost unbearable willpower. It certainly fit the *Zeitgeist* of the 1960's. So many people were influenced by Tolkien's work back then. Do you have any sense of whether your mother read him?"

"None. And I was surprised to see that there were so few of my mother's things left here. Wouldn't it have been nice if I'd found Tolkien's works sitting on a shelf?"

"Any other poems that might contain clues?" Sirona asked hopefully.

"Not really. I need to read through this again, and try to read between the lines, not that I understand all the lines themselves. But it's getting late...." Much to Sirona's disappointment Raina returned the Yule Poems to the side table, and repositioned her reading glasses on top of the book, as though locking it for the night.

The hint at calling it a night didn't escape Sirona, but she wasn't quite ready to leave. True to her nature, she was ready to push the envelope, if just a bit. Her glance went up to the mantle where the pottery sat that had caught Art's eye days before.

"And this is the work that Art so admired?" she said, rising from her chair to get a better look for herself.

"Yes, but I don't see that there's much to admire. He said something about the designs being similar to Neolithic pots, but how would he know that?"

"Because he has seen some. There are examples of Neolithic pots in the gift shop at Stonehenge in England. We've both been there. I have a little apartment in Glastonbury where I spend a good bit of my time. A charming town...."

Sirona chose not to mention just how beyond "charming" Glastonbury really was, and her reason -- indeed her need -- to sojourn there every year. There was much to tell but it had already been stated that the night was getting on. Nor was she exactly sure how to approach all that she was dying to share with Raina, still not entirely sure Raina was *the one*. For now, she would probe what was within easy reach.

"So, what made you choose these designs?"

"I don't really feel that I chose them at all. It seems more like the clay did the choosing. Whenever I'd finish a pot, the semi-dry clay -- "leather hard" they call it -- just seemed to call out to me to cut a design into it and when I did, these are the lines that came to me. After a while, I'd promise myself that I'd do something different, but as soon as I set my tool to the clay, I'd make those lines again. It didn't matter to me enough to fight it -- I had no agenda for the clay work other than to have a focus and to let go enough to get dirty." If Sirona saw Raina blush, she didn't acknowledge it. For Raina's part, she shut her mouth as though trapping the rest of the story behind her lips.

"May I hold one?" Sirona asked.

"Of course..."

A mottled blue glaze dripped down from the rim of the small pot Sirona picked, the glaze stopping short of an alternating zigzag design that marched around the perimeter, the rest of the pot glazed clear so that the sandy colored clay body was its own expression. Sirona ran her finger over the etching, feeling a faint energy in the play of the lines.

In that moment, even if she wasn't absolutely certain that Raina was *the one*, she was convinced that, at the very least, Raina was part of the story, and most likely held clues, whether she knew it or not, to finding what Sirona and Art so ardently sought. They were painfully aware that they were not getting any younger -- running out of time. If they did not find the Third in this lifetime, what would be the chances of doing so in the next? Still holding the pot, Sirona fixed her eyes on Raina, watching for whatever she could glean from the other woman's gentle but troubled eyes.

"It's beautiful," Sirona almost whispered. "You have a gift."

Having held Sirona's gaze for longer than she thought she could, Raina finally looked away.

"I doubt that very much, but if you like that piece, it's yours."

A gaze from Sirona made Raina add, "a return gift for the beautiful brooch, then." Sirona dropped her eyes and nodded in thanks, a regal gesture, Raina thought.

And now the evening was truly at an end.

At the door, Sirona turned and, taking Raina's hand said, "Don't doubt yourself, or your gift. You mustn't." Then turned and left before Raina could protest.

Tired as she was there was no turning in, not yet anyway. Waves and waves of undercurrents washed over Raina's thoughts as she considered the night's conversation.

Sirona, so stunning and graceful and....timeless. Not at all out of place in this world, but had Sirona stepped back centuries, no one would be the wiser. In so many ways she was not the kind of woman Raina felt comfortable being friends with, and yet...and yet...she knew she would accept this connection and carry her part of it as best she could.

And there were Sirona's parting words, her admonishment to Raina -- not patronizing, but a genuine appeal. Clearly Sirona saw something in Raina that Raina was blind to, or that had been obscured by all that she had gone through, like grime on an old window. But beyond the window, dirty or clear, the world awaits in all its beauty. For a moment, Raina was acutely aware that her mother had spent years sitting in the same room Raina sat in now, and a jolt of something, like a whiff of a passing fragrance, stirred her heart.

Picking up the slim volume, she turned to the first entry. November 26th.

In measure sweet this ancient creed
Twenty-six couplets rule the Rede

From now 'til Yule, in days the same
Let us play a mental game

For each day hence in simple rhyme
Cast a thought in space and time

With ancient lore when such we find
To set our souls with ancient mind

And in the doing if we see
What greater sense in life there be,

Then praise we will the Lore of Old
For casting out the bitter cold

Of a world that's lost the simple way
Of living well as well we may.

To the Lord and Lady, I give my hand
Guide my words as best you can.

Raina's eyes fell on the words, "*Set our souls with ancient mind.*" Why did those words evoke in her the very personhood of Sirona? It hadn't escaped Raina that Sirona had an affinity for the Yule Poems, would have read more in the book if Raina had let her. Her own possessiveness shocked her in a way -- it was unlike her, but it wasn't for what the poems said so much as it was her inclination to believe that her mother had written them.

Such concerns weren't shared by Sirona; her interest in the book had to do exclusively with the poems themselves. But illogical as it was, Raina couldn't help but feel that she needed to keep the small volume protected from others in order to keep intact whatever thread there might be with her mother. Silly, silly thoughts, as the night wore on.

Unaware of the transition, Raina drifted into a light sleep and dreamed. *The pillars of Stonehenge were golden in the late afternoon light, casting shadows that twined into roots burrowing deep into the ground, a counter-balance to the huge stones above. Amid those stones stood two figures, one clearly a woman, the other cloaked. As Raina's dream-self approached, the woman turned and held a slender hand out to her. It was Sirona but mixed into her face was the face of a crow. Beside her, the cloaked figure remained with its back to Raina, the wind pulling at the cloak, billowing it into black wings of fabric, as though whatever or whoever was inside was barely there. Then the cloak swirled in the wind for a moment and collapsed, a heap of black emptiness. The face that Raina knew to be Sirona's twisted in agony and called out "you mustn't!"*

13

Arthur

Either she had not previously paid much attention, or this was truly the most amazing January thaw of her lifetime. The air was unmistakably spring-like and water lay upon the ice like a gauze apron on a silver dress, rippled by the wind as its foundation lay unmoved...but threatened Raina thought. The ice would not survive another day or two of this kind of weather or the cheery gaze of sunshine that brightened all that had been so drear for so long.

Not even trying to be remorseful for the early call, Art had awakened Raina with a proposal of a picnic in what he said was a "secret place."

"Trust me, you won't be disappointed."

And so, by 11:00 am, Raina was dressed for a muddy trek. There was nothing else to prepare but herself as Art had promised her a delightful repast of his own design.

"Secrets. Everywhere secrets," Raina said aloud to the room. But Art was revealing his, little by little, as she kept hers well-hidden, her explorations continuing, but not gaining her much insight.

Last night she had lingered on the Yule poem for December 14th...

Arthur, King, I know your name,
I know your pride, I know your shame

The ruling king of all that's good
Who finds his solace in the wood

To make it right all eyes on thee
In neither mind nor act be ye free

Your human shape so prone to err
While all around you people stare

And lay their sins upon your head
Upon your soul so blithely tread

Return to us they say you must
Arise and live from ancient dust

But are we wise to put our store
On one man's head who is no more?

Perhaps the King we now await
Is in our hearts -- be it not too late.

It was the name, of course, that caught her eye. Loath to admit it, nevertheless she had actually been missing her neighbor. She'd seen him splitting wood from time to time and sensed that for a few weeks he had been gone. Without him around, she'd felt a bit bereft, if the truth were known. She'd taken a few walks down the lake road on days that weren't too foul in the hopes of catching him out, but she never did.

And now this invitation to some secret place, in the muddy woods no less. Had it been anyone else, she would have declined, but the thought of seeing Art again turned a January picnic into a not-to-be-missed event.

They ambled down the road, past a half dozen cottages, then Art turned left, away from the lake onto a path that Raina would never have found on her own. Brambles and deadfall obscured the path and made the going difficult, but only for a few feet. Suddenly, they were in a clearing filled with the crisp January light. Without hesitation, Art made his way toward the upper edge of the clearing, again, not a path the casual hiker would have easily found on their own, but Art navigated toward it without hesitation.

Once on the path, Raina was surprised to see that it was not as muddy as she would have thought. Bright green moss that looked like millions of tiny trees covered the way and cushioned their steps. The slope was gentle and eventually the path widened enough for the two of them to walk side by side.

They made small talk as they ambled along, but mostly Raina was besotted by the smell of the woods and the uncanny warmth on her face. She breathed deep, as though she could pull the very essence of the woods into herself and be transformed by it, healed by it. Why do those who minister to the emotionally distressed think that drugs and sterile walls will drive away the demons that plague the unwary when, she thought, twenty minutes in a woods like this might well be enough to clear away the creeping tendrils of fear and confusion from the mind and wash it clean and alive again.

A touch on her arm.

"This way my lady," Art said as he steered her onto a side path. It was then she heard it.

"A stream?" she asked.

"Ah yes...we'll be at our spot momentarily. It's great to be out here isn't it? Makes me feel like a kid again, playing knights and dragons in the woods, slashing at menacing weeds with a stick for a sword."

Raina's heart lifted and she let herself fall into the carefree memories Art was evoking. They were not hers, but her imagination could conjure them, if imperfectly. And yes, it was delightful to be out here. She pulled off her hat as if to get closer to all that was not her. Now they walked to the rhythm of the flowing water that was still out of sight, but which sang louder with every step. Then the trees opened up and they were standing on the edge of the stream.

"There's a large rock up ahead that makes a great picnic spot." Art stepped off the path and offered Raina his hand as they stepped over rocks and branches. Raina could see a large, flat rock in the near distance just on the edge of

...

"...a waterfall!"

Art let a smile escape unrestrained.

"Pretty, yes?"

"Yes!"

Once they attained the rock, Art swung into action.

"Let's see if these sandwiches are any good," he said as he shrugged off his backpack and started pulling things out of it like it was a magic sack, holding more on the inside than the look of the outside indicated was possible. A blanket, wrapped sandwiches, plastic glasses and a bottle of Chardonnay.

"There's some water in here too if you'd prefer..." but Raina eyed the wine with delight.

"No. The wine is perfect." She plunked herself down on the rock unable to remember the last time she felt this content. But what was happening here? Art had been absent since Solstice, and now this, seemingly out of the blue. *Don't over-think it*, Raina admonished herself. Sitting in the middle of a stream, feeling the warmth of the rock and the friendship of a good man...she'd be nuts not to just go with it.

The two of them tore into the lunch like starving children.

"This is perfect, Art. Thank you so much."

"My pleasure. I come up here a lot. It's nice to have someone to share it with. Too buggy and overgrown to get here in the summer, so I make the most of it in the other months."

Art set the glasses on a flat part of the rock and carefully filled them with wine. For just a moment Raina was mesmerized by the honeyed glow as the sun's rays ignited the liquid. Sometimes little things are almost too beautiful to bear, she thought.

"Well, here's to the rejuvenating powers of nature." Art raised his glass and waited as Raina gathered herself to do the same.

"Yes," she said, "and getting out of the house."

Never had a sip of wine tasted so good, at least not in recent memory. Everything seemed to sparkle with a crispness that was clearing away the cobwebs. *I must be losing my mind* she thought as for a brief moment she imagined filling a glass with the water of the stream that burbled all around her -- surely it would taste as scrumptious as the wine.

"When I'm out here," Art was saying, "I like to imagine the trees are seeing me, just as I see them." Art glanced at her shyly.

"That's a charming thought," Raina said, eyeing the trees with wary appreciation. "What do you think they make of us?"

Art let out a hardy laugh, relieved that this woman didn't seem to think him absurd. "God only knows. Probably that we move around too much!"

"…that we lack sophistication and grace…"

"…running around like little kids with ants in our pants…"

"…shallow, no roots…"

"…no center." Their mirth slid into something else.

"But we're not shallow," Raina said, serious now, "or rootless. But I would say we don't always make the best use of our gift of mobility."

"Quite possibly," Art replied, carefully folding his empty wrapper, "but it got us up here, didn't it?" He flashed Raina a quick smile. No doubt Art was quite handsome in his youth, or at least handsome enough, but now his face looked not unlike the bark of the trees he seemed so fond of. Worn and wrinkled, but there was a hint of youthful handsomeness under it all, or at least so Raina thought.

Then it occurred to her, the poem from December 14th, about Arthur the King. Just as Sirona had known of the Tolkien books, so might this Art know something about his namesake. Raina told herself it was part of the puzzle. It was worth the risk to broach the subject head on.

"Perhaps you were named after Arthur the King?" She meant it to sound casual, taken as a jest, but the look on Art's face suggested that the question unnerved him somewhat. He reached for the Chardonnay and refilled his glass to the brim, then drained half of it. Had she spoiled the day? Her heartbeat quickened. In that moment she realized beyond a doubt that she had grown fond of Art and was ready to be more than a little angry at herself if she'd ruined it. But now Art had a strange smile just peeking out around the corners of his lips.

"Ah, King Arthur and the glorious knights of the Round Table. You know the stories?"

"Only vaguely. I've seen the motif in various movies, as have most people, but I never really got into it much. Wizards and knights -- that kind of stuff has always made me uneasy." Something was dawning in the back of Raina's mind, but she pushed it away.

"Really?" Art was genuinely surprised.

"Well, you know...I'm a modern woman through and through." She meant it to sound casual, but it didn't. Cautiously, Art launched into a little lesson on the Once and Future King. He introduced her to the major players of the tales, explained the significance of the sword Excalibur, the Round Table, and Arthur's dream of the unity of England.

"Of course, there were romantic intrigues and pesky women involved, and that's where things got messy," Art said with a grin. "But what on earth brought this up if you've never spent much time with the tales?"

Raina took a deep breath.

"The Yule Poems. The December 14th poem speaks of Arthur the King and depicts him as a rather complex figure, both mythically heroic and fallible."

Raina couldn't help but notice that Art's eyes shone with the same intensity as Sirona's did at the mention of the book.

"Well, he was complex, which is why the myth is so powerful and persistent. I believe it's a primal, existential story. It deals with the struggle to keep a pure heart while wielding power, the wayward impulses of love and attraction, and questions of personal sovereignty. It also sits at the nexus between the old pagan ways and Christianity.

It's been told and retold probably more times than any other single story, changing each time as the teller tries to tease out the complexities of the human heart. One could spend their whole life studying it, reading all the various tellings, and still there would be more to think about, more pieces of the tale to imagine."

"You speak eloquently about it...and knowledgably. How is that?"

"I've *lived* it!" The words came out more forcefully than Art had intended. Then, more calmly,"...I mean...I told you, I used to play knights and dragons as a kid and I've read I don't know how many versions of it."

So, you *were* named after him!"

"Actually, I think it's more that I was innocently named Art and I lived into the name. But the day is waning. We should be getting back, but I'm wondering if you would sit here for just a moment while I venture up stream for a bit? With any luck, I won't be long."

Of course, she would wait. She had plenty to think about as she considered what Art had told her of the tales, and thought, too, about what he had said earlier about the trees watching her. What did they see as she sat there, aged and worn but feeling on the verge of something new blossoming in her? For a moment she fantasized that she might ask the trees what *they* thought -- what *they* saw.

Perhaps she dozed, the wine getting the best of her, but it was unclear to her how much time had passed when a rustling on the stream bank alerted her to Art's return, which was none too soon as the sun was going wintery silver in the west and the warmth of the day was noticeably ebbing away like a tide.

What on earth was that thing he was carrying?

"It's a beauty, isn't it?" Art was beaming, holding the stick like a staff. The wood had long since been debarked, now grayed and polished smooth by water and time. It was surprisingly straight, but at its top (which, Raina realized, was really its bottom), five large, dried roots arranged themselves like antlers. The effect was arresting, and Art, standing there holding it at his side, was even more so.

"It suits you," Raina said, and meant it. "Wild man of the forest."

"So you might think, but this is for you." He held the staff out toward her.

Before she could think to be polite, she blurted out, "What in heaven's name would I do with it?"

"Just be with it, let it be with you. Its purpose might become clear at some point."

Just like his *if you're meant to bring something, it will come to you* comment about the Solstice gathering, Raina thought. But clearly Art wanted her to have it, had gone into the woods to look for it. It seemed important to him somehow, or...anticipated. When Art held it out to her, she had no choice but to take it. Admittedly, the smooth wooden staff felt delightful in her hand, if the antlered crown was a bit intimidating. But upon reflection, perhaps a walking stick might be useful as they made their way home, which, Raina realized, they'd best do soon or they would be finding their way in the dark, not a circumstance Raina relished.

"Shall we depart my Lady?" Art said.

It was dusk before they were out of the woods, but Art seemed to know exactly where he was going. That's not to say, however, that it wasn't a bit tricky navigating roots and rocks in the deepening gloom.

"Is the staff a burden?" he asked. "I can carry it until we get to the main road if you like. It's a bit unwieldly."

"Actually, I've been using it to steady myself. The going is a bit tricky."

But Art reached over and gently took the staff from her, then offered her his hand.

"Here, let me steady you if I may."

Willingly, Raina took his hand, much rougher than the weathered wood, but warm and reassuring, and constant. So connected, they made their way together for the rest of the descent. A hand in the darkness. How Raina would have appreciated that when she needed it most. But here it was now, at any rate, and with it came a flood of relief that Art could never have guessed at. For Raina, it was like she could take a deep breath after eons of shallow breathing, always just enough to keep her alive, but never all that she needed.

Alone again in her well-lit cottage, Raina built up the fire and set her staff against the side of the fireplace, then made a cup of tea and fetched her computer. Warmed by the dancing flames, she dove into a search on King Arthur, and was soon lost in history, myth, books, movies, television series', and an overwhelming cast of characters each with his or her own branching stories. But one in particular snagged her attention. A dark, craggy, hooded figure holding a staff.

Merlin. Advisor to Arthur. Magician. Often pictured holding a staff not unlike the one Art had just found in the woods which was now leaning against the fireplace in her living room...her living room.

If she had thought it strange that Art would have given her such a thing just a few hours ago, it was downright creepy that it so resembled something this mythical magician was often pictured with. Raina stared at it, daring it to move, not sure that it didn't, given the play of light from the fire across its surface. Wasn't there something in the Yule Poems about the wizard? Yes, in the final poem...

Wizard rests in winter lair, stars for robes, tangled hair.

It wasn't a hard image to conjure. There was familiarity to it. Raina couldn't help but think of the Mother Room and the illusion of stars across the firmament. But there was also a quickening of her pulse that unnerved her. Why did the image of a wizard make her tense? True it was that her interest in literature never wandered toward the mythical or fantastical, but rather was focused on the contemporary. Maybe a little magical realism here and there but always in the service of the modern landscape of the human condition. But that wasn't cause for an elevated pulse. Maybe. But, by design, all she remembered of those months of terrifying dreams and even waking visions was the darkness, the lack of control, the hint of power too intense to handle.

A tinge of the vertigo Raina had felt in the Mother Room made her close her eyes and grip the arms of her chair. Too much wine in the woods perhaps? Tears pushed at the edges of her eyes. Alone in this shell that had been her mother's refuge she wanted for all the world to cry out

"Why Mother? How could you leave me so bereft of your guidance? How is it that I cannot see clearly? What is this box in my chest that I dare not open, that keeps me only half alive in this world?"

Then the tears started in earnest. Let them fall, she thought. Too exhausting to hold them in, to pretend that they weren't a constant threat. She raged, she cried, she doubled over in pain. A lifetime of grief spilled out of her and flowed into the lake, and watered the trees, and reminded the dried wood leaning in the corner that it was once a living thing. And when it was over something in Raina had changed. As the grief tumbled out, so did some of the fear, the caution, the hesitation of doing more than just dipping a toe into the waters of life.

Tomorrow she would walk back into the woods where Art had taken her. She would go alone and take the staff with her. She wasn't sure what she was looking for -- perhaps the childhood joy Art felt there, or maybe it was something else -- but she would go there, alone, open, daring the world to help her to see what she could not see on her own.

14

A Shimmer in the Woods

Raina was on the trail before sunup, intent on avoiding prying eyes, carrying the antlered staff and heavily dressed against the more typical January cold that had returned. At first, she thought she might not find the turn into the woods, overgrown as it was, but their walk yesterday had disturbed the brush enough that a close look told Raina she was on the right track. Well rested and determined, she forged through the web of understory with little trouble and soon found herself in the clearing. She remembered that Art had headed off to the edge of it at the upper right-hand corner.

Again, with little difficulty, she soon found the path and delighted all over again at the charming tree-like moss under foot. Kneeling, she brushed her hand over it gently and felt an unexpected gratitude well up in her. How amazing nature was. Such perfection and detail on such a small scale; such beauty imparted to something mostly unnoticed by humans. Now she felt a tinge of regret that she was trampling all over these tiny, precious little beings. Gently, she pushed her hand down upon them in mimic of a footfall, then lifted it again to see that the moss sprang back as though nothing had disturbed it. Still, as she stood up and resumed her ascent, she willed herself to step more lightly.

As she neared the place where she thought they had turned off toward the stream, Raina did not bother to seek out the spot. Today's destination was not yesterday's. Instead, Raina's interest lay in the continuation of the path. Whether it was the staff that drew her on (which, she surmised, had itself come from somewhere beyond), or her own curiosity, didn't matter. She was drawn to find out where the path led. And so, she travelled on. The path rose more steeply as of course it would, she thought, otherwise how came the lovely waterfall? Now she was using the staff in earnest as she trudged over the rising terrain.

For a time, the sound of falling water dominated her senses as the path swerved closer to the stream. Stopping to rest, she let the sound wash over her and breathed in the fragrance of the shimmering spray that flew off the plummeting stream like wraiths...or snow geese, Raina thought, remembering the beauty of their departing flight in a similar morning light.

As she continued on, she saw that she was nearing the apex of the waterfall. Perhaps the slope would gentle some after that, or so she fervently hoped. Her aging legs were beginning to threaten her success in going much further. But her hopes were dashed as the ground rose even sharper still and became rockier so that she had to pick her way carefully around boulders slick with a scrim of dew turned to ice. Now, she had to rest after every dozen steps or so and, despite the morning chill, she could feel the sweat gathering beneath her hat.

During one such rest, she thought she saw a glimmer in the woods, a few feet off the path. At first, she was inclined to pay it no mind, but it continued to flash and recede, a teasing wink impossible to ignore. Pulling herself to her feet, she cautiously stepped off the path to make her way toward it, weaving through the understory as best she could, until, by some trick of the twists and turns, the flash seemed to move behind a giant oak. Game on, she thought, and, reaching the oak, held out her hand to touch the immense trunk, then slid around it to where she was sure she would catch up with the shimmer at last, but what she found instead caught her breath -- a ring of stones around a dark pool.

What happened next defied reason. It was as though her mind shut off and her body took over, threatening to melt away, then and there, as unbidden tears sprang from her eyes in a flood and her heart felt as though it would burst. Amid scattered twigs and acorns, she dropped to her knees on the verge of the pool, unable to do more than let the fierce emotion roll over, around, and through her. Helplessly, she clutched her chest as though to hold on to whatever it was that wanted to fly out of her and meet the swirling energy emanating from the pool. A potent mix of agony and bliss tore at her. Trembling, she closed her eyes and, in the darkness, imagined a wispy figure, like an... angel. And when she opened them again, the image still hovered over the pool. It could have been just the morning mist rising into the cold sunlight, but it seemed to Raina that it held out open palms to her. An invitation or a blessing.

A part of her never wanted to leave, never wanted to return to whatever world she had left, but the cold eventually intruded, forcing her to her feet and turning her thoughts toward home, as though whatever had had her in its grasp relented at last. The otherworldly beneficence she had felt rising from the pool, however, lingered.

Steadying herself against the oak, she backed away slowly, reluctant to take her eyes from the pool, but knew it was time to leave. Sighing, she turned to make her way back to the path, but all she saw before her was woods. Surely, she hadn't gone that far off track. She tried not to panic -- this wasn't a huge fairytale forest, just a wooded area around a lake with a stream somewhere to her...left, she thought. If she went downhill, like flowing water, sooner or later she was likely to emerge on the lake road. Confident in her strategy, she began her descent, and was soon pleased to see that she was indeed on a path. Relieved, she swung her staff out to meet the slight swagger in her step.

After a bit, however, she started to feel like this wasn't the same path she had taken on her ascent and when she started seeing bits of cloth tied to the trees here and there, she was sure of it. Despite the fact that on the way up she had mostly kept her eyes on the ground to avoid the rocks and roots, she would have seen what appeared to be markers regularly and carefully placed to catch the eye. So, this was a marked trail, but not the one she had come up on, not the continuation of the one Art had brought her on the previous day. For a moment, she debated turning around and following the trail back up to where, she reasoned, it might intersect the original path. But she was tired, exhausted, she realized. And what if she was wrong? She would perhaps spend the last of her energy getting herself even more lost. If this trail was marked, it had to lead somewhere, and a somewhere where there were people, or at least a person who had gone to the trouble to mark the trail.

Downward she continued, almost numb with fatigue, questions, and wonder. Before long, she heard what sounded like a car, and soon after that, she could see the lake, the blessed lake, through the trees. The cloth markers had ceased some time back, but the trail was clear enough and though now it was disappearing into understory, the view of the lake would lead her to the road and home.

When at last she emerged from the woods, she had all she could do to keep from collapsing, but she could see her cottage in the near distance. Almost too late, she thought to mark the trail in some way, for nothing that she could see did so and she was fairly certain she would want to return this way at some point. Looking around, she noticed a half-dead tree that sported a low branch sticking out like an overgrown nose. Were she younger she could have climbed up on it and pretended it was indeed a grandfather ready to tell her marvelous tales. She would easily remember this big-nosed grandfather tree.

When Raina reached her porch, she found that she could not yet shut herself behind doors. Moreover, her customary tilt toward doubt was presenting itself, and reality was re-asserting itself rather jarringly. What was it that she had experienced at the pool? Could she trust the beneficence she had felt, or would it dissolve into the darkness she was all too familiar with? Was she sliding back into madness, lured by the promise of angelic grace? She stared at the lake, taking deep breaths, joy and fear waring inside her.   In the near distance, Art's cottage sat on the edge of her vision, waiting.

Raina was tired of holding everything in.   It was exhausting and it was becoming abundantly clear that she wasn't an island. Would Art know of the pool? She had to know...now.

Storming wasn't exactly the right word for the determined steps she took to get herself to Art's front porch, but it did take courage, as she had never come to his house without an expressed invitation. It seemed rather bold, but a page had turned. It was time for Raina to take her life in her own hands. Late though it was, the time had come.

"Raina!" Art was clearly surprised to see her and suddenly she realized that on top of coming unannounced, she was probably muddy, sweaty and somewhat disheveled, but so be it.

"I have a question for you..." she pronounced, more aggressively than she had intended.

"Well, come in, come in.   But those boots have to stay in the hall," he said with an amused smile. Where had she been? They were caked with mud.

"Tea?" he offered, "Stout?"

"Tea I guess...no... make it stout if it's that horrible stuff of yours."

"Ha, you've been hanging around with Sirona too much, picking up on her indelicate ways."   Art seemed delighted to be hosting Raina on the spur of the moment. She was relieved that he was in a good mood. He had mugs out in a flash and was pouring their libation when Raina jumped right to it.

"So..." she began, "what's with the pool in the woods?"

Art froze in mid-pour. Not "what pool?" or "where?" just a painfully long silence, but Raina could wait, arms folded. Clearly, he knew exactly what she was talking about.

After a pause, Art finished the pour, picked up the two glasses and turned to face Raina.

"I wondered if you'd find it...eventually. This morning I gather."

"Clearly." Why was she angry? So, Art hadn't shown her this pool. Big deal. But it was more than a pool wasn't it? And they had been so close the day before. Why hadn't he taken her to it then?

"And...?" Art asked, taking what was supposed to be a nonchalant sip of his stout.

And? She was the one asking the questions here! But he wasn't giving anything away until she did. It didn't seem like Art to be so cagey.

"*AND? And,* I had some kind of mystical experience, that's all!" Now she was shouting, waving her hands, pacing around the kitchen. It was a good thing Art was still holding her drink. Then she stopped and turned to Art, tears on her cheeks.

"What was that Art? What is going on?"

Art put the drinks down and went to her, drew her to him and let her cry into his shoulder.

"What's happening to me? Am I losing it?" Art had no idea the depth of fear that lurked behind those words, but he was clear that Raina was seriously troubled.

"Look...you're not losing it, not even close. There's much to tell about the "pool" as you call it, but if you're ok with it I'd like to call Sirona. She should be in on this conversation. I've got some leftover stew on the stove. Why don't we have a bite while we wait for her?

In that moment Raina realized that she hadn't eaten breakfast. She had started out on her jaunt at dawn and the world had turned upside down since then, but she had had nothing to eat.

"Food would be good," she admitted.

Art steered her to the kitchen table, placed a bowl of stew in front of her then went to call Sirona.

"On her way," Art said as he re-entered the kitchen and scooped a bowl for himself. Raina was eating like she hadn't seen food in weeks and Art left her to it, but hoped fervently that Sirona wouldn't dally. It would take the two of them to negotiate what was coming, but in many ways, Art was relieved that they were going to get into it.

When Sirona arrived, Art ushered them into the living room, having poured a round for all three of them.

"Now then," Art said, leaning forward in his chair, "tell us about your morning..."

From the first step outside earlier that morning to the eventual emergence on the road, she recounted every detail of her hike, and every thought and emotion she could find words for. If Art or Sirona had any questions along the way, they kept them to themselves, not wanting to derail Raina's story in the slightest, although if Raina had looked up rather than telling her story to her hands, she would have seen Sirona's eyes grow immense at the revelation of what Raina had experienced at the pool.

"Well...there it is," she ended, finally. "Do you think I'm mad?"

Sirona and Art exchanged a look, silently deciding between them that Sirona should begin.

"What you found is more than a simple pool...as you seem to have discovered. It is a holy well."

"A holy well? I thought that was the stuff of fairy tales," Raina said, almost whispering.

"Well, maybe so in America, but there are holy wells all over the Celtic lands and we'll get to that, but Raina, I have to say that what you experienced today is...unusual."

At that Raina stiffened. Sirona could not know how often Raina's behavior had been deemed "unusual" and to what extremely disastrous result.

"But not bad," Sirona rushed on as she saw Raina's reaction. "Many people go to holy wells for spiritual inspiration and have done so, in fact, for thousands of years. What you seem to have experienced is what is known as the 'Gift of Tears' -- that can happen when one is brought into the presence of the Holy Spirit, the touch of which is so tender that one is brought to tears. Raina, many long for what you experienced today, but few are blessed as you have been."

"Blessed..." Raina mused. "How, why, has this happened to me?"

Sirona looked beseechingly at Art, who shrugged his shoulders. How much to tell her when they weren't entirely sure themselves? But today's events had pushed the envelope.

Art cleared his throat. "Do you recall asking me about King Arthur yesterday?"

"Of course," Raina answered guardedly.

"Well...Arthur was known as the Once and Future King."

Raina could feel something tightening in her chest.

"There are those who believe that Arthur's spirit returns," Art continued, "perhaps has done so again and again, hoping to find a host and a circumstance conducive to the realization of the reign of hope, goodness, and equity that Arthur stood for..."

Raina raised an eyebrow..."Don't tell me..."

"We believe so, yes, that in some way at least I am connected to Arthur's spirit."

"There's more," Sirona said, leaning forward in her chair. "Some tales suggest that Arthur's sister, the healer Morgan le Fey will return as well, and to complete the triad, the magician and advisor, Merlin. Together, the three represent Sovereignty, Healing, and the sacred connection between the Earth and humankind. Sirona is the name of a Celtic goddess of healing..."

A weighty silence fell over the room like a cloak that Raina felt trapped in. Even if she could wrap her mind around the ancient spirits alive and well in her new friends, what role did she play in all this...unless...

"That leaves Merlin. Surely you don't think..."

"Much points in that direction," Art said trying to hide his excitement.

"But Merlin was a man!" Raina protested. This much she knew from the little bit of research she had done.

"Well, Merlin was a shape-shifter, or so it is said. And, anyway, shouldn't we assume that spirit is not gender-defined?"

"Me... Merlin...utterly ridiculous."

Sirona stepped in. "We're not sure, exactly, that Merlin's spirit inhabits you as we believe Arthur and Morgan le Fey do us. But we're convinced that you have come to us as the key and that in some way you will be instrumental in completing the triad. Your experience at the well today suggests that you have a spiritual power and connection that is not typical."

"The question now is," Art said gently, "are you willing to help us pursue this?"

They waited. They had said all they felt they should at this point. It was now up to Raina to take it all in and walk forward with them or run away.

When Raina finally spoke, it was not either of those choices that she addressed.

"There's something you need to know about me," she said. "I have a deep fear of madness. I've been in treatment -- it was years ago. You offer me this story that touches that fear, as did the experience today at the well. And yet, I feel a strong affinity to the both of you and while my episode at the well was overwhelming, it did not exactly carry the fear and darkness of my past. I'd like to tell you my story, then we'll see if that changes your thoughts about me."

Raina waited for their response; it was Sirona who gave their reply.

"You have listened to us with an open heart. We can do no less for you."

"I've been in treatment, years ago, " Raina began, then continued with the story that defined her life, broke her heart, and chained her soul. She told of the horrible nightmares she had had since puberty, terrifying dreams in which she wielded power that she could not control. She might appear as a bear, a hawk, a boar, but always she knew it was herself and more often than not it ended in blood and death that she was somehow responsible for. She blamed the dreams for her mother leaving and yet she knew that her mother had not been at peace either...ever. That she herself may have suffered from similar visitations Raina eventually grew to suspect.

But alone as she was, and troubled, Raina did her best to live a normal life. She finished college, got married, had a precious daughter...at that she paused in her recitation. Her daughter. April. How thoroughly she had tried to wipe the loss of her from memory. She could have stopped her narrative there for all the pain the memory of her sweet child caused her, but forced herself to continue.

After the birth, the nightmares, the visitations intensified, attacking her in her waking hours as well as in sleep. She became erratic to the point where both she and her husband feared for the safety of the baby. Her husband's solution was to have her committed straight away, without any attempt at other solutions. Raina was institutionalized, a divorce was finalized, and custody given to the father, who then disappeared from her life.

Raina struggled for months to regain control. With no husband, parents or friends to support her, she was at the mercy of the mental health professionals. Her therapy consisted mostly of drugs, some of which helped, others made matters worse. Had she had the where-with-all she might have done herself in, so desperate did she become, but one day, in the midst of the worst of the darkness, the dreams left her. It was as though they had given up. In retrospect, she wondered if it was because she hadn't given in to them, hadn't manifested the dark nature they seemed to want from her, but had clung doggedly to her sense of right until she prevailed. Wherever she had found the strength to do that, she had no idea, but was thankful for it.

Nevertheless, it was months before she could convince the doctors that she was better. There was nothing in their experience that could explain the sudden change of events and so they continued to pry into the corners of her mind, looking for the malaise they believe lurked there until finally, failing to find it, they let her go.

She went back to college, received a degree in literature and found a post at a small college. During those years she tirelessly sought the whereabouts of her ex-husband and daughter but to no avail. They were nowhere to be found and eventually she gave up and buried herself in her teaching and her constant vigilance against the madness that had once possessed her.

Her narrative complete, Raina sat with her eyes closed, afraid to look into the eyes of her friends and see rejection there. A hand grasped hers and she felt two strong hands on her shoulders. Art had come to stand behind her and Sirona now held her hand in both of hers.

"We are saddened by your story," Sirona said softly, "but not entirely surprised."

Art spoke from behind her, a protective stance.

"We have thoughts about what you've shared, but it's been a long day and you've been given much to contemplate, as have we. Shall we plan to meet again tomorrow?"

Turning to look into Art's eyes, Raina was taken aback by the affection and care she saw there, and the pain. If this man held the spirit of an ancient King, what a compassionate and troubled King he must have been. The flood of emotion that had filled her at the well threatened to overcome her again, but she fought it back.

"Yes, we should meet tomorrow." Raina managed, then, "If you're willing to come to my cottage, I have something to show you."

15

The Healer and the King

It had snowed during the night and the sunless morning did nothing to warm the lake room. Raina sat wrapped in a blanket, gripping her hot coffee cup with gratitude, and stared out at the white expanse. This was not her favorite kind of day, when the world looked all black and white. Amazing, she thought, how, without sunlight to color them, the pines on the far shore might as well have been etched with charcoal.

Then, like a liberated hunk of snow, a seagull took on that special quality white sometimes has on cloudy days as it flew across the wall of trees. Even on a black and white day, Raina thought, smiling slightly, there can be beauty if one looks long enough. But the seagull was soon gone and Art and Sirona were due shortly. She rose to shower and dress and prepare herself for what lay ahead.

"Did you sleep well?" were the first words out of Art's mouth.

"Surprisingly, I did. Dreamlessly even. It's almost as though my mind had enough dream-like stuff to deal with in my waking hours yesterday and needed a rest!"

Laughing, Sirona inquired, "So are you ready for more? There's so much we want to share with you."

Maybe she really was ready, Raina thought. She had carried her personal agony for so long, so alone. To unwrap all that she had kept bottled up was appealing.

"You said last night that you had some thoughts..." Raina said.

"Well then, imagine if you will, coming to the realization that your soul, your inner being, carries something of a previous life, or lives, and moreover that those lives were of a pretty fantastical nature," Sirona began.

"We were lucky, in a way, that we were siblings," Art continued. "Unlike you who struggled with your visions alone, we at least had each other for consolation."

"Was it terrifying? Did you think you were mad?"

"No," Sirona said, "not terrifying, just...different. The realizations came slowly, gradually, over the years. As Art said, we had each other. When we were young, our play reflected our essential natures. What fun we had in those years, carrying on like we were mythical beings from some past time, roaming the woods, living in a fantasy realm of what we thought was our own design..."

"...until we got older," Art continued, "and started to have experiences that suggested it was more than just our imaginary play."

"And your parents?" Raina asked.

"They were oblivious," Art answered. "They just thought they had wonderfully imaginative children. As we grew, things became more complicated, but Sirona's beauty was her cover. I swear, she bewitched people with it. One toss of that raven hair or stare from those dark eyes would silence even the most brazen. No one ever dared question her or get too close..."

"Both a blessing and a curse..." Sirona interjected. "But Art had it worse. He was a magnet for the opposite sex. They flocked to him, fawned on him, to the point where I had to intervene. We risked being accused of having an unnatural relationship, but "normal" ones just never worked out, so we eventually abandoned them. All our energy was spent trying to figure out what was going on with us."

"And how *did* you figure it out?"

"We learned about the transmigration of souls or metempsychosis as it is sometimes called -- the transfer of a soul from one body to another. Then, through research, dreams and eventually just *knowing*, it came to us whose souls we seemed to be carrying." Art was looking at Raina with a questioning look. Why had this not been her experience?

Then Raina asked the question that had been haunting her.

"Did you not, at any time, think you were insane, delusional?"

"No, that never occurred," Sirona said, apologetically. "Again, having each other was an immense help. True, we lived in our own world, but we filled that world with research and discussion, comparing our dreams, our feelings, our visions. Sometimes, especially if we were in the woods, we would have a shared vision. And, in truth, while some of those visions raised troubling questions or presented challenges, they were never dark or terrifying."

"And as we aged," Art added, "the fact that we, as biological brother and sister, housed the souls of two who were also siblings, we began to wonder if the souls always travelled such, or if we were a fortunate exception. If so, then perhaps we existed at an auspicious time in the life of the prophecy. It became our obsession, our life's work, to seek out the third soul of the triad, as we have explained. Our dreams, our hearts, were full of that longing which gave us purpose. We were convinced that Merlin's soul had to be here somewhere and that we were destined to find it.

"When I found the well in the woods," Art continued, "I believed that it was a sign -- a very powerful one as you found out, and that it was directly connected to finding Merlin, odd as that may seem. So, I've rooted myself here, keeping watch over the lake, the well..."

"And my mother's cottage..." Raina said, things making more sense now.

"Yes, and your mother herself, for that matter, but she was so reclusive, I couldn't connect. There were signs, but I felt that if Merlin's soul inhabited her, that it would sense Sirona and I, and at least make some movement of connection. But all I ever got from your mother was a reclusiveness that I didn't feel it was my place to impose upon."

"And so," Sirona said, taking up the narrative, "we came very close to giving up hope. We are aging; time may well be running out. Then when you showed up, there were signs, and that you found the well and had the experience you reported...perhaps we have been too forthcoming, too quickly, but you must understand, this has been a lifelong quest for us. We apologize if we've come on too strong or made you feel cornered, but in you we think we have found the treasure at last. To keep our excitement under wraps is a bit more than we're capable of."

Sirona smiled her endearing, enchanting smile. Raina sighed heavily. She couldn't help but envy the siblings their shared experience. To have had company with which to sort out the confusion and terror would have been such a blessing.

"If I carry the soul you are looking for," Raina mused, "why was my experience so different?"

"That's a good question," Art replied. "Merlin wasn't exactly a light-hearted kind of guy, but to have such unremittingly dark visions...it doesn't square at all with our own experience. And it seems that you never had any sense of your soul connection to a former life?"

"Not at all. I never even had an interest in these tales you talk about, or much of anything mythical. I just always felt like there was some dark force within me that wanted out, or to turn me into something that I didn't want to be. I've always had a fear of getting angry or wanting something too badly, that if I got too passionate, well, it was almost like I could have spit fire. I don't know why I thought that, I just did. That's a big part of why I submitted to being committed without a fight. I was terrified that I'd hurt someone, especially my daughter."

Tears threatened. Raina could not speak, or even think about her daughter, without acute agony. That hole in her would never mend, regardless of how much self-awareness she managed to gain, or how the years passed, one after another. When she could safely speak again, she ventured, "So maybe I'm not what you think I am, some 'third' in your mythical triad. Maybe I'm just a crazy woman who has seen enough...difference...to accept your strange story."

"That doesn't explain the discovery of the well," Art mused.

Sirona bit her lip and Art edged up in his chair. The room grew painfully silent as each, in their own way, struggled with how to move forward. Finally, Art spoke, and when he did there was a hint of a different tone in his voice, the tone of one on whose head leadership rests, with all its urgency of necessity and sole responsibility. Failure was not an option, lest something precious and unredeemable be lost.

"This much I am sure of, you are not crazy. We may not entirely understand the nature of your visions -- and I'm profoundly sorry for the pain you have suffered -- but there is something here that must be faced and understood. As for being our completion, you may or may not be the vehicle of Merlin's soul -- that we must seek to determine -- but that you are a key to bringing his energy into consciousness so that we might complete what it is our purpose to do in this time and place, is, at least in my opinion, indisputably true."

"But..." Raina tried to protest, though weakly. Art was growing in stature and power before her very eyes. The man who had been so gentle with her, so helpful and kind, was now somewhat intimidating.

He held up his hand, "There is no argument here. I could spell out for you all the little things that had started to add up since we've met you, but your experience at the well is proof enough. In fact, that you *found the well at all* is incontrovertible proof."

"What do you mean?"

"He means," Sirona said, tempering Art's intensity, "that the well has its ways. The casual hiker would never find it. You were drawn there, were you not? Like a willow branch in a dowser's hand, you bent in the direction of the Source."

Did she? She thought she had been merely exercising her own curiosity. She certainly wasn't seeking the well; she never would have guessed such a thing existed. But she had to admit, she had been seeking *something* although she had no idea what.

Clearly, Art was waiting for a decision from her. Would she join this quest or would she not? Her thoughts went to her little attic office at the university, the safety of hiding in academia where eccentricity was mostly tolerated. Safe, unremarked, all her questions pushed to the back of her consciousness. Now, she'd met these two who not only accepted her as she was but were willing to help her sort out the controlling mystery of her life, and that in so doing, she would be helping them as well. What was the point of safety when it was so empty? Furthermore, she had to admit, if she was being *pulled* it was in the direction of these two people. There was something comforting, right, about being in their presence.

"Alright then. I guess I don't have to fully believe what you think about me to explore this whole thing further. I do know that I feel an attraction and trust toward the two of you that I've never felt before. And having a purpose wouldn't be so bad. Right now, I'm adrift. I can't help but wonder if my life has had any purpose at all."

Sirona smiled. "I think we can put that notion to rest now."

Raina let her mouth curl up into a wan smile. "Then in that case, we might as well get this thing into gear. I have something I want to show you."

As she led them up the stairs to the loft, she felt a lightness she could never remember feeling before. However off-beat this quest was, it promised to give her some relief from what had kept her living a half-life, a life afraid of itself. The joy of being free from that was creeping into her, filling her chest with a feeling like carbonation.

As Raina pulled the cord that illuminated the Mother Room, Sirona gasped and Art exclaimed, "I wondered!" Raina watched as the two explored the room, her heart pounding. If anyone might understand what this room was all about, it would be them. Sirona ran her fingers over the painted walls while Art examined the scattered artifacts on the shelves. Raina was about to explain that this is where she had found the Yule Poems when she heard steps on the porch. Absorbed in their explorations, the two had not heard it, so Raina slipped out to investigate.

A figure stood at the door, shadowy through the glass. Raina did not hesitate to open it, curious.

"Well, there you are Raina..."

"Malcolm! What are you doing here?"

The unthinkable sight of her ex-husband standing on her porch, invading the serenity of her precious home, made the bile rise in her throat. The wave of vertigo kept her from closing the door in his face.

"I lost track of you for a while there. So, you've left the university then? Didn't take me all that long to find you though, did it?"

"You knew where I was?"

"Oh sure, I've kept track of you. Never take your eyes off the serpent, right?"

Raina felt the blood rush to her face. Perhaps there was a chance...

"Where's my daughter! Tell me where April is!"

"Well that's the point, isn't it? I've kept my eye on you to be sure that she never found you, or you her, although I'm pretty sure I've made it so she'll never want to look."

"You bastard!"

"Better a bastard than a devil." Malcolm tried to look past her into the house. "Aren't you going to let me in?"

"Absolutely not. What the hell do you want anyway?"

"Just wanted to know if I had to adjust my game plan. Have to understand the lay of the land so I can make sure April never looks for you."

"You have kept her from me all these years!"

"It's been an interesting game, that's for sure. The stories I've spun to make her hate you. There's a beauty to a poisoned well -- the more one thirsts, the deeper the poison penetrates." Malcolm paused, a shadow passing over his face. "But she's a young lady now and getting ideas of her own."

Raina fought the tears with everything she had, but they came anyway. So lost was she in her own sorrow that she failed to see the hint of fear cross Malcolm's face.

"Oh, don't worry," Malcolm went on with false sympathy, "I'll be sure she never finds you, even if she looks."

Raina felt the hair on her neck rise. She knew that Malcolm was a hard man, but now it looked like he had been the one drinking from a poisoned well all these years. A well...her mind flashed to the holy well a short walk from where they stood. The image of Malcolm defiling it made her shudder...and panic, not just for herself but for the Well... and for her daughter.

"You need to leave," she said, trying to keep the fear out of her voice, but he heard it, sniffed it out like a hungry predator.

"Oh, come on now Raina honey. You should welcome the visit, living out here all by yourself like this. What if those bad dreams of yours come back and you're all alone?"

"Oh, she's hardly alone..." it was Sirona who spoke as Raina felt Art and Sirona on either side of her.

"You going to leave under your own steam or should I show you the way to your car?" Art said as he moved toward Malcolm, who had taken a step back, but still hesitated. Another step forward from Art and Malcolm turned down the stairs, failing to muster the swagger he desired. But Art wasn't satisfied. He followed Malcolm into the yard.

"I trust you know you are never to return here, yes? This is not a place for the likes of you." They were stern words, but it was Art's stature and baring that drove the point home to Malcolm.

Art watched Malcolm's car shrink to nothingness, then made his way back into the house, hearing Raina's sobs before he even reached the door.

"He's gone Raina, and I don't think he'll be back."

"You don't know him," she raged. "He's taken everything from me, everything! He's known where I was all this time and has kept my daughter from me -- poisoned her against me. And now even this..." she said, waving her arm to encompass the house, Art and Sirona, "this final bit of comfort he will find a way to destroy. He can't just let me be, he has to suck the life out of me." Through her tears, Raina looked longingly at the little house she had grown to love, that held her mother's spirit and perhaps some clues to her own being. As her gaze took in the beloved cottage, she looked up into the loft and saw that the door to the Mother Room had been left open, the string lights glowing like fireflies. Had Malcolm seen it? Fearing for everything that was important to her, she prayed that he had not. Then a horrible thought came to her.

"What if he finds the well? He will defile it!" Her heart beat wildly. The thought of him getting anywhere near the well, desecrating it with his mere presence or worse, panicked her. If he had found her, what kind of uncanny ability did he have to find anything that she had touched, loved?

"Raina," Art said sitting beside her and taking her tear-soaked hands in his, "he cannot find the well. We've told you -- the well has its own defenses. Even if he were as...prescient as you imply...were he to go into the woods, he would more likely meet with misfortune than find the well."

"However true that may be," Sirona argued, "I fear this man, this...

"Malcolm."

"...this Malcolm may be more than he appears. Consider the role he has played in Raina's suffering. Perhaps he was instrumental in blocking Raina's ability to deal constructively with her visions, to work through them and become whole."

Raina was shaking her head..."No, no, that's all me. It started even before I knew him. He had nothing to do with it."

"I wouldn't be so sure about that, dear one," Sirona said. "Your visions are truly yours, but your ability to find their meaning and your purpose was stifled by his treatment of you. And now that you've found some peace, it seems he has come here to intimidate you, to suss out your current situation and find a way to inject the poison of his fear into your mind."

"Look Raina," Art said, sternly, "no more hiding. No more fear. You have a destiny to fulfill. If Malcolm is a malevolent force working against you, you have to face that head on. You aren't alone any more. You have Sirona and me to help you and we are not without our resources. We need to move ahead and keep our wits alert for whatever threat Malcolm intends, but we cannot let him intimidate us and keep us from achieving our purpose." Art dragged his weathered hand through his mop of gray hair.

"This isn't just about us..." he continued. "There's something bigger here. I'm not entirely sure what it is, but now that you're here with us, I trust it will become evident with time, which, as we are all too aware, is not an infinite resource."

Sirona shifted in her seat. "I have a thought," she said. "Why don't I take Raina to Glastonbury for a while. Prescient or not, Malcolm won't figure that out right away, if ever, and I believe that's where we should go anyway to begin looking for some answers."

Then, suddenly delighted, "Oh, Raina, you will love Glastonbury."

Raina looked at Art, and seeing both his power and compassion, knew she did not want to be far from him.

"You will come, too?"

There was a sadness in Art's eyes, as Sirona answered for him.

"Art's place is here, Raina. He is the keeper of the well, the lake, and this cottage and the mysteries it holds."

Raina tried to smile through her tears but was pitifully unsuccessful.

"So, more than just a neighbor checking in on the place, then," she said, suddenly aware of the depth and importance of Art's sacrifice in the name of a centuries-old prophecy.

"Much more, I'm afraid."

Book Two

Pam Collins

16

Ceara the Potter

Ireland
circa 1000 AD

Ceara was a paradox. She was blessed with the most beautiful red hair anyone in her village had ever seen. It flowed across her shoulders and down her back like waves of flame. When she stepped into the sun it was as if her head had caught fire. No one could see her thus and not stop to take in the terrifying beauty of it. But it was also fire that had disfigured her, rendering what should have been the prettiest lass in five counties only a curiosity. Her scarred face and arm had defined her since she was twelve.

She had been helping her father at the kiln. It must be said that he cautioned her against it, but Ceara would not be dissuaded. She had been fascinated by her father's craft since she could walk and had been throwing on the wheel since she was ten. In those years, she was willing to let her father do the firing, but then came the day of misfortune. She had made a special pot, fluted and perfectly shaped, etched with interlacing vines and berries. It was, to her mind, the most beautiful thing she had ever made. She had placed it lovingly in the cold kiln and now wanted to be the one to experience the thrill of removing the finished piece.

The fire was spent, but the stone walls of the kiln still held the heat, enough so that when in her haste she tripped and fell against them her young skin was singed. Stunned by the fall, she lay there, her face against the stinging stones, until her father could get to her and snatch her upright, leaving flakes of her tender young skin behind.

To Ceara's advantage, the village healer was skilled. She kept Ceara's burns covered in calendula poultices and fed her soothing drinks that eased the pain. As for Ceara, the fiery red-headed child endured her pain stoically, lest she upset her father. Nevertheless, the potter was inconsolable. From that day forward, he let the kiln lay cold and unused while the wheel gathered dust. What was left of his store of pots and cups, he sold for a song and soon there was little left to sustain their small household. For the love of the child, the village folk did what they could, bringing whatever they could spare from their own tables, but it was a meagre existence for the potter and his child.

"Father," Ceara spoke, though it gave her pain to do so. "You must work again. The generosity of the people cannot last forever. You are the best potter in five counties. Please, take up your craft as you should do."

But the potter only stared into the distance. Had Ceara's mother lived, she would have known how to deal with him, but Ceara's words fell off him like crumbs.

And so, it came to pass that, before she was fully healed, Ceara fought against the pain and began to take her father's place at the wheel. Her work was nothing like the potter for form and decoration, but her bowls would hold gruel and her mugs would deliver ale to the thirsty. They would not bring people from far and wide as her father's had, but they would serve the needs of the village and she could use them to barter for the things they needed, though in truth, remembering the generosity of the villagers, she always took less than she gave.

In the beginning, she would urge her father to help her, but as soon as he cast his eyes on her face, tears would come and he would turn away from her. As for Ceara, it wasn't her disfigurement that broke her heart, but the loss of her father's affection and companionship. But she was young, with a life ahead of her and so, despite the pain and loss she had endured at such a young age, she took responsibility for the maintenance of the household as her father shriveled into himself and died within the year.

The years passed and Ceara grew in mastery of her craft. Because of her disfigurement, there were no suitors to complicate her time, so in the freedom of her days, she indulged every creative notion that came to her. She most loved etching and carving the leather hard clay. The ease with which the clay gave way to her imagination thrilled her. Nothing was spared from her creative eye as she sought new design ideas from the world around her.

Lately, she had taken to sketching the faces of the children of the village who would often come to her cottage in the hope that Ceara would give them a hunk of clay to play with. As they formed little bowls or animals, Ceara would do her best to catch their intense and sweet expressions on her stone tablet, then in the evenings, by candlelight, she would render their faces on the sides of bowls and flagons. Sometimes an ear or nose would extend and become a handle or a spout. In truth, Ceara's work was as beautiful as she was uncomely, as playful as she was somber.

Eventually, Ceara and the clay she loved became as one entity. Everyone who saw her work marveled at the life in it, as if the very landscape had come to Ceara's feet, waiting to be lifted into her work and once there, to transform the vessel into a part of the landscape in turn. There wasn't a household in the village that didn't eat and drink from her vessels. Beautiful as they were, Ceara insisted that they were not to languish on a shelf, but were to be put to daily use. And in truth, for many it seemed that mead and milk tasted sweeter, stew went further, bread stayed fresher in Ceara's pottery. And while no one willfully broke any of that precious crockery, accidents do happen, and when they did, a new piece appeared that was, if possible, even more beautiful than the last.

It didn't take long for word of her craftmanship to spread beyond the village and soon Ceara had all she needed of material wealth. She had a new studio room built on the sunny side of the cottage with a large door she could open in good weather. There, she set her wheel close to the threshold so that she could be all but outside as she worked. Half the room was shelved to display her work to anyone who came to buy, but the other half was full of a strange and abundant array of "inspiration objects" that she continually collected.

Truth was, it had gotten so she hardly needed most of the compensation she acquired for her work, so she found ways to share her wealth with the village. She hired people to dig her clay and wrap the finished pieces for travel, and she had silver pieces for any child who brought her an interesting shell or flower or any other found treasure. She was beloved by the people not only for the beauty she created for their tables, but also for her generosity. She appreciated the general affection but as she grew into womanhood, she hungered for the love of a special one with whom she could share her heart. But she could never forget that her father died from the grief of her disfigurement. How could she expect any young man to overcome what her own father could not? She told herself her craft was her love, but when she was forced to finally admit exhaustion at the end of the day, the darkness of night was a deep well of loneliness.

It was on a particularly beautiful day when Ceara was glad to have her workroom wide open to the blessed air that her life changed irrevocably. She was nearly finished centering a particularly large piece of clay, her legs furiously working the peddles of the wheel, her hands covered in slip. Bent over her wheel, she smelled the scent of lavender before she saw the finely made boots out of the corner of her eye.

"Excuse me. I didn't mean to startle you."

Ceara brushed her hair from her face with the back of her arm and looked up to see the most beautiful woman she'd ever laid eyes on. Raven black hair framed a silken white face that held grey eyes the color of the sea in a storm. The woman's clothes were like gossamer, grey and pale blue layers, flowing around a tall, slender form. *Perfect symmetry,* Ceara thought, always aware of form before anything else. Then...

"Are you one of the faire folk then?" Ceara heard herself ask then was sorry for the words the moment they were out of her mouth. If this woman was fey, she wouldn't appreciate Ceara blurting it out.

"I wouldn't say so," the woman smiled.

Suddenly Ceara was painfully aware of how she must look, covered in clay, ragged clothes, hair a disheveled wig. Out of habit, she turned the burnt side of her face away from the stranger as she gathered herself.

"Please, make yourself at home in the kitchen, or the garden...there's a seat there. But I must clean up a bit."

"Of course. The garden will do just fine. 'Tis a fine day, isn't it?"

Ceara rushed to make herself presentable, then prepared some ale and bread for her guest. On the way to the garden, she remembered to throw a damp rag over the lump of clay she'd work so hard to center. No matter who this woman was, there was no point in wasting a morning's work.

After the food had been set before her guest, Ceara did her best to compose herself. *If not fey, then what?* Ceara wondered. It wasn't as if she hadn't met plenty of finely dressed people who had come to buy her wares, but this woman was uncannily different. Ceara gave the appropriate time to the ritual of hospitality before she spoke.

"If you'd like to see my work..."

"Oh, I know your work," the woman smiled. "Most folk do. You're quite well known, out there." She waved her hand as though to encircle the whole of Eire.

Ceara nodded. She never knew how to take compliments.

198

"I expected a rather grand house for someone so well known."

"I don't need much...and I like it here in the village," *because I need the company,* she thought, but managed not to say.

"And your garden is as lovely as your pottery. You live alone?"

"Ever since my father died. I was quite young."

"This is all beautifully tended for one person alone."

"The village children come and help me. They'll do anything for a chance to play in the clay. There are few homes in the village that don't have a collection of little clay animals."

"So, you are important here in more ways than one."

Ceara shrugged.

"No doubt you would not be comfortable leaving all this?"

Ceara hadn't expected such a turn of conversation.

"No, this is my home," she said, pulling herself up straighter, but then she wondered, *would I?* "But you have told me nothing of who you are, or what you have come here for."

"I'm called Liadan, and I've come here for you."

Ceara found the courage to look into the sea grey eyes of her visitor.

"What is it you wish?" she said in what sounded to her like a very small voice.

"I....we....need a special vessel. A ritual vessel. It must be made of clay and by one who has known the elements in special ways -- the tears of grief, the air of generosity, the clay of the earth, and....the touch of transformational fire."

Ceara's hand went to her face as tears slid from her heart into her eyes.

"You, Ceara, are such a one," Liadan proclaimed.

Liadan had given her a week to get things in order, but it hardly took Ceara that long. She had been promised all the tools she needed so she packed only her very special tools and a few other oddments. As for clothes, she realized she hadn't a single dress worthy of wearing among strangers. There wasn't a single unstained garment among the rags she called clothes. She had had no need of anything else...but now...well, it would be what it would be. She made an agreement with one of the young men in the village, Naoise, who seemed most interested in working the clay, to watch her house, the studio and the kiln. He was free to use everything as he might, so long as he took care of it as his own. He readily agreed, and in that moment, Ceara realized that she had taken on an apprentice...just like that.

Liadan returned in the week, as promised, but only with an extra horse, not a cart. Had she known that Ceara had so little to bring? But surely, she did not know that Ceara had never ridden. Liadan seemed to read her mind.

"Not all of our trip will be on open roads. This beast is well trained and is brother to my mount. He will carry you well." And then, with a little smile, Liadan added, "This is only the first challenge you will face, my crafty friend. You have a world of new experiences awaiting you."

Not for the first time did Ceara wonder if she was making the right choice to accept Liadan's proposal, and yet there seemed no way to refuse, no room in her mind for anything other than acceptance. Who was she to imagine that it was appropriate for her to choose her own destiny? Is it not the way of Destiny that when it knocks, only the unwise would naysay it? It could be argued that she had freely chosen to take up her father's craft, but had there really been a choice? The craft had chosen her at her birth, and later marked her in such a way as to claim her, for with her scarred face, there were many doors closed to her.

Liadan helped her secure her bundle to the horse, then showed her how to mount and hold the reins. Ceara's heart was tapping an alien rhythm, but soon it slowed to match the hoofbeats as the two women made their way out of town. Other than settling Naoise into her house, she had not said any good-byes. She trusted that Naoise would hold her place until she returned, for return she fully believed she would.

The journey passed as though in a dream. Ceara lost track of days and direction, Liadan's voice flowing over her like the sound of the sea, rhythmic, continuous. It seemed to Ceara that they saw many wonders and ate delicious food, but she could never remember any of it or give it a name. She often wondered how she managed to stay astride her horse, so dreamy was she, but her mount was carrying her securely. Then, one night at their campfire, Ceara's focus sharpened a bit and reality came back to her, gently, but with urgency.

"Are we not nearly there then?" Ceara asked.

"We are."

"In all this time, we have not talked about the task ahead of me," and now Ceara wondered that she had not asked any questions up to this point. Liadan had told Ceara that she was the one they needed to make some kind of ritual vessel and, as though enchanted, Ceara had accepted this as a given. But now the questions and doubts came flooding in.

"How will I know how to make what will be right for this special vessel?"

"You have already begun on the path of knowing. Now you must undertake an *imram*, a journey to the eternal invisible world. Tomorrow we will arrive at Bru na Boinne where you will sequester for five days, five being the sacred number of the elements. I will be near throughout, bringing you water, a little food, and herbs to enhance your journey of imagination. I cannot say what you will learn, where you will travel, but it is for us to trust that the ancient ones will speak to you and you will emerge knowing what it is you need to do."

"And what if I don't? I don't think the faire folk have ever spoken to me."

"Have they not? Your pottery is all but alive. If you don't know that, others surely do. You have been marked — to you a hideous scarring that the uninitiated turn away from, but others know the gift of which it is the insignia. You are on the verge of doing what every artist can only dream of — taking what appears to be inert material and breathing life into it, a life that will have generative power."

Ceara opened her mouth to speak — to protest — but found that she could find no words. She fought a strange kind of ecstatic terror that tried to well up in her. Was coming face to face with Destiny always so terrifying? As though reading her mind, Liadan said, "You faced worse than this when you were recovering from your burns. You were only a child and yet you did not succumb to a trauma that could have killed you. Your father, an adult, was less strong than you."

At the mention of her father, Ceara felt her heart constrict, but Liadan's fierce eyes, lit by the firelight, seemed to warn her away from grieving for what could not be changed. So, she wrapped her cloak about her and did her best to invite sleep.

It was midday when they reached the mound. To Ceara's eyes it was nothing more than a large earthen mound ringed with standing stones, but it was clear from Liadan's purposeful approach that this was the site she was seeking. Nearer, she saw a large stone on its side, almost as though a standing stone had fallen. Swirls, some in sets of three, covered the rock. Liadan went to work removing rocks and branches from the mound, but Ceara stared at the rock, rivetted. Perhaps it was the long journey, or the sparseness of their repasts, but she could have sworn the lines were moving, pulsing, reaching out to her.

"Come." Liadan beckoned to a small entrance in the side of the mound, barely big enough for a person to enter. How long had Ceara stood staring at the entrance kerb? For Liadan had also built a small fire just to the side of the opening and now held a torch toward the passage as she motioned to Ceara to follow.

Down the narrow passage Ceara followed the amber light until they came to an alcove. Therein, evenly spaced around the semi-circle, were three smaller alcoves and in each a large smooth rock, like an open palm. Liadan handed Ceara the torch and lit another small fire in the center of the space. As she worked, Ceara studied the markings on the wall which danced and swirled in the torchlight. Again, she felt light-headed and mesmerized. The power here was palpable, leaving her both exhilarated and terrified, but whatever awaited her, she was determined to meet it head on, despite the weakness in her knees.

"There," Liadan said at last. She had made a alter-like arrangement of drinking vessels, a plate, and candles. "This space is the Womb of the Moon, and it will be your safe place for spirit dreaming. Make yourself comfortable on whatever stone you choose. When you're ready, I have prepared a concoction of herbs that will help you on your journey.

"For the next five days, I will come and go, bringing you small meals and drink, keeping a torch lit, but we will not speak and do not rouse yourself from wherever you are traveling. I will be camped at the opening of the passageway and will never leave you. Rest in the knowledge that you are safe here in the womb. Whatever travels you take will be travels of the mind. Your physical body I will protect and keep safe, and the herbs I give you will keep your spirit from being severed from your current existence. In short, you are safe. Learn well from what is shown to you and remember, you are a chosen one."

Liadan touched Ceara's cheek, running her finger across the pattern of scar tissue there. Not since the healer who had cared for Ceara after the accident had anyone except Ceara ever touched her face, and certainly not with the tenderness that Liadan now bestowed. So, this is what it felt like to be cared for. Here in this stone womb Ceara let her heart open. *Chosen* she knew not for what, but being chosen implied a task that, if completed successfully, would be of some use to others. She drank the herbal mixture Liadan had prepared and nestled herself on the eastern stone, the highest and smoothest of the three. She was ready.

"Will you be safe outside?" she asked Liadan, although her limbs were already heavy.

"I will. I am well protected. You are not to worry about me at all. It is almost night. You will sleep well I think and begin your journey tomorrow..."

Ceara thought she would speak more to Liadan before she left, but sleep pulled her into its folds and all was nothingness until the dreaming began.

17

An Otherworld Journey

Day 1

She heard the wind before she felt it, a soft breath against her face, not emanating from the tunnel as one might expect, but from the pores in the rock, swirling around her, teasing, whispering. It carried a multitude of scents, some she recognized, others that were foreign to her, but she clung to their elusive beauty. Forest and sea, flower and vine, hearth fires and cooking pots. No images entered her mind to accompany the scents. It was as though she could live on scent alone, as the wind must. Wind eyes, wind heart. Is this what it is like to blow across the land, carrying each fragrance with you on a separate stream of the air that is you — like invisible strands of hair, flowing, flowing?

Lost to time, Ceara was the wind, meandering, bellowing, drifting, raging. Scent was soon joined by touch — trees, water, people, fields, all that the earth holds and yet again without the sense of sight, only smell and now touch. As she travelled thus, timelessly, incessantly, the essence of each thing she touched entered her, each leaving its tiny dot of being in her memory. But what was most thrilling was the sense of freedom and effortless travel. In a small corner of her consciousness, she remembered Liadan telling her she would be safe, that her spirit would not permanently leave her body. But what if it did? To fly like this forever, would it be so bad?

"Who's there?" A male voice intruded in her flight, bringing her to a standstill so that the wind pushed against her, as it always had. But still she hung suspended, with the wind, but no longer the wind itself.

"Who's there I ask, and I want an answer!" The voice was not angry, stern rather, and carrying an authority that Ceara was loath to disobey. But how could she answer when she had no answer to give? A moment ago, she had been the wind, incorporeal. She would have preferred to stay that way, but the voice would not be ignored, so she struggled to regain at least a shred of her identity. "A potter," she managed.

"Humph. A *potter* indeed. What is it that you seek here?"

"I'm…not sure. I…need to…make something…."

"You wander these realms with no more intention that that? Take care *Potter* that you are not lost."

Ceara wanted to answer, though she had no idea how to defend herself. But at that moment, she felt a cool hand on her brow gently easing her back into gravity.

"Shh…do not speak. Drink this." Liadan held a cup to Ceara's lips. The liquid was sweet and satisfying. Ceara struggled to bring Liadan's face into focus against the amber glow of the chamber, but with little success. Easing her back onto the basin, Liadan gently covered her. Ceara tried to reach out to her, to beg her to stay, but the weight of sleep was too heavily upon her.

Day 2

A lake below and a throbbing in her ears. Her shoulders ached and the lake was speeding toward her. Closer, closer, she was going to....glide into the waters and fold her wings. What was this? Her long neck arched gracefully toward the surface of the water and there she saw her reflected self. Orange beak, black mask, beaded eyes against a snowy white head. A swan! One push of her huge webbed feet sent her gliding across the lake with exquisite grace. She was so beautiful! Pride swelled in her feathered breast. She arched her neck as though she was royalty and swam on, and on. The day was misty, soft. Ceara's whiteness shone with an unearthly glow against the grey skies. As Ceara swam, the mist swirled around her in coils reminiscent of the swirling patterns on the stones where she dreamed.

Although there was no one on the shore to see her graceful beauty, Ceara could see it as though she were two — the swan and her sleeping self. Such beauty with no human eyes to verify it. What was the point then? So much beauty like this on earth, in the heavens, that goes unseen by human eyes, except for rare glimpses. Did it matter that it was unseen? Is there some extra-human reason for the heartbreaking beauty of the unspoiled world? As the swan, Ceara thought she would know, but there was only silence and a vague urge to find something to eat.

"What did you expect then?" That voice again, accusing this time. Ceara opened her mouth...her beak...to form an answer, but was mute.

"Did you think then that all this is put here for the sake of humans? How humans came to such folly I'll never know, and never is a long time for me. Beauty *is*, because *isness* is beautiful. Rather simple and lacking in philosophical depth, don't you think? Oh, to be fair, there's a bit more to it, but that's for you to find out. Isn't that why you're here, after all?" The voice faded, leaving behind a hint in Ceara's mind of a cloaked figure, hooded, carrying an oaken staff.

Ceara woke to dancing shadows and a fierce hunger. No hand on her forehead, no soothing voice. Liadan was not there. Feebly, she edged out of her nest to put another stick on the fire. As the light flared, she saw the cup and bread that Liadan had left. Ceara fell to, almost forgetting to use her hands, the vestiges of her swan self still in her memory. The bread and liquid were surprisingly filling, but she almost didn't make it back to her nest before falling back into the dream world.

Day 3

Panic gripped her. She couldn't move. Her legs felt like they went on forever, holding her solidly in place. Her arms ached, arched as they were into the air, reaching as though there was something they would grasp, swaying a bit in the wind, but otherwise fixed.

"No use in struggling, Potter." That voice again, familiar now. "And anyway, this time movement isn't the point. You are beautiful though. Would you like to see?" As before, now Ceara seemed to split into two, a disembodied consciousness looking down upon a large oak.

"A little better, then?" The voice came from a heavy, tattered cloak, from which emerged a withered hand that held a gnarled staff. With a start, Ceara realized that she felt a kinship with the staff — more than kinship. It was as though it was part of her, and yet there it was, in that hand.

"Oh yes, my staff came from you, or rather the oak you are a part of, for now. You must be quite special, Potter, or at least your task is, to be allowed to meld with *this* oak. One might live inside it, but that's not the same as *being* it, is it? But I'm distracting you. Not sure how long you'll have here, so I'd best not use up your time with idle chatter. Know this. There is a link between you and I. I see that now." And with that he was gone and Ceara could no longer see anything. No movement, no sight. This was special? It was the most horrible experience Ceara could imagine.

"Relax. Soften into it." The voice, echoing through the forest, touched her like a kiss of wind. Ah, the wind, making her branches sway like hair beneath the waves. She remembered her time as the wind — the wind that now embraced her in return. Slowly, tentatively, she did as the voice had bidden. Deep breaths, releasing the fear. Now the branches that had been aching gloried in their reaching and swaying, an ecstasy of dance. Never mind that she had no feet with which to move, there was a world of life in her that never tired as it was showered with thrilling and continuous sensation.

And the breathing. Had she ever really breathed before this? Her whole self was involved in the act of drawing in all that was around her. She was awed by the seamless connectedness she felt with everything — wind, rock, plant, animal, stream…human…somewhere…it all belonged to her as a child in the womb belongs to its mother. And when she exhaled, all that beingness leaned in, absorbing the exhalation with joy and gratitude. Give and take, in and out, the joy of it was excruciating.

Then she wiggled what might have been toes, but was roots, reaching, drinking, curling, alive in the living earth. Rooted, rooted, rooted. What had initially been terrifying was now perfect being. Reaching into the air and into the earth, and between it all, her entire being in perfect communion with everything. Stillness was what made it all possible. To move would be to pull the roots out of the earth, to let go of the sky, to breathe in the service of exertion rather than all life. Her human consciousness remembered what it was like to be perfectly still — to better hear music, or prolong the sight of a family of deer in the woods. The still point where the clay is centered on the wheel, ready to take form, where the essence of the individuated self dissolves into the universe of being. Perfect, infinite stillness…

"Ceara, wake up." She heard the voice as though from a great distance, well beyond the woods. She did her best to ignore it, but it persisted, growing louder and more insistent. It wasn't the harsh voice of the man in the cloak, but the sweet voice of…

"Liadan…" Ceara managed, pulling away from the stillness with heart-rending regret. But her friend had her own pull on Ceara.

Sternly, "Ceara, come back now."

"I don't want to…"

"But you must. You may travel, but you must keep a foot in this world, lest you are lost and your destiny remain unfulfilled."

This time Liadan stayed with Ceara while she ate and refreshed herself, washing in a basin of sweet water tinged with the scent of rosemary. She hadn't realized how much tension she was holding until her body loosened. Having Liadan there was a blessing, a respite from the intensity of her dreaming. Eager to share her insights with someone she opened her mouth to speak, but Liadan laid a finger upon her lips.

"Not yet," she said, though Ceara could see the concern and curiosity in Liadan's eyes. "Let this be a time of rest, but you mustn't break the spell of the dreamtime." With that Liadan began to sing a soothing song in a minor key. Ceara leaned back into her nest, but didn't sleep yet. She lay there, listening, watching the spiral motifs on the wall dance in the firelight as she felt her mind clear. No need to cling to the dreams or puzzle out their meanings. They were a part of her now and their meaning would blossom in her as needed. This, it seemed, was what Liadan's song told her.

Day 4

Surrounded by a riot of flowers and greenery, Ceara climbed a gradual incline. The day was clear and sunlight sparkled through the branches of the trees. In the near distance, she could hear the fall of water, musical, as though tiny sprites were chattering to one another, perhaps calling her to join them. But something urged her on, up the hill until she could climb no more without a rest.

Just off the path she spied the perfect stone on which to sit a spell. So much foliage! Flowers and herbs filled the air with their perfume, reminding her of her time as the wind, only now she was nearer and their scent was heavier and full of color.

As she searched the ground, naming the various plants, she saw it. A small concavity amid the foliage on the forest floor. A well. A sacred well. And with that realization, there was movement among the trees and, as though a sapling had gotten legs, there stood a woman dressed in green, as much a part of the forest as a woman could be and still be human. Moving closer to Ceara, she opened her hands in a gesture of grace.

"Welcome my child. You have travelled far and in many forms. How unusual! And here you are at my well. What is it you seek?"

Ceara was surprised to find her own voice for the first time since she began her journey. "I've been charged with making a sacred vessel, but I know nothing more than that." Ceara searched her mind. What indeed was it that she wished to know?

"What makes a thing *sacred?*"

The Guardian smiled. "I think you already know, you who have been wind, bird and tree, but you are here and I am not disposed to deny you whatever the Well has to offer. Drink then." The Guardian then bowed slightly and gestured toward the Well. Tears she couldn't explain were pouring from Ceara's eyes as she knelt at the Well's edge and dipped her hands into the water. It tasted like the smell of the forest floor, but sweet, too, and more refreshing than anything she had ever known. She thirsted for more, but politeness stayed her hand.

As though reading her mind, the Guardian said, "Drink all you need. The Well is inexhaustible so long as I am here to protect it. Drink until your heart is full."

And so Ceara did and when she awoke, her hands were still wet, tears still trickled down the sides of her face, and beads of water still sat on her lips, a kiss she would never wipe away if only that were possible.

Day 5

The forest was deep and tangled, but not menacing. There was an air to everything that suggested life out of time, primordial, alive on two planes at once, the concrete and the imaginative. In her dream state, these things did not trouble Ceara's mind; she did not struggle to make sense of it, but accepted it as it was. She walked on, drawn to what she knew not, but inexorably drawn, nonetheless.

When she came upon the woman in the clearing, leaning over a huge pot, she had no fear. The beauty of the pot caught her artist's eye. Its shape was so perfect, it excited her spirit; the designs so alive in their rendering they seemed to undulate and dance around the rim.

"You like my pot then?" The woman asked, clearly taking pride in her possession.

"It's perfect!" Ceara exclaimed, or thought, her admiration opening her heart.

Eyeing Ceara carefully, the woman seemed to come to a conclusion.

"I believe you are here for a sacred purpose and so I will trust my identity to you. I am Cerridwen, Welsh Goddess of Transformation, Rebirth and Inspiration."

Ceara's eyes grew wide.

"Oh yes, I see that these are things you seek," Cerridwen continued, "and not for selfish reasons. Truth be told, in your precious being, you hold enough inspiration for ten humans, but now you have been given a task for which you will need to call on...more."

Ceara tried to speak, but had no words. Her hands, however, began to tingle and grow warm. She imagined the clay spinning beneath them, her fingers pulling it up, higher and higher, shaping it, beautifully, perfectly.

"Come closer," Cerridwen beckoned. "Look into the pot."

Unafraid, Ceara obeyed the Goddess, looking into the swirling blue-green mists of the cauldron, while Cerridwen's words sounded inside her head.

"'Tis true, 'tis a cauldron you will be called upon to fashion. When the time comes, you will have all that you need -- the strength, the vision, the will.

"Know this, child of clay, the cauldron is the perfect symbol of the marriage of the concrete and the ephemeral. The earthly vessel holds that which nourishes not only the body, but the spirit as well. The cauldron is the locus of sacred alchemy, in which discrete elements are combined to create wondrously new things." Cerridwen paused to let her words take root. When she was confident that they had, she added, "You may think the potter nothing more than a craftsperson, making the utilitarian tools of domestic life, but know this deep in your soul and carry it forward. The crafting of vessels brings together all the elements -- earth, air, water and fire...and from you, the potter, spirit. And in the design and the form which you fashion, rests the power, as you have felt here, to awaken that which only beauty can."

There was more -- Ceara wanted more -- but the Goddess and her cauldron were fading, swirling back into the elements from which they were formed.

Ceara awoke famished, not just for food, but for the tools of her craft. Never before had she felt such a burning need to *make*, to bring together all that she experienced over the past few days: the aching beauty of avian nature, the interdependence of the woods, the transformative power of water, the freedom of wind to go beyond the silly limitations so dear to humans. Of fire, she had no need of instruction -- that she literally carried in her skin.

She tucked into the food Liadan had left, sucking the honey out of the pores of the bread before devouring it. As she lifted the cup to drink the pure water it held, she laughed aloud. A simple clay cup, onto which someone had carved a swirling pattern that delighted the touch. Simple and not simple at all. The very act of drinking became a ritual act of renewal and grace. After a long draught, she set the cup down reverently and whispered a prayer of gratitude, for potters, water, visions, and the hands that could make them a reality. She *had* to get to work. With renewed energy, she gathered together the things Liadan had brought into the mound, piling them into the basket Liadan had left, then smothered the fire and, feeling her way along the passageway, emerged from the stone womb, ready to make the most beautiful pot she could manage.

As Ceara stepped into daylight, Liadan saw her and emerged from the rude shelter she had constructed for herself. The moment she looked into Ceara's eyes, she knew that her journey was complete and that the task that lay ahead was likely to meet with success. Letting out a cry of joy, she went to Ceara and embraced her. As she did so, she felt the energy that coursed through the other woman's being and realized the need to make haste. Ceara was on fire with inspiration and was in dire need of the means by which to express it.

The pot, when finished, was indisputably the most beautiful anyone had ever seen. The process had been a gentle one. Liadan assured Ceara that there was no hurry, that the destiny of the vessel would not be realized for years to come, but that it's making had to happen in Ceara's hands, that there was a connection between the two, the nature of which it was unsafe to divulge at this time, lest it be more difficult to keep the vessel safe through the ages.

Perhaps the ability to live with such mystery was part of what Ceara had learned on her spirit journey, for she was sufficiently content with her work and the company of Liadan's people to let the questions go unanswered. By day, she would joyfully toil at her work, first forming the pot, piece by piece, shaping, smoothing, then with each new section, securing it by running the whole beneath her hands, making the unification complete, blessed.

When at last it was fully formed, then came the decorating -- carving, incising, laying in colored clay made from a watery clay slip mixed with minerals. At the end of each day she would carefully mist the vessel then cover it to keep it moist and ready for the next day's inspiration.

While Ceara did her work, the young men of the community were busy building the kiln that would fire the finished piece. Ceara might have wondered where they had gained the expertise for their work, but in truth she trusted to them, and to the sacredness of their task. They would know how to build so that the pot would be fired at just the right temperature -- the balance of fire and air in their hands. The thought that the pot might break in the firing was not entertained -- no one could bear the thought.

In the evenings, Ceara would feast with the community who never once asked more from her then the work she was doing on the vessel. In truth, they delighted in waiting on her and sharing her company as poetry, music and dancing filled the torch-lit nights.

Often, it was Liadan who sat by her side, but others were attracted to this gifted person, and vied for her attention. One young man, indeed the one who seemed to take the lead on the construction of the kiln, took an interest in the potter he saw himself in service to -- to the point of not just seeking to share the evening's festivities with her, but to leaving gifts at her workplace as well. Shells, flowers, branches twisted into compelling designs.

Without making a fuss, Ceara made them a part of her day, decorating the studio with them. But in her heart, she was feeling something else coming alive. In the atmosphere of Liadan's joyful community and the contentment of her own work, Ceara's disfigurement faded from her concerns so that the possibility of love had room to enter.

When the pot was finished at last, the whole community gathered for its unveiling. Liadan declared it "a true Cauldron" as a cheer rose up from the crowd. The clay shown warm in the sunlight, as the yellows, blues and greens in the design sung out their magnificence, and the swirls, vines, and knots shifted and danced around the circumference, just as Ceara had seen in her vision. Pride wrestled with wonder in Ceara's heart. Had she really done this?

But now came the time of letting go. That night, as the cauldron was placed in the center of the common area, surrounded by torches whose light played across the surface in a wonderous show of dancing color and design, Liadan explained to Ceara that soon they would have to take the cauldron to a place of safety. The camp would be struck and there would be no sign of what had been done there. Ceara and the rest of the community would have a week to celebrate, but then the leave-taking must be accomplished.

Deep in her heart, Ceara had been harboring a wish to stay on with Liadan's people, especially the young man with whom she had developed a mutually loving relationship, and yet, she wasn't surprised when she learned that all this had been temporary -- almost as though it had been a prolonged, idyllic dream.

"Your village needs you," Liadan explained, "as does the future. What you have learned has application beyond what you have created here."

And so, the day came when Ceara's masterpiece was wrapped and hidden among the common goods of the community as they began their travels in one direction while Liadan and Ceara travelled in the other. No words can describe the pain of the sundering of the lovers, but that it must be so was written in the destiny of which they were all players. Still, in her heart, Ceara would carry the joy of their union forever, and in her womb, she carried the seed of the continuation of her line.

18

Glastonbury

Glastonbury
Somerset, England
The Present

Charming wasn't quite the right word for Raina's first impression of Sirona's apartment. There was a warmth and comfort to it that wasn't easily accounted for by its decor, which, Raina realized, she couldn't quite find the right words for. None of the standard categories applied. *Eclectic* was the only word to describe it, but that didn't describe the feelings Sirona's choices of decor and decoration inspired in Raina. As she scanned the room, it occurred to her that the unifying theme was not a theme at all, but rather what pleased the inhabitant, and in this case, that seemed to be the beautiful, the different, the unusual. That Raina had been invited into this gave her comfort -- assurance that her strangeness was welcomed here. *A place where even I can fit in,* she thought.

Still, she felt a wrenching ache for all she had left behind -- her mother's house, the strange attic room, the promise of summer on the lake and...Art. All of those things were just beginning to open up in her, just beginning to fill the void it had been her lot to carry for so long. To leave them now...but Malcolm had found her and seemed intent on re-entering her life with full-on malevolence. Sirona was right to fear him and to draw Raina away from him. Yet, even Malcolm's reappearance had a hint of promise for Raina, for where Malcolm was, April surely was as well, or at least nearby. She had buried the yearning for her daughter so deep it had almost scarred over, but Malcolm's presence brought it to the surface again so that the notion of seeing her daughter permeated the very air she breathed. In the States, that was a possibility, but here?

"It's small, but it's all yours," Sirona said, showing Raina to her room, whose lace-curtained windows looked out on an infinite green landscape on one side, and the edge of town on the other. Sirona's apartment sat on a verge, one foot in the electrifying energy of Glastonbury and the other heading into the verdant countryside. Over the coming months, Raina would see this place as a metaphor not just for Sirona herself, but for the entire zeitgeist of a cultural shift.

"I expect you'll want to rest," Sirona continued. "Make yourself comfortable. I'm going to nip out and collect something for dinner."

So typical of Sirona, Raina thought. It was as though Sirona could read her mind. During the trip, she had been wonderfully sensitive to Raina's distress. Raina could tell Sirona had a million things to share with her, but somehow understood that Raina's emotions were raw -- too raw to touch -- and so she let her be. Instead, she was like the mother ship pulling Raina's rudderless skiff along, safely and deftly through strange waters. And how confidently Sirona navigated them herself. Raina was struck with the deference that absolutely everyone showed Sirona. Neither fear nor attraction but something that combined the two. As Raina closed her eyes and began drifting off, she wondered that those reactions to Sirona were not hers. True, Sirona was one of a kind, but for Raina, Sirona was just...

Unnamable but delicious smells pulled back the lid on Raina's bottomless slumber, letting in the afternoon light and the trappings of entirely new surroundings. As Raina waited for the rest of her body to wake up, she wondered if this might be what Alice felt like when she fell through the looking glass. Things were the same enough for one to function, but pervaded by a sense of one not being quite fully present.

"Ah, there you are, and just in time," Sirona said as she motioned Raina to the beautifully set table -- wine decanted, two perfect settings of stoneware plates offset with water goblets sparkling as though lit from within. The center of the table was adorned with a small collection of delicate flowers and greens arranged in the pot Raina had given Sirona.

"My pot." Raina said, amazed that Sirona would have chosen to bring it.

"Lovely, isn't it?" Sirona said, smiling.

"You brought it here..."

"Of course. It belongs here," Sirona said with a small wave of inclusion.

"Am *I* really here?" Raina said, as much to herself as to Sirona, feeling that she was caught behind a veil of some sort. Was this just jet lag or something else?

Laughing, Sirona replied, "You are here and this is all very real, as much as anything is defined as "real" in Glastonbury. You might as well get used to a sense of being between worlds here. It is indeed disorienting at first, but if you let go of the fierce and limited view of reality, there is much to learn and experience in this place. But...first things first. Let's get some food in us."

The two tucked into the food with pleasure and raised their glasses more than once in toasts to friendship, new adventures, and Art, poor Art. Raina missed his anchoring presence, terribly, palpably. Then again, knowing he was watching over things in the States was an essential tether. However strange this place was, she was not adrift here. All that she had left behind was in good hands, awaiting her return, or so she fervently hoped.

"So, tell me about this place," Raina invited as Sirona refilled their glasses.

"Ah," Sirona was beaming. Obviously, she had been anxious to share this with Raina. "Glastonbury is hard to describe. It's a place to be experienced, but I can at the least prepare you for its uniqueness.

"Long, long ago, this area was a marshy, inland sea, at the center of which was a hill -- an island -- once known as Ynis Witrin, the Isle of Glass, or Avalon. As you will learn, the "Isle of Avalon" figures prominently in the Arthurian tales as a place of wonder and connection to the Otherworld. For centuries, this place has been set apart as a place of mystery and the sacred. Even the Romans were awed by it, despite their hatred of Druids and all things Celtic.

"Today, Glastonbury is a mecca for all manner of beliefs and expression of mystical notions and beings. When we go out, you are apt to see people dressed as fairies or zombies, or...whatever." Sirona laughed heartily. "There are more festivals here than you can count, celebrating all manner of things. There are those who dismiss all this as hippie foolishness but," and here Sirona grew serious, "there is much to be learned here and much that is as real as it is mysterious, hiding in plain sight. This I tell you in confidence, but then, you are living with a manifestation of it -- and you may be, or become, one yourself, so, with time, you will come to see and feel the power and importance of this place." And now Sirona was smiling again, and looking at Raina as if to say, *are you ready for this?*

"And our goal here is...?" Raina asked, swirling the inch of wine left in her glass, feeling the rising of a strange excitement tinged with apprehension.

"Well, to get you sorted, of course! Raina my dear," Sirona said, learning forward in earnestness, "you are the key to something momentous. We have come to the one place in the world where there will be clues. We may not find everything we need to know here, but there is no better place to start. We will study, talk to some people I know -- and I trust be directed to some I do not, yet. And... I have one really special surprise for you."

"Oh?"

"I'm keeping that under my hat for now. But I won't make you wait long. For now, come see this." Sirona rose and led Raina to an alcove off the kitchen, lined from floor to ceiling with books, and holding both a desk and a comfortable reading chair. On the desk were a few carefully placed volumes.

"You are welcome to look at anything that's here. I've chosen a few books to get you started, but follow your instincts. Whatever speaks to you. Oh, and there's a blank book in the top drawer of the desk you can use to take notes."

Stepping back so that Raina could freely wander the room, Sirona saw that she was thrilled. When Raina pulled the journal from the drawer, she noted the beautiful design on the cover -- two intersecting circles with an arrow rising through the center. Raina traced it with her finger and felt a thrill.

"I assume there's a significance to this design?" she asked, never taking her eyes off it.

"Oh yes, indeed."

"Let me guess, you're not going to tell me right away."

Sirona's silvery laughter was all Raina was going to get as an answer.

"And now," Sirona said with a slight bow, "I'm going to leave you to it. I've been gone for longer than usual -- I have some people to connect with now that I've returned. You will meet them all soon enough, but for now I'll spare you our silly reunion rituals. You're comfortable alone here?"

"Of course," There was no doubt in Raina's mind that she would prefer this quiet study to meeting a bunch of new people, though she hated to have Sirona leave. Her presence was so calming.

After some reading, and musing over the blank pages of the journal, Raina found that she could not keep her eyes open. Intending to wait for Sirona's return, nevertheless, she found herself stumbling gratefully into her bed, eager for oblivion. But that's not what awaited her. That night Raina was visited by a dark dream, like those that had driven her to desperation so many years ago. The darkness was a weight, pulling her into it, like a black hole sucking her soul into fragments. A swimmer in roiling midnight waters, she struggled to attain the surface, pumping furiously without even a glimmer of light to indicate in which direction release awaited.

When she finally awoke, sweating and panting, she wondered, had she called out? Holding her breath, she listened for the faintest sound. If Sirona had heard her, she wouldn't ignore it. But the apartment was silent except for Raina's beating heart. Raina fell back onto the pillow, distressed and confused that the dreams had returned after all these years, and here of all places. She lay awake, staring at the ceiling, waiting for daylight.

When at last the room lightened and Raina heard Sirona moving about in the kitchen, she escaped her bed to the relative normalcy of brewing coffee. Such a relief it would be to tell Sirona of the dream, and yet, what kind of cloud would that put on the hope that had been shining in Sirona's eyes ever since they had stepped foot in England? Perhaps the dream was no more than an effect of jet lag, or so she told herself.

If Sirona noticed Raina's edginess, she didn't let on, but laid out the plans for the day. A restful morning, reading, chatting, then, when the day warmed, they'd visit the shops on High Street. Perhaps, Sirona suggested, Raina would like to buy something flowy for the Imbolc celebrations that were just a few days off. Indeed, the haste with which Sirona had prepared for her and Raina to leave the States was not just to escape the evil designs of Malcolm, but also to arrive in Glastonbury before the February 2nd celebration of Spring and the Mother Goddess in all her forms.

Respectful of her friend's enthusiasm, Raina did her best to hide her discomfort, and, if truth be told, Sirona's excitement was infectious. By the time they had entered their third shop of crystals, incense, and plenty of flowy clothes and fairy wings, the dark dream had faded into the rainbows and glitter of Glastonbury. Overcome by all the choices, Raina finally settled on a hooded cloak in swirls of blue and green, accented by subtle slashes of yellow, edged with a dark green braid of Celtic knots gliding up and around the garment like a living thing. The inside of the hood was lined in azure velvet and when Raina pulled it over her head, for all the beauty and brilliance of the cloak, she felt hidden, invisible. If she'd had her way, she would have worn it for the rest of the day, delighting in the spell it seemed to wrap around her, but Sirona gently insisted that they save it for Imbolc. After that, she assured Raina, she could wear it day and night if she wished.

The rest of the day was spent in friendly delight, Raina clutching her "fairy cape" in one arm as Sirona took the other and led her, part tour guide, part participant, through the magic of the shops, until, exhausted and perishing, they stopped at a pub and ended the day with meat pies and ale.

That night, as the friends retired, Raina crawled into the cool sheets, grateful for the rest, giving little thought to what might await her in sleep. All the more terrifying then, when she found herself standing on the top of a hill surrounded by a raging storm that she herself seemed to be causing, directing. She watched in horror as her dream-self drew fireballs from the sky and tossed them onto a village below with just a flick of her wrist. Then she raised both hands and drew waters from the earth, raging waters that lifted the flaming buildings and tossed them about, still alight, while people both burned and drown, screaming...or was that her? She awoke to find Sirona on the edge of her bed and a dim light shining in from the hall.

There was no thought of returning to sleep. Sirona drew Raina into the kitchen, made a floral smelling tea, and sat her down, insisting that Raina tell her every detail of the dream.

"Oh, don't make me!" Raina pleaded. "You don't understand."

"I believe I can, if you let me."

"But this is what drove me mad, stole years of my life and cost me my precious daughter!"

"And clearly could do so again if you run from it. Listen to me. Our dreams are our unconscious selves and our connection to cosmic energy attempting to speak to us. Push them down and they will haunt us, follow us like serial killers down the dark alleyways of our lives. You know this. You've lived this and it has cost you. But you survived it because of your goodness and your strong will." Raina sniffed at this, but Sirona was not to be deterred.

"And now they have returned. You must see this as a gift..." Sirona continued.

"Why now and why here," Raina interrupted, "in this magical place?"

"Because of the power here, where the truth cannot be hidden or hidden from. In the shadow of your dreams is the truth of your power, waiting to be revealed. And know this, you are not alone with this anymore. I am here with you and I will bring all my healing knowledge and the energy of this place to bear on discovering what has crouched in you all these years."

When Sirona grabbed Raina's hands, she could feel the energy in them and see the intensity in her eyes -- those dark eyes that held such mysteries. As in a waking dream, she remembered the vision she had had in the Mother Room of Sirona amid standing stones next to a cloaked figure that had withered like a leaf falling from a winter tree. Remembering it now, she was filled with dread, as though it had been her in that cloak who had drifted away like smoke.

"What have I got to lose?" Raina whispered, surrendering at last.

"Tell me your dream, dear one -- every detail before the sun comes up and whisks them away."

As Raina narrated her dream as best as she could remember it, she noticed that sitting here with Sirona, in her charming little kitchen, gave her a bit of distance from the horrors of the dream -- almost as though she was recounting a movie, something outside of herself. From time to time, Sirona would gently ask clarifying questions so that as the dreamscape was fleshed out, Raina could make more sense of it, rather than just feeling the terror.

When at last she had finished, Sirona asked, "If you can remember, what about this dream is similar to the dreams of your past. Is there a unifying theme?"

"Yes -- and this is easy. It's that I have a horrible power over people. It's like I can hurt people with a flick of my wrist, or make them do things that they do not want to do."

"Well, we can all do that -- and we do it both intentionally and not so."

"But I hate the thought of that. I never want to intrude on people's...."

".... sovereignty?"

"Exactly."

"That's an honorable attitude. Most people are all too ready, even pleased, to step on the self-determination of others."

Raina shuddered.

"It makes my skin crawl to think of it. Keeping people from becoming their full, authentic selves seems like a great sin, not just against individuals, but against society as a whole. How much joy, insight, and innovation has been lost that way?"

"You should know as well as anyone. Your light has been all but extinguished, and yet, obviously, you have much to share."

"But that's just it! I don't! I have nothing but pain to offer! My dreams..."

"...are just that, the shadow side of a great power. What if you saw them not as inevitabilities or definitions of you but as warnings...reminders of exactly what you just expressed to me...the horror of stealing people's sovereignty. And yet, couldn't such power be used for good? Aren't there times when we can actually increase people's light by being a mirror for them -- calling out what they cannot see for themselves?"

Thoughtfully, Raina had to admit that that might be true, but still, "It's tricky, though," she said. "How do you know what is helpful and what is not?"

"I think you know the answer to that," Sirona answered. "Wisdom, an open heart, connecting with the Sacred. But it seems to me that there's a bigger question here. To what extent do you actually have such power? Have you ever actually *done* anything even remotely like what you see in your dreams?"

"NO! But the dreams are so real, so intense, it feels like I have. I used to awake surprised that I wasn't covered in remnants of my evil deeds."

"And this last one?"

"Not so intense...no."

"Good. We have much work to do. I have told you that I have a surprise for you, and it is something I believe will help us with this, but we can't get to it until after Imbolc when the town's activity dies down a bit. In the meantime, I can concoct a draft that will enhance your sense of distance from your dreams, so that we can work with them, but you will not be so consumed by them. Are you ok with that?"

"I am, but I can't help but be afraid, nonetheless. These dreams make my heart ache, and terrify me not just because of the images in them, but because of the fear that stays with me like an aftertaste. I don't think I've ever felt free of being perpetually vigilant, lest I bring that terror into this world."

"That must be terrible, that constant tension. I am at your side, dear one. Perhaps I can help you carry that load until we can find ways to take it from you completely."

Raina sighed, "Do you really believe that is possible, that I can be free of this?"

"It is my sole goal in life at this point," Sirona said, and as she said the words, her face grew fierce, her eyes darkened, and her arms raised, like a bird ruffling its feathers. "Perhaps it has always been my purpose."

19

Imbolc

Despite Raina's resistance to Sirona's idea of plaiting greenery into her hair, she had to admit the effect was arresting. The violet blossoms and spring greens made her gray hair look silvery, like falling water, and brought a lightness of spirit to her that was pure delight. If she'd worried about having the dexterity to do the same for Sirona in turn, she needn't have. Sirona pulled her raven tresses up high in the back and let them fall like feathers between her shoulders.

"Twice a year I get to dress like myself -- Samhain and Imbolc," Sirona explained as she raised her arms and let the long black gauze of her dress spread like wings.

"Like yourself?" Raina asked, a bit alarmed.

"Oh yes," she said, dancing around the apartment and laughing heartily, "I'm part raven, don't you know? Beware! Hide your glittery things out of sight lest I purloin them and add them to my stash."

Sirona's merriment was so infectious Raina could not resist and so the fairy and the raven danced about the room like young girls, ready and eager for the party that awaited them.

Once there, however, Raina's joy tempered into an anxious awe. Not a single person in the room looked anything like a twenty-first century human. Fairies and wizards, gnomes, birds, foxes, high priestesses, green men. It was as if they had stepped into a magical realm and, as she leaned toward Sirona's ear, that's exactly what Raina said.

"Brilliant! Then we have succeeded!" Sirona exclaimed, leaning into Raina in turn, but at the same time eyeing the room for familiar faces.

"Fall into it and enjoy it, my dear." She advised. "Tonight, we celebrate the re-emergence of life after its winter slumber. What can be more joyous? And you! You look like spring itself! Reign here tonight as you were meant to, dear one."

"While you fly around like a dark shadow?" Raina teased.

"Always vigilant, dear, always." Sirona spoke it as though in jest but Raina knew there was a profound seriousness in Sirona's words. How was it that she was blessed with such a supportive friend, Raina wondered, not for the first time. She only hoped that the day would come when she could return to Sirona even half of what she had been given.

"Oh, and stay away from the pink punch," Sirona warned with a wink, "you're not quite ready for that one yet. And the baked goods should be consumed in moderation, but all else is as normal as we are not."

With that, Sirona whisked Raina into the middle of the crowd and the merriment began. Introductions were made, but Raina suspected she would never remember any of the names, or match them to all the decorated faces that came and went throughout the night. Sirona seemed to know nearly everyone in the place, and their behavior towards here was one of friendly admiration. Clearly, Sirona was a person of significance here in Glastonbury though her behavior never revealed that -- only the reaction of others toward her gave it away.

Laughter filled the room and from time to time some magical being would raise their voice above the general din and recite poetry -- always in rhyming couplets -- about the joys, the beauty, the mystery and the power of the natural world. Where had she heard that style before?

"So like your Yule Poems," Sirona said at her ear. *Yes, that was exactly it,* Raina realized. There was a lilt to the style that was pleasantly dreamy, like a chant. She found herself eager to hear more and vaguely wished she could regale the crowd with her own inspirations.

"Can you do that?" Raina asked her friend.

"Me? I can only caw. *Caw, Caw,"* Sirona said, raising her arms and twirling Stevie Nicks style. Raina was beginning to wonder just how much of the forbidden punch her friend had imbibed, when across the room she saw something that brought her up short.

On the edge of the frivolity, standing alone and deadly serious, was a man dressed all in white, with long white hair pulled back in a tight ponytail. Of all the people there, he was the least fabulously outfitted, and yet, somehow, he seemed the most inhuman of all -- and, he was staring straight at her. It was not a malevolent gaze, exactly, but he held her eyes with an intensity that both attracted and repelled Raina. Not sure whether she was unable or unwilling to break the gaze, she stood frozen in time, as the party swirled around her. Was it only a moment, or long into the night that she stood thus, as though she were two people -- one, shy and wishing to be released, the other wanting desperately to be seen -- to be known.

Hardly did she notice the gathered assemblage thinning around her until Sirona touched her arm.

"We're all headed to the Great Hall for the concert," Sirona said, taking Raina's arm. "Hey, are you ok?" she asked, sensing her friend's awkward stillness.

Raina turned to Sirona as though coming out of a dream.

"Do you know that man?" she asked.

"What man?"

"That one," Raina said, turning back to where he had stood, only to find no one there.

Hang drums and koshi chimes, hammered dulcimer and fiddle -- mystical sounds and earthly rhythms put Raina in a trance.

While others danced and swayed around the room, Raina sat in the corner, the hood of her fairy cape pulled up and over her brow, rendering her safely unremarkable as she let the music carry her away. She flew, she swam, she rode on the back of a silver stead...no, she *was* the hawk, the dolphin, the horse. Her senses touched everything, nothing was alien to her and she was at home everywhere. In contrast to the darkness of her dreams, here, everything was shimmering light, suffused with a power to bring joy and growth to everything.

When at last the music stopped and she could feel Sirona at her side, she could have wept to be called back into the every day, and yet, she realized, she was exhausted from the ecstasy of her visionary experience.

The two walked home in companionable silence, each marinating in their individual experience of the night. Revelers passed them by, sparkling in the moonlight like fireflies having one last go at brilliance before the night was over.

Once home, they instinctively went to the kitchen where Sirona prepared the "night tea" as they had come to call the concoction that eased Raina's slumbers.

"Did you enjoy the celebration?" Sirona asked, although she was pretty sure of the answer.

"I did, very much! I've never experienced such a thing!" Then, rather shyly, Raina asked, "Was that someone special I saw you dancing with at the concert?"

Sirona hesitated just a beat before answering.

"We are soul friends. We don't choose to live together, but there is a deep connection."

"I'm sorry, I don't mean to pry..." which Raina clearly felt she had done.

"Not at all," Sirona said, bringing the tea to the table. "You are now an important part of my life. Before this is over, I expect you will know more about me than you wish to. But now, tell me about the man you asked about. I didn't seem him, but if you describe him, I may know who he is. It would surprise me if there was someone at that gathering that I didn't know."

Raina was about to answer when suddenly words came into her mind that spilled out like an exhale.

Beware the man all dressed in white
So like an owl that prowls the night

In you he sees not what you guess
A hidden soul from you he'll wrest

Beware his gaze, his eyes of gold,
In thrall to him yours they hold

Until he knows for sure and true
the wonderous thing he sees in you.

Sirona stared at Raina, while Raina covered her mouth in shock and tears filmed her eyes.

"What the hell was that?" Raina finally whispered.

"I'd say it was a poem similar to the ones you heard tonight. You did say at the party that you wished you could do that..."

"But to just have it come out of me like that..."

"It is a tad surprising," Sirona admitted, "but it is Imbolc, a magical night, and you heard and enjoyed poems like it at the party, many of which were, I suspect composed on the spot. The style is an ancient one and has persisted for good reason. It comes naturally and easily to us -- well, some of us anyway. And then there are the Yule Poems. You are inclined to believe they were written by your mother, are you not? Not so surprising then that you may have inherited the gift."

Raina stared into her tea, doing her best to process the night, and the creeping feeling that this was just the beginning, that Alice's world behind the looking glass would pale in comparison to what awaited her in Glastonbury.

Sirona gave her some space, sipped her tea and waited as patiently as she could before bringing up what really concerned her, and that was not the arrival of the poem, but the content.

Raina, however, beat her to it. Heaving a huge sigh, she explained, "So, I guess that's a description of the man at the party. As the poem says, he was dressed all in white and his hair was long and pulled back. He didn't take his eyes off me, which was bad enough, but he was uncannily handsome. I wanted so badly to look away, but I couldn't. I don't know if it was just animal attraction or some kind of spell he was casting, but he held me prisoner while he...I don't know how to say it...it was like he was trying to see into my soul."

"Just like the poem says," Sirona observed. "Does it feel like his intent was malicious?"

"I'm not sure...alien, I guess you'd say. I didn't know what to expect, or how to act. It was like I was frozen to the spot. So...do you know him?"

"I do not. But I will ask around and keep my eyes open. Will this trouble you or disturb your sleep?"

Raina had to laugh and some of the tension drained off her.

"I guess extemporaneously spouting poetry isn't the worst thing that could happen to a person, nor should I worry about our mystery man -- for now anyway."

It was the last line of the poem that had Sirona's attention, but she wouldn't bother Raina with that tonight. It had been the best Imbolc since she could remember, in no small part because she was sharing it with Raina and clearly seeing something blossom in her. This unassuming woman was fitting into Glastonbury much better than either of them had imagined. The sight of her sitting wrapped in her beautiful fairy cape, lost in the music, tickled Sirona.

But more than that, it suggested that she and Art were right about their new friend, and that her connection, her purpose, was on the way to being discovered. Sirona rose from the table and cleared the tea cups, then gave Raina a light kiss on the cheek.

"Sleep well, dear one. May the sweet magic of the night follow you into the dreamworld."

The next few days passed in cooking, reading, and just being lazy, as Sirona insisted they wait until the Imbolc crowd had cleared out and Glastonbury was somewhat back to normal before she would take Raina to a special place. Raina knew better than to rush Sirona -- there'd be no point in it. And anyway, it was good to read and relax. Something told Raina she would have more than her share of adventures soon enough.

"There's an email from Art," Sirona announced one morning. "He says he's seen a woman at your cottage, but was not able to catch up with her before she left."

"Hmmm. Isn't likely anyone I know." But Raina couldn't help but think of Malcolm. She felt safe from him here, an ocean away, but the man was devious and apparently intent on doing her harm.

Sirona, too, thought of Malcolm and wondered if he was up to any mischief through a proxy of some sort, but if

Raina hadn't already thought of that she would hold her tongue. Instead she announced, "I think tomorrow we will venture out."

"To that special place you keep hinting at?"

"Could be..."

The day began with rain, but cleared to a cool brightness by the time the two women began their walk into town. Narrow roads, quaint houses, bowls of water left along the sidewalks for thirsty dogs. There was an easy acceptance of the common place here that was hard to find in America, Raina thought.

When they arrived at the gardens, Raina was immediately delighted. There was something about admission, but Sirona just nodded and ushered Raina through the gate and up a path lined with spring foliage. The morning rain had awakened the aroma of growing things to an intoxicating level. Sirona waited patiently as Raina tarried and took in every little bit of it.

Up a gentle incline and around a charming tree and suddenly it was there -- a small stone patio with a bench beside an ornately decorated wooden lid tipped up to reveal a grated well, still decorated in greenery for Imbolc. Raina's knees buckled but Sirona was right there to keep her upright. Tears burst from Raina's eyes and her heart swelled like it would burst with love, awe, and an overwhelming desire to turn to vapor and become one with the place.

Sirona led Raina to the bench and the two of them sat quietly until Raina's emotions settled somewhat. But the tears were still streaming down her face. She neither could nor wanted to stop them. They were like an out pouring of blessing and gratitude.

"Did you see her?" Raina whispered after a time.

"I have at times, yes," Sirona answered in a similarly hushed voice, "but today my attention was all on you. Was this like your experience at the well at the lake?"

"Yes, only far more intense, and this time, instead of just sensing a presence I felt like I could see her."

"And?" Sirona was doing her best to draw Raina out without leading her. She wanted to know Raina's experience unalloyed by her own.

"It was like a voice in my head was calling me to remember something I'd forgotten -- something I'd loved deeply but had forgotten to cherish. And I feel it, like an ache, here" she said, putting her hands to her heart.

"Is it too much? Do you want to leave?"

"Never. I want to stay here forever." Then Raina turned to Sirona and their eyes met in an intensity of connection Raina had never experienced before. Mystical experiences aren't easy to share with another person. That Sirona never seemed to shy away from Raina's strange visitations was a wonder to her...and a blessing.

"What is this place?" she asked at last.

"This," Sirona said, with a deep reverence in her voice, as she left the bench and knelt by the well to caress the rim of the opening, "is the Chalice Well. Perhaps the holiest of holy wells. People have been coming here for centuries -- over two thousand years some say, to pray, to drink it's healing waters, to experience all manner of connection with the Divine."

243

"I'm amazed at the power of the feelings I had -- am still having. Is it like this for everyone?"

"Some no doubt, but I think the intensity of your experience isn't common. Still, the Well has a presence that is uncanny and undeniable. You see how it is dressed for Imbolc. Love and reverence surround it."

"And it's just out here like this? Anyone can come here?"

"Well, there is a gate and," she chuckled, "an admission fee, but this isn't America where wonders are cordoned off -- or fake and over-played, and over-priced. Also, I think the Well has a way of protecting itself. Those whose hearts are not pure would, I suspect, have no interest in it, or they'd see it as just another vaguely interesting tourist trap, snap a picture and move on."

"What they would miss..." Raina said dreamily.

"Well yes, what is missed every day, everywhere," Sirona said, waving her hand at the gardens. "But here it is focused, concentrated."

"What is here," Raina said, searching for the right words, "is what people long for, but don't know how to find, or what it looks like. And yet, it is just *here*. Open and accessible..."

"Raina, dearest one, I don't think you realize how blessed you are. You have an acute sensitivity to Divine presence..."

"...as do you!"

"To some degree, but not like you."

"But the darkness, the madness," Raina protested, not really wanting to recall that aspect of her life, especially in this remarkable place, but it was never far from her thoughts, and something about this place called it out. Raina gnawed at her lip and tasted the salt from her tears.

"I don't completely understand it," Sirona admitted, "but over the next few weeks, we are going to work at puzzling it out. For now, I will say that I think it comes of fear and misunderstanding. Everything has its shadow side, even the good, and when the good is overwhelming or has no clear way to express itself, the shadow gains ascendency. And there is the question of power..."

In that moment, the wind came up and stirred the spring greenery, perhaps diluting some of the enchantment surrounding them.

"Let me show you the rest of the garden," Sirona said rising and holding out her hand to Raina.

Wandering down the path from the well, they followed the course of the spring, to a spout erupting from a sculpted lion's head. Sirona took a sip of the iron-rich water, and encouraged Raina to do the same. They spent a few moments of reverence there, watching the water spill from the spout into a trough stained red from the iron-rich waters. From there, they continued their descent through the ancient, reaching arms of yew trees, to where the flow forms carried the water, twisting and turning, into a level pool of two interlocking circles.

"How is it that we are alone here, wonderful as that is?" Raina asked, tipping her head back, striving to pull everything she had experienced into herself through all her senses. All these years of suffering and confusion, caution and loneliness were falling from her like a chrysalis falling away to reveal the gestated butterfly, wings still stiff, but promising flight.

"I expect the rain has kept folks away," Sirona suggested, "and many may have gotten their fill throughout the holiday. We are lucky indeed to have it to ourselves. As you might guess, that's not always the case."

It was then that Raina saw a flash of white, but before she could alert Sirona, it was gone.

Before they left, they visited the giftshop, where Sirona encouraged Raina to browse around while she talked to the woman behind the counter. The conversation was earnest, that much Raina could see, but the two women were careful to keep their exchange private, and Raina was content to let it be so. That this was Sirona's home and that she was an individual of some importance here was growing increasingly obvious to Raina, who, it must be said, was just delighted to be a part of it and let things unfold in their time.

That night, the women stayed up late into the night. Sirona pulled books from the shelves and shared some of the history and myths around Glastonbury -- the Isle of Glass -- Avalon, where Arthur was supposedly taken upon his death to await the time when he would return. Struggling to take it all in, Raina thrilled to know she was actually in a place that held such history and such powerful and persistent mythological significance. America had nothing to compare. At least from the perspective of European settlement on, America was an infant compared to other nations. Any deep historical and mythical roots were in the keeping of the Native peoples and, tragically for all concerned, all but lost in the horror and ignorance of colonialism.

Raina's head spun, but of this she was certain. Tales of holy places, power places, were not superstitions or flights of fancy but very real indeed. Now that she had some distance from it, she could take a bit more critical look at what happened to her at the Well and there was no getting around it. On all levels -- physically, emotionally, spiritually -- there was a power there that was greater than her. Not only did she feel it, but she was forever changed by it. Exactly how she was changed, she couldn't really say, but she instinctively knew that she was, that this day's experience and the spirit of the Well would never leave her.

There was so much more that Raina wanted to know, but the day had left her exhausted. She began nodding where she sat until, laughingly, Sirona insisted that they retire. Raina staggered from her chair, readied herself for bed as though in a trance and fell into the deep waters of the unconscious, dreaming of flowing, carnelian waters carrying her through woodlands, grasslands, into the sea and eventually into the very heavens.

She awoke refreshed and ready to continue their conversations and reflections from the night before but was brought up short by the sight of a suitcase in the hall. Had a visitor arrived while she slept? But she knew better; she knew whose suitcase sat by the door and her heart beat hard at the thought of what it might mean.

"What is this?" she asked Sirona, her voice choking.

"Ah, dear one. I must travel for a few days..." Sirona began, but Raina's tears cut her off. Such an intense response was not exactly what Sirona had expected. Moving quickly to her friend, she grabbed her hand and wiped at Raina's tears with the corner of sleeve.

"This won't do, dear one. We both have our work to do. There are folks we will need to engage in our quest but they are typically those who like to keep to themselves. I need to make some gentle forays and plant some seeds, all of which is best done alone for now."

"And what of me? What am I to do without...while you are gone?" Raina's voice sounded more shrill than she would have liked, but she wasn't ready to be left alone in this strange place. Just when things were evening out for her, was she to be left alone again?

As gently as she could, Sirona challenged the other woman.

"I think you know what your work is...what you are called to do."

"Sirona," Raina was pleading now, "whatever I need to do is best done with you here to help me. You have brought me this far, shown me such wonders...if you go now..."

"...if I go now, none of what you've achieved will be lost. Besides, I'm not going forever -- a few days at most. Listen, dear one. Something has opened in you and you need time to explore and nourish it. The work you have to do is between you and the spirit of this place. I have no role in this other than to get you here and stand by your side as you find your footing...which you have done.

"How did you sleep last night, by the way?" Sirona asked, not really changing the subject, though it may have appeared so to Raina.

Sleep...had she actually slept last night Raina thought? Or did she just ride mythical waters through the dark hours?

"I...travelled...pulled along on a flowing stream..."

"There it is," Sirona said, with triumph in her voice. "The journey has been initiated. Listen carefully. I have made arrangements at the Chalice Gardens for you to have access any time you like, preferably during the off hours when you won't be disturbed by others. The Gardens, the Well, are yours to explore. You will know what to do. And here, wear this."

From her pocket Sirona drew a chain holding a replica of the design on the Chalice Well lid and fastened it around Raina's neck.

"The spirit of the Well recognizes you; now it is time to recognize yourself. Wear this as a comfort, and don't forget your fairy cloak. The weather will not always be fair. You'll be glad of its warmth and its...cover."

A quick toot of a car horn intruded on the moment.

"That's my ride," Sirona said, gathering herself and her baggage. She kissed Raina's cheek and flowed toward the door. With her hand on the latch, she turned to Raina.

"Remember, the sacred mystery is indwelling in every aspect of the Garden."

With that, Sirona flew out the door and into the waiting vehicle. Raina hurried to the window, wrestling with the ache of Sirona's departure and wondering who it was that was ferrying her away. But she needn't have wondered. As she watched him help Sirona stow her belongings, she was fairly certain it was the man she saw Sirona dancing with on Imbolc.

20

In the Garden

Hanging around the apartment without her friend had little appeal, so she might as well do as bidden. The garden awaited. Mercifully, though the weather was cool and overcast, it was not raining. Her cloak was perfect for the day, and her spirits lifted the moment she put it on, almost as though she was donning a different persona, like an actor in a play. And yet, Raina wondered, can't it be said that however fanciful the personas we take on, they nevertheless become a part of us, at least in some small measure?

"Good morning!" the woman at the Garden enthused, smiling at Raina as though she had known her for years. "Delighted to see you. Sirona and I spoke yesterday; she told me all about you." The look she gave Raina was a bit unsettling. *All about her?* What exactly would that be? "I will show you the way to enter should you want to come when no one else is around..."

As easy as that, Raina thought, marveling at the casual attitude despite the value of what it protected. Then again, it seemed that Sirona had established Raina as some sort of person of importance. Under the folds of her cape, Raina shifted her shoulders somewhat. *A person of importance* did not fit comfortably on them, but if it got her into the garden to prowl at her leisure, so be it.

Once in the Gardens, Raina didn't head to the Well right away, though she longed for it. Rather, she wanted to explore the rest of the grounds, take in with fresh eyes what yesterday she could only see through the mist of heightened emotions. Was it only yesterday?

She started at the ground level pool, situating herself on a curved bench that reminded her of the yin yang symbol, glad of her cloak insulating her from the wood, still damp from yesterday's rain. Gazing at the flow form structure that guided the gushing water from the heights into the circular pool, she could see more clearly the unmistakable feminine form of the construction, the final section clearly "birthing" the water...water of life...water of spirit...giving it to, what? The world, the earth, the generations to come?

Whatever it symbolized, there was a clear and indisputable nod to the unconditional generosity of nature and its systems. Such a contrast to contemporary society. She thought of the literature she had taught for so many years, the product of humankind's development here in the 21st century. How convoluted the contemporary voice was, so mired in the degradation of modern life, wrestling with form in order to create something new, original. And yet here was nature, doing its thing, the same thing, day after day, unconcerned about novelty and in its sameness offering a consolation that was priceless...and pure.

She knew the arguments about not hiding from the disfunction, degradation, and unmoored lives of contemporary experience. Of course, one cannot heal what one refuses to see, but where was the healing? So often the ugliness became a perverse form of entertainment and was left at that with no path to healing offered or even imagined. Cynicism and despair defined the zeitgeist of the age, the future most often imagined dystopically. The positive and the beautiful were mocked as naive, and yet here was nature, consistently pouring out the essence of life at the rate of one thousand gallons an hour. Which was more real? Which safer to trust, the existential despair of humankind or the persistent beauty and renewal of nature?

The water drew her. Despite the chill of the day, Raina longed to immerse herself in it. Her thoughts turned to Aries Lake...and Art... the lake she had yet to swim in and the man who...

With a sigh she heaved herself off the bench and made her way up the side of the pool, past a small statue of an earth goddess, and underneath the yew trees, so expressive in their formation. She would be at the Lion's Head soon and there she would take a drink of the healing waters. Were they really, or did people just believe them so? And was the difference between the two possibilities as mutually exclusive as many would think?

She tasted the iron rich waters, then reached down for another palm full, hungry for the sweetness, the *rightness* of the taste. Of course water had healing properties. One didn't have to be a mystic to believe that. It was scientific fact; the purer the water, the fuller it was of necessary minerals, the more healing potential it carried.

Raina's intention had been to move directly on to the Well, but why hurry? She felt a strong need to rest, to fold herself into the environment. She sat down on the ground, heedless of the damp, and lay her head back, cushioned by the hood of her cape. How simple, how sweet, how welcoming this garden. As she lay there, she felt her anxiety melt off and soak into the vast and porous earth, there to be composted and transformed into more earth, more garden, sweet and welcoming. She may have dozed off, she wasn't sure, but when she opened her eyes, she felt that the day had advanced. Sitting up slowly, she couldn't help but smile as one does at the beginning of a recognition of kinship.

Up the hill now, to face the Well. As she approached, she took a deep breath. Stepping into the recessed patio, the tears came again and her heartbeat quickened, but she was ready for it -- longing for it.

She knelt at the edge of the Well and put her hands on the stone rim, closed her eyes and breathed deeply. How one opens one's heart is hard to describe, but she knew she was opening to a deep receptivity and an offering of love and commitment. She peered into the Well's depth and tried to empty her mind. If this was prayer, so be it. All she knew was that she was there to listen, receive whatever the spirit of the Well had to offer, knowing she was safe and in a loving atmosphere. Then, in the stillness, she waited.

A slight breeze came up, lifting Raina's hair as a lover might, sweeping it off her forehead. With the breeze came the scent of spring blossoms, the natural incense of the sanctuary of earth spirits. The touch of stone beneath Raina's fingers was inviting. She went deep -- not asleep, but not entirely present to the mundane world, listening not with her ears, but with her spirit, the nexus of head and heart.

Suddenly the sky darkened and she felt as though she couldn't breathe, as though she was surrounded by earth, buried alive. She felt the panic rising in her. Darker still the day became, and more stifling was the air around her. Not stifling, but nonexistent! Instinctively, she knew if she took another breath, she would inhale not air but earth. She held her breath until she felt her lungs and head would burst. Dizziness engulfed her. A darker black than the earth itself threatened to overtake her. She had let her guard down, trusted the beneficence of the Well, only to come to this place of certain death. The shadow place.

"*Hold fast,*" a faint voice spoke from deep in her unconscious. "*Become a worm, at home in the darkness.*"

How absurd. She was the farthest thing from a worm. Desperately, she wanted out. Why wouldn't the Well, the loving Goddess she had seen rise from its depths, hear her and release her? Fool to have given herself over to such naive belief. One small moment of respite that she thought would turn it all around, all of her suffering, had now dissolved into the terror that had been her life. Why should she be surprised? Let go then, breathe in the darkness, have done.

Less faint now, *of earth you were born, to earth you shall return, become as the worm that was there in the beginning and will be there in the end.*

At the point of ultimate desperation, what did she have to lose? She let the image come to her. Surrendering, she let go of fear, identity, outward appearance. She imagined herself a worm and as such, found herself moving through the soil as though swimming through water. Bits of earth brushed her body, caressed it. She found pleasure in the undulation of her body, no more than a ribbon of being in the vastness of the universe. Slowly, joy and freedom replaced fear and the need for control. How long she stayed like that, she couldn't say, but the return to her own consciousness came gently, naturally.

When she opened her eyes, the world seemed alive in a way it never had before. Every leaf and blossom, the edges of stone, everything stood out as though outlined in a delicate brush of silvery light. Joy tumbled into Raina's being as though she was drinking it from the very air. At the same time, in contrast to the light, the shadows were darker, prominent, indissoluble. And the thought came to her...*All the world is a play of darkness and light, neither to be feared, but faced and understood.*

Raina descended on the opposite side of the Well from her ascent. Here, the garden existed in profusion. Amid the tangle of green, she spied a particularly beautiful carving of an ammonite shell. Stopping, she stooped to run her fingers over it, delighting in the swirling shape and the undulating ridges. In that compelling form, she saw a metaphor for life, starting at an outer edge, arising from apparent nothingness, then gradually curling toward a center of understanding and wholeness that then defines the whole and gives it meaning, the progression to that point a swirling dance with ridges of experience, ups and downs, but each one moving inexorably toward a center point, the ground of being.

Overwhelmed with the revelations of the day, Raina now quickened her step, ready to leave the intensity of the gardens and melt into the everydayness of life, at least for a while. In her hurry, she failed to notice the blur of white some distance from the path, and the two golden eyes intently following her descent.

Over the next few days, Raina made frequent trips to the gardens, often taking with her the journal book that Sirona had given her, it's purpose now clear. So many thoughts were coming to her that she thought it best to record them. In truth, it was often a compulsion to do so -- to resist would have been futile. Without Sirona there to share her insights, they begged to see the light of day in the only way available to her. And for a time, it was enough, scribbling away on a bench in the gardens, or sitting in Sirona's apartment in the evenings, drinking her concoction of night tea.

But as the week progressed, Raina became increasingly desirous of her friend's return. As so often happens when one returns to health after an illness, Raina was bursting with energy and a passion for getting on with life, which in this case, meant their quest. Whatever awaited Raina, whatever her role was in the mysterious quest Sirona and Art alluded to, she was ready to endure it.

Nor did she now need to go to the Well during off hours. She'd had her time of intimacy with it, established the bond, and found the inner pathway between her spirit and that of the Garden. Now it gladdened her heart to see others strolling among the yew trees, sitting by the well, drinking the healing waters -- although she did wonder how many of them may have had an experience similar to hers. Could she see it on their faces? After some time of clandestinely searching for signs, she gave it up. Not for her to know she guessed. But despite her attendance to the visitors at the Garden, her eyes never seemed to fall upon one particular visitor, stunningly handsome, always very aware of Raina.

On the fourth day since Sirona's departure she ended her time at the Well in the gift shop, perusing all the treasures there. Art had been strongly on her mind all day. It had occurred to her that he must be connected to this place in some way, and yet he was stuck in the States. And, truth be told, she missed him -- his easy laugh, his gentle strength. What would he make of her experiences here?

Perhaps she would use her lonely night to write to him -- an old fashioned, written letter, penned on a card that might evoke a bit of what had transpired for her. As she looked for just the right image, her eye caught on a print. Raina's hand flew to her mouth, for there, beautifully and perfectly rendered, was Raina's vision on that first day -- an ethereal goddess rising from the Well, her arms outstretched in blessing. Could it be? Then she was not alone, after all.

Yes, she must write to Art. She chose a card and asked the clerk for a copy of the print, evidence that she hadn't over-reacted, that her sense of a presence at the Well was at least imagined and appreciated by others, and perhaps even directly experienced. She stowed her purchases in her bag and made her way home, imagining another night alone, but not entirely, as she would evoke the presence of Art as she wrote to him of all that had come to her since she had left the cottage.

As she fumbled for her key at the door, it opened of its own accord and there stood Sirona, home at last.

"Where have you been?" Sirona said, feigning accusation, then smiling broadly and moving aside as Raina bustled into the house and, dropping her bag, flung her arms around her friend.

"How I have missed you! There is so much to tell you."

Sirona put her hand on Raina's face and looked into her eyes, seeing there exactly what she had hoped to see.

Raina, in turn, in that moment had yet another insight.

"You left on purpose, didn't you?"

"The time was right. And it wasn't like I didn't have to get out and make those connections," Sirona said, smiling.

"But if you'd been here, I could have shared so much with you," Raina protested.

"You needed to do this on your own, to work things through and find your own way. If I'd been here, you would have measured every new insight against my approval. In my absence, you had no one to trust but yourself. And you do trust yourself now, do you not?"

"I do. Yes, I do. Oh, Sirona, how can I ever thank you for all this?"

"Ha! Well, that's to come! We have some intense work ahead of us, but first I must hear of all that has transpired for you these past few days."

Rain misted the windows as the two women spent the afternoon in deep conversation, moving from room to room and thought to thought as the weather insulated them from mundane interruption. Later, as they worked together preparing an evening meal, Raina shared her desire to write to Art in the evening.

"Perfect." Sirona agreed. "And while you do that, I'll read your journal. I'm so glad you've used it. It may be important to others, to the future. And as we move forward, to the extent possible, we should record everything we learn."

Sirona wanted to say more, to give Raina a glimpse of what lay ahead, but forced herself to let the day be what it was.

Dearest Art,

I have so much to tell you. Would that I could do it in person, on the edge of the lake or in the woods by your waterfall. But perhaps you will not recognize me when at last we return...

Breakfast was already set when Raina finally arose, her journal placed next to her plate, as though being served as part of the repast. Leaning against the counter, coffee in hand, Sirona greeted Raina with the most serious expression she had ever seen on her friend's face.

"What?" Raina asked, biting her lip. Had Sirona read something in the journal that troubled her?

"Coffee?" Sirona asked, turning to grab a cup.

"Not until you tell me why the dour expression..."

Submitting, Sirona said, "It is clear to me now, and should be to you as well, that the dark dreams that have plagued you -- indeed ruled your life -- are the shadow side of an exceptional brilliance. The brighter the light, the darker the shadows. I am not surprised, dear one, at the power in you. What concerns me is why -- and how -- it has been so repressed in you, so unavailable to be used as a balance against the dark. Often, we fail to see our own brilliance and muddle through life being half of what we could be, but in your case, with such heightened powers, the shadow nearly did you in, and, so thoroughly, so unnaturally, that it suggests some kind of external malevolence at work."

The color drained from Raina's face.

"I'll take that coffee now..." Raina said, fumbling with the kitchen chair.

Sirona filled a cup and came to the table. Raina drank in silence for some time, then, setting her cup down with a trembled hand, insisted, "Say more."

Sirona reached across the table and took Raina's trembling hand in hers.

"I wish I knew more. You are intelligent and strong. In the natural course of events, it would seem likely that you would work some of this out on your own, or at least seek help in doing so. That you pulled yourself out of the mental collapse you suffered after April was born is a wonder. I expect that took a great deal of effort as did what came after. Still, you survived, though you did not thrive and you most certainly did not find your power or even have an inkling of it."

"Until I went to my mother's cottage and met Art...and you."

"Your mother's cottage drew you. One might imagine that while she could not help you in her life, in her death she provided for you a sanctuary of sorts."

"Which I was just beginning to explore when Malcolm showed up."

"I've given much thought to him," Sirona said. "Certainly, he exacerbated your troubles, but something larger seems to be at work...of which he might be an agent, wittingly or not."

"But who or what would be that concerned with me? I'm no one."

Sirona's eyebrows rose nearly out of her head. Her visage darkened and her shoulders twitched as though she was ruffling blue-black feathers.

"NO ONE?" she said, her voice deep as though something or someone else was speaking through her. Raina pulled back.

"You're forgetting what Art and I have told you! Then again," her voice returning to close to normal, "we may not have been clear, because we ourselves are not entirely clear." Then Sirona straightened, fixing Raina with full intensity.

"Art and I have felt from early on that you are the key, the final piece to the destiny that surrounds us. Now, more than ever," she said, glancing over at the journal. "I am convinced that you are in some way connected to Merlin."

At this, Raina opened her mouth to object, but Sirona silenced her with a raised hand.

"Exactly what that connection is, I believe we will get closer to understanding in the coming weeks. I've made some connections and we will leave as soon as you are ready to deal with what we learn. In the meantime, know this -- whatever it is that the three of us are meant to accomplish will undoubtedly have its foes, forces that have a vested interest in keeping the power and perspective of what we represent silenced."

"And what is that exactly?" Raina felt like her insides were quaking, out of fear or excitement, she wasn't entirely sure. But it was clear that she had not gone as far as she was intended to, and now was the moment of truth. Either she had the courage to face what was coming, or she would fall into her habitual mode of being -- unobtrusive, small and safe.

"But you already know!" Sirona said, picking up Raina's journal and slamming it on the table. "You know! You've felt it, seen it, been healed by it! It is the sacred power of the Earth." Now tears were streaming down Sirona's face, which frightened Raina even more than her anger.

"For over two thousand years, humans have been moving away from their essential being, denying the fullness of divinity and forcing it into the *ridiculously limited* image of an off-planet god, male, selective in his grace, greedy for reverence for himself only at the expense of the feminine, the four-legged, the winged, the rooted..." Sirona's fury was terrifying.

"Do you have any idea how important this image is?" she asked, waving at the picture on the table. "That you actually *saw* this means that you *could* where most cannot. *You know it to be the way of being.*"

At this the fire in Sirona calmed as she slumped into her chair.

"Raina, the survival of this planet and everything on it depends on recovering what has been lost, forgotten, denied. Perhaps it is already too late, but you are here, perhaps in the nick of time. It was prophesied that Arthur the King would return, and in my Art, we see that that may have happened, may have been happening through the ages as his soul was reborn over and over again.

"In me, the spirit of Morgan Le Fay has persisted, struggled to remain pure of the taint of sterile religion. But of Merlin, who was also prophesied to return, we have heard nothing...until now. The depth of the light and dark in you is evidence of his nature, diluted through the centuries, perhaps, but the nature of it is like a signature.

"In Merlin, the fullness of the light and the shadow were unbounded; his magic lies in his unique ability to balance them, but ultimately that ability came from a oneness with the Earth itself, for it is there, and only there, that one finds true balance."

21

Familiars

For over an hour Sirona had been navigating her car down narrow roads bounded tightly by stone fences and hedgerows that blocked out the rest of the countryside. With no vista to focus on, Raina began to feel queasy and was forced to close her eyes to preserve her dignity. In the stillness behind her eyes, she finally had the chance to review the startling events of the morning.

Taking a quick glance at her emails before leaving, Sirona had found a message from Art in which he explained that he had at last learned the identity of the woman who had come to the cottage. It was Raina's daughter, April, looking for her mother. She knew the cottage from having spent some time there with her grandmother and knew as well that her grandmother had left the cottage to Raina. From time to time, when she could slip away from Malcolm's incarcerating gaze, she would come hoping to find her mother. This time, Art was able to intercept her, and so a connection was established between the two. April was now in college, Art explained, and so had gained some independence from Malcolm.

She will return whenever she is safely able to do so -- that is without Malcolm's knowledge -- and when her studies permit. She and

I have much to discuss, and the strange little room in the loft holds particular interest for her.

Naturally, Raina longed to hear more, and envied Art his time with her daughter. Her precious daughter whom she hadn't seen since she was a baby...the thought of seeing her, touching her was almost more than she could bear. But there was little time to dwell on that as Sirona was whisking her out the door, explaining that they had to make a stop as part of their journey.

Near the neighboring town of Street, they pulled onto a side road, little more than an alley, and stopped at a green sign with gold letters that announced the shop as "Tuttle's Time Emporium." Inside, there were clocks everywhere, the cacophony of ticking and chiming quite overwhelming. Behind the counter, a man who appeared to be older than time itself, but sprightly, perhaps even beyond time, greeted Sirona familiarly.

"Ah, the healer. Merry Met, Lady Sirona. I trust you are well. Going to visit Rowan, are you?"

Raina could neither hear Sirona's reply nor see her facial expression, as her back was to her, Raina wisely standing near the door lest she disturb any number of precariously situated timepieces.

Whatever Sirona's response was, it resulted in Tuttle ducking into a back room and reappearing after a short while carrying a small blue bottle of the type to dispense a misty spray. Sirona slipped the bottle into her purse and paid Tuttle. For a brief while longer, they engaged in conversation which seemed to include Tuttle raising his eyeglasses and looking around Sirona to get a good gander at Raina.

Once outside, Sirona took the bottle out of her purse and bid Raina close her eyes while she gently sprayed the mist over her, then doused herself in the same way. When Raina questioned her, Sirona replied,

"It takes time to work...I'll explain its function when we get closer to our destination."

Back on the road, with her eyes closed and the morning rattling around in her head with a million unanswered questions, Raina focused on the subtle aroma of the mist -- woodsy and sweet, like the inside of bark. A lovely scent really...

The sound of gravel under tires woke Raina from an oblivious slumber.

"Welcome back, sleepy head."

"Did you drug me?" Raina asked, trying not to sound too accusing.

"Depends on how you define drugged," Sirona said, her easy laughter returning at last. "You've been sprayed with a concoction made mostly from the juices of the cambium layer of trees and a few other proprietary ingredients known only to Mr. Tuttle, master of time that he is. You are about to meet Rowan -- a very interesting person, as you will soon see. Tuttle's mist has shifted our vibratory levels, slightly slowed us in time as it were, which will aid our purpose here."

"And our purpose here is what?"

"Rowan should be able to tell if you are Merlin's reincarnated spirit..."

"As simple as that."

"Hardly simple. She wouldn't do this for just anyone, but she has a vested interest in any sign of Merlin's influence returning to the world. But we tarry. Here, let me give you another dose." With that, Sirona misted Raina, the earthy smell easing Raina into a relaxed, receptive mood.

As they approached the dwelling, Raina could barely tell if it was a tree or a house. She wondered if she wasn't still half asleep, as things seemed to move and shift as though they weren't sure themselves exactly what they were.

They were met by a woman whose skin was the color of bark, her hair a tangle of the reds and oranges of fall leaves, and her limbs and fingers long and slender, graceful even in stillness. She was not beautiful in the way human beauty is typically judged, but in the abundance of life-force she radiated. Raina felt her own energy quicken in Rowan's presence, drawing in the atmosphere around her as though it was the breath of life.

"Do come in," Rowan said, her voice like the hush of wind.

Rowan led them through the dwelling and out a back door into an alluring grove in the center of which was a single chair made of woven branches. Rowan gestured for Raina to take a seat while Sirona drifted into the circle of trees, leaving Raina, for all intents and purposes, alone with Rowan, who squatted before her and held her eyes intently with her own. After a time, Rowan took Raina's hands into her own gnarled and dark-skinned fingers. Her eyes closed as she spoke.

"Speak to me your name."

Raina opened her mouth to speak, but nothing came out. Rowan tightened her grip slightly, then..."You are safe here, we would know your name."

Again, nothing.

Rowan let go of Raina's hands, stood up and circled her chair three times while Raina sat mute and empty. Returning to her position at Raina's feet and taking her two hands in one while she placed her other on Raina's heart, Rowan intoned, "*In the name of the ancient and perpetual forest, we implore you to speak your name.*"

Raina's body tensed, and her head shot up as though seeking the sky. Rowan struggled to keep her hand on Raina's chest, when a small, anguished voice came from Raina's lips.

"*I've been known by many names...too many to speak, but women all.*"

From her outpost at the tree line, Sirona inched a step or two closer, tense with anticipation and restraint.

Thinking the interview had concluded, Rowan moved to take her hand away from Raina's heart at last, but Raina grabbed it roughly, pulled it back tightly against her chest and hissed, "*Release the curse...please...release us!*"

Rowan shook where she knelt, like a tree quaking in the wind, then slowly stood and pulling her hand from Raina's grasp, raised her arms into the air, swaying, weaving patterns against the sky while Raina slowly opened her eyes and looked around, clearly oblivious to what had just transpired.

Rowan turned to Sirona.

"Gather her and let us move inside," she instructed, then slowly made her way toward the dwelling.

Sirona took Raina's hands and gently pulled her up, then the two followed Rowan in silence.

Rowan prepared a tea, similar, it seemed to Raina, to the one Sirona called "night tea" and let her guests take a few sips before she spoke.

"Here is what I see. This one does not house Merlin's spirit, or it would have spoken, of that I am certain. But that there was a response to the invocation of the forest implies a connection. I sensed Merlin's hand in this in some way, but exactly how is not clear."

"What of the curse?" Sirona could not help herself from blurting.

"What curse?" Raina said, startled.

Taking Raina's hand, Sirona said, as gently as she could, "You spoke of a curse, dear one, from which you begged to be released."

Raina's eyes widened, her insides trembled, but she could find no words. Looking from Sirona to Rowan, she hoped that one of them would disclaim it, explain it away, but that wasn't to be.

"It would seem," Rowan began, thoughtfully, "that the lineage of 'many names' carries a curse. Does that seem likely to you?" Rowan asked, looking searchingly into Raina's eyes.

"I'd like to say 'no'," Raina said, her voice shaking and subdued, "but the truth is, if that is true, it would explain a lot. But why in heaven's name would my lineage be cursed?"

Still dealing with the disappointment of learning that Raina did not house Merlin's spirit, Sirona now struggled to put the pieces together as best she could.

"So, now we know you do not carry Merlin's spirit, but Rowan is convinced there's a connection that we still don't understand. But that your line has been cursed, suggests that there may be a connection between that curse and Merlin.

Raina drew a sharp breath.

"God help me! Do you suppose an ancestor of mine was cursed by your wizard? It would *certainly* explain the horrifying dreams." Raina's heart was beating wildly. If that was so, then she was surrounded by potential enemies, when all this time she had reveled in their friendship and support.

Sirona's face darkened at the thought, but nowhere in her heart or mind could she grab onto anything that would support that conclusion. She could see, however, that Raina was on the verge of a serious panic. She grabbed Raina's shoulders and held them tight, boring her raven eyes into Raina's.

"I see absolutely no evidence for such an assumption. Neither Art nor I have ever felt even a hint of anything like that around you. Nor would the Goddess of the Well have presented herself to you so openly if you had been Merlin's enemy. Do you hear me?" Sirona came close to shaking Raina, but instead held her as tight as she could.

Rowan moved toward the two and laid a gentle hand on Raina's shoulder.

"I, too, would have felt Merlin's enmity, if any there was. I am sure of it. More likely, it seems to me, your ancestor would have drawn a curse from someone opposed to Merlin. On that, however, I can gain no further insight."

Still embracing her friend, Sirona could feel that Raina's heart was calming, so she backed away, giving Raina room to breathe.

"I have something that might help," Rowan said, releasing Raina as well. "Give me a minute if you would."

As Rowan disappeared into a room curtained by drooping branches covered in almond-shaped leaves, Sirona moved closed to Raina.

"Whatever this curse is, you've gotten this far...and of late, you have flourished. Rowan can help you, as can -- as already have -- the waters of the Chalice Well. We will not rest until we get to the bottom of this, but please, foreswear any notion that you are in any way at odds with Merlin."

The two women watched the play of light and wind move through the strange dwelling Rowan called home. There was harmony here, and air that was fresher than Raina had ever experienced. In such an oasis of pure life force, perhaps even a curse might be out played. Raina's insides were still trembling, but the women's assurances were believable. Besides, the alternative was so fraught with despair that Raina was all too willing to be dissuaded from it.

When Rowan returned, she took Raina's hand and in it placed a small wooden, leaf-shaped amulet, etched with the design that Raina recognized as that of the Well cover. A deep red ribbon attached to the amulet dripped through Raina's fingers.

"This amulet is made of the Rowan tree, the ribbon dyed with Rowan berries. It is a ward against enchantment. That, and the Rowan berry tea you've been drinking here and at Sirona's will further support you in warding off the effect of the curse. I should say, in addition, that if this curse is as old as I suspect, it's power may be waning somewhat. Hold fast to your quest. You have a destiny that is connected to bringing Merlin's power back into the world. You must complete it, not only for the world itself, but for you as well. It may be that in so doing you will release the curse, which I suspect applies to your offspring as well as to yourself."

April! Raina let out a choked sob. The thought of her precious daughter cursed was unbearable. If she had any lingering doubts about continuing on whatever this thing was that she and Sirona had begun, they vanished at the thought of April. Sirona read her mind and nodded in agreement.

"Then let me send you off with this as well," Rowan said. "Here is the name of someone who may be able to help you take the next step." Handing Sirona a slip of paper, she asked, "You know him?"

"I do. We've had our differences, but yes, now that we know what Raina *isn't,* he may be able to help us puzzle out her connection."

"Good. And this...I think you can safely up the dose some." Rowan handed Sirona a rather large jar of dried red berries.

"Straight from the source," Sirona said, smiling. "You are a dear. Thank you."

At the door Raina hesitated and turned to Rowan.

"I....is there some compensation due?"

"Only that you complete this quest. May the strength of the Goddess be yours, Raina of the many names." Then Rowan bowed slightly and retreated into the shadows.

At the car, Raina dropped into the passenger seat like one completely drained. Seeing her friend in such a state concerned Sirona, but there was little more that she could do except promise her that she would take a less torturous route home. And while they were in Cornwall, she would treat Raina to some Cornish pasties and stout. At that, Raina roused herself some, having no idea what she was in for, but realizing that she was famished.

Raina soon learned that a "pasty" was a deep-fried meat pie, delicious enough on its own, but married with stout, all thoughts of ancient curses receded in gustatory delight.

"This stout...I've never had better...except for..."

"Art's home brew?" Sirona winked. "Where do you think he got the recipe?"

"You *stole* it!" Raina said, feigning shock.

"Of course not! How could you imply such a thing? Rather, you could say that I *replicated* it. And if the truth be known, I may have had a hand in perfecting the original recipe. Anyway, no one, except the three of us, will ever be the wiser."

The stout went down like silk, washing away the intensity of the day, but half way into her second one, Raina was emboldened enough to ask, "What is the story with Rowan?"

"A rare being, that one, as you could see for yourself. No one -- at least no one currently living -- knows how it all came about, whether she was always like that or began as a human who spent so much time with trees that she became one...or if she was a tree that took on human qualities. It is a puzzle that will never be solved nor has she ever, to my knowledge, shared her story. In the end, it doesn't matter. What matters is that she is a wonder, and just as trees speak to one another beneath the ground, she is able to connect with the spirit inherent in all beings."

"So that's what she did? She connected to my soul?"
"Exactly."

"But I felt nothing in the garden. I wish I had been more awake -- there are so many things I'd like to know."

"But that would not be for you to do. Our souls, spirits, are complicated things -- both inside us and outside, ours and not ours. Rowan knows how to be discreet. We came to her with one need for which she made one request, keeping her intrusion to a minimum. That we learned more than we had asked for was a gift. Distressing though it was, we need to see it as a blessing, for every bit of self-knowledge we obtain moves us closer to being in harmony with spirit."

"Hmmm." It took Raina a stout-inspired minute to process that, then, "And what of Tuttle's mist? Has it worn off?"

"Hard to say -- it's different for everyone. But I would venture to guess that your rather enthusiastic appreciation of the stout might imply that you're still vibrating a bit more slowly, savoring the moment in slow motion as it were. Cheers!"

Bright lights and the intoxicating smell of new books didn't seem like the kind of place where they would find the Arthurian scholar, but that was where Abernathy Whitestone had reluctantly agreed to meet the two women.

"You told Rowan that you haven't always agreed with this Whitestone fellow," Raina said on the day before they were set to meet him. "If I may ask, what is that all about?"

"He's arrogant as hell -- thinks he knows everything about the Arthurian Age, but he's all about the men and discounts the women, who, if one knows the truth of it, were the real movers and shakers of the time. While the men were busy with their politics and war games, it was the women who held together the web of connection, healing, and spiritual growth. When I'm with him, my spirit trembles with barely concealed rage at his omissions and misrepresentations, and I think he senses that.

"He was not eager to meet with us, but I dropped hints of information that I knew would pique his interest. I did *not* tell him that "my friend" was a woman who has some kind of connection to Merlin. He will resist that, I suspect. I only hope that his desire to reawaken Merlin overrules his aversion to the feminine."

When Sirona asked at the counter for the scholar, she and Raina were led to the back of the store, down a "staff only" corridor, to a door marked "private." There the clerk knocked seven times and waited, sharing a wan smile with the two women. When the door opened, the delicious smell of the bookstore was overtaken by that of ancient tomes and old man. The clerk gave a slight nod and vanished back into the present day, leaving Raina and Sirona alone to manage Abernathy Whitestone as best they could. Stooped and wizened, the scholar did not offer the women a seat, forcing Sirona to ask, as politely as she could manage, if they might sit. Whitestone waved his hand vaguely at two rickety chairs piled with books and papers while he made his way to the only upholstered chair in the room, his back turned to the women who quickly gathered the detritus and set it on a nearby table among a disordered array of books, maps, skulls, and whatever else the two women tried to avoid seeing.

Once seated, the old man stared at the two women, obviously not inclined to begin the conversation. Sirona began with the only card she knew they had to play...

"As I mentioned on the phone, we have been to see Rowan..."

"The only reason I'm seeing you now," he interrupted. "Go ahead, tell your tale and be quick about it."

And so Sirona did, as concisely as she could, but leaving out no detail, hoping against hope that as feeble as this man appeared, his mind was still sharp enough to snag on anything that would have some meaning for him...and them.

"And so, you see, we believe there is a connection, but if not one of ensoulment, then what? Rowan trusts that you can help."

"Humph." The old man sat slumped in his chair as if half asleep. Sirona began to despair, but something stirred in Raina.

She took as deep a breath as she dared in the stale air and, looking directly at Whitestone said, "You want to help us, for in so doing your life's work will achieve its true purpose."

Whitestone stirred and his eyes opened wide behind his glasses. He stared at Raina with renewed interest, or more accurately, any interest at all.

"You?" he barked. "Why you?"

He didn't have to say, *you're just a woman*. It was implied in his tone. Sirona bristled, but Raina stayed cool, focused.

"I have no idea 'why me'," Raina said evenly, "I only know that it is so. I am connected. You must search what you know and help us complete the tale in any way you can. To what end all this," she asked, waving her arms, "and all your years of study if not to find the key that unlocks the mystery of Merlin's return?"

Clearly, she had hit a nerve. Abernathy Whitestone leaned forward in his chair and stared at Raina intently. As he did so, it was as though the years fell away, and he was left with renewed vigor and clear sight. His hand went to his chin which he rubbed meditatively.

"Is it possible?" he asked, as if to himself. Then he left his chair and began rummaging through books and manuscripts.

"What is it?" Raina asked, rising from her chair and joining him as though she was as likely to find the answer as he was. Sirona eyed Raina with admiration. Not only was Raina not intimidated by the scholar, but it seemed he was beginning to see her as worthy of his attentions. Whatever powers of persuasion Raina had conjured, it was working beautifully.

"There are some tales...not given much credibility, mind you...of a... daughter."

Raina's heart quickened. The very word 'daughter' made her heart ache. At last he pulled a thin, fraying volume from the shelf and carried it to the table. As Raina and Sirona surrounded him, he explained, "This is one of the few surviving manuscripts from a nun in tenth century Cornwall. She was given to visions so they say, and most considered her quite insane..." a look passed between Raina and Sirona, "...but safe inside the convent walls. From what has survived of her work, it is assumed there was much more, which was lost, or destroyed, it being considered unseemly for a woman to write, you see..."

Gently, Raina drew Whitestone back to the issue at hand.

"And what does it say here?"

Whitestone ran his grubby finger down through the text until he found what he considered relevant. "Ah," he said, then read on...

"It is given to me to know, through the blessings of the Lord our God and his messenger the Holy Spirit, that in his later years, the Druid known as Merlin, lay with a common woman and begat on her a daughter, after whose birth, the woman, weak in spirit and body, passed from this mortal shell, leaving the child to be cared for by a kind and childless couple.

Whether the child ever knew her father was not given to me to know, but around her glowing spirit, I have perceived age upon age of daughters, into the present time and beyond. God be praised that in this way something of the ancient sage is preserved, despite his ungodly ways, and so it is in this way that we know the largess and mercy of the Father of Christ, may his name be ever reverenced on our lips and..."

"And so it goes on..." Whitestone said, snapping the volume shut.

The three stood speechless, staring at the table, absorbing what they had just heard. Whitestone was the first to speak.

Pulling back and scanning Raina from head to foot, he mumbled, more to himself than his guests, "Can it be?"

Sirona whispered, *"I've been known by many names...women all."*

Raina shivered. Images from all the years of dark dreams and visions flew through her mind...the cloaked figure so often present...longed for and feared simultaneously. Could it be that all the questions came to rest on a single answer? She was Merlin's descendant.

"Not his soul, but his blood..." she whispered.

"Let us consider this!" Whitestone said, suddenly full of enthusiasm. "There are implications here."

"Do you suppose she ever met her father?" Raina asked, the words sounding strange in her mouth.

"Possibly," Whitestone said, "but it would have to have been before he became entangled with Nimue. From what the tales tell us, Nimue would have been furious to hear that Merlin had had a dalliance, with a common woman no less and worse, a child by the union."

"Well, the *tales* as you say, don't always get it right, especially about women," Sirona said, speaking up at last. "And yet, what you say about Nimue might well be true. I've sensed the spirits of other women of power of that time, but there is a shroud of mystery around Nimue."

"It might be that the power she stole from Merlin, it not being hers to have, seriously damaged her," Whitestone suggested.

"That might mean age upon age of a regressed soul, rebirth into lowly beings..." Sirona mused.

Raina struggled to keep up with the metaphysics of the conversation, and yet, as she relaxed, she felt something begin to quicken in her, something that knew all too well of what they spoke.

"What of the curse?" Raina asked, trying not to choke on the word.

"That is a mystery to me. The logical one to blame for that would be Nimue, but if Merlin never knew his daughter, then Nimue likely didn't either. But here is what is occurring to me as we speak. As the legends tell us, Nimue used Merlin's own magic to trap him into a tree or a cave somewhere in the forest of Broceliande in Brittany, then called Armorica. Might one surmise that a daughter of the magician might try to interfere with Nimue's plans?

There is not a hint of it anywhere in the legends, but who is to say?"

The scholar sat pensively for a few moments, then seemed to be shaken by a new thought.

"What if..." he began, "what if a descendant might have the power to release him from his ensorcellment?" Whitestone looked at Raina with a greedy stare.

"Come now." Sirona intervened. "Even if an enchantment could last fifteen hundred years, I doubt that human flesh could. To even entertain the idea that Merlin could be released into his original form is madness."

At that, the scholar lifted his chin and squared his shoulders, obviously taking umbrage at Sirona's words.

"But we were never expecting to find his *body*, were we?" Raina said. "We, you, have been on the hunt for his soul. But...if he was ensorcelled rather than killed, so that he never actually died..."

"...then his spirit could be trapped in limbo. Raina, that's brilliant," Sirona said, delighted.

At that, Abernathy Whitestone got over Sirona's insult rather quickly, finding a foothold in the new theory.

"Might we suppose then, that someone of Merlin's own flesh and blood might have efficacy in releasing his soul?"

Raina glared at him.

"And what makes you think I would have any idea of how to do that?"

"Oh," Whitestone said, raising a hand, "that kind of metaphysics is beyond my area of expertise."

But while the two academics sparred, Sirona was hatching a plan. Rising from her seat and taking Raina's hand, she enthused her gratitude for the scholar's assistance, while clearly in a rush to leave. But with her hand on the door, she paused when she heard Whitestone's parting words.

"It may be worth a trip to Tintagel, to the cave beneath it reputed to be Merlin's retreat. There is nothing there now but rock, but who knows? Perhaps some deep memories might be stirred..."

A good recommendation, she had to admit, but insufficient to entice her to linger a moment longer.

Once outside, the friends took deep draughts of the fresh air to clear their lungs of the malodorous atmosphere of the scholar's rooms. Thus refreshed, Raina saw that her friend was distracted by a tangled woodland of thought.

"Ok then," she said, "what are you thinking?"

Whether or not Sirona would have given her a straight answer, she never knew for at that moment a handsome man dressed all in white was approaching them.

22

A Gathering of Twelve

Such masculine beauty, such mesmerizing eyes, should be illegal, Raina thought as she tried, unsuccessfully, to retreat from the oncoming individual.

"I assume you're coming from a visit to Abernathy," he said, making no introduction or pleasantries.

Impatient with the interruption, Raina snapped, "What business is it of yours?"

"I could have saved you some time and... unpleasantness," he responded coolly. Is there somewhere we can talk?"

Raina bristled. "Why should we trust you?"

But at that moment, Sirona stepped up, her eyes turned raven black.

"He is avian," she said, "have a care. And I believe we should hear him out. He would not approach us for any trivial reason."

"Appreciated, my Lady. Allow me to introduce myself. I am Percy Smith. Perhaps we could take a seat in the park across the way?"

Percy offered Sirona his arm and let Raina follow like a willful child, not an attitude Raina took kindly to.

"I trust Whitestone was able to tell you that this woman..."

"...Raina," Raina supplied, more affronted by the minute.

"...Raina," Percy continued, "...is the descendent of Merlin..."

"Why yes," Sirona said, "But how do you know this?"

"And why didn't you tell me that night if you knew?" Raina blurted out.

"What night?" Sirona asked, then, realization dawning, "Oh, is this the mystery man from the Imbolc gathering?"

"The very same," Percy answered before Raina could speak. Then, looking directly at Raina, "If I had walked up to you that night and told you that you were the descendent of Merlin's daughter, would you have believed me? You would have thought me mad, which would have complicated my efforts to be sure about my suspicions. But watching you in the gardens..."

"You were spying on me!"

"Observing. I'm fairly good at it. But had I spoken to you I would have known sooner. You have the same fiery temper as Annwyl..."

"Who..."

"Merlin's daughter -- your ancestor."

"Merlin's owl." Sirona said, her eyes alight. "You carry the spirit of Merlin's owl. Well met..."

Percy made a slight bow. Jealousy rose in Raina as she watched a look of mutual admiration pass between her friend and the *owl*. Even more irritating was hearing that Merlin's daughter wasn't all sugar and spice, and apparently had gotten on the wrong side of an owl. Raina began to wonder -- perhaps hope -- that this day was a very long, very lucid dream, well awakened from.

"Raina," Percy said, now turning to look directly at her, "I apologize for being flippant. All this must be a lot to take in. Yes, from what I can gather, your distant grandmother was an untutored, frustrated child, but that was down to Merlin himself. Had he schooled her, given her sufficient love and attention, who knows how different things might have been, but Nimue had the best of him at that point."

"And you know all this how?" Raina asked, still skeptical.

Sirona intervened. "Souls can hold memory, released through dreams, visions, what I guess one would call *knowings.*"

"In my case," Percy said, his beautiful face wrinkling into distress, "it comes through a repeated dream. Annwyl is at the cave where Nimue has ensorcelled Merlin, and has tried, unsuccessfully, to release him. Nimue suddenly appears, taunts Annwyl and casts the owl and a knight up into a whirlwind of undoing. I watch as my dream self, but I can also feel the shattering of my being. Quite discomforting.

"But it must be said that in the end, Annwyl proved to be quite brave and ready to sacrifice her own life for Merlin. Miraculously, while Nimue was distracted by torturing the owl and the knight, Annwyl was able to get away. At the last minute, however, Nimue threw a curse at her retreating form."

"The curse! So, it *was* Nimue..." Raina exclaimed.

"And the nature of the curse?" Sirona asked.

"Of that I have no sense. I believe the owl was senseless at that point," Percy said, a look of pain crossing his face.

"And what of the enchantment on Merlin?"

"Nothing, I'm afraid. I've seen glimpses in my dreams of the owl finding Merlin in a cave, rather *interwoven* in a tree, but no more than that. There is so much suffering around the visions that..."

"Say no more..." Sirona said, placing a hand on Percy's. "You've given us more than we could have hoped for." Sirona noticed that Raina had gone deathly pale.

"We must take our leave, I fear. It has been a trying day for Raina...for all of us. Merry part dear Percy. Let us not be strangers."

When Raina awoke from a much-needed nap, she found Sirona pacing the floor, her usual self-assuredness replaced by more than a slight agitation. Raina hated to see her friend so distressed. She had come to count on Sirona's confidence and calming ways, her easy laugh, and ready answer to whatever difficulties presented themselves. Now all she saw was an agitated crow, wearing a trench into the floor.

"Perhaps we should get Art to come..." Raina offered.

"Not wise," Sirona said. "He is needed where he is, especially now that April has turned up. There is so much at stake..." Sirona trailed off back into her troubled thoughts.

"What has you more agitated," Raina asked, "the curse, or the notion of trying to release Merlin's soul, about which we haven't a clue?"

"Both," Sirona replied, as she ceased her pacing and threw herself onto the couch, exhausted by all she didn't know. "But in different ways. The curse explains, I suspect, why it is that while you carry Merlin's blood, you are stifled in the expression of it. As for releasing Merlin's spirit -- *finding* it was one thing, a quest I felt was manageable, but *releasing* it, even figuring out *how* to do that will take the concerted effort of every wise person I know."

"What if," Raina began, unsure of how to express what she was thinking, "as you say, the human body, even ensorcelled, would, after centuries, degrade. Would that not mean that it eventually dies and therefore releases the soul after all?"

"Possibly, but also possibly not. My instinct tells me that an enchantment encompasses both the body and the soul and even should the body dissipate, since spirit is not subject to material degradation, it would persist, and do so perpetually enchanted, until...until *what* is the question.

"Furthermore, if the spirit is still under enchantment, that would explain why Art and I have not sensed it all these years, as hard as we've tried."

"Then, where from here?" Raina asked.

Sirona dropped her head into her hands, her fingers clutching her beautiful raven locks, as though doing so could yank the thoughts from her mind. Raina sat silently, holding the space while her friend struggled. Having no ideas of her own, it was all she could do. What if there were no answers? How would she console her friend if it turned out that her

life's work was for naught? In the face of that, whatever
"curse" Raina was under seemed to pale in comparison.
She'd gotten by well enough, after all. Sure, she could have
done better, but isn't that true for most people? But the
thought of Sirona...and Art's...life-long hopes, indeed their
purpose, dashed...

"I need to convene a gathering," Sirona said, raising
her head at last. "Many of the wise and sensitive friends I
have made over the years...now is the time for them to come
together, to bring their collective wisdom and energy to bear
on what might be the most important project of their lives.
It will take some time to contact everyone, but it's worth a
try. To *not* try, to turn our back on what we have
discovered, incomplete as it is, would be a sin against the
ages. And, we have our key, our magic charm, my dear.
We have you."

"Me?" Raina couldn't imagine how her total
ignorance of all these metaphysical intrigues could be of any
help whatsoever.

"Still you don't believe how important you are?"
Sirona said, smiling beatifically at her friend. "You are of
Merlin's blood, diluted over some fifteen hundred years, but
still there, encoded in your very being. I've told you right
along that you are the key and now it is obvious exactly what
kind of key you are...and what doorway you fit! But you are
right about contacting Art. I've left him in the dust of all
these revelations. I need to tell him of what we've learned
and hear what he has to say."

With that, Raina saw a change in Sirona's mood.
Something must have turned, for now her agitation turned

into cautious excitement. Perhaps, what she and Art had sought all these years was now on the cusp of coming into being. At least the nature of the task ahead was clear, if the doing of it was not.

Now that Sirona was back in action and quite literally on her feet, Raina's thoughts returned to yet another discovery -- that of April having made an appearance and a connection with Art. The knowledge that her daughter was well, grown to independence and within reach, filled her with joy.

As Sirona was busy emailing Art, she would pen a letter to her daughter, pouring her love and her hopes into words crafted by her own hand.

Dearest April,

I hardly know where to begin, nor am I even sure how it is I hold the pen in my shaking hand, so thrilled am I that there is the potential to see you, hold you, shower upon you all the love held in bondage these long, painful years.

There is much to tell, to dispel the false images I expect your father has created of me, but I will not dwell on them here. Rather, I'd have you know me and see for yourself that your mother is no monster, but only left you for what she believed at the time to be in your best interest. If you have been duped by your father, know that I was as well. Some of my story you may learn from Art, as I have shared much of it with him, but I'd rather you spend what time you have with him getting to know him as the gentle man he is. You can trust him. He is a dear friend, as is his sister, Sirona, with whom I am now here in Glastonbury.

Our work here has been to discover the source of the psychological malaise I have struggled with my whole life -- and which

I had hoped I would protect you from. What we have learned is stranger than what I could ever have imagined, but that is a tale for later. Let me only say, that it appears -- at least I hope -- that we are nearing the end of our work here and now I long only to be able to return to you, in the hopes that you will find it in your heart to know your mother at last.
Love and Blessings,
Raina

Over the next few days, Sirona was glued to the computer, making connections and writing frequently to Art. She made it clear to Raina that she was free to read all of the correspondence, but Raina was overwhelmed by it all, and quite frankly, too trepidatious about what lay ahead to even think about it, only caring to know if there was news of April. More aware than Raina was of what might lay ahead, Sirona left her alone, encouraged her to visit the gardens and rest however much she liked.

In less time than allowed for a return letter from April, should there be one, Sirona announced that the gathering had been set. They would meet at Sirona's mid-afternoon of the following day and leave for the Tor in order to make the summit before sunset, as the ceremony should be done in the liminal space between day and night.

"The Tor?" Raina asked.

"You see it all the time. It dominates the landscape. It's the hill with the tower at the summit -- St. Michael's Tower. The magic inherent on the Tor cannot be overstated. If those who have agreed to come, combined with the magic of the Tor, can't give us what we need to know, nothing or no one can. But dear one, I sense that Spirit is on our side, that it wants this to happen. The time is ripe and you have been discovered. I should tell you, there is much excitement about you among the community. You are quite the celebrity, having inspired both hope and determination." Then, lightheartedly, Sirona added, "let's just hope the weather is with us as well."

Half way up the ascent, Raina understood Sirona's concern about the weather. The wind blew with such force that Raina feared for her footing as well as that of most of the assembled company, not one of them being younger than she. But the one she had worried about most seemed to be doing just fine. Rowan was delighting in the wind, bending and twisting and humming to herself. In that way, the group of twelve women made their way at an elderly pace up the side of the Tor.

Twelve women. When only ten arrived earlier that day, Raina had been concerned. Where was the eleventh that, with Sirona, would make twelve? But Sirona laughed her contagious chuckle and informed Raina that she, indeed, was the twelfth woman.

"Me?" Raina had protested. "But I have no magic!"

"Oh, my dear one!" Sirona said, her merriment uncontainable. "*You have no magic?* Through your veins runs the blood of one of the greatest magicians of all time! No magic indeed! Why, it is only because of you that we can hope to have any luck at all in our quest this night."

One of the women came forward, gray-haired as were most of them, with a round face and sparkling eyes and a visage that was so full of compassion, Raina could hardly keep from hugging her on the spot.

After explaining that she had done a Tarot reading in preparation for their task, she told Raina, "Now I better understand the appearance of the Nine of Wands. It represents your disposition for what is to come. You have emerged from a great healing which has given you an enormous reserve of power. Believe in it, trust it, stay the course. Daughter of Merlin, how precious you are." She touched Raina's cheek as though in blessing, then humbly moved away, back into the assembled collective.

As she pushed against the wind, Raina touched her cheek, remembering the blessing. It wasn't easy believing she had such phenomenal power when for so much of her life she had felt just the opposite. But it was as Sirona had said, the greater the one, the greater the other. She must stop doubting that truth, doubting herself. Over the past few days, the realization that April was a part of this had weighed heavily upon her. Like Raina herself then, April was also a descendent of the great wizard, or whatever he was. Knowing so little of April's life, she had no idea how this was manifesting in her child. Did she suffer the dark visions, or some other plague? The question had pushed at her mind as she wrote the letter to April, but a letter was not the right place to open the discussion -- at least not yet. Whatever life was like for her daughter, Raina knew that whatever she was facing going forward, she was doing for her. It was that thought that gave her enough courage to overcome her doubts...and fear.

It was a long climb, but the women took it with determination, resting when they needed to. Sirona had timed it well. They would reach the summit well before sunset. They passed some folks, coming and going, but as the day wore on, visitors dwindled to a trickle until the twelve women were on their own, as they had hoped they would be.

At the crest of the Tor, the wind made a wild scene of the elderly group, blowing their hair and garments into wings and swirls. Sirona's dark locks rose upwards off her head like a crown, giving her, for a moment, a most uncanny look. If there was any question that these women were here to commune with the spirits, it was dispelled by the sight of them, transformed by the intense weather into creatures of the air as they began their preparations.

Then, as the sun neared the horizon, the wind calmed and all but died. It appeared that Sirona was right -- a force was working in their favor. As the last light of day colored the western sky, Raina breathed easier. She could do this. No, more than that, she *wanted* this, had waited all her life for it.

She took her place within the circle, as the women began to sing, some shaking strings of bells, a few tapping a gentle rhythm on small drums. The music rose and fell like the undulating movements of nature, but always, magically, harmonious. Raina found her voice and added to the chorus, surprised that it came so easily to her as she lost herself in the swirling sounds, swaying slightly, feeling her spirit literally rise in her breast. Someone had lit a small fire in the center of the circle which emitted a delicious aroma of wood and herbs.

Raina felt surrounded by all that was good -- good made manifest. Then Sirona's voice rose above the singing which subsided as she gave praise to the four directions, and called upon the spirits of rock and tree, water and earth, fur and feather. A hush and then the ask...

By the power of blood and bone, and the will of those faithful to Earth Mother, Divine Spirit, we pray for guidance in our quest. We would release an ancient curse, not for our sakes, but for the good of the whole earth, your generative and sustaining creation, which we poor creatures have so put at risk. We seek the return of the spirit of Merlin, that such knowledge, so long lost to us, be restored.

Within this circle, we hold blood of his blood and bone of his bone, newly aware of her lineage and desirous of releasing his spirit, if such is possible and within your power to grant. Guide us, Great Mother, show us the way, if such be your will.

Blessed Be.

The air had stilled as though listening to Sirona's supplication, the only sound that of the crackling fire. Darkness wrapped its arms around the Tor as Raina held her breath, waiting for what, she had no idea.

Then, one by one, voices rose around the circle...

...a cauldron...Rowan branches...oak grove...marriage of rock and tree...it must be three...the youngest first...the poet speaks...release the soul...see beyond...deep within...embrace the curse...promise me...

Twelve voices, twelve directions, then silence. When the wind rose slightly and she was sure there would be no more direction given, it was Rowan who raised her rustling voice to close the ritual, giving thanks to the four directions, the spirits of the earth, and the Divine Mother. As though on cue, a deep sigh arose from the twelve. It was finished.

In silence, the women broke the circle and gathered closer to the fire, then one by one, they began sharing the visions that had come to them. They talked late into the night, each adding a piece to the puzzle, generating a rough plan that the coming days would flesh out. Most of it made sense to Raina, but one thing troubled her. The woman who had spoken "the youngest first" had had a vision of a young adult woman being the first to enter the cave -- clearly not Raina or Sirona whom everyone had agreed were logically two of the three to attempt to release the curse. Sirona felt Raina tense beside her, but what must be must be.

"Who would the third be?" the woman asked.

"Logically, that would be Raina's daughter April, especially as she carries the blood as well," Sirona said hesitantly, dreading Raina's reaction.

"I'll not put my daughter in harm's way," Raina said, the tears in her voice hard to hide. "This is my job to do...for her sake. We can find another third."

Sirona took a deep breath in preparation for speaking, but it was Rowan who spoke.

"It is not for us to make such decisions. If the Mother says it must be your daughter, then so it must be."

"She didn't actually *name* her. How can we be sure?" Raina protested.

"It is a knowing, Raina," Rowan spoke, her voice reaching deep into Raina's chest. "It is the kind of knowing one learns to trust if one is to work with Spirit. Our human will serves us well when we use it to maintain our courage and resolve, but it disadvantages us when we wield it against Spirit. To assume that what we *want* takes precedence over the harmony of what *is* causes immense damage, the result of which is all around us." Rowan paused to let her words sink in, then, "Given your concern for your daughter's well-being, what is more important than to seek the undoing of the curse which, I believe, is intertwined with Merlin's enchantment?"

No one had yet to mention the curse or the instruction to "embrace" it. A voice from the darkness asked, "Who spoke the words concerning the curse then?"

In a small voice, Raina answered, "Me...it was me."

The women talked long into the night and, as the weather had become hospitable, it was decided they would wait until daylight to descend the Tor. One by one, they dozed off, wrapped in shawls and blankets. The fire burned itself out, but the moon had risen, a sky-sailing currach that bathed the Tor in a gentle light.

With her beautiful fairy cloak wrapped tightly around her, the hood bunched up into a suitable pillow, Raina lay on her back, enjoying the novelty of laying under such a huge expanse of cosmic brilliance, feeling sleep slowly wrapping her in its net when she suddenly let out a cry and sat upright.

"What is it?" Sirona asked, startled out of sleep.

Raina was trembling.

"A blackness moved across the sky, then swooped down, inches from my face, and dragged an icy finger across my forehead...or so it felt." In the darkness, Raina was spared the sight of concern that twisted Sirona's features, but her voice was soothing.

297

"I am here, dear one," Sirona said, moving closer to Raina. On her other side, she heard Rowan rustling closer to her as well, then others pulling in tighter, so that Raina lay in a circle of twelve women.

"She can threaten, but she has no power over you, dear one. You are among many allies, each with her own positive energy, all of which, tonight, is at your service, daughter of Merlin. Sleep."

23

Low Tide

"Are you ladies hungry at all?" Niall called from Sirona's kitchen as the twelve women filed into the apartment, exhausted and perished from their long trek down the Tor and through town. The table was piled high with fruit, cheeses, eggs, and a variety of baked goods, all presumably baked and arranged by the man Raina understood to be Sirona's "soul friend." Raina cast Sirona a glance of raised eyebrows and a mischievous grin, in response to which Sirona just shrugged.

Elated chatter filled the room as the women tucked into the abundance, but once stomachs were filled and toes were warmed, they returned to the work at hand which was to discern who was doing what over the next few weeks, and setting a deadline for the journey of the three. Raina's spine tingled at the realization that they were actually going to do this.

Rowan agreed that she was the obvious one to provide a Rowan branch and some well-considered herbs as well.

"And," she added, "I think a trip to Mr. Tuttle would not be wasted. The option of slowing down time a bit might come in handy. My, my, I've not been this active in ages!" she concluded with glee.

Beatrice claimed obtaining the cauldron as her task.

"I've heard stories of an ancient cauldron, made, so the story goes, for some future ritual purpose...a very important and mysterious one. Sounds like what we're about, does it not? It was originally crafted in Ireland, so they say, but spirited away for safe keeping. I know someone who may have a sense of its location..."

Liselle had family in Brittany. "I'll get maps of the forest, and ask around among the locals to see what tales still exist. It is widely accepted...and a point of some pride...that Merlin is enchanted somewhere in Broceliande, so no one will be alarmed by my questions." At that she giggled. "Who in their right mind would expect that anyone actually intended a spiritual jailbreak for the old wizard?"

Raina appreciated the attempt at levity, but was too tense to join in the merriment.

The rest of the women agreed to be at the service of "The Three," as they were now named, in any way required. Sirona thanked them all sincerely for their help, but knew in her heart that it was she and Raina who had the most work to do to puzzle out the rest of the message from the spirits.

They settled on two weeks as a final date to have everything in place, then drifted out into the late morning and away to their various tasks. Now Raina's heart was in her mouth, and the absurdity of what they had planned hit her full force. She, a college professor from the 21st century, was planning to undo a spell supposedly cast fifteen hundred years ago. Her tendency to madness had taken a strange turn indeed. Perhaps it was she who was under a spell, cast by the compelling and hypnotic Sirona...who at this moment was quite affectionately thanking Niall for his domestic consideration that morning. Raina slunk off to her bedroom to brood, and without realizing it, to fall into an exhausted sleep.

"Raina, you have to read this!" Sirona's words through the door were accompanied by a rapid knocking. Jolted out of sleep, it took her a minute to pull herself together.

"Come to the study as soon as you're awake..." Sirona demanded, her voice trailing away as she flew back to whatever had so aroused her.

"I was about to write to Art, to tell him about all that transpired on the Tor, when I saw this email from him. You must read it for yourself," Sirona said, directing Raina to the computer.

My dear ladies,

I have to wonder what might be going on with the two of you, as the ether here seems much excited. April visits frequently, and we have shared much, but what I need to tell you urgently is this. April has taken to sitting for long spells in the little attic room, staring at the walls. She says she sees words swirling in the paint, most of which make little sense to her, but this morning she ran to my cottage in quite an agitated state, insisting that she's been told she must join you in Glastonbury. As fortune, or the spirits, would have it, she has spring break soon, and so can get away without jeopardizing her studies, though I do believe if she felt she needed to leave immediately, she would, her studies be damned.

She can tell me little else, knowing nothing more herself than that she needs to be with you. I know she is curious about her mother, and it may be no more than that (no more I say, when the magnitude of that importance is obviously beyond my humble understanding), but I sense something else is afoot, that perhaps you might shed some light upon.

I'm willing to get her on her way in a few weeks' time as long as that is acceptable to you, so I await your response. But I beg of you, do not delay. I'm not sure how best to calm this highly agitated young woman of whom I have grown quite fond.

I close by relaying to you that today the lake is a blanket of diamonds, the Goddess's best dress draped out upon the waters. A portent perhaps?
Best,
Art

Pushing herself away from the computer, Raina moved to the window, speechless. April coming here of her own accord, and on the eve of the perilous task they were about to undertake...reunited with her daughter at last, but what would that be like? Art had said she was "curious" about her mother, which left much room for disappointment, if not revulsion. And how would she respond when they told her upon her arrival that they were hoping to use her for their own means, taking her into a forest to free an ensorcelled spirit? If Malcolm had convinced April that Raina was mad, would this not prove the assessment?

Raina put her head against the cool glass of the window as tears of frustration blurred her vision. However it was that Raina had imagined a reunion with her daughter after all these years, it surely wasn't this. She gritted her teeth and clenched her hands. What had she gotten herself...and her daughter...into? Oh, to be back at the University, teaching half-asleep freshman, numbering her days in semesters, and living a boring, simple, invisible life...

"I'm writing back...is there anything you want to say?" Sirona called from the computer, too full of her own positive vision of events to notice Raina's anguish. "This is perfect! April already wanting to come...and arriving here with time enough to get her up to speed...Raina?"

Pivoting from the window, Raina had all she could do not to rage at Sirona. Doing her best to keep herself in check, she faced her friend, her cheeks red with fury and tears.

"This is anything but perfect! I've waited all these years to see my...daughter...a sweet gradual reuniting...not on the verge of putting her in danger! And what if she hates me? What if she's coming here to spew the venom that Malcolm has surely been pouring into her all these years? What then?"

She bit off her words, lest she say more and be sorry for it.

There was no way Sirona saw this coming, nor did she know how to respond to Raina's reading of events, so different from her own. Then again, she reminded herself, she and Raina had lived in vastly different realities for most of their lives. In her excitement, she'd let herself ignore that. Now came a critical test of her healing powers. She must put herself into the troubled heart of another, even to the point of letting go of her own most cherished dreams, if it came to that.

Sirona took Raina's hand and led her to the couch, giving Raina time to calm down and herself time to know best how to frame what she would say. Once they were seated, she began hesitantly, but firmly, deciding that truth would be the best way forward.

"I've been selfish, dear one, blinded by my own desires. When we began this, April was not in the picture, and you were at a turning point in your life, ready, or so I thought, to take a leap, especially as that leap might bring you some respite from years of torment." Sirona paused to try to judge Raina's response, and give her a chance to speak if she so desired, but Raina's tears had not ceased, nor had her head raised in recognition that she was even listening. Sirona had no choice but to continue.

"But now, Goddess be praised, April has found some measure of independence and has sought you out. Concurrently, but maybe not entirely coincidentally, it appears she has a place in our quest."

At this Sirona could feel Raina tense. She rushed on.

"Clearly, April wishes to come here, to see you. I assume we do not want to deny her that, even if we could, but now I see clearly that we cannot and should not compel her to join us on our mission. That must be her decision, freely made."

At that, Raina finally raised her head, the relief on her face so poignant that Sirona was ashamed of herself for not having seen Raina's perception of events earlier.

"And anyway, a spell of undoing would be in jeopardy should any member of the company be there under duress."

"But you have powers of persuasion..." Raina said, not as an accusation, but as a statement of fact. Still, Sirona felt the sting. She bowed her head and struggled with the observation she knew to be true. In that moment, Raina understood that Sirona wrestled with the same conundrum she did -- how does one keep power, whether it be minor or miraculous, from hurting others, from treading on their sovereignty, no matter how well-intentioned one might be?

Now it was Raina's turn to console. She took Sirona's chin in her hand and turned her face toward her own.

"Thank you. We will await April's arrival, see how she...feels about me...give her a chance to understand things and then let her make her own choice, doing our best not to influence her decision. But...if she chooses not to join us, what will we do for a third?"

"We'll figure that out. With the guidance of the Mother, we'll figure it out."

Together, the two women worked on a return message to Art. They decided to tell him everything -- agreeing that he should know, and hoping he might have something to add to their insights. But for now, he should not tell April about the project. Let April come to Glastonbury with nothing but her own desires in tow and see where it goes from there.

By the time they finished, it was well into the day and both women were exhausted from all that had transpired as well as their own emotions about what lay ahead. Rest seemed called for, but Sirona knew that they had at least one more thing to accomplish, and that was to follow Abernathy Whitestone's suggestion that they visit Tintagel and Merlin's Cave. The sooner the better Sirona thought -- a good way to pass the time until April's arrival and, should anything come up as a result of the visit they would have time, hopefully, to deal with it before it was time to turn all their attention to Raina's daughter. She would bring it up at breakfast tomorrow morning. For now, the two friends needed some time alone.

"What say you to an adventure today?" Sirona asked at breakfast, striving for the airiest tone she could muster.

"You mean for a change?" Raina teased, then, "Sure. What do you have in mind?"

"Tintagel and Merlin's Cave. Whitestone suggested it and, for once, I agree with him. If nothing else, it's a delightful trip to the sea. And I think it would be useful, grounding, to actually visit the site. Moreover," Sirona said, pausing for effect, "I can promise you a culinary delight that you won't soon forget."

"Better than pasties and stout?"

"Well, nothing is *better* than that, but this can hold its own...a different kind of delight."

"I suppose you won't give me any clues?"

"Not a one."

"A cave, the ocean, something delicious. I can't imagine refusing that. Is it far?"

"About two hours. Best to time it with the tide, which will be low by early afternoon. Let's say we leave at 11:00?"

Raina smiled, glad the two friends were back on somewhat of an even keel. An outing was brilliant in more ways than one.

Tintagel rests on a cliff, high above the sea, but Sirona guided Raina to the stairs leading down to the water, rough and wild, but well retreated for the time being. Raina couldn't resist. Rolling her pantlegs up past her knees and casting aside her shoes, she waded into the surf and immediately soaked her pants despite having rolled them up, but little did she care. She'd never dreamed she would be wading in the sea off the coast of Cornwall. Then again, she'd never imagined any of this.

"Want to see the cave?" Sirona called, her voice wavering in the wind, aware that they were bounded by nature's clock.

Reluctantly, Raina trudged back onto the beach and picking up her shoes, made her way around rocks and detritus to the mouth of the cave.

It wasn't much, depending on what one's expectations were -- an opening in the rock that if one were persistent, one might climb through to a smaller opening on the other side. Raina and Sirona were content to go some distance in then find rocks that allowed for a halfway comfortable seat. Behind them now, the light from the cave mouth had transformed into a luminescent tear in the darkness, soft-edged, hiding the beach beyond, but graciously sharing enough light with the interior to cover the two women in a grey half-light. They were alone; what few tourists were wandering around were more interested in climbing the heights to the ruins of Tintagel.

A strange awe settled over Raina, the knowledge that she was connected to this place slowly worming its way into her.

"What do you suppose he did here?" she asked.

"Spy on the Duke of Cornwall, according to the legends," Sirona answered, with no small dose of irony. "Tintagel, right above us, is the site of the Duke's keep."

"Do you suppose this was more...habitable in his day?"

"Hard to say. Fifteen hundred years is a long time, even for rock."

"So, if Merlin had a daughter all those years ago, and if the line remained unbroken until my time, that's..."

"...forty-five generations give or take."

"Forty-five women, carrying Merlin's blood through all those years," Raina mused. "Curse or not, they must have had some impact."

"One would hope so, but women have not had free reign to realize their potential even unto this age. And anything that had a hint of magic to it...the witch purges were no joke. Any woman who stood out in any way was fair game for all manner of danger. Best to keep any talents under wraps, or, if revealed, done so cautiously...often allowing or being forced to have men take the credit for it."

Unbidden, the thought of her Wonder Woman figurine came to Raina's mind. Women's power safely expressed in a fantastical figure -- relegated to fiction.

"Odd, don't you think, that Merlin's child was female rather than male?"

"Well, even a magician, apparently, cannot control what happens in the womb, but on a metaphysical level, Merlin having a daughter makes for some interesting sense."

"Explain."

"May I?" Sirona asked, reaching for Raina's necklace.

"Of course." Raina reached around and undid the clasp then carefully handed the pendent of interlocking circles to her friend. In the dim light the silver shone as though lit from within. Sirona lovingly traced the two circles with a finger, then traced and re-traced the central almond shape where the two circles overlapped.

"This symbol is one of the most dynamic, revelatory symbols known to us. It holds...everything. It is known as the Vesica Piscis with the central vesica referred to as the mandorla. The entire form is a multiplicity of sacred geometry, its proportions and harmonies produce phi and mirror relationships seen in nature. There is so much more to say and discover about its geometrical meanings, but it is the metaphysical aspect that concerns us here."

Again, Sirona ran her finger around the lower circle. "Imagine this as the physical world, the world of the material, what we might refer to as *immanence*. And this," a loving touch to the upper circle, "the world of spirit, transcendence..."

Raina tentatively reached out her hand, "and this," she said, pointing to the mandorla, "the meeting of the two?"

"Exactly!"

Raina felt a thrill of recognition, awakening, course through her.

"The central vesica," Sirona continued, "represents the essence, the ground of being, the marriage of immanence and transcendence, material and spiritual, the true nature of all being..."

"...the dark and the light, masculine and feminine...all the dualities in relationship..." Raina said.

Sirona looked at Raina in admiration and relief.

"My God," Raina exploded, "where have I been all my life?"

Sirona's laughter bounced off the cave walls, encircling them like the music of the fairy world.

"You've been living in -- mired in -- a world that clings to dualism like life itself, when in fact, true reality is the very opposite. Our dualism will be our undoing."

"But it comes to us so easily, is it our nature then? Are we doomed?"

"I don't believe so," Sirona said, serious again. "It takes some work to live in the space of unity, but I believe it's only been the last two thousand years or so that dualism has been so pronounced. Indigenous peoples all around the world understood -- understand -- that spirit inhabits all matter, and matter can be the pathway to spirit. And that perspective, much to our purpose here, is central to Celtic thought."

"Merlin," Raina breathed.

"Yes."

"My experience at the Well..." Raina said as pieces fell together in her mind.

"A rather powerful example of actually feeling, even seeing, the unity of matter and spirit," Sirona agreed, "and the attendant power and beauty of living, if ever so briefly, in the wholeness."

"So, it is not lost entirely," Raina mused.

"Not lost at all! It is around us all the time, but most are blind to it, or afraid of it. Our modern world is increasingly structured so that spirit and matter do not meet, except in the hands of and by the *permission* of the select few."

"So how did that come about?"

"Perhaps the roots go deeper than what can be known from this perspective, but there is no question that Rome and the form of Christianity it created -- and spread -- swung a cleaver through the mandorla, sundering the immanent from the transcendent."

"But haven't I seen Christ represented by the fish symbol, the mandorla itself?"

Sirona sighed, "And there lies the tragic irony. You're right -- Christ has been represented as immanence and spirit in one -- the holy trinity of God, Man and Spirit. But the tragedy is that the vision of unity he could have brought to the world is trapped in his being, and his alone, externalizing the path to wholeness, so that people worship the man rather than seeking the unity in themselves..."

"...trapped in one man. Like Merlin, ensorcelled, trapped..." Raina said, her voice hushed in half-formed thought.

Had there been more light in the cave, Raina would have seen the look of wonderment on Sirona's face, but her mind was spinning, knitting together what had only been disparate thoughts until now.

"From what little I know of the church," Raina mused, "while they might represent Christ as the mandorla, their rules all denigrate the material, essentially making our humanness a sin. It's always troubled me -- made no sense. I guess that's why I've never been a church person. I could never explain it well to those who were, but so much of what churches taught just went against the grain for me."

As it did for Merlin, Sirona thought, but kept it to herself for now.

"I once saw a bumper sticker," Raina continued, "that said *Love God Not His Creation.*"

Sirona shivered. "There lies our doom."

The two sat in silence for a spell, listening to their own thoughts and the distant pulse of the ocean, until, tentatively, Raina broke the silence.

"So, there is a connection between releasing Merlin -- or rather his spirit -- and healing the dualism, bringing us back to integration."

"Precisely. At least, that is the hope," Sirona said, handing the pendant back to Raina. Before returning it to her neck Raina ran her fingers over every inch of it with renewed appreciation. As she sought the mandorla, however, she felt the piece of metal in the design that bisected it vertically.

"And what of this?" Raina said, a bit distressed by the interruption of the almond shaped vesica.

"That is a Christian addition...the Sword of St. Michael which is often seen as representing *purpose* and its importance in living a full life."

"Or of binding the free flow and interplay of the two worlds."

"Oh, my dear," Sirona said, unable to contain herself any longer. "It appears your mind has caught fire. You could see it that way, or resist it, as some of us have resisted the Christian overlays for centuries, keeping our pagan rituals and understandings alive and seeing them as true, regardless of efforts to obscure them. Still, the idea that *purpose* is central to a life well lived is an essential teaching, of which there are a few -- perhaps many -- in the Christian way."

"So then, what is the ultimate purpose of releasing Merlin's spirit, if we are able to do so? We cannot turn back the clock, Mr. Tuttle's inventions notwithstanding. We cannot wipe the slate clean and return to the pure world of the ancient past."

"True enough. And I doubt the pre-Christian world was all that pure, for all its metaphysical insight. Our proper relationship with the past is to learn from it as best we can, but not be bound by it. That, too, is represented in the Vesica Piscis. Life is interplay, interconnection, things combined to make something entirely new and, hopefully, better. Evolutionary alchemy. Our world is broken, and anything that is severed which was meant to be whole is plagued and full of contagion, the only remedy for which is reunification."

"So, releasing Merlin's spirit is a step in that direction..."

"Merlin represents the old ways," Sirona said, her voice full of longing, "reverence for the earth and the knowledge of its power, as well as the necessity for balance and integration. You've seen the Magician card in the Tarot deck? *As above, so below.* The magician is the physical image that represents the mandorla, the marriage of heaven and earth, immanence and transcendence, and the role of humanity to foster the connection. With Merlin's spirit lost to the world, so too is lost the locus, the impetus, the energy of those understandings. I have no idea how it will play out if we are successful, but releasing that energy to be free in the world again, unrestrained, is a beginning."

"And Nimue's curse on his offspring?"

"Much the same. Imagine releasing all that potential? While we don't know exactly what Nimue's curse was, we know from your experience, and perhaps your mother's, that it kept Merlin's descendants in thrall in some way. To release that..."

Now Raina squirmed in excitement.

"I've had a thought. Who is to say that there was only one offspring per generation? Even if here and there, there had been a second child...or more. Over fifteen hundred years, Merlin's bloodline would have exploded..."

Sirona sucked in the generative air of the cave.

"Imagine the potential waiting to be unleashed," she exhaled.

The two friends sat, overwhelmed by their thoughts. Then, of one accord, they rose from the rocks and made their way to the light, pausing at the mouth of the cave to let their eyes adjust to the brilliance of the day and take deep draughts of the sea air.

"Do you think we can do it? Break the curse?" Raina asked, almost afraid to voice her fears. But Sirona answered with conviction.

"Every curse has a counter, some action that will release it. Remember the words on the Tor -- *embrace the curse*. Think of all the fairytales you know. Bastardized as they are, they all hold a kernel of the truth of curses. The prince kisses the cursed princess, the fair young woman kisses the beast-man. To run from a curse cements it. To embrace it, to see the good behind the veil, vanquishes it."

"Only love can overcome evil...and the fear that feeds it..." Raina whispered.

To speak would unleash centuries of pent up emotions, so Sirona only grabbed Raina's hand as they stood silently, letting the sea speak for her as each wave brought it closer and closer to the shore.

Raina's stomach rumbled.

"I believe you mentioned a *culinary delight?*"

"Indeed, I did! Shall we ascend?"

At the cafe, Sirona ordered them "creamed tea." What Raina expected was a cup of tea with cream in it...a disappointment as tea wasn't going to satisfy her hunger and moreover, she liked her tea unadulterated. But what appeared was something else altogether. A cup of tea, yes, and black, accompanied by a large scone topped with clotted cream and jam. Raina's mouth literally watered at the sight of it.

"Go ahead," Sirona laughed. "Tuck in!"

Raina's pleasure-centers erupted. The marriage of jam, cream and pastry was like nothing she had ever tasted before.

"This cream -- it's better than any whipped cream I've ever tasted."

"Because it's not whipped cream. True clotted cream is made with unpasteurized milk -- not a common item in the States."

Talking around another mouthful, Raina asked, "Is everything in England so delicious?"

"I wouldn't say so, no," Sirona admitted. "We're not really known for our culinary skills. But if you're finding our food so delightful, you'd best beware of France."

As soon as she'd said it, she regretted it. Soon enough they'd be venturing into the ancient woodlands of Brittany, to encounter what, they had no idea. Raina bore the tremor, then let it pass. She was determined to enjoy the moment, the way the bitter tea bit into the sweet. The play of opposites, she thought. The essence of life.

They watched the sea below, the waves crashing against the rocks, the spray like birds or butterflies, something magical taking flight, then falling gleefully back into the sea to do it all over again. The sight caught Raina's spirit. She thought of children, doing the same thing over and over again for the pure joy of it.

"Such beauty," was all she could manage.

Sirona leaned toward the window, as though she would fly out and join the dance below.

"Beauty is the handmaiden of the soul..." she said.

Once away from the magic of Tintagel, more personal concerns began to crowd back into Raina's thoughts.

"I'm terrified of meeting April," she said at last.

"But it's been your dream for years," Sirona objected.

"I know, but now that it's actually going to happen, I'm terrified. What if she hates me? I left her after all, and Malcolm has had all these years to poison her against me."

"No one could hate you dear one," Sirona said, her heart full of love for her friend.

"Ha! Not true. Malcolm does."

"He fears you. That's a different thing."

Raina sat with that for a minute. Sirona continued, "At worst, your daughter is not sure of her feelings, but the longing for the mother is primal. She will want to know you and once she does...well, your beautiful being will do the rest."

24

April

April arrived in Heathrow at 10:00 am, barely functioning from lack of sleep. If Raina had been afraid she wouldn't recognize her, she needn't have worried. Picking out the auburn-haired girl who looked quite like her memory of her young mother would have been easy even in a crowd twice the size. Her heart jumped at the sight of her, her young body lithe and obviously home to abundant vitality even as it dragged itself toward them. Raina wanted nothing more than to run to her and sweep her off her feet in the hug that had been waiting nearly two decades to happen, but she hung back, not having any idea how this daughter of hers would react to her after all these years.

Raging anxiety had left Raina nauseous that morning, the long drive to the airport doing nothing to ease her distress. Better if she had let Sirona meet April on her own, she couldn't help but think. But here they were. Busy with luggage and jostling crowds, however, made it easier to by-pass awkward greetings and potentially unwanted hugs.

Once in the car, April crawled into the back seat, apologized for being nearly narcoleptic and immediately fell asleep, for which Raina was eternally grateful. Having the first conversation with your daughter in nearly twenty years in a car, after a trans-Atlantic flight, was not, in her mind, the best situation. Sirona and Raina rode in silence, honoring April's need for sleep, which didn't abate until they were nearly home.

As April stumbled through the door of Sirona's apartment, she mumbled one word.

"Food?"

Luckily, Niall was once again providing a delicious repast. The four of them silently buried themselves in the comfort of food, although Raina found it hard to eat, her anxiety tightening her throat like the strings on a pouch. When the meal was finally over and April seemed to be coming around a bit, Sirona declared that she needed to help Niall clear and wash and that perhaps Raina would like to take April for a stroll in the Gardens, giving Raina a clandestine look that said, *You know the power of the Gardens..."*

On the way, Raina chatted nervously about Glastonbury and how much she was enjoying her stay with Sirona. All very casual stuff. But once in the gardens, Raina hoped that April would find her voice. They took a seat by the pool, the final fall of the Chalice spring providing a soothing background to their talk.

"So," Raina began, "you've been spending time at your Grandmother's cottage. It's a lovely place isn't it?"

April nodded, "I miss her. She was wonderful to me."

A knot formed in Raina's throat. So, her daughter got the motherly nourishment that she did not. She was both grateful and a bit jealous at once, but gratitude won out. That her mother stepped in to cover for Raina...what a blessing.

"I'm surprised that Malcolm allowed that," she said, risking getting into troubled waters.

"Grandma had money, and Dad wanted it. Anything she gave us was supposed to be for me, but Dad always found a way to use it however he saw fit. Still, he was careful how much time I spent with her, but every moment was precious to me. And, he had his own leverage. He made Grandma swear she would never say anything to me about you, or she would never see me again. Of course, I knew nothing of this through the years, until Grandma got sick and knew she didn't have long. At that point she felt she had nothing to fear from my father, so she said what she wanted to say. We didn't have much time, but she told me that she had watched you through the years."

Despite her efforts to hold them back, tears rolled down Raina's cheeks as she bit her lip. April put her hand on her mother's.

"She loved you."

"But she never...why did she never..." Afraid she would begin to pour out years of pent up grief, Raina clenched her teeth and stayed silent.

"She was ashamed of herself for leaving you. Then, the more time passed, the more difficult it was for her to imagine you would want anything to do with her."

Raina could only shake her head and let the tears come. When at last she could speak, she whispered, "and I did the same to you...but I tried, I really tried."

"Dad made it impossible for you, I know that now. I don't blame you. Whatever it is that plagued both you and Grandma...it must have been horrible, and to be so alone through it all. In her final days, Grandma did her best to explain it and made me promise to find you. But it wasn't until I was in college that I had any freedom at all to pursue that...but always with Dad on the lookout."

"But now you're here..." Raina said, her anguish subsiding in the face of the miracle of her daughter's presence.

"I am, aren't I?" April said, her cheerfulness on full display. "Now that I'm older, I'm finding ways to get around my father. And, finally, here I am with you in this beautiful place!"

Glastonbury, the Chalice Well gardens, the perfect setting for this blessing -- her daughter's presence and a sense of her mother's life, and love for her, at last. Drying her eyes, she asked April what she now longed to know.

"What was your childhood like?"

April was all too eager to pour out her story. Her earliest memories were of a doting father, who kept a comfortable and happy enough home. But as the years passed and April grew more conscious of living without a mother, things changed. The more April grew in curiosity about her mother, the deeper Malcolm sank into quick anger and meanness.

"He would tell me horrible stories about you, but something in me resisted them. Especially as they became more malicious and disjointed, I sensed that they were fictions. By the time I was in high school, he began turning his venom on me, claiming I was 'just like my mother,' a claim which, contrary to his intentions, I welcomed, though I never let him know that. Eventually, he came to the edge of violence, but when he'd raise his hand, a look from me would make him retreat. It was as though I could look right through him to see the small man inside, and I think he somehow sensed that."

"It must have been very difficult for you to grow up essentially parentless," Raina said, remembering the pain of her own childhood, basically raising herself.

"It wasn't easy, but I had Grandmother...and my books. I read voraciously. I loved fantasy novels, buried myself in them, and was particularly drawn to the Arthurian legends."

At that Raina's eyes went wide. Wait until Sirona heard this! Then again, knowing what she now knew (although it was still taking some getting used to), it made all the sense in the world that April would read the legends around her own ancestral heritage.

"And..." April continued, "there were my dreams."

"Dreams?" Raina exclaimed, her heart nearly jumping out of her chest. Then she asked, though she dreaded the answer, "What were they like?"

"So beautiful! It was like all the stuff of the fantasies I so loved followed me right into my dreamworld."

"Nothing...dark?" Raina barely knew how to broach the subject of her own night horrors.

"Of course, everything has its dark side, the villain who wants to stifle all the joy in the world," April said laughing. But then serious again, she continued, "but whenever anything like that got close, there was always a woman there to protect me. She was never far away, as though she was hovering over me, around me, like a mist, but capable of dispelling the darkness -- almost like she sucked it into herself and turned it into light. I loved her, counted on her."

Raina's heart twisted. All she had ever hoped for was that April had known a good life. Now, despite the knowledge that Malcolm had been a destructive force, April somehow had had the ability to rise above his malevolence and find a peace of her own making. A weight the size of a lifetime dropped from Raina. April was whole and healthy, and now she was here.

"Come," Raina said, holding her hand out to April, "I have something to show you."

Taking her mother's hand, April followed her mother up through the yew grove, past the mother goddess statue, and straight to the Well. As they stepped down into the recessed area, Raina stood back and watched her daughter walk to the edge of the Well. Standing behind her, she couldn't see how April was reacting until at last April turned to her, tears in her eyes.

"It's the most beautiful thing I've ever seen!" April exclaimed, the tears running down her youthful skin, adding a sheen to her already rosy glow. *There are the tears,* Raina thought. *Are there always tears at the Well? Are they our inner springs rushing out to meet their source?*

Raina moved up to stand next to her daughter, the two of them staring into the Well. In a hushed voice Raina asked, "Do you see her?"

"Who?" April answered.

"The Goddess of the Well" Raina answered, lost in the memory of her first experience there.

April turned to her mother.

"All I see is you," she said.

That night, after April fell into a jet-lagged sleep, Raina told Sirona everything the two had shared in the gardens. When Raina spoke of April's dreams, Sirona's face wrinkled in thought.

"Is it possible," she said, finally, "that somehow you took on the darkness for her? It would explain, at least in part, the depth of your own suffering."

Raina took in a shaky breath.

"If I'd been knowingly offered that opportunity, I would have done it gladly, and if that is the case, then..."

Sirona placed a gentle hand on her friend's cheek. The thought they shared needn't be spoken aloud.

"May I ask a favor?" April had bounced out of bed, all the effects of jet-lag apparently overcome, thanks to youthful vigor.

"You can always *ask*," Sirona replied, already playing the sardonic aunt.

April took it in stride, then blurted out, "Could we go to Stonehenge? Oh my God, I've always wanted to see it! Is it far?"

"About 80 kilometers -- a little over an hour's drive. You're ready to get back in a car?"

Apparently, the answer was too obvious for April to bother with.

"Then can we?"

Sirona and Raina looked at each other -- here it was, that youthful energy, always wanting to be on the go.

Stonehenge was old hat for Sirona, but Raina had never seen it either and now the prospect seemed delightful to her.

"Well, *Auntie Sirona,*" Raina said, enjoying the play, "what say you? May we? Pretty please?"

Unable to hold back her smile any longer, Sirona suggested they invite Niall along and beg him to make a picnic lunch to boot.

"I'll get online and be sure we can get tickets and reserve our time," Sirona added, the old pro having the outing well in hand.

Within the hour, they were ready to go. Niall agreed to drive to give Sirona a break after having made the trip to London and back the day before -- an offer that Sirona gratefully accepted. When Raina stepped out of the bedroom wearing her "fairy cloak" April was delighted.

"Mom! You look fantastic!"

It was the "Mom" that caught her. Perhaps the sweetest word in any language.

The journey was full of happy chatter, ooh's and ah's from April as they whisked through the undulating green of the English countryside.

"Giftshop first or straight to the stones?" Niall asked as they bundled out of the car, but April was already on the path, nearly running toward the famous site, leaving the elders no choice but to follow behind. By the time they had gotten to it themselves, April had already fairly skipped around the entire circumference. Out of breath, red-cheeked, she threw out her arms and proclaimed, "Isn't it wonderful?"

Indeed, it was. Raina had no words for what she felt, but kept imagining that, for all the splendor above ground, even more was going on beneath, though she had no idea what that might be. The four made their way around the stones together, mostly speechless, each in their own world of wonder.

"Can't we get any closer?" April asked finally, straining like a filly on a tether. "I want to touch the stones!"

"Alas," Niall answered. "So many people have done just that, that they have had to rope it off for protection. It is a shame, though, that such an important place is off-limits to folks."

April stared at the stones as though she was trying to touch them with her eyes.

"There are things to know here," she said, "but I can't get to it from this distance."

"They call to you..." Sirona said, half question, have statement.

"They do."

Just then, two crows swooped down and landed some distance away from the foursome.

"Look," April said, "it's Morgan le Fay and Merlin, come to see us." Glances exchanged among the three.

"Imagine," April continued, "that they suddenly took on their human form and approached us. What would we say to them?" After a strained silence, Sirona came to the rescue.

"I think if they went to all that trouble," Sirona began, "that it wouldn't be us old folks they'd want to hear from, but you. What would *you* say?"

"I'd ask them to tell me where we went wrong...how we've made such a mess of things." All April's playfulness seemed to have melted away, and in its place stood a very serious young woman.

"Or maybe," Sirona said, as much to herself as April, "maybe they are the ones who would want to know what *you* know...how you see the world and what they could have done to alter the outcome of our present time?"

April gave Sirona a strange look, and in that moment, something passed between them. Raina watched the exchange with curiosity and renewed wonderment that this was her child.

After they finished circumnavigating the stones, the women went into the gift shop while Niall went to the car to retrieve the lunches. As people do, each wandered in their own direction, seeking out what interested them most, but April and Sirona soon tired of the goods, and sought out Raina, who, they discovered, was transfixed in front of a display case.

"What is it?" Sirona asked her friend as they came to her side. Raina pointed to a replica of a Neolithic pot etched in a linear design.

"Yes, it's like yours." Sirona said. "Don't you remember us telling you so?"

"But, how...?" Raina was clearly struggling with her discovery.

Sirona put her finger to Raina's head and tapped it. "There's more in here than we can ever know the extent of. Ancestral knowledge my dear. No surprise that it came out in your pottery."

"You're a potter?" April squealed a bit too loud for the gift shop.

"Not a potter really. I've only just played around with it some."

"She's a potter," Sirona said, "she just hasn't had the freedom to know it or practice it."

April eyed her mother with renewed admiration, while Sirona and Raina exchanged a glance pregnant with all the unsaid things that would, sooner or later, have to be shared with April. And time was running out.

That night Sirona and Raina let themselves be delighted by April's monologue about her love of the Arthurian tales. After seeing Stonehenge -- myth come alive -- she was bursting. Sirona was bursting as well, dying to tell April that she was, indeed, standing in the land of Arthur, but for now, it was April's time. Moreover, Sirona could see that Raina was delighting in every word that came out of her daughter's mouth. So they let her talk, until they could hold their eyes open no longer.

At breakfast the next morning, Sirona had some interesting news for her guests. She had just received an email from Beatrice -- she had found the cauldron and was hoping to bring it to them later that day.

"Cauldron?" April asked, her curiosity more than a little piqued.

"Long story, luv," Sirona said, as nonchalantly as she could manage. "We'll fill you in when it gets here." Well, that was that. For the rest of the day, the tension in the apartment was palpable, each woman full of anticipation for her own reasons. No day had ever been longer. Mid-morning, Sirona pulled Raina aside to tell her that she had thought she should contact Rowan.

"How do you think April would handle that?"

"How is April going to handle any of this?" Raina said, the protective mother on full display. Then, "I'm at a loss here. Perhaps we should let Rowan decide for us. If she wants to be here..."

By 2:00, the front window was never without one of the women on watch. When Beatrice finally arrived, they would all have crowded into the doorway, but Raina gently pulled April aside as Beatrice made her way into the apartment carrying a wrapped bundle as though carrying a babe.

Once inside, she placed the bundle in the center of the room while the three women gathered around. Carefully, Beatrice unwrapped the precious artifact, revealing a large pot decorated in swirls and interlaced knots, stained in hues of blue, yellow and green. Its shape was perfect and for something that was over one thousand years old, it seemed to have suffered not the slightest crack or nick. Nor was it heavy, considering its size.

What was most amazing, however, was the effect that it had on the women. A skeptic might put it down to the pot's beauty and age alone and perhaps that was all it was, but the women felt a kind of reverence that was hard to describe. One by one, they reached out to touch it, gently running their hands around the rim and tracing the flowing designs with their fingers, and when at last they drew back, their skin retained a tingle, a presence, as though someone, or something, still held them in its grip.

But of the four women, it was Raina who was most affected. When it was her turn at the artifact, she got down on her knees and held her hands on either side of the vessel, as though she herself was forming it on the wheel, and when she did so, she felt the pot spin beneath her hands, slippery, malleable. She pulled her hands away, afraid she had damaged it in some way, but the pot was as it had been, complete, perfect, beautiful. Hungry for what she had felt, she held the pot again and closed her eyes. Again, the cauldron spun beneath her hands as though it was alive, perpetually in a state of becoming.

It was April who broke the spell.

"I've never seen anything like this. What is it?"

It was time then. They could wait no longer. Either April would accept what lay ahead or not. It was Beatrice who began.

"This is a thousand-year-old artifact, according to the stories, fashioned by a particularly gifted potter for some important future need..."

"And that future need," Sirona continued, "we believe is upon us." She took a deep breath and studied April's youthful, innocent face.

"You know the legends...know what is said about Merlin's demise, how he was ensorcelled by his own magic at the hands of Nimue..."

April's eyes went wide. "Yes..."

"Well..." Sirona began.

Now April was looking anxiously at each of the women in turn, moving from face to face, seeing the deadly seriousness that sat on their features.

"We believe," Sirona continued, "that it has fallen to us to try to...release Merlin's spirit at last, in the hopes of bringing his ancient wisdom back into the world."

April was speechless, but Raina had a sense of what her daughter would ask if she had been able to find the words. Taking April's hands in her own -- still throbbing from the touch of the cauldron -- and fixing April's eyes with her own, she said, "I know you are going to find this hard to believe," there seemed no way to break this gradually, "but we have discovered that, though it wasn't mentioned in the legends, at least the ones we know of, Merlin had a daughter. And I, and therefore you, and your grandmother, are descendants of that daughter." Silence sat on the room like a lid. Raina held onto April's hands as though ready to pull her out of whatever deep waters she might fall into.

"You're not kidding me?" April asked, her voice so hushed Raina couldn't quite get a read on the emotions behind it.

"About such a thing..."

A knock on the door interrupted what Sirona was about to say. It was Rowan. As she entered, April's eyes went larger still if that was even possible. Rowan took in the scene in an instant, and while the cauldron called to her, she sensed that it was April that needed her attention most.

"You've told her then?" she asked Sirona, who nodded affirmation.

Rowan went to where April sat, and knelt beside her, her knees creaking and groaning as she did so. Raina still held April's hands, tethering her, so Rowan lifted a gnarled hand and placed it gently on April's shoulder. With a voice like the sound of a gentle wind in the trees, she spoke soothingly to April.

"Hush child, hush. All is well. You are safe here, sheltered by more love than you can imagine."

April closed her eyes and took a deep breath, drawing in the comfort Rowan exuded.

"Reach within," Rowan intoned, "feel the ages inside you, like the rings on a tree. You are here because of all that went before, all the women who carried a gift of insight, wisdom, and deep connection to the natural world -- carried it despite the winds that blew against them. Your grandmother, your mother, and so many women before, and now you are here in this moment of recognition and reconciliation. You are blessed beyond all imagining."

Not just April, but Raina as well, linked as she was to April, fell into Rowan's words and was strengthened by them.

Slowly, Rowan withdrew from April's side and Raina took away her hands, giving April the space to digest this new information about herself. When April opened her eyes, her face creased into a cautious smile.

Looking at the four women in turn, she said, "So, what's the plan?"

25

Of Blood and Bone

There was no holding April back. Typical of youthful plasticity, April absorbed the whole story like a plant drinking up the rain. Before the women could even put to her the role they hoped she'd play, she begged to be a part of the adventure.

The next few days were spent putting everything in place. Liselle had sent maps and everything she could gather about where it was rumored Merlin was "buried." Niall gave his attention to gathering what they would need for the journey, and Rowan had collected herbs and Rowan bark, as well as a time-slowing tincture from Tuttle, taking April with her who did *not* stand at the door, but scoured every corner of the strange man's shop.

Evenings were spent going over the directions gleaned on the Tor.

"*A cauldron* and *Rowan branches* we have," Sirona said, ticking off a list she had memorized. "*It must be three* thankfully has resolved itself."

"There was some doubt?" April asked.

"Your mother was concerned about putting you in harm's way," Sirona answered, while Raina gave a blushing shrug, doing her best to hide the fact that she still wished April could stay safe at home.

"You should know, however," Sirona said, holding April with her eyes, "it also says *the youngest first.* It is not clear yet in what way you would be *first*, but be warned that you may be called upon in some manner to stand alone."

If Niall had been there, he might have reminded them how April had plunged out ahead at Stonehenge, her eagerness on full display. This, however, might be quite a different thing.

"What else," April asked, skipping over the *first* issue.

"Well, there's *the poet speaks...*" Sirona continued.

"I've had some thoughts about that," Raina said, pulling out the slender volume of Yule Poems.

The minute she saw it, April exclaimed, "I know that book! Grandmother used to read it to me, especially around Christmas time."

"Do you know if it was she who wrote it?" Raina asked, excitement in her voice.

"Oh yes, it was her work, and she bound it herself as well. I remember watching her do it."

"Was this at the cottage?" Raina asked.

"No. She had a small apartment in town and only went to the cottage from time to time. I only got to go there -- to the cottage -- once or twice in her later years. It was as though the cottage was a secret, a hiding place for her."

This was information it was going to take Raina time to digest, as was the surety that her mother had written and bound the small book she now held with a new reverence.

A slight shake of the head helped to bring her back to the work at hand. "There have been phrases here and there in the poems that seem to speak to the issue at hand...like this...

Magic folk of ancient time
Held in verse, sung in rhyme

Circle round like swirling mist
Our eyelids they have sometimes kissed

Yet our world to them is gray
Their eyes can only see that way

Lest we light the brightest flames
And sing aloud in joy their names..."

Sirona moved to the edge of her seat. "Brilliant" she said. "This suggests that we should wear bright colors, bring fire..."

"And call out his name..." April added, her excitement growing as well. "Is there more?"

"Maybe," Raina said. "There are lines here and there, like...

A heart that's true, a mind that's free,

and

One and the same are youth and age,
Time is timeless, knows the sage..."

"That could be about you and me, Mom, one young and one...ah...older...but we both share his blood and in that way are the same."

"And," Sirona chimed in, "*time is timeless* -- Merlin's spirit is trapped in time. That might be very important to consider..."

"There's something here about the poetry itself," Raina continued.

> *There's more in this than first is thought,*
> *With care the ancient rhymes were wrought.*

"Then, in the same poem it says,

> *Mystery craves unearthly dance,*
> *Some things best seen through sideways glance."*

"So," April said, afire with thought, "the poems are supposedly about the time between Thanksgiving and Solstice, but maybe there are indeed clues running through them, like a single special thread running through the weave of the thing."

"My mother couldn't have known about all this and kept it to herself...could she?"

"Who knows?" Sirona said. "Or maybe she just wrote these things without realizing their significance to our quest."

"Or maybe," Raina said, tentatively, "the ancient blood was speaking through her without her being conscious of it." Her head reeling, Raina set the book aside.

"May I?" Sirona asked, remembering the early days when Raina was somewhat possessive of the little book.

"Of course," Raina replied, glad now to have the help of other eyes to plumb the secrets that suddenly seemed to be tumbling from the poems. Sirona let the book fall open in her lap and read,

Swirling time in spiral coils,
Spinning out in life's drear toils,

Merry met and meet a friend,
What was once is yet again.

"Destiny. Is it possible we are caught in it, acting out something that was decided by something other than us?" Raina asked, feeling the possibility of being part of a prophecy pushing at her, urging her forward.

"I think," April said, tentatively, "each of us should read through the book on our own and make note of what speaks to us and come together again tomorrow. As well as these little Easter eggs we're finding, there may be an overall, how can I say it, *attitude* revealed that might be useful to us."

"Someone else can take it tonight," Raina said, yawning deeply. "I'm up to the brim."

"Auntie S," April offered, "you want it first?"

Sirona raised her eyebrows at the nickname, but was already well under the spell of this young woman's delightful blend of intellect and merriment. She could live with *Auntie S.*

"I'm not much better off than your Mom at this point -- it's all yours, sweetheart, but don't stay up too late."

Hugs all around and off to bed with the elders, while April curled up on the couch, running her hands across her grandmother's book, as though she was caressing her dear, wrinkled face. "Miss you Grams," she whispered, then opened the little book, ready to read it with new eyes.

Disheveled hair, dressing gown askew, a pool of spilled coffee left untended, Sirona sat at the kitchen table furiously scribbling. Raina had never seen her friend so unkempt.

"Good heavens? What's happening here?"

Sirona looked up at her friend, struggling to bring her into focus.

"Have you been up all night?" Raina asked.

"Just early this morning," Sirona replied, still only half returned to her surroundings.

Raina moved around to Sirona's side and saw the Yule Poems open on the table amid hastily drawn images and notes.

"You've found something..." Raina said, as April stumbled into the kitchen, yawning and stretching, then clearly alarmed by the intensity of the two women.

"Come here, honey...I think your Auntie S has found something important if I can only get her back to reality in order to share it with us," Raina said.

"It's all here!" Sirona said at last, a tinge of mania in her voice. "All through these poems, the theme of marrying heaven and earth, the transcendent and the immanent, and drawing the knowledge of the pre-Christian past into present awareness, all in the context of the return of Arthur, the Lord and Lady...and of course, by extension, Merlin. Either Morgan was a prophet or a conduit through which the universe spoke...or both. I think we can forgive your mother, Raina, for her failings if this was the destiny she was carrying. A heavy load indeed. As I read these poems, any doubts at all about what we hope to accomplish have been dispelled."

"But these aren't new ideas...this could be a coincidence..." Raina said, her skepticism rising in an urge to protect her friend from false hope.

"What is coincidence? The context for our quest coming together like this belies coincidence. And there's more," Sirona plunged on. Her hand shook slightly as she turned the pages of the book.

"Here, in the poem you noted last night that talks about the *sideways glance*. A few stanzas before that reads,

That wine within the goblet pour
Then look therein and you'll see more

"In the poem, the wine refers to the poems themselves, the *ancient rhymes*. But coupled with the mention of the goblet and the sideways glance, it gives us direction on how to proceed with our ritual of release."

"Are you sure?" Raina said, worrying that her friend was reading more into things than was called for.

"Absolutely! I've been struggling with what exactly we're supposed to do once -- and if -- we find the cave. As I read this, my neck prickled. It's all here. The goblet is the cauldron, not a far-fetched correlation that, as through history the two vessels have often been named interchangeably. The wine is the concoction we'll make of herbs and whatever else Rowan chooses – and very importantly, a drop of time tincture, just enough to slow things down, ever so slightly. Finally, some water from the Chalice Well, and the whole thing stirred with the Rowan branch. Then..." Sirona looked up to be sure that Raina and April were still listening. "...then, we look askance...we look into the cauldron rather than anywhere in the cave itself, and there, we will *see more*. We'll call the spirit out."

Now April was wide awake. "Auntie S! That's brilliant!"

But Raina's skepticism was still running wild. "How will we *call the spirit out*?"

April was all but jumping up and down where she stood..."*With ancient rhyme* of course."

"And I suppose that ancient rhyme of release is also somewhere in these poems?" Raina said, feeling like she was the only realistic one in the room.

Sirona stood, faced her friend and, leaning against the table, folded her arms and said, "No. Not in these poems...in you."

April clapped her hands joyously, but Raina's doubt was evident on her face and her stony silence.

"Mom! You can do this!" April enthused.

"Remember the poem that literally fell out of you on Imbolc?" Sirona reminded her. "It's part of your inheritance dear one. You really must accept that, embrace your power. The success of our mission depends on it -- it really does."

Then Sirona turned to April. "And so, my dear night owl, did you discover anything last night?"

April struggled to pull her eyes away from her mother, whom she'd been looking at with deep admiration and affection.

"Nothing like what you've found," she said at last, "but I did find something."

"Do tell," Sirona said, smiling broadly.

"Well, I was thinking a lot about the youngest -- me -- being first and these words jumped out at me...

To turn life's wheel fore or back,

Walk the wood on thine own track

"I think I fell asleep with the book in my hands, because the next thing I knew I woke up and the book had fallen to the floor, but in the meantime, I had had a dream. I was walking in the woods, not alone, but ahead of everyone else and every step I took turned time backwards. I could tell because fallen leaves were flying back into the trees and summer leaves were turning into buds. All very interesting, but not frightening, because I knew the people behind me literally had my back, and the turning back of time was part of why we were there."

"So... when we get to the forest," Sirona said, "you take the lead."

"It appears so," April said, smiling from ear to ear.

Sirona was beaming. "I think we have a plan! The pieces are fitting together too perfectly to be incorrect."

Raina heaved a huge sigh. "So," she said, looking at Sirona, her face not yet ready to smile, "if I go write a poem, will you at least comb your hair?"

"And I'll make breakfast!" April said, twirling away from them and heading to the refrigerator.

"Is that safe?" Sirona asked.

But Raina was already out of the room, and April was busy cracking eggs.

Over a delicious breakfast of "garden omelets," as April called them, Sirona suggested that they take a stroll in the Chalice Gardens. They'd been working hard and had discovered much. Best to give their minds a rest and seek some renewal at the Well. April had not been there since she had first arrived, so the excursion appealed to her, and Raina needed little excuse to be in that cherished place.

The day was stunning for mid-March and the sun on their faces was a balm. They ambled and chatted, and watched other people doing the same. All three took a drink from the Lion's Head then playfully tossed droplets of the sacred water at each other, anointing each in turn in friendship and shared purpose, delighting in being free for the moment of the stress of what lay ahead.

When they arrived at the Well, they found themselves alone, the awareness of other visitors receding into stillness. Instinctively and without a word spoken, they clasped hands and circled the Well. Whatever each was experiencing, they kept to themselves as they gazed in silence into the depths of the sacred waters. How long they stood that way was hard to say, but eventually a group of tourists could be heard making their way up the path. Hands dropped as silent thanks were offered and the three slipped away, returning to the mundane world.

At the pool, they lounged, April sprawled on the ground, Sirona and Raina comfortably arranged on a bench, their eyes closed in rapture under the warmth of the sun.

"You'll get burnt if you're not careful," came the voice, nudging into their serenity.

Percy stood before them, all in white, his hair gleaming silver in the sun. Shading her eyes to see him against the light, Sirona motioned him to sit down, which he did, folding his legs and gliding to the ground with a grace Raina could only dream of.

"Well met, Percy," Sirona said, "how have you been fairing?"

"Well enough, Lady, and yourselves?" he asked, nodding at Raina, but sliding his eyes toward April, not sure if she should be included in his inquiry. But April was already on her feet, not one to miss a thing, and came to lean against Raina where she sat. Putting her arm around her daughter, Raina felt pride warm her insides.

"This is my daughter, April," Raina said.

"Well met," Percy said, holding his hand out from where he sat, which April bent to meet, the movement looking almost like a bow. Polite enough, but April was uncharacteristically silent, which didn't surprise Raina. Percy was an alarming specimen of humanity. For his part, Percy strove to keep his expression friendly but as neutral as possible. If this young woman was truly Raina's daughter, likely he knew more about her than she knew about herself. But he had already erred in how he had approached Raina with what he knew. Best not to repeat the error with this special young woman, the next in Merlin's lineage. Gently dropping her hand, he feigned a casual interest in their doings.

"And what are you three ladies up to on a fine day like this?"

A thought was taking root in Sirona's mind. It wouldn't hurt to have Percy as an ally in their scheme.

"The *three* of us are taking a rest from planning a... trip. You might call it a forest adventure..." Sirona said, hoping Percy would catch on, and so he did, the slight raising of his right eyebrow being all the confirmation Sirona needed.

Percy took in each of the three women in turn.

"I wish you well on your journey. May the Goddess be with you, and if there's anything I can do to assist you, I am at your service."

With that he arose, as gracefully as he had descended, quickly brushed the back of his trousers, and made a tiny bow to each of the women.

Holding out his hand again to April, he said, "May you enjoy your stay in Glastonbury. There are many wonders here to experience. When you return from your journey, perhaps we can chat some more."

April managed a hushed, "Thank you. That would be lovely."

With that, Percy turned and ambled across the lawn, back into the cover of the gardens. As he left, Raina couldn't help but think he looked somehow like a retreating bird, an image that seemed to stir a memory that appeared and dissolved again in the blink of an eye.

"Spring Equinox," Sirona said, suddenly.

"What about it?" Raina asked, turning to her friend, while April continued to stare in the direction of Percy's retreat.

"That's when we should go...at the Equinox."

"That gives us a few more days to prepare. Do you think that will be enough?" Raina asked, aware, as the other two were not, that she had been painfully unsuccessful at coming up with any kind of magical poem.

"I think it will have to be. Our discoveries have raised our energies. To tarry too long would risk letting that essential energy dissipate. And the Equinox is a power time, a time of rebirth, and the perfect balance between light and dark. It would be wise to tap into the cosmic energies as well as our own."

As they walked home, April striding into the lead, Raina asked Sirona what made her think they had raised all this energy.

"Percy," she responded.

"What's he got to do with it?" Raina asked. Was it her own anxiousness about what lay ahead, or were Sirona's utterances annoyingly ambiguous these days?

"Strange that he just showed up like that, isn't it?"

"I guess," Raina admitted, "but Percy makes your average "strange" look normal. And I believe he does like to prowl the gardens."

"Yes, but *prowl* is the operative word here. He likes to stay in the shadows, but today he came right to us, drawn, I would propose, by the energy we're emitting."

Raina shook her head. "If you say so." If they had raised energy, Raina couldn't feel it, her own anxiety vibrating at a frequency that was no doubt drowning out everything else.

At Sirona's suggestion, the three women agreed to enlist Niall and Percy in their plans, a participation the two men took on with enthusiasm. While the three women went over the steps of the ritual and all the materials they would need for it, the men concerned themselves with the more mundane aspects of the trip -- food, lodging if they decided they needed it, ferry schedules and tolls.

It would take roughly eight hours to make the trip to the forest, and time after that to actually find the location which wouldn't be, they'd agreed, the place where the tourist information claimed Merlin's tomb to be. Instead, they relied on the stories of locals and the hints from the night on the Tor. An attempt to get more specific information from Abernathy Whitestone had been met with waved arms and dismissal. Odd considering the enthusiasm he had shown on their visit, but the group concluded that either he was embarrassed by the holes in his knowledge, or his mind had fogged over and left him lost to his previous insights.

How to transport the cauldron was of considerable concern. Wrapped, it could barely be stuffed, ever so gently, into a large backpack which Niall agreed to carry. A gallon of water from the Chalice Well had to be procured with special permission -- a heavy item that Percy volunteered for. The herbs and the makings for a small fire fell to Raina to carry, the hope being that she would be the least likely to draw attention, an assessment that she wasn't altogether pleased with. Sirona would carry the Rowan branch, lest it become confused with the detritus for the fire, and April drew the straw for carrying food for snacks along the way. Each carried a small electric torch -- a must for cave exploration. The time tincture Sirona hid among her person -- it wasn't something they wanted to try to explain to security on the ferry, not that some of their other items weren't rather sketchy as well. As they considered that, Sirona and Percy simultaneously turned to Raina.

"What?" Raina said.

"The voice thing..." Sirona said. "You used it with Whitestone, you could use it with ferry security as well, if need be."

"I have no idea..." Raina objected.

"But you do," Percy said, boring her with his golden stare. "You do. If the need presents itself, you will know what to say, but only if you believe in yourself, believe in your power to persuade."

April was staring at her mother, her mouth open. "You can do that Mom? That kind of Jedi misdirection thing?"

"So I'm told. I don't like the idea of it..."

Sirona all but stamped her foot. "Get over it, Raina! We have a higher purpose here and you won't be changing the course of history, or the trajectory of a security guard's life, just causing a little distraction, tossing a verbal rock to draw curious eyes away from us!"

With that, the fivesome let out a collective sigh. Rules and regulations would be one less thing to worry about -- or at least they had a plan. It was also collectively decided that, while the trip would be arduous, they would not interrupt the journey -- or their energy -- with sleep. To do so would likely dissipate their focus, and held more potential for drawing unwanted notice. Instead, they would rise early and accomplish the trip and the ritual all in one day and worry about resting later.

The night before their departure, the men stayed at Sirona's, camping out in her living room. The five were determined to stay together, to build the psychic energy needed for the coming day. Before retiring, they would devote the evening to telling stories about Merlin and calling to mind the things he stood for. Sirona and Percy took the lead, with April supplying modern day representations of him, especially as they emphasized his role as teacher and protector of nature.

Niall and Raina listened intently, enjoying the tales but also enjoying the way the others became increasingly animated as they brought the beloved wizard to life. Merlin the caller of mists; Merlin who could speak to the beasts and birds; Merlin who protected the forests; Merlin the shape-changer, striding through the world of humankind, drawing the winds of magic and mystery in his wake, and keeping alive the dream that there is a world beyond the veil. More so, that beauty, harmony and wisdom are right here, beneath our feet, at the end of our fingertips, within our own souls if we but look closely.

All the beauty of the utopic world of King Arthur's vision of equality, might for right, and justice -- how much of that was Merlin's vision in the hands of a great and selfless King? As their stories spun out through the night, it was as if the wizard himself was listening from the shadows, wrapped in his ragged cloak, holding his staff, nodding in appreciation that at least these five knew his heart, his soul, and his vision for the world...and, it was hoped...would act upon it.

Then, before they called it a night, they performed a ritual unwrapping of the cauldron, which neither Percy nor Niall had seen. In the dim light of Sirona's living room, the cauldron seemed to glow of its own accord, speaking to each of the five in turn, assuring them that their plans were sound and that it was the very vessel required for their purpose -- indeed, that their purpose and the vessel's purpose were one and the same. When sleep at last made its insistent demands, before Niall could re-wrap and stow the cauldron, April reached out and touched it reverently, her young soul moved to awe by its beauty and antiquity.

Fierce winds and torrential rain woke the five even before their intended early awakening, battering the windows and dousing their spirits. Everyone was thinking it, but it fell to Niall to say the hard thing.

"Perhaps we should postpone..."

"Absolutely not!" Sirona said, putting her hand on Niall's arm, signaling that she understood that caution had to be voiced, if not entirely sincerely felt. Niall would walk through fire for Sirona and they both knew it. "It must be today."

"You have said you felt that Spirit was with us on this," Raina said. "I don't suppose it has changed its mind?"

"There are all kinds of forces at work in the Universe," Sirona countered. "I don't doubt for a minute that there are those who would dissuade us from our purpose."

"All the more reason to persist," Percy added.

"Then we'd best dress for the ill weather and pray the ferries will still run." Niall said.

Despite the storm, the ferry kept its schedule, though the crossing was not for the faint of heart. As they approached the coast of Brittany, however, the storm tempered, but did not abate entirely.

They drove as far into the forest as they could, then shouldered their respective burdens and stood sopping at a trailhead while April squatted down and, putting her hand onto the earth, intoned words that had come to her, unbidden and urgent.

Sacred oak grove, marriage of rock and tree, deep within. I'm coming for you ancient father, show me the way...

Over and over she spoke it, then she rose, as if in a trance and began the trek. The others followed at a near distance, careful not to break April's focus, her inward listening. For a long while, they stayed on a path, but suddenly, April veered from it and took off into the dense woods. Sirona panicked a bit. She knew of the tales of people getting lost in this forest. She hung back from time to time to rip bands of cloth from her brightly colored scarf and quickly tie them to a branch. At the same time, she tried to pick out remarkable formations of rocks, clumps of understory, whatever she could hold in memory to lead them back out should April's inner compass only serve her in one direction.

The going became more difficult, rocks and roots slippery from the rain, forcing them to travel more slowly. It was obvious that all were tiring -- all but April. Then suddenly April came to a dead stop. Looking up, Sirona saw that they were in the middle of an oak grove of absolutely massive trees. She looked around, but could see nothing that even remotely looked like a cave. April turned to the companions, her eyes still glazed over in trance.

"It is here," she said.

No one dared speak, but it was clear that a single word united their minds.

Where?

Then Percy stepped forward, his arms outstretched like divining rods. He rotated slowly, splaying his fingers, as though reaching for some unseen hand. Then, "Come," he said to the group as he headed toward a rock face behind a tangle of understory. Before the rest could reach him, he began tearing away at the brush. The others joined him, following his lead, all of them being as careful as possible to push the tangled foliage to the side rather than uproot it. Before long, an opening in the rock appeared. A nod from April. They had found it.

The five set to work unpacking the elements of the ritual. As they worked, Sirona leaned close to Raina.

"I forgot to ask -- you have the poem, yes?"

Raina was rummaging furiously in her pack. "No," she said in a hushed croak. "Not yet...but it will come. Don't worry..." she assured Sirona, although she was not, herself, assured at all.

When everything was unpacked, Niall declared, "We'll keep guard out here, against what, I don't know. But at the very least, though it seems unlikely, should some lost soul wander into this grove, we will keep them out of the cave."

Sirona nodded in agreement and appreciation.

Nothing more needed to be said. The three women, with April in the lead, bowed their heads and squeezed through the small opening. It was pitch black inside, the opening through which they had just come appeared like a luminescent egg behind them, but gave little light to the interior. They each lit their electric torches and made their way slowly into the interior, until Raina let out a gasp. Wordlessly, she flashed her torch at a rock face that looked as much like the bark of a tree as rock. Then, dropping her light, Raina clutched at her chest and fell to her knees.

"Mom, are you ok?" April asked, rushing to Raina.

Raina leaned into her daughter's arms. When she could speak, she did so through tears. "I feel him," she said. "Oh my God, I can *feel* him."

Sirona knelt on the other side of her friend, trying to sense what was going on with her. The three sat quietly until Sirona at last ventured to ask, "are you able to proceed?"

"Yes," Raina replied, having recovered some. "I have to be. There is so much...visions or memories...we must do what we came here to do. *We must.*"

Supported by April and Sirona, Raina rose on trembling legs. "We must continue the ritual as planned. As soon as we can, we should douse our lights and work with the light of the fire...remembering to look askance."

Turning their backs to the wall, they worked quickly. Sirona set the fire, Raina and April positioned the cauldron, caressing it as they did so, running their fingers over its designs. Then Raina poured the water from the Chalice Well into the vessel, thanking the Goddess under her breath as she did so. April, thinking about Rowan, whom she had come to adore and honor as a teacher and protectress, sprinkled the herbs into the water. Drawing a vial from her blouse, Sirona closed her eyes and called on the ancient carrier of her soul, Morgan le Fay, healer, enchantress, sister to Arthur and contemporary of Merlin, then dropped three drops of the time tincture into the cauldron.

As the women circled the vessel, Sirona took three brands from the fire, one for each of them to hold while they took turns with the Rowan branch, stirring the waters, peering into the cauldron, careful to look nowhere else than into the depths, and waited for Raina to speak.

And waited...and waited. Panic was rising in Sirona. To get this far...

Suddenly, Raina took a sharp indrawn breath, then, throwing her head back, her voice echoing in the darkness, her voice thick with emotion, intoned,

"Father, wizard, druid, mage,
We come to you in modern age,

Our love we bring, our hearts alight
To see your hungry soul set right.

Merlin, mage of Arthur's heart,
Your wisdom now you must impart,

Your soul's despair we've come to heal
Our promise here we will reveal..."

Here Raina paused, to catch her breath Sirona hoped, but the pause was more prolonged than any inhale should be. Raina's hand shook, causing the flame of her torch to dance, but in the next moment April grabbed her mother's hand, steadied it, then spoke,

"To give our hearts, our minds and hands,
To Nature's way across the lands,

For as above, and so below,
Is the Way that all must know

From your blood and bone are we,
Your spirit now, we do set free."

Together, the three women repeated the last line, stirring the mixture, their eyes stinging from the wood smoke and constant vigilance. Slowly a mist began to form on the surface of the water, swirling, flowing in pale greens and blues tinged with white. It curled and spiraled, snaked around the Rowan branch, coming close to the hand that held it, but stopping just short of touching it. The women raised their voices and continued speaking the charged words. As they watched, the mist gathering itself into a flame-shaped density in which there seemed to be vague images of trees, rocks, water, and moonlight, all pulsing, shifting, writhing, then suddenly it stretched, reached, and lifted into the air.

As one, the women watched it rise, until it disappeared into the infinite darkness above them. At the same time, they heard a sharp crack and looked down to see that the cauldron, the ancient, finely wrought, uncannily beautiful cauldron, lay in pieces at their feet. April stifled a cry and fell to her knees, soaking them in the spilled waters. She hovered her hands over the shards, as though she would magic them together again, but they didn't move.

"Hold fast!" Sirona said, with hushed urgency. "Quick, lean your torches against the shards, then bathe your hands in the spilled water. Quickly, quickly, now stand with me and join hands, and whatever happens, do not let go."

Mother and daughter did as bid, then with pounding hearts clutched hands as Sirona raised her voice in a piercing keen.

"*Nimue, I feel you near. Hear me, daughter of the Mother Goddess, as are we all. I stand here, vessel of the soul of Morgan le Fey, sister to you of the ancient ways. Whatever has turned your soul, for that I am sorry, but know this, here stands two of Merlin's blood, mother and daughter, united in love, strengthened by the knowledge of their lineage at last. Your curse is broken. Let the power of the mage be released in these and those who will come after for the good of all. And for you, sister, may your own soul be released from darkness and misery. In the name of the Mother Goddess, may you be healed at last."*

Sirona's words bounced off the walls of the cave and swirled around the three, who stood, barely daring to breathe, fiercely clutching each other's hands. When the air fell to silence at last, Sirona released her companion's hands. "Come," she said, "Our work here is done. We must leave without delay."

"But the pot," April said, stooping to gather up the shards.

"Leave it be, dear one," Sirona said, kindly, but with urgency. "We cannot tarry here, lest we unwittingly undo our sacred purpose."

Even as Sirona spoke, the three heard a hiss and looked to see that the shards were dissolving, returning to the earth from which they came.

One by one they tumbled out of the mouth of the cave and fell, exhausted, to the sodden earth. Niall went to Raina and Sirona in turn, helping them to sit up while Percy tended to April who was crying piteously. Then the men joined them where they sat, the five of them in a rough circle, unable for the moment to do more than sit upon the wet ground and contemplate what they had done. Niall was the first to speak.

"Can you speak of it?"

"Not here, not yet," Sirona answered.

They all felt it as one -- an urgency to leave the forest. No one would soon forget what they had just experienced. The telling could wait. For now, they needed to pull the brush back over the cave mouth and erase any sign of their presence. Once done, they made their way out of the forest, Sirona's scattered threads shining like prisms, catching the golden glow that emerged from behind the clouds at last.

26

The Promise

A heavy mist rolled down off the Tor and pooled in the town of Glastonbury, hiding neighbor from neighbor, and obscuring the passing of time. From her window, Sirona saw nothing but gray.

"A strange morning," Niall said, coming up behind her, whispering so as not to wake the others.

"Not sure what to make of it," Sirona agreed. "Is it just weather, or something more?"

"Cloaking mists were Merlin's signature calling card, were they not?" Niall observed.

"Indeed it is so..." Sirona mused. "He did his best...or worst...work under cover of them, tricking Dukes, confusing armies. It makes me wonder. Have we romanticized the Mage and forgotten his use of trickery and misdirection? Have we unleased on the world a power for chaos that might have been best left alone?"

Niall put his arms around the modern-day enchantress and buried his face in her hair, drawing in the scent of her. Loving Sirona was never boring. Though it was her way to present an unfailingly cheerful demeanor in public, he knew no one who took life more seriously than did Sirona. Now, in the aftermath of accomplishing a remarkable feat, worthy of celebration he would have thought, her hyper-vigilance was alert to unforeseen and undesirable ramifications of their actions.

"Maybe it is just the weather...after the storm..." he whispered into her ear, knowing that his words would do nothing to ease her concerns, but saying them anyway. And who knew? Maybe it *was* just the weather.

The two stood thus, watching the laden air move like a cat stalking its prey, while Niall tightened his arms around his lover against the chill they both felt.

By the time the rest of the house awakened, Niall and Sirona had prepared a breakfast fit to fill everyone's bellies as their stories from the day before would soon fill each mind and soul. As for the strange mist, as the day warmed most likely it would dissipate and with it any suspicious fears, or so they hoped.

As one, the five drifted toward the living room, leaving the remains of breakfast unattended to. Since leaving the forest, they'd barely spoken, each one processing events in their own way. But now, there was a felt agreement that it was time to talk.

Sirona looked to Raina to begin, if she was willing, but a look from her told Sirona that she would rather not evoke what swept over her in the cave. And so Sirona told the story from start to finish.

"What caused you to address Nimue as you did?" Percy asked. "We had not planned that."

"Nor had I," Sirona admitted. "But I felt her presence in the cave, strongly. And I felt her anger at Raina and April. I was terrified for them, but also for Nimue. For her to hang on to that for so long...it confined her soul. The words just poured out of me, out of my heart. I hope I broke the curse, but I also hope I released Nimue's soul. In hindsight, I pray I haven't loosed a malevolence upon the world, but it seemed to me that Nimue deserved some forgiveness, a chance at redemption."

As Sirona spoke, Raina realized with a start that they had not yet told April about the curse. She must be wondering now, but as Raina looked at her daughter, she saw no signs of confusion, just the sadness about the cauldron breaking that had been sitting on her mercilessly, like some clawed thing. Best to leave it alone for now then as they processed the rest of the day.

"Well, I can tell you this," Niall said. "At a certain point, there was a gust of wind from the cave and a shimmering mist shot out and up into the trees and suddenly the whole forest came alive, the branches all swaying every which way and the trees literally singing, their leaves like so many windchimes."

"There was an uncanny light," Percy added, "like sunshine but more golden and there was a feeling in the air of...jubilation."

Raina and Sirona shared a relieved smile. Perhaps this, added to what they saw in the cave, was sufficient proof of their success. Still...

"I guess there is no way to know for certain," Sirona said, "but we've done what we could. Only time will tell for sure. It will be up to us to be alert to signs."

"Art..." Raina said, but could not finish the thought.

"I know." Sirona said, reading her thoughts. "But we will share every tiny detail with him and, who knows, perhaps he felt something of what transpired in the cave, even as far away as he is."

"But we lost the pot," April spoke now, the sadness in her voice heartbreaking to hear. "The beautiful cauldron broke!"

"I believe that is as it should be," Sirona said, her voice tender but stern. "If we can believe the tales, the cauldron was lovingly crafted specifically for the purpose to which we put it. For one thousand long years, it waited, idle, used for nothing else, until the time came to fulfill its purpose. If the pot had survived, it would have become a totem, a relic, an object of adoration which people, being what they are, would have worshiped, making it a frozen, lifeless icon, thinking that was enough, rather than doing the hard work that now awaits us to set things right."

Reaching to her daughter, Raina said, "More pots are easily made, and the act of making is an act of reverence, an opening of oneself to the spirit inherent in the material." And in that moment, Raina felt her hands ache to touch clay, to build form and decorate it with the things of nature.

But there was something else she realized as well. "While we were in the cave, I had a vision. Nimue certainly played a part, but I think it was Merlin's own despair that trapped his spirit as much as anything else."

Percy looked at Raina with unadulterated admiration.

"Merlin lived at a time when the old ways were passing away," Percy began. "Actually, I should say, they were intentionally destroyed. The Romans made it their business to annihilate the Druids, to erase their knowledge and replace it with the new religion. He may well have been the last, or nearly the last of his kind."

As he spoke, a profound sadness swept across Percy's features. Seeing it, Raina realized that the sadness always lurked there, was part of what made Percy so unusual, so difficult to look at.

"I see now," Raina said, so much becoming clear to her at once, "that much of the darkness that has haunted me was a deep and suffocating despair. I thought it was my own, and it was to the extent that it ran my life, but now I suspect that it may have originated from Merlin. Of all that he may have passed on through his lineage, despair overwhelmed it...as it did him."

"For fifteen hundred years that despair held sway," Niall said in a hush.

"But we have taken the responsibility for releasing that burden from his soul," Sirona said with conviction. "As we heard that night on the Tor, *promise me.* We must do everything we can to heal the rift between the earth and ourselves, to make the Celtic triad of body, mind and soul the trinity that we hold sacred, and to live into the unity of immanence and transcendence. Such was the Druidic way and so it should be again. That is the promise we make and that is the promise we must keep."

"So what will that look like?" April said, voicing the question on everyone's mind. It was clear by the silence that followed her question, however, that the answer was going to be a work in progress.

"My first thought was a massive party," Niall finally offered, more to break the silence than provide a viable answer, "but now I'm not so sure."

"Nor I," Raina agreed. "It seems like I should feel celebratory, and I do feel up-lifted to a degree, but cautious as well. Thoughtful. More like we're just beginning than ending something."

Sirona eyed the window. So far, the warming day had had little effect on the mist. At least, she thought, she wouldn't have to talk folks down from broadcasting yesterday's activity on social media.

"I think caution is well advised," Sirona began. "We have no idea what our actions have set in motion, nor am I eager for any kind of notoriety." As she glanced at each of her companions, she was certain that they were of the same mind.

"Nevertheless," Percy said, "our intent was to bring to the fore the missing pieces of contemporary consciousness that Merlin represents. It doesn't need to be announced that his spirit has been set free after all this time to accomplish that, but..."

"...how do we make that knowledge work for us, right?" April asked.

"This much seems obvious though," Raina added. "We must bring the other players in this drama up to speed. I suspect we should have another gathering of the twelve, if you agree, Sirona."

"I do, absolutely. We should do it soon, and as much as I hate to say it, we should include Whitestone as well."

Hesitantly, Percy leaned forward, "I know we want to keep the circle small, but I'd like to invite my son, Tanan, to the gathering. I have a feeling that he will have a role to play going forward."

"I trust your instinct completely," Raina said, then, "that is, if the rest of you agree?"

"Unquestionably, we will need alliance with the younger generation in this. Tanan is most welcome. Agreed?" Sirona asked, looking at April and Niall in turn, both nodding in the affirmative.

That afternoon, at Percy's request, Raina joined him in the Chalice Gardens.

"I hope you are comfortable with meeting like this," he began.

"I am. What's on your mind?" Raina's feelings for Percy had softened considerably. Indeed, she welcomed the opportunity to get to know him better.

"I want to reiterate my apologies for any discomfort I have caused you," he began. "I tend to be a fairly reclusive person, not really great at knowing how to behave in social situations. When I saw you at the Imbolc gathering, I was blindsided by what I felt. Something in me called out to you with such an urgency I had no idea how to deal with it. I froze, but apparently that looked much different to you."

Raina smiled, a genuine, relieved, smile.

"Apology accepted," she said, "and one offered in return. I'm too easily disposed to mistrusting men, and, quite frankly, I felt a pull as well and it frightened me."

"Well then." Percy replied, his features softening, taking the danger out of his good looks. "Friends then?"

"Friends, of course."

The morning mist had finally melted under the warmth of the sun, leaving the gardens alive with springtime enthusiasm. Amid all that abundant increase, the newly established friendship took root.

"Tell me of this son of yours, Tanan you said."

"Ah, my son," Percy said. "He is everything to me. Our relationship is much the same as that which I see between you and April. It is a pleasure, is it not, to enjoy our offspring that way?"

"A new pleasure to me, I'm afraid, but one I'm very much looking forward to living into."

And so the two shared the details of their parenthood, Raina learning that Percy's wife died when Tanan was young, leaving him to raise a son on his own. In turn, Raina told her story of being forced to leave April and the manipulations employed by Malcolm to keep them separated. It was a surprisingly easy sharing, the wounds of each being different, but equally deep.

"You think Tanan will have an interest in our quest then?" Raina asked at last.

"I do. What I've learned about April mirrors what I know of my son. I can think of no better people to guide us in bringing the wisdom of the ancient past into the contemporary world. I look forward to them meeting."

"And you wanted to be sure that I'd be ok with that," Raina said, smiling, "that I didn't continue to harbor any suspicions about you or your intentions..."

Percy shrugged. "You've found me out."

Raina could have let him off the hook, told him that over the past few days she had developed an admiration for him, and valued the insight he'd brought to the quest, most particularly what he knew about the curse. But for now, a simple smile would have to do.

By evening the men had left, giving the women time to get some much needed, uninterrupted rest. Sirona busied herself writing a long message to Art then contacting her ceremonial collective and AW. The plan was to meet the following afternoon. April seemed somewhat restive, but buried herself in books and sleep. For her part, Raina's thoughts turned to the matter of the curse. She longed to discuss it with Sirona, but wasn't ready to burden April with this new issue after all she'd been through in the forest.

Perhaps she shouldn't burden her with it at all. Sometimes, Raina thought, curses were given power by the cursed believing them, thereby creating a self-fulfilling prophecy. Ever since learning of the curse that day at Rowan's, it had plagued her, made the skin on her back crawl when she thought of it. If she could spare April from that, she would. And if, Goddess willing, Sirona had been successful in the curse, what need at all for April to know about it? Still, there was a tiny part of Raina that thought it best for April to know everything, to move forward with every shred of information possible. Secrets have a way of eating away at the foundations of things, however grandly conceived, as Raina well knew.

Full to bursting, Sirona's little apartment buzzed with anticipation as the invited guests crowded in, each one eager to hear the opinions of others in the aftermath of such a momentous accomplishment that now opened a future of unknown ramifications and possibilities. Giving no explanation, Abernathy Whitestone had declined the invitation, a blessing perhaps, thought Raina, given the forced intimacy of the group. Beatrice had brought the keeper of the cauldron, and, as suggested, Tanan was present as well.

Once everyone was settled, the five began their narrative of the events in the forest, each taking a part in the telling. They had made it clear at the start that they wouldn't mind interruptions if anyone had questions, but so rapt was their audience that not a single one was willing to pause the story, even for a second, although Beatrice did let out a sigh when she heard of the breaking of the cauldron.

At the conclusion of the account, Sirona addressed the room.

"So, we are fairly certain we were successful in releasing the spirit, but the path forward is unclear. We have even had some doubts about whether we've done the right thing. I know that's hard to hear at this point, after all everyone has done to aid our success, but we suspect it would be unwise not to consider the full range of possible ramifications of what we have done."

Rowan was the first to speak. "I agree that vigilance is called for, but I don't think you've done the wrong thing in releasing the spirit. The enchantment was unnatural, and the loss through the ages of such critical energy as Merlin possessed, well, we all see the perilous imbalance of the modern world. The return of Merlin's spirit alone cannot be expected to correct the imbalance. To do so will require the creative and eco-sensitive work of an army of knowledgeable and caring folk. But that Merlin's soul has been returned to the web of spirit energy could be...should be...profoundly helpful."

"The trick will be," Liselle began, "to connect with that spirit. I agree that it would be inadvisable to shout from the rooftops that Merlin's soul is free, but rather than shout it, we have to somehow live it."

Muriel, the sweet-faced woman who had invoked the Tarot that day on the Tor, spoke next.

"Just as Merlin's spirit has been suspended in enchantment all these centuries, so too has his story been frozen in the past. There have been inklings of it in various fantasy tales, like Tolkien's Gandalf and the wizard school of Hogwarts, but to my knowledge a full expression of what Merlin represents, most particularly his deep understanding of and reverence for the earth, has not been fully articulated."

"I agree that we must find a way to bring Merlin into the present." It was Jemma, the keeper of the cauldron who spoke. "It is to be hoped that the liberated spirit will find a home in a prophet for the modern age, but even if we should be so lucky, it will be years before that can be realized."

April couldn't contain her urge to ask a question of Jemma.

"Are you upset about the cauldron breaking?"

"Not at all," Jemma replied. "Its beauty was outstanding, unearthly even. The stories that have come down about its maker are wonderous. But I agree with Sirona's assessment that, should it have survived, it would likely have become an object of worship, another *thing* that we spend our energy adoring rather than turning that adoration to the earth itself and its well-being. It was never meant to be an object of worship. Indeed, it was almost constantly kept wrapped and hidden away. It was made for a single purpose -- the one you used it for. With its purpose complete, it is in keeping with its magic that it has returned to the earth."

April's eyes glistened with tears at the memory of the cauldron, but she agreed with Jemma's position.

"I have a proposal. May I?" April asked, deferring to the elders.

"Of course!" Sirona enthused, delighted that April appeared ready to take the lead.

"I propose that the people gathered here form a collective -- a group committed to the on-going work that began the minute the spirit rose out of the cauldron. There are sixteen of us. If each of us forms their own small group of trusted and committed folk, and we all keep in touch sharing information, ideas, and experiences, our answers to 'what comes next?' can evolve."

A ripple of approval floated through the room. Slowly, Rowan rose.

"It is fitting," she announced, "that youth take the lead, with the support and wisdom of the varying ages and knowledge that is represented here. I suggest that April lead this group. Will you take on that task, dear one?"

April hesitated and glanced at her mother, who subtly nodded in the affirmative.

"I'll do my best," April said, hoping that she could live up to their expectations. "I think, however, that I wouldn't mind having a partner..."

"Let us trust that such will emerge," said Rowan, her eyes alight as though with some hidden knowledge.

"And feel free to delegate," Jemma said. "I'd be happy to develop a communications network if you like. My wife and I are good at Internet stuff. She even has a blog -- the whole works. We're on the ground and ready to run."

April smiled her assent. She liked Jemma from the first, admiring her role as Cauldron Keeper...and her strength in letting go of such a rare and wonderful thing.

"Well then," Rowan announced, "it's settled."

With that, applause and quiet calls of 'cheers' filled the room.

"Snacks in the kitchen everyone," Sirona announced, "and plenty of Rowan berry punch!"

As the group broke up into smaller clusters, Percy took the opportunity to approach April, Tanan at his side.

"April, I'd like you to meet my son Tanan. Like you, he's at university. Tanan, this is easily one of the bravest women I've ever met."

Fortunately, April thought, while plenty good looking, Tanan wasn't as otherworldly gorgeous as his father. That made it easier for her to greet him with a relatively calm demeanor. Percy slid away like a ghost and left the two young people to chat freely. Finding a quiet place amid the clamor of the guests wasn't easy however, and it wasn't long before the two decided a walk was in order. April pulled her mother aside to tell her they were headed to the Chalice Gardens, a move Raina was grateful for, as she was for Percy's announcement of his intentions the day before. In fact, having April out of the house worked to her advantage for what had been nagging at her.

As the two left, Raina sought out Sirona.

"Do you suppose we could get Rowan to join us in the study and discuss the issue of the curse?"

But Sirona never got a chance to answer, as Rowan appeared at Raina's side as though she'd been there all along. Moving into the relative privacy of the study, Raina began.

"I'm torn about telling April about the curse. Should I spare her the concern, or should she know...and do we think we've released it?"

"As you know by now," Rowan said, "I believe that facing reality honestly is the only way to live a whole and spiritually connected life. So, yes, April should know, but you shouldn't have to bear that burden alone dear Raina. It should be us three who tell her and support her with our beliefs to this point."

"And those are?" Raina asked.

Sirona folded her arms across her chest. "Despite my words in the cave, I'm not sure we can know for sure if the curse has been broken. Nor are we yet or will we ever be fully aware of the exact nature of the curse, though we can make a pretty good guess. I have come to suspect, however, that perhaps you, Raina, have already broken it, or at the very least seriously diminished it. My brave words in the cave were based on that assumption."

"How so?"

"April has told you that she has never had the horrible dreams that have always plagued you. Do you remember our discussion in the cave? I believe that your fierce and unwavering love of April, despite all that you have gone through, drew off the tentacles of Nimue's malevolence, and pulled them into yourself. You suffered doubly so that April would not suffer at all."

"That's a theory, but..."

"And how have your dreams been of late?" Sirona pressed.

"Truth is, I can barely remember them. But I attribute that to your night tea."

Rowan had been listening carefully to Sirona's words.

"We could, if April is willing, bring her to my garden and I could gently petition her soul..."

"Is there any danger in that?" Raina asked.

"No, not as long as April is willing and clear about what we're doing. There would be, in my opinion, more danger in not doing it."

A heavy sigh escaped Raina. How she longed for the turmoil of her life to be over, but, she suspected, that was not to be her lot. Rowan's comment about facing reality honestly hit home and stirred her blood, the blood that carried Merlin's DNA. Suddenly she knew that that was the way Merlin had lived. Unlike so much of humankind that creates infinite distractions from the truth, Merlin never closed his eyes, never hid from anything and that was both his great wisdom and, undoubtedly, the source of his despair, at the last.

"I'd like to give her the day, but she has to get back to the States and her studies. I suppose since you're here now Rowan, we should tell her this evening."

And so it was agreed. Raina's heart went out to her daughter. To go from the life of a relatively average young woman to all that she'd been through and learned about herself in the past week, must require quite an adjustment.

Then again, since April was also of Merlin's blood, perhaps there were resources there that could handle these startling revelations. Raina consoled herself with the thought. Indeed, ever since the release of the spirit, a new awareness was growing in Raina. More than that, a new sense of strength. It was as though her connection with Merlin was liberated. The shadows were graying, manageable, instructive even. If this was happening for April as well...best to acknowledge it. It was, Raina realized, part of the effect of liberating Merlin's spirit. This evening couldn't come fast enough.

By the time Tanan had left April at Sirona's door, all the guests had left except for Rowan. Wondering that she was still here, nevertheless April was delighted that she would have more time with this precious woman. As April entered the living room, she sensed that the three women were doing their best to act disinterested in her return, but were anything but. They were probably dying to know how Tanan and she had "got on" since both of the young people understood that their meeting had been orchestrated. But this was something more. She could cut the tension with a knife. Not being the kind to hold her tongue or tolerate a mystery, April addressed it head on.

"Ok ladies, what's up?"

They sat her down and much the same way as they had a few days earlier to tell her of her lineage, now, as gently as they could, they informed her of the curse that seemed to be attached to that lineage. They discussed the dreams, Percy's visions, Sirona's theory, and Raina's experience in Rowan's garden. They did their best not to leave out a single detail, now realizing that April was more than just a vessel for their teachings, but also a source of wisdom and vision in her own right.

"So, Auntie S," April said, "That's what you were about in the cave. I was so upset about the cauldron breaking I was only half connecting to your words. What you said about Mom and me being connected with love...that sounded so good. It's interesting too, your theory about Mom taking on the darkness for me. There was always a woman in my dreams who protected me from whatever evil lurked. I imagined that she was my mother. Even though my mother couldn't be with me in real life, she would come to me in my dreams. There was no question in my mind that she loved me and would do anything to protect me.

"I believe that's what helped me resist my father's negative influence. And now that I've met my mother in real life...well, I'm getting that same feeling of safety and protection." April paused and as she looked at the three women, there was a depth to her visage that suggested a woman more mature than April's years. "You surely don't think I would have joined your escapades so readily had I not felt safe...like my mother would do anything to protect me?"

Sirona slipped her arm around Raina, more certain than ever that love can knock the wind out of malevolence.

"So now, one more thing needs to be considered," Rowan said. "It's your decision entirely, but if you'd like to come to my garden, I could do for you what I did for your mother. I could gently petition your soul and maybe thereby learn whether or not the curse has been broken. I can't promise you that we will get the information we seek, but it's worth a try. As I say, it's up to you."

April was a bit shy of letting Rowan know just how fond of her she had become, but the thought of going to her garden to let her work her magic thrilled April.

"I'm game," she said. Then, "and because I know you're dying to ask, yes, Tanan and I did hit it off. We have much in common...and...he has agreed to be my partner in leading our collective."

That the women didn't seem entirely surprised at that news wasn't lost on April. Clearly, she was caught up in something special, precious, and mysterious. Best to let it unfold as it will.

The women agreed that they would meet at Rowan's the following afternoon and that Raina and April would leave the following day for home. That didn't allow much time for leave-taking but April needed to get back to classes, and Raina felt an urgency about connecting with Art. Sirona was torn. She would have loved to return with them, but also felt there were loose ends that needed attention.

Among other things, Raina had made a case for telling Abernathy Whitestone about all that had transpired. Whatever his reasons were for avoiding the gathering, he shouldn't be ignorant of this latest chapter in the legend of Merlin. Raina would have been willing to go, to play the fellow academic, but she was running out of time. It would have to fall to Sirona to deal with the cranky scholar.

After Rowan left and Sirona retired, Raina and April enjoyed some time alone in the dim light of the living room.

Raina took April's hands in hers, marveling at the slender, graceful fingers, so comforting in her own.

"You've been through a lot. How are you fairing?"

"I'm ok Mom. It has been a lot to take in, but I'm ok. And I wasn't as surprised at the things you revealed to me as you might have feared. Remember, there was Grandmother, and her special little room in the loft. There were inklings there that made more sense as you shared your story with me here."

"Well then, we have a lot to talk about, I think."

"Tons."

"I was thinking...when we get home...there's room at the cottage. I don't even use the two rooms in the back..."

"I love the cottage..."

"...then, would you like to stay there...at least consider it your home base as your future takes you here and there?"

Squeezing her mother's hands so tightly it made Raina wince, April whispered, "I'd love to!"

"It's settled then."

"Most of my stuff is at school, but I do have some things at Dad's house..."

"Don't worry about Malcolm. We'll handle him. Don't forget about the power of misdirection. *We aren't the druids you seek.* You can practice it on him."

"Really? You think I can do that?"

"Positive."

A Lineage Begins

Wales
circa 500 AD

     Making her way in the pre-dawn light, and carrying a babe wrapped tightly but carefully across her chest, a young woman rode into Wales from the south. As she neared the familiar croft, her heart beat faster and tears threatened to spill from her eyes, but she fought them back, as she had learned to fight every other urge to surrender to life's disappointments.

     At the edge of a wood she whispered a command, in obedience to which the trees moved just enough to make way for her horse. Her destination was a large, three-trunked oak not far from the edge of the woods if her memory was correct.

     As the sky lightened some in anticipation of the rising sun, the tree appeared, blocking her path, and sending a flood of memories through her soul. Careful of the child she held, she dismounted and kneeled at the base of the tree. An arrangement of sticks and twigs marked the threshold of what might have been a fairy door, formed by the arch of a root. Quickly, the young woman swept away the detritus and pushed her hand into the opening thus revealed. After some pawing around in the dirt, her fingers lit upon something round and cool -- a copper coin.

     Rising from where she had knelt, she tucked the coin into the folds of cloth that swaddled her child, then mounted her horse and with some urgency, retreated along the spell-cast path which closed behind her, leaving no trace of her visitation.

     Worrying now that she had come too late, she hastened toward the humble dwelling that had been the best part of her life. Sliding quietly from her horse, she listened for any sign of wakefulness in the two she had been assured still lived there. There...a slight sound, the creaking of a floorboard. Quickly but gently, she laid the bundled babe on the doorstep, then pulled herself back upon her mount and kicked it into a gallop, reaching the main road just as a woman, aroused by the sound of hoofbeats, opened the door.

The End

Coming in 2022,
Vol. 2 of the Rowan Branch Trilogy...

The Book of April

So secret was the society that even its full name did not appear over the medieval-looking door, only the letters SPH were carved into the lintel. The door itself was secured with a secret code, thereby ensuring that only the initiated had access to the ornate interior of the meeting place of the Society for the Preservation of Heaven.

On this day, all the members were present in the chapel. Lit by the surrounding windows, the chapel ceiling was radiant in its domed imitation of an angel-studded heaven, its arc enfolding the assembly in the embracing promise of a joyous afterlife. On the chancel, robed in purple and gold sat the high priest, accompanied by a rather unkempt individual, a rare guest, but tolerated for the ominous news he was there to impart.

Though perhaps he had made a mistake, thought Abernathy Whitestone, intimidated by the atmosphere in the chapel. Yes, hearing about the assumed release of Merlin's spirit had raised questions in his mind that troubled him. He had always been comfortable dealing with Merlin as a legendary figure of the past, fixed in time, the definition of him only changing according to research or creative recastings that were safely confined between the covers of books -- stationary, manageable, dismissible if one so chose. But to imagine Merlin in any way *living* again, in the present time, haunted Abernathy's thoughts. To tell the truth, he had always found the character of Merlin to be terrifying. The things he was purported to do -- raise mists, disguise himself and others, shape-shift, talk with animals, get into another's mind. To live in a world where people might have such powers was just too inconstant and undependable for the likes of Abernathy. It would be like living among vipers, slithering around in hidden places until they rose up and buried their fangs in one's face. As a Merlin scholar, studying that which he feared gave Abernathy a feeling of control over his subject, as though he had his specimen in a cage.

But now it appears the object of his study has escaped, and is loose upon the world. If, for a brief moment that day in his study with those two women he had thought it would be thrilling to have the mage released, ever since that moment he regretted that enthusiasm and any role he played in the success of the venture. And so, through channels known to those whose lives are spent preserving a certain worldview, he had contacted the Society for the Preservation of Heaven, and shared with them his fears -- fears which they shared, but for their own reasons.

Now, however, he wondered if he hadn't made a mistake. As he sat amid the cloaked and unsmiling (as long as one didn't count smirks) men of the Society, he sensed an unwavering zeal for a profoundly narrow interpretation of the "good" that outdid even his own. Mostly, he was fearful for Raina. Perhaps because she was a fellow academic, but more, he believed, because she exhibited an appropriate humility and gentle femininity that made her tolerable, as women go. Sirona, however, was another thing altogether. He could barely tolerate her presence, so much did she remind him of the evil enchantresses of the legends. Oh yes, he did have to admit that perhaps the Lady of the Lake could be excused, having, after all, provided Arthur with Excalibur. But the rest of them -- trouble every one. Seduction, trickery, witchcraft. Abernathy Whitestone shuddered where he sat just thinking about it.

Pam Collins